MIRACULOUS BOUNTY

As the kin neared the top of the slope, sunlight glistened on something small and red wavering at the tip of one gaunt branch. A tiny scarlet sphere was growing on the end of the branch, swelling and darkening under the silver sky.

The object began to tremble as the creature came closer. A moment later it dropped to the ground.

Without slowing, the kin bent, extended its arm, and retrieved the redfruit in one motion. It walked on through the trees, eating in small, precise bites.

The Alchemists

Geary Gravel

A Del Rey Book

BALLANTINE BOOKS • NEW YORK

This book is dedicated with love and thanks
to my father, Harold R. Gravel,
and to the memory of my mother, Nina C. Gravel.

The
Alchemists

PRELUDE: THE MURAL

How is an eon captured? What thickness of chains will bind a century? Which unraveling of the design reveals a single perfect year, complete and untouched at its heart?

A year. What are its colors, and how loud its cries, and where does it begin and end?

There is a museum on Commons, the Great World, which has grown so famous in the past few centuries that it is referred to simply as The Museum on eighty-seven of the two hundred and twenty-eight Worlds of the Human Community.

If you are reading this, there is a good chance that you yourself have been to Commons, a fair chance that you have visited The Museum, a chance that you have strolled along the rose-crystal skywalk connecting *Musical Instruments of Old Earth (A.D. 1646–2308)* and *Unidentified Artifacts of the Years of Expansion*. If, in the course of your promenade, you had chosen to pause at the approximate midpoint of the skywalk and turned to face the rising suns, you would have found yourself staring directly into the Belthannis Mural, that last creation of the pan-imagist Mig which has become almost as widely known as The Museum itself.

The mural, which towers forty meters above the curving glass and sculplate of the Grand Mall, is in the form of a huge tessellated disk, somewhat reminiscent of the Aztec stone calendars found in the *Terminal Cultures* exhibit on the sixteenth floor of the White Wing.

Visible to the thousands arriving daily at Green Tower Landing Stage as a faceted, multicolored medallion, the mural resolves itself when approached by way of the eastern ramps into a vast spiral constructed of more than four thousand individual tiles, beginning at the upper rim of the disk and circling grandly inward till the last tile stares out triumphantly from the exact center of the mural.

As a prime example of the pan-imagist ideal, the paintings combine narrative, philosophy, aesthetic achievement, and personal expression in one coherent statement—a masterpiece of overwhelming unity composed of four thousand and seven discrete works of art. It is a tribute to Mig's craft that each fragment of the spiraling mosaic is at once totally subjective and brilliantly evocative; it is Mig telling himself The Tale of the Lonely Man in symbols which none of us should fully understand.

And yet we do.

As different as ash and seaspray we come, no two of us alike, to gaze awhile at a spiraled complexity, a nautilus shell of shape and color. We stand before fragments, hints, shadows, and we comprehend the whole and it is beautiful, superbly flawed, the history of our worlds and of our people.

The first square captures the eye immediately: a dark gleam from the distant past. Here is chaos personified, the grinning devil of confusion and mistrust which the folk of Antique Earth let loose upon themselves in the final devastation of the Sigh Wars, the last chapter in the dream-time of prespace human history. Self-destruction is a bloody tide in these days, and humankind is swept before it again and again, till hope is all but quenched. Among the record keepers a new word is coined combining suicide and genocide into a single act: crime and punishment skillfully wedded at last. Nation-states are smashed into rubble and then the rubble is smashed, changing places into names, names into memories, with the relentless regularity of an automated scythe.

But humanity is tenacious: a limpet on a battered rock. Each sweep of the tide leaves survivors to crawl erect once more, to stretch their mouths in rage and build new instruments of war until, finally, a limit of some sort is passed and silence falls: peace born not of maturity, but of exhaustion.

Beyond all odds the silence lengthens, old angers forgotten or obliterated. One more try at civilization is cautiously scraped together from pieces of the shattered past. Peace reigns; yet the legacy of fear is an almost palpable presence in this curve of the mural, and the ancient cautions flow unbidden into the viewer's mind. *Know thyself*, old chronicles admonish, *but not thy neighbor. Froy's dead: Stay out of my head!* Mig's skill transports us through time to an era when psychological manipulation was the chief obscenity, and the slightest attempt to influence the will of another human being was met with swift and deadly punishment. The scars of captation—mind control—lay deep in the people of Earth, and they took many years to heal, many thousands of years to be forgotten.

Humankind grew restless in the lull following this latest in a long succession of Last Wars, and the mural's next segments suggest an overcrowded, minutely factioned society which teeters on the verge of yet another conflict. Dark-webbed, clouded, these tiles are rescued from despair by the tiny glimmer of color, the bare hint of precious order just beginning to emerge. In the next section the glimmer has become a radiance; the hint of structure has crystallized into an image, a dash of vivid pigment.

Space travel!

A sudden sense of movement, of purposeful growth, of breaking free and bursting outward. Here is the miraculously recovered, newly vigorous Man as he appeared at the dawn of *Mirin*—literally "the wave," in the Lower Tongue of World Hinderlond—the Years of Expansion, building the massive Cold Ships that would ferry him to the stars in centuries-long voyages, the passengers frozen into cargo and stacked like kindling in the holds.

And then a tile devoted to the silent agony of the Wait and

the Watch, the Look and the Listen. No one could say with certainty which Ships, if any, would find haven at the end of the passage: it is said that there were so many "ifs" involved in the first Expansion that those who waited back on Earth made a new religion out of their uncertainties and chanted them in long litanies before they went to bed at night.

But the next scene is bright, lit by the flickering glow of both joy and terror that accompanies the early colonization, with the ancient Ships crawling finally, one by one, into grateful orbits around a double handful of newfound worlds. Names whisper in the mind: Cibola, Weldon, Green Asylum, New World, Chalice, Stone's Throw, Maya, Babel, Dunbar's World, Street of Dreams...

It is the first fruition of *Mirin*. Each world is unique, and each is beautiful, clothed by Mig in radiance as if seen through the eyes of the voyagers themselves, newly roused and peering for the first time through the eye devices of their great-bellied Ships. Look with them: a new world!

Many feel that the underlying emphasis in these segments of the disk is on separation and isolated metamorphosis. The Cold Ships were snails crawling between the stars. Centuries would pass before the first word of success reached the dreaming Earth, and all the while the child-planets grew, each one different and each alone.

Struggle.

Solitude.

Change.

This is the lexicon of the Expansion.

Yet some say that it is paradise that flickers briefly through these scenes, a dance of exultant discovery that humanfolk were destined to learn, and for them this turn of the spiral grows wholly joyous. World after world is discovered, possessed, catalyzed. Millennia pass in a dozen tiles.

Mirin-time ends abruptly with the completion of the first great circle of tiles. The painting begins anew, as does the history of humankind, with the Encounter, the first meeting between Man and Otherman on a nameless planetoid, a numbered speck near a dying star strung like a bead between ancient Earth and the galaxy's distant center.

First Meeting.

Mig presents us with a swirl of dark colors, an eternal moment of frozen shock as a lone explorer comes face to face with the most unexpected sight of all: her own image.

In image they are like us. In essence they prove unfathomable.

Soon after the Encounter they are given the name which they will bear through history: the Elyins, we call them, the Others. From the beginning they are the gift-givers, we the recipients, for they come with ships that skip like thoughts between the stars, making ours snails indeed.

They come among us unafraid, sharing all but themselves and their origin, picking up our languages like playthings, curious but not prying, reserved but never cold, bringing us crashing together in their wake as they visit worlds which have remained isolated since their first colonization thousands of years before.

They are like Man to the hundredth power: stronger, smarter, more beautiful. They are like Man as an abstraction or a pure concept: focused, distilled, clarified. They are enough like Man that often their appearance is greeted with hysteria. Old doctrines are reexamined: *And humankind was made in the image of God.* . . . Is this the pattern to which we were shaped? Is Elyin the name of the master template?

From the humans come fear, hatred, distrust, mingled crazily with envy and near-worship, blind love and reasoned affection. From the Elyins come reactions for which we have no reliable labels.

One thing seems clear: they are here because they wish to be, not because they need to be. Trade is proposed, but they will not trade with humanfolk; they bring their gifts with no thought of recompense, gifts which shake our many cultures to the roots. Along with the snatches of oblique advice, the quiet encouragements and cryptic cautions, comes a golden gel that tastes of fire and slows the human aging process till Man's days promise to extend beyond his dreams. A device given casually to a child on Cibola begins a communications revolution that will link world to far-off world through Screens of liquid light. And the ships: the Darkjumpers themselves, miraculous vessels capable of skimming beneath the skin of normal space to span impossible distances, leaping through light-years which the ancient Cold Ships had translated into human centuries.

With these gifts come the tantalizing possibility and gradual reality of an interstellar empire—though "empire" seems too strong a word for those worlds wary of subjugation or loss of autonomy. An Imperial Trust is formed, complete with many-layered bureaucracy and coordinated by an elected Trustee whom custom immediately retitles Emperor. The Great Years begin with the establishment of the Blue Shell Council, a representative body which attempts to oversee the actions of the many human worlds from the one Great World, Commons.

In time, other sentient races are encountered by Man, some incredibly alien in thought and form, others deemed more humanlike—though none are found which share the look-alike bond of Man and Otherman. Now comes a long quiet time, the period of almost four hundred years which some have called the Pax Elyannin, and peace prevails among the worlds touched by humankind. Peace dominates these tiles, yet through the artistry of Mig there is a subtle undertone, a contrast between the human men and women, and their Elyin counterparts, the beauty of whose faces is touched in the paintings with an absent, faraway cast, as if the entire race shared a single consuming desire, a yearning for something unknown to Man.

Peace.

In a flash of jarring hues, the second great ring of the spiral is concluded and Man crawls from his too comfortable bed, rubs the dreams from his eyes on a too pleasant morning, and finds that he is once again alone. In the span of a few hours, on every world, planetoid, construct, ship, or bit of rock trod upon by Man, the Elyins have vanished.

It is the Day of Departure, and there is no return. Man calls this day *Ansat*, the Hinderlond Low Tongue word for a small wound which, though initially insignificant in appearance, causes eventual death.

Mig devotes this entire turn of the spiral to the Departure, correctly gauging its importance in the history of humanity. The next scenes detail the years of painful adjustment as Man— the deserted child, the abandoned lover—attempts to cope with his loss.

Contemplating Mig's portrayal of the chaos that follows the

Departure—the swift and shocking suicide of placid Fleyn, human Emperor of the Imperial Trust; the massive shifts in population created by the expanding Drifter class; the brutality of the Blink Wars—one recalls the analogy of the historian Boesgaard:

> We made wonderful candles for Hearth Day when I was a child. We began by pouring the hot colored wax into containers already filled with chunks of ice. For a time there was equilibrium and the mass appeared solid. But when the wax had hardened and we removed the candle from its container, we found that all of the ice had melted away, leaving sudden gaping holes. We were amused and charmed. Such grotesque creations are fascinating as children's candles, unsuitable as governments. We should have been prepared for the ice to melt.

Mig delineates the situation in harsh, decisive strokes. Faced with disaster, Man is the creature that improvises. A Human Community is proposed to replace the Imperial Trust. The three most respected Secretaries of the Trust's administration are drafted as a temporary triumvirate to rule in Fleyn's stead, and the few alien races involved in the old federation are by various methods discouraged from joining the new Community, as a slumbering xenophobia reasserts itself on many worlds.

There are two turns left to the spiral. The first is a tableau of increasing horror as it becomes apparent that humanity's new and solitary realm may yet contain an unknown quantity of "ice."

The scene is ten years after the numbing blow of the Departure, the three hundred and sixty-fifth Great Year, according to the now ironic reckoning still standard throughout the Community. The luxurious *Via Maria*, a Darkjumper bound for World Babel out of old Earth, ceases functioning without warning in midjump and erupts convulsively into normal space, fantastically off course. Attempts to regain power prove futile; before another ship can arrive to evacuate the forty-two thousand passengers, the *Via Maria* drifts leisurely into a small white sun and explodes.

Three months later, the *Pourquoi* enters the Dark near Chalice, never to be seen again. Lost and presumed dead are thirty thousand passengers, colonists en route to the frontier worlds of the Maren.

Eleven months later, the *Dustapple* detonates gracefully on its landing stage on Weldon, leaving thousands dead or injured. Other Darkjumpers die less dramatically in the months and years to come, as engines sigh into dust or wheeze into permanent silence.

For three and one-half centuries, humanfolk have looked upon the Darkjumpers as the paramount symbol of those Others who had come among them. They were the Gift, the Legacy, the unquestioned and unquestioning servants. For three hundred and fifty years it has seemed neither imperative nor possible to unravel the fantastic complexity of their functioning. Now they have begun to die, and no human possesses the knowledge to build new vessels with jump capabilities, or to diagnose and cure the ills of the present finite shock. The Darkjumpers continue to malfunction at unpredictable but increasingly frequent intervals. They voyage in pairs whenever possible, and still it is a gamble. One-tenth of the total number of Darkjumpers give up the ghost in slightly less than five years.

The Cold Ships lie in their storage orbits like hibernating snails. Centuries from star to star. Visions arise of a civilization utterly sundered. The gnawing questions, never wholly stilled, grow louder. *Did they plan this? Are they watching us, perhaps? Is it some immense genocidal joke—slaughter by remote control?*

Twenty years after the Departure, two factions dominate a frightened humanity. The Builders are a decided minority, mostly Scholars who speak of lengthened lifespans and counsel patience and ingenuity, seeking to calm the babble of fear while attempts are made to repair or recreate the dying ships. More numerous by far on most worlds are the Expansionists, called the Parad Mir from the Hinderlond Low Tongue word for "wave unending." The Parad Mir predict a shattered, scattered humanity and point to the glorious days of early colonization. If Man is to be so cruelly fragmented, they cry, should he not be allowed a final chance to fill the Galaxy with his seed before the last Darkjumper's death brings impotence and isolation?

With an evangelical fervor not seen since the death or metamorphosis of the old religions, Parad supporters initiate a relentless drive for the acquisition of new worlds, and Survey ships are dispatched by the administrators on Commons to comb the Galaxy for planetary systems. Increased levels of population are encouraged on many Community worlds, justified by the promise of adventure on rich new planets.

But the habitable planets encountered by Survey are few; when one is located it is a precious discovery. During the Great Years of the Trust, planets inhabited by any but the most primitive forms of life had been routinely classified [CLOSED] and left monitored but untouched to develop without interference. Now, spurred on by the politically powerful Expansionists, the Surveyors find themselves reluctant to give up these rare jewels, and a frenzied humanity becomes dangerous. New amendments to the ancient Laws of Man are passed which establish a Code of Human Criteria, to be applied to advanced life forms on all newly discovered worlds. If there is conformity to the requirements of the Code, the indigenes are declared "human beings" and grudgingly left alone. If they do not conform, they are pronounced animals and confined, evacuated, or eliminated.

Very few races survive the Code, for Man is a singular creature in many respects, and an extra appendage or a plumed tail is enough to condemn as the zeal of Survey grows. In a few cases there is sufficient doubt, and the Builders pounce on these. Decision-makers are brought in from World Lekkole, also called University, a hearthplace of the Scholar class devoted to the accumulation and dissemination of knowledge. Though the participants' sympathy lies with the planetary indigenes, all decisions are bound by the inflexible Code, and in case after case the final verdict is the same. Thus, the penultimate turn of the spiral ends on a note of frenzied exhilaration for some, of horrified remorse for others, of barbaric cruelty and cold fear.

The final cycle of tiles, ending in that famous scene by the river beneath the silver sky, is devoted entirely to a single year, to GY 380: the Year of Belthannis, the time of the Lonely Man.

It begins, of course, with the Survey Ship *Ecco*, drawn by a dim notation on an ancient Elyin starmap to the single habitable satellite of Pwolen's Star: an Earth-sized planet christened Belthannis Autumnworld by a poetic crewmember. "Habitable" becomes "inhabited" when robot probes betray the presence of a highly developed form of animal life. The viewscreens are employed, and Mig gives us a discovery scene to rival the Encounter with its frozen shock and emotional intensity. Word is sent at once to University requesting a Special Evaluation Team, there follows the brief visit and quick decision of old Emrys, the subsequent arrival of the Group Resolvent, the unexpected addition to the team, the evolution and enactment of the great plan, and so forth.

Those with an eye for detail and some knowledge of Mig's craft are drawn like spinflies to this final turn of the mural, for it is here that the Master surpasses himself. No one familiar with the events of GY 380 can fail to be stirred when presented with this vivid, unparalleled portrait, as if with the very substance of the year preserved for eternity. . . .

It was the year 9718 by a very old calendar; it was the year 380 by a newer one. The parachristians called it 4472 and the Cults of Isis 1118. To the catpeople of Marik it was the Blue Mosaic Year, and to the men and thieves on Street of Dreams it was the Long Day of Great Promise.

Civil disturbances on Frond threatened to spread to a nearby neighbor, the pleasure world of Penny Arcade, as violence flared in empty warehouses and interstellar tourism dropped steadily. The venerable Societé Philosophique on St. Sang was temporarily disbanded. The Velvet Scythe and the Sad Smile, two of the ultrapopular Net Personalities, made known the conception and geneshift of Sum and Som, incredibly identical and theoretically perfect twins. A subsea volcano erupted on Dunbar's World, permanently killing eighty-one humans and three Augmented dolphins. Da-no-ka-Fen, Builder candidate for World Voice on Sipril, was struck by a clay brick and seriously disoriented during a campaign speech at a *mulel*-processing plant. A species of carnivorous mammal, *Felis domesticus*, was declared officially extinct on old Earth while continuing to thrive on numerous other worlds, and a Babellian athlete established a new record for the reticulated spin at the Holy Games on Chalice.

It was the year they legalized suicide. The year Tom Mencius, sometimes called Ta Meng Tse, completed *And Birds About You*, his most influential historical drama. The year Atlantis rose again under a vitreous dome and a different name to become a resort colony for the very rich somewhere in the middle of the vast Ondoyant on old Earth. It was the twenty-fifth anniversary of the Departure of the Elyins, and the great ships continued to die, one by one. Paranoia sent tolerance hopping like a toad before an angry dog, while common sense chased its tail in the corner. The Human Community was expanding and contracting like something about to give birth, and a man was discovered where there were no men.

It was an ordinary year, greeted with a thousand prayers and a hundred thousand curses. A protean year, bearing a million names and wearing a billion shapes, or no shape at all. A mirror, reflecting only those who knew how to look for their faces.

Where does a year begin?

In the mind, in an instant, in the flicker of a jeweled eyelash. Perhaps this one began in the slums of Heartsdesire, on Street of Dreams, where hungry children drift like fog through the constant drizzle, and can surround and rob a stranger in less time than it takes to sigh. Perhaps among the scented rooftop gardens and underground pavilions of a planet called the Great World in the languages of a dozen races, in the childish chatter of men and women trapped in gaudy imitation of a dream which had vanished utterly two and one-half decades ago. Or on the Secret World, in the many-hued darkness of Maribon, where emotion is measured in mathematical units, and speech is only for the very young.

Perhaps it began on Belthannis, at sunset.

CHAPTER 1

They came in bright colors, these saints, these
meddlers, falling like leaves through the false autumn
air. Singly and in pairs they came, and each one
brought a world with him. Flashing through the
sunset, they spilled light and laughter freely, singing
as they fell.
And there was one waiting . . .

FROM AUTUMN MASQUE,
BY FO-NA-VO-REM

1

Jon Emerson Tate, called Emrys in the abbreviated style favored by the Scholars, craned his neck as he trudged up the
grassy incline, trying halfheartedly to relocate the small red
star that had flared on his Screen a few minutes before. The
air seemed thinner, colder than usual, with a sharp hidden edge
that had him coughing in short, painful bursts by the time he
had gained the top of the small hill. He paused at the edge of

the forest, head cocked in a listening attitude, while his breath
erupted in brief silver clouds on the early-evening breeze. Except for his muffled coughing and the angry piping of a cluster
of thimblewort by his sandaled foot, the world was wrapped
in silence like a gauze, fragile and expectant.

I have been away from people far too long.

He shook his head slightly and started toward the faint path
that twisted into a shadowy grove of tall black-barked trees.
He squinted at the ground until his feet recognized the vague
trail, then he turned his eyes skyward again, peering anxiously
through the latticework of treetops. There: a crimson pinpoint
winked sullenly at him from behind the high black branches.

*They will probably try to call me Sessept. They will definitely
call me Emrys, though one among them will know my old name,
my true name. . . .*

*And what will they call me when I've told them the real
reason they were sent here?*

He glanced over his shoulder at the sunset, a pale golden
bruise spreading slowly on the gunmetal sky, then checked the
time on his wrist and hurried forward, picking his way instinctively through a maze of tiny ferns and brush that clawed at
the hem of his long robe. In his hand was the block of dark
waxwood he had been carving when the signal came. He had
brought it with him unthinkingly when he left the Hut; he
clutched it between fingertips and palm, kneading it slowly as
he half ran, half stumbled through the forest.

The trees were beginning to give way to patches of thimblewort and the faintly luminous bluemoss when suddenly he
glimpsed the clearing a few meters ahead. His footsteps slowed
as if the air about his ankles were thickened by the growing
shadows, and he hesitated in the final fringe of half-grown
saplings. He was conscious of an irrational desire to remain
hidden in the trees, to observe those who were coming without
being seen himself. A quick glance upward showed him the
tiny red star, flickering dully. He took a tentative step toward
the open field and cursed himself when he wavered back beneath the sheltering black boughs.

These are my own people, he insisted silently. *I have nothing
to fear from them*. He kept his rebellious thoughts from adding
yet with an effort. *As long as I can have time to properly*

prepare them. They mustn't see it until—

But he had checked with the Screen before leaving the Hut: the creature was safe, far to the west by the river that marked that edge of its territory; there was little chance of its wandering this far tonight.

He tensed as a faint lilting sound filtered down from somewhere high above his head. *They're singing!* he thought with a start, craning his neck.

And then he could see them, dark smudges against the tarnished silver as they fell slowly into visibility. The last rays of the sun caught them, reveling in the flashing bits of color here and there on their garments, and they twinkled like a string of lanterns as they drifted down over the meadow. The songs had stopped, but they called back and forth to one another, laughing as the ground rose under their feet, and he remembered his own lonely descent of several months past, before even the Hut had been planted.

Their voices grew louder, bringing him snatches of their conversation:

Newborn Isis, have you ever smelled such a breeze! Not a city, not a road, not a single landing stage . . .

"A savage place, as holy and enchanted
As e'er beneath a waning moon was haunted
By woman wailing for her demon lover . . ."

Tcha! All I'm wailing for is a dram of sweet blue wine with a warm chamber wrapped around it.

Speaking of moons, is there one?

Yes, three of them, but it's early yet. . . .

There—is that our meadow, that silver shimmer?

Closer, closer: the outlines of their packets became faintly prismatic and they glided past the treetops like wavering soap bubbles.

"Notice anything that resembled food on the way down?" a voice called out, quite clear. "I haven't had a decent meal since we left the 'jumper." There was scattered laughter.

The sound of jesting voices in the quiet ever-autumn of Belthannis was shocking. Startled finally into awareness of his undignified position under the trees, Emrys forced himself to move toward the clearing.

"Record that," a male voice descending to his left was saying, "the first soul on Belthannis was thinking of her stomach."

"So was the first soul on old Earth," retorted a woman on his right, and they began to touch ground in an uneven circle. Grappling for balance under unfamiliar gravity, each one pressed the small stud at his or her neck and the transparent packets stiffened and fell away like the petals of night-blooming flowers to sparkle and dissolve. Emrys took a deep breath and stepped out into the meadow.

He spread his hands in a tentative greeting. "You'll find there's plenty of warm food in the Hut."

He heard gasps. One of the wayfarers cursed, stumbling over the remains of her packet as she spun around.

Emrys felt a warm flush creep up his jaw. "Forgive me, that was stupid," he said. "I've been here by myself so long that it seems I've forgotten how to make a proper greeting."

"Not at all. It's just a surprise to see someone so soon." A sober, young-looking man with dark hair and neatly trimmed beard extended his hands. "Sessept Emrys it must be, correct? Or would you prefer High Scholar?"

"Just Emrys, please." He touched fingertips briefly with the dark man as the others approached.

"Here, Jack," one woman murmured over her shoulder. "Here's your first soul on Belthannis, not me."

The ring of travelers clustered around Emrys as if he were a heat source. He got a jumbled impression of fine Sipril silk near red plaid homespun; splashpattern biosynthetics brushing faded machine-wear; sturdy black boots precariously close to dirty bare feet; cloaks, patched breeches, one extravagant hat, dusty protectalls and burgundy velvet finger-sheaths. It had grown too dark to see their faces.

"In fact we weren't expecting a welcoming delegation," a new voice said from the shadows. "You needn't have come out. They gave us a map."

Emrys waved a deprecating hand. "No trouble. I'm glad for the walk and eager for the company. It darkens quickly here, and I didn't want to chance losing someone. You'll find these fields experience quite a drop in temperature once the sun's down."

"*Sta*, it's chilly already."

A woman with bright golden hair moved closer to Emrys, running her hands along inadequately covered arms. She wore sole-sandals and an iridescent garment like blue butterfly wings that draped her from throat to ankle. "Pwolen's third, the Autumnworld," she said in a singsong murmur. Then, in a different voice, calculating: "Half an hour's time will have it near four degrees Old Basic, I would say."

"That sounds right," Emrys said. "Would you be the planalyst? Ah, I've some data I'd like to show you after you're rested from the journey—say tomorrow or the next day."

"You mentioned the Hut. Is it nearby?" asked the bearded man. He was turning in a slow circle. "Over there? I've lost my bearings. It looks quite different from the ground, doesn't it?"

"My guess is this way." The velvet voice spoke from the shadows behind Emrys. "Beyond those domed bushes near the blue glow."

Emrys forced himself to keep his eyes to the front, and summoned a friendly chuckle from a throat gone suddenly dry. "I'm afraid you're both disoriented. Our rather sketchy path begins between those two blackbark trees—see there?"

He slid a thin disk from his belt and grasped it between thumb and forefinger. Light leaped forth in a painfully bright white arc. Emrys fiddled with the object and the radiance dimmed and narrowed to a pale milky shaft, which he pointed toward the forest.

"Perhaps we should go in now." He paused in thought. "Did they drop everyone?" he asked. "I thought I counted six, but in this light . . ."

"There are six of us," a woman answered, "but one's come only for the scenery, so to speak, and not as a member of your Group Resolvent. He styles himself an artist, and I thought it might be amusing—"

"It's true, Sessept," dark-beard volunteered. "I know for a certainty there were only five of us aboard ship who'd been summoned for the Evaluation. I asked one of the captains."

"Five . . ." mused Emrys. "I had six replies, six confirmations. The artist—you wouldn't be a Scholar also, would you?"

There was a snort of laughter. "If he were I'd have University investigated for incompetence," said the woman who had spoken before.

"I see." Emrys glanced up at the blackened sky, where a faint dusting of stars was already visible. The red pinpoint had vanished. *If we're missing a member they could force selection of another team*.

He sighed and tightened his collar against the wind.

"Well. We must hope our tardy member is en route aboard a different ship. The important thing now is for us to get to the Hut."

He aimed his lamp between the trees, and the travelers moved off slowly, threading a single line through the high silvery grass.

2

Raille waited in the room that had been her father's library before his unexpected death. Five long years ago a bolt of lightning, rare on placid Weldon, had tickled a lemon tree in the full bloom of spring and Raille's existence had collapsed in a graceful arc. Since that day she had avoided the library as much as possible, for it still contained so much of her father's life that his physical presence was an almost visible lack: a ragged hole in one of the intricately carved walls, a patch of vacuum in the scented air.

But now she sat in her father's favorite bodyhug, looking curiously at those pieces of his life which had been left behind with the twisted body they found beneath the tree. Her gaze wandered up the neat shelves of holodots and recordings, lingering over the prized collection of real printed-word reconstructions of books, some of them ancient volumes dating back more than seven thousand years, written in Antique tongues like Sude and Anglefrank.

Memories rushed in to supplement the sight of the familiar leather-bound copy of *Home Again*, bringing with them the texture of the pages and the smell of the printer's ink. She passed over the red and gold binding of the Parachristian Bible, the green of *Isis Reborn*, and the calm blue of the Taoist texts to a slim volume of favorite short stories by the reclusive Gerel Varyga.

In the far corner of the room, hidden discreetly by the shadows of the heavy homewoven hangings, was the stylized coffin of the family *bain-sense*, trimmed in ebony and ornately carved candlewood, and lined with soft velvet of the purest pearl grey.

Raille leaned back, and the lounger moved with her, unobtrusively altering its structure to fit the contours of her body. She closed her eyes and let her fingers drum idly on the dark polished wood of her father's desk. A few inches from her hand a tiny filament vibrated noiselessly in its holder, simultaneously cleansing the air and releasing a fresh, subtle perfume.

She heard a click, and her mother entered the room, arms burdened with a cluster of bittersweet and firestem. She brought the flowers to a ceramic vase on one corner of the desk and began to arrange them with quick, birdlike movements of her slender fingers. She kept her eyes carefully lowered as she worked, and Raille realized that she was trying her best not to look at the small white message card lying conspicuously on the leaf-colored blotter.

When the flowers had been arranged to her mother's satisfaction, the older woman seated herself carefully on the other side of the desk, avoiding her daughter's eyes. She was still a beautiful woman, Raille realized, looking at her closely for the first time in months. The long brown hair that swept back and up in an intricate, eye-teasing design had only a few strands of silver, and the smooth face betrayed no sign of age save the five precise little lines that had been neatly etched into her mother's high forehead. *One for each year since his death*, Raille thought.

Her mother looked up suddenly, and their eyes met. The older woman's lips were tension-tight, her dark eyes slits, as if she were awaiting a painful blow. The expression was unpleasant, a schematic interpretation in tight horizontal lines of her mother's inner emotional state. Raille watched the tiny muscles flash and disappear in her jaw as she relaxed her mouth for speech. The voice when it came was querulous, and much higher than she had remembered.

"If the ship should stop out there in the Dark and Empty—"

"It won't." Raille felt her own jaw stiffen.

"It might even explode on the landing stage like that one—"

"I'm going, Mother," Raille said evenly. "I've already sent

my acceptance through the big Screen at Gammelstad, and I'm
going to Belthannis."

"To study some creatures! Your father—" She fell silent,
studying the deliberate disarray of the flowers.

Raille looked past her mother's rigid shoulder to the small
circular window between the *bain-sense* and the bookshelves.
From her position in the lounger she could see the tops of the
lemon trees like emerald domes shrinking in precise rows toward the blue vastness of the Midmonth sky.

"—why you would want to leave your—"

In a week, she reflected, it would be Greenmonth and the
peak of the long summer's growing season. The ripe lemons
would fill the estate with their memory-laden fragrance, re-
calling so many Greenmonths and so many long, happy summers.

"—think your grandfather and I can manage without—"

Is it only twenty? Raille asked herself, surprised. *Have I
seen only twenty summers on this blank blue world?*

Outside a flock of golden birds dipped lazily into view above
the orchards.

"—let me read the cards."

"What?" Raille shifted in the bodyhug and stared blankly
at her mother. The older woman was searching for something
in the bottom drawers of the desk.

"A reading," she said. "If you're determined to go, you'll
at least let me do a reading. There are so many things that
might happen—ah!" She placed a small silk-wrapped package
on the blotter, pushing the message slip from Gammelstad to
one side with a *tsk* of disapproval. "These cards," she murmured, untying a small cord and folding back the cloth with
great care, "these very cards belonged to your several-times-
over great grandmother, who was a blood cousin of the Founder
himself and spent a quarter of her life on the First World before
the Settling." She caressed the top card with a reverent fingertip.

Raille looked with distaste at the stack of yellowed rectangles resting on the keepweave. A tiny muscle tugged at the
corner of her mouth and she said softly, "Please, Mother, I'd
rather you didn't."

Her mother had begun to shuffle the deck slowly, deliberately. "Nonsense," she said coldly. She dealt the cards swiftly, and Raille shivered as the pattern completed itself. The Alchemist. Queen of the Cups. Queen of the Staves. Death. She looked away. Her mother leaned forward expectantly, wetting her lips. "The cards never lie, you know."

I know, Raille thought, *I know, I know*. From the corner of her eye she glimpsed the flock of golden-winged birds as they lifted from the orchard and wheeled gracefully toward the east. She watched them intently.

"How very odd," her mother murmured.

Half an hour later Raille was walking through the great front door and down the wide marble steps. "Come to me before you leave," her mother had called from the half-completed reading, still seated at the desk as if trapped there by the unfinished future. "Come to me and we'll talk."

She found her grandfather in the lemon orchard, working with his hoe at the base of one of the larger trees. The soil was rich and dark where he had already dug; she felt it cool and solid beneath her bare feet. After watching the slow, patient patterns of his work for several moments she leaned forward and tapped his arm. A bright gold tooth gleamed in the smile above his white beard. He set aside the hoe to free his hands for conversation, leaning it against the trunk of the tree.

"Good morning, my-Raille," he said with a flick of calloused hands. Raille thought of her mother's soft white fingers making meaningless patterns in the bittersweet and firestem. "Have you seen your mother?" he continued, the signs flowing clear and liquid from his hands in concert with the soft, roughened voice.

She nodded, calmed as always by the gentle movements of his speech. "In the library," she signed. "She wanted to read the cards, but I wouldn't let her finish."

Her grandfather shook his head, smiling. "Obstinate child," he signed with a click of his tongue. "Are you going?"

"Yes, yes, yes!" Her fingers swept the air like moths. "And I'll bring you back a plant, a strange one from Belthannis!"

He smiled again, and the light sparkled in the gold tooth. "Just you come back. Just bring yourself back."

"Oh, I will, I will! I'll be back before next Coldmonth.

You'll never even notice I've been gone." She stretched up on her toes in delight. "Grandfather," she asked suddenly, dropping down on her heels, "what is it like out there? You were Out once."

"A long time ago, that was. Before my hearing had gone completely. Hard to communicate if I went out now. Hasn't been much deafness since the Others came and went."

"Do they all speak Inter? I'm halfway fluent in that. Or will I have to learn more new languages? I don't have the time!"

He inclined his head toward the base of the tree and tugged at his beard. "You'll be working with scientists, I imagine, educated people, and all those from the Centermost worlds speak Inter anyway," he told her. "The children, they learn it from a machine in most places now."

"What about the people themselves?" Raille asked. "What are they like when you're among them?"

"Like a million different things. The Community is large, large." The old man shrugged. "One thing is: they don't have a great affection for the dear folk of Weldon."

Raille's enthusiasm sagged abruptly. "What do you mean? Why? What have we ever done to—"

His hands interrupted her. "It's more what we haven't done. Do you know how many of the other human-settled worlds don't belong to the Community? Two, maybe three? Our blue jewel has been a private world since the earliest days of the Wave of Expansion."

"But surely that's no reason to hate us."

"Those that dislike us—I did not say 'hate'—do so because we are different, in a way that is outside their own differences. Partly because we refused to be poured into their Community stewpot. Partly because we never worshiped the Others, nor took much notice of them at all. And because we sent back their longevity drugs and chose death over life, as did few others, chance over security. Although"—he leaned back, pressing his shoulder against the tree trunk—"some say death was the easier choice, the greater security, and immortality the frightening prospect."

"But the Darkjumpers still come, from time to time." Her fingers stumbled over a new thought. "I have to take passage on a Darkjumper to Belthannis," she said wonderingly. "I have to pass through the Dark and Empty."

"That would seem to be the best way to get there. Did you have them send your yes-note to Lekkole?"

"Yes, this morning." Her signs were clumsy; she was trying to picture the voyage through space and nonspace.

Her grandfather shook his head, watching her with a smile.

"No chance to back out now, then. They've probably already rerouted a passenger ship or two to come pick you up."

"Back out?" Her vision faded. "I don't want to back out— oh, Paba, can you imagine it? A ship coming here, for me?" She squeezed the dirt between her toes and closed her eyes, watching the great starship settle ponderously, delicately, on the single landing stage at Gammelstad. "I wonder if I'll be the first one there."

Her grandfather shook his head and picked up his hoe, returning to work at the base of the tree. Above them, a second flock of birds, rust-colored with brown-barred wings, had appeared out of the west and begun to circle lazily over the orchard.

3

In the sixth year of his life, somewhat later than was common for a novice of his classification, he had stopped using his audible voice.

He had taken up residence at this time in the central barracks at Delphys, largest of the three Cities of Maribon. There were gathered the five levels of communicants: the novices, beginners like himself, just embarking on the mastery of shellscan and self-delineation, or already venturing into the twin realms of delve and affect; the rarely glimpsed anchorites, living in their careful seclusion, coded each to his bondsman and shuttered from outside contacts; the adepts, perfected and certain, walking the dim corridors wrapped in *stet* like a cloak of cold flame; the imagoes, less numerous than the rest, oblique of bearing and unmistakable in their garments of deepest jet and purest white; and the noumena, mind-patterns of deceased communicants carried in the brain of adept or imago, no less real for their incorporeality than the other four strata.

He had been inquisitive for a short time, midway through his fifth year at Delphys, undertaking lengthy journeys of exploration and indulging in periods of solitary pondering deemed unsuitable for a rising communicant. On one such excursion, while prowling through a long, shadowed corridor not meant for those of his slight attainment, he had encountered a tall, striding imago, oblivious of the boy's presence and cloaked in protective motes, the broad white forehead emblazoned with the irresistible symbols of the *rorshock*.

He had sunk to his knees as the other passed and remained there in the dim hallway for several days in a barely living state, his thin body twitching, his mind wheeling obediently about the commanding pattern.

They found him before he starved and took him to a lesser adept who removed the image of the symbol and performed a series of adjustments upon his young mind to rid him of his lingering handicap. The adjustments involved illustrating the ways of gaining mastery over those motes within him which were responsible for initiating the inquisitive impulse. Once he could understand the urge, it was believed, he could also manipulate it.

The power to engender an emotion in his own mind or in the mind of another, and the concomitant ability to banish it with a twist of his will, shattered utterly emotion's dominion over him. Thereafter he progressed through the novitiate stages at an accelerated rate, attaining anchorite status at the age of sixteen and entering seclusion with his bondsman, a slight young touch-woman from the eastern settlements, for a period of eighteen months.

He emerged an adept of the first reach, well acquainted with *stet*, his days devoted to exercises of perception and control, his evenings given to meditation upon selections from the ancient book of wisdom known as the *Eng Barata*.

Six months of training and contemplation of the *Eng* were ended for the young man by a summons from an adept. He was informed that he would shortly be implanted with a noumenon, the mental configuration of a deceased communicant, with which his own mind would thenceforth share the habitation of his brain. Then there had been a brief meeting with an aged imago who told him of his upcoming journey to another world.

Instructions concerning the performance of his mission there were spare and enigmatic: Follow the guidance of the *Eng Barata*. Allow necessary actions to reveal themselves in their own time, and fulfill the *stet* of each moment.

When he sensed the interview was at an end and turned to leave the room, the imago halted him with a small gesture.

A sheet of micapaper lay squarely on the basalt table. At the old one's nod, he stepped forward and took it up into his hands, gazing at the row of precise phonetic characters that divided the paper like a column of marching insects.

"Chaaasssmaaannn," he said in a voice thick and grating from twelve years' disuse. "Chassman."

The imago signified acceptance, an end to the audience. By the time he had moved to the door her eyes were closed and she had retreated into meditation upon *stet*.

Chassman returned to his bare cell and began to practice speaking. For two-thirds of his life he had used his voice less than a dozen times, at the infrequent drills, when with the others he said *Aaaaaaa* and *Ooooooo* and *Rrrrrrr* so that his vocal cords would not atrophy.

He never asked whether the word *Chassman* had been his own original name when he was a child in a touch-man village before his selection as a proto-communicant, or whether it was the name of the noumenon he now bore, or whether it was a new word altogether, manufactured moments earlier, perhaps, because the sounds had impressed some adept as being particularly *stet*.

4

It was a traditional Hut: candlewood and sculplate, white stone, battleglass and plax, all blurred and bent at the edges by a high-effect weathershield. Lights were beginning to glow dimly through the tinted windows as Emrys and his followers grouped around the doorway. When Emrys touched his thumb to a bit of ornamental scrollwork they heard a faint chime, then the thickly paneled door slid open with a muted hiss. When they were all inside, a voice spoke from the shadows above their heads.

"Welcome back, Emrys. I trust your companions arrived with a minimum of discomfort. Did you have a pleasant walk in the night air?"

Emrys glanced at the ceiling with a wry smile. "Yes, thank you, Hut, quite pleasant. I must go to my room for a minute. Would you show my friends around?" He nodded to the others, then disappeared behind a room divider in the guise of a continuous veil of cool rain that evaporated centimeters above the carpeted floor. The walls of the foyer were of natural stoneling, the so-called living rock of World Obun, terraced with ivy and niched with clumps of pterodendron.

"Certainly, Emrys." The voice was calm and beautiful, an androgynous mixture of crystal whisper, golden hum, and high silver flute. "Welcome, travelers! Allow me to introduce myself: I am your habitable University terminal, identification code available upon request, a machine intelligence placed here to provide and to serve for the duration of your stay."

"You're one of the new volitional units, aren't you?" The dark-bearded man was inspecting the pterodendron, which trembled and flexed slightly as he touched it. "I'd heard that was a prototype model, not yet in use."

"Semivolitional," the voice corrected gently. "But you are quite right. I am one of only six of my level currently in operation.

"You must excuse Emrys," it added after a moment. "He sometimes suffers from frightful headaches. Nervous tension, mainly—he worries too much. And now, if you would walk up the ramp to your immediate right, please."

The interior of the Hut was furnished much like the main salons of a Community Darkjumper: in the Grand Eclectic mode, incorporating influences from many cultures, with heavy ornate sofas clustered around shifting erotic flame sculptures and a pearl-gray *bain-sense* in the Library. The rooms seemed open and sprawling to the untrained eye; persons versed in the architechnical sciences would have become gradually aware of a scrupulous conservation of space. Outside, the Hut was a hazy-edged dwelling reminiscent of the pre-Commingling period on New World, executed in great blocks of beige, black, and earth-color. Inside, it was a comfortable retreat, a museum, a laboratory, and a self-sustaining life-support system, all under the meticulous guidance of a sophisticated machine mind linked via Screen to the great datapools on University.

Manufactured by the skilled crafters and master architechs of a planet called Bluehorn, the Hut came as a completely preseeded unit, its intellect in place from the early stages of composition to ensure proper integration and to encourage the development of an ambience. Most Huts could adapt themselves to a wide range of environments, with a standard month the usual span from installation to optimum performance. When Emrys had witnessed the initial implantation of the Hut on his second visit to Belthannis, he had found it to be a four-room shelter far too preoccupied with its own growth to engage in more than perfunctory conversation. In the months that followed he had watched it mature as both the habitation and the companion-servant it was designed to be.

"And this is our Music Nook. Yes, you certainly may touch that: it's a genuine baby grand, a very ancient kind of musical instrument now reproduced exclusively on Alba Mundus. I do hope some of you like to create or experience music. There are flame-sculpting materials in that cabinet, and the wall with the mural becomes an old-fashioned kinetic-image screen when you tap the elbow of the largest nude. No, the purple one. That's it.

"We have an extensive library of reconstructed sound-and-visual presentations from the back-before, including the Antique *Belle et la Bête* and several versions of the highly influential pre-Expansionist *Cielo Argenta*. There is also a set of military training films from the Collapse on Melkior if anyone is really interested in classics.

"The Orrery is at the end of this corridor—it's marked with a blue glass oval on the floor—and the Garden of Earth is just beyond that silk hanging. I'm quite pleased with the way it's turned out; you can smell the pine from here, I believe."

Through irised doorways and up and down tightly spiraled staircases, over shadowed colorplays dancing in panels of transparent flooring that chimed intricate melodies when trod upon, and along halls hung with textures, clouded with mists, and

scented with aromas from a dozen different worlds, the voice
of the Hut led them through its chambered complexity, seeming
always to emanate from a point slightly above and in front of
them.

"And this is the very center, our Hearth Room," it said at
last, leading them through an archway flanked by fierce stone
lions. The chamber was large and circular, domed, so that it
resembled half a sphere. A golden dragon in the Vegan style
curled in rich mosaic menace on the floor, and portraits in oil
and brass peered down from the incurving wall, each one precisely placed so that all appeared to gaze at the immense, round
table set in the center of the golden dragon's tiled lair. The
rest of the room had been artfully organized through the use
of furniture and decorative objects to form sequestered areas
of various shapes and sizes, some large and open enough to
encourage social interaction, others of a more solitary, con-
templative design.

The men and women wandered about the room with languid
interest, pressing a grim statuette here, caressing a length of
polished wood there, until, as if by common consent, all began
to drift inward along the dragon's glittering spine, and they
found themselves face to face around the massive table.

"There's no hearth," a dark, slender woman said with a
shake of her hairless skull. "There never is."

"What's hearth?" murmured the young man with his arm
around her shoulders.

"It's a pity, I know," the Hut commented. "An incongruity,
a definite flaw in the basic concept." There was a pause where
a person might have sighed. "I've tried my best to give it a
sense of warmth, nonetheless, albeit only spiritual. That table
is real *oke* from Prinnetwar, and fully automatic. And the blue
circle just to the left of the Picasso hosts the Screen which is
our link to civilization. It may be employed for local observations, and is also capable of bringing in the Net clear as a
bell."

"Oh please," said the woman with the white-gold hair and
butterfly dress, "couldn't we limit its use to planetary observations? I was hoping the Net wouldn't have to follow us this
far out."

There was a trace of bitterness in her voice, a childlike

quality to her movements. The woman had a serene and fragile beauty that was highlighted by the pale blue tulip embossed on one cheek. Her true age was impossible to determine, though careful *noia*, the analysis of gestures and expressions to determine chronological age, would have argued for considerably more than the nineteen or twenty years immediately evident in the delicate features. The upper limits of Ember, the Elyin longevity drug, had yet to be established.

"Unofficially, my dear Person Scholar, I'm in total agreement," the Hut said in a confidential tone. "However, the Laws are quite specific in requiring that the avenues of communication be kept open for those who wish to utilize them."

"So the old Laws operate on Belthannis Autumnworld, *aussi*?" the bald woman remarked. "Comforting. With Laws and the Net, this might as well be home. *Nicht wahr*, machine?"

"This really Picasso?" the curly-haired young man asked before the Hut could comment. He had wandered away from his dark companion and stood next to the opaqued Screen, inspecting a small painting with casual interest.

"Why certainly," the Hut said. "*The Woman in White*. We have her on loan from The Museum. Do you paint, perhaps?" It chatted on, warming to the subject. "I'm pleased to find a fellow art enthusiast out here in the wilderness: we shall have to have a talk sometime! Did you notice the Fan Felsing half-white in the Library? Have I done justice to the brass with my arrangement, or do you find it self-indulgent?"

"Yours? I thought—"

"Oh, most of the practical planning is done by the architechs on Bluehorn. They do give us a modicum of artistic control once we're installed, however. I did so try to get a real hearth . . ." A note of true regret crept into the beautiful voice.

The sound of clicking sandals spiraled down the anteroom stairs and Emrys entered briskly, rubbing his hands and humming as he crossed the tiles. Striding directly to the table, he reached under its rim and ran his fingers over a recessed keyboard. There was a sound like a distant gong and seven cushioned seats looped down and outward from the underside of the table. He tapped another combination of keys and the sound was repeated on a higher note, as panels slid open and seven place settings rose into view. Wineglasses filled from the bot-

tom up and linen napkins unfolded themselves on the wide
tabletop. At a final tone, like a small silver bell, Emrys waved
them to their seats.

"Three bells for evenmeal," he said. "Two for midday, one
for breakfast, though of course you're all welcome to eat when
you please; the table is quite simple to operate from the panels
in front of you or through direct commands to the Hut. Now,
who wants *bouillabaisse*?" His fingers played on the hidden
keyboard and fat, steaming dishes rose like balloons.

When everyone had been served, Emrys put the table on
automatic and turned to his own meal. As he ate, he allowed
himself furtive glances at each of his companions. That the
others seemed to be engaged in the same sport reinforced his
belief that most of them were strangers to each other as well
as to himself. A Darkjumper was the size of a small city; the
members of his team might not have seen one another until it
was time to be packeted for planetfall.

They ate in silence, eyes rising and dipping, spending exactly the right amount of time studying a neighbor's face so as
to seem casual. Emrys searched his memory of the acceptance
cards, trying to recall if any of the members of this group were
noted as being particularly religious. He had learned from experience, long ago on World Chalice, that certain sects could
be notoriously sensitive concerning personal privacy. With such
people it was always better to look than to ask, better still to
keep your mouth *and* your eyes shut. But the others were doing
enough looking: he grinned behind his napkin as the bright-
haired woman stole a wondering glance at the man across from
her, a somber-looking individual with skin and tightly cropped
curls of an odd, sandy-golden monochrome. He didn't seem
the sort to follow current fads in tint and brow paint and the
subtle alterations in hue when he shifted position supported
that observation; his skin had almost certainly been *panked*,
the dermis impregnated with a photosensitive dye. The rich
coloring was not easily removed and Emrys wondered if the
man had indulged in panking for reasons other than decoration.

The bright-haired woman was watching the golden man
intently, a small frown troubling her exquisite features.

Emrys looked away and found himself staring directly into

the eyes of the curly-headed boy seated half the table away. He automatically shifted his gaze to the portrait above the other's head, but not before the boy had flashed him a wide and friendly grin.

No embarrassment there, he thought ruefully, *except my own.*

The man on the boy's right, he of the sandy flesh and stern, almost scowling face, was not participating in the common inspection, being much too absorbed in the contents of his plate. Emrys watched shamelessly, fascinated, as the other chewed a mouthful of crumbly cheese-in-cake in small exploratory bites. With a mental shrug, he reexamined his own plate; palm-sized mushroom slices, asparagus with a citrus sauce, translucent wafers of the omnipresent *mulel* grain; all complemented by an assortment of mild drugwines, steaming chetto, and bowls of fruitwater. He had let the cuisine of old Earth guide his choices for their first meal together; surely there was nothing here which a University Scholar should find unusual.

A flicker of dull green: Emrys saw that the ravenous diner had but one eye. The man's left socket was occupied by a smooth-fitting oval of milky green. When the light struck it at a certain angle, he could discern scratches of some sort on its surface, but he was unable to see them clearly.

Noticing that the others were nearly finished, Emrys concentrated on his own meal for the next few minutes. After the table had swallowed most of the utensils and empty platters, he pulled the thin white squares out of his pocket and placed them on the table in front of him.

"Well!" he pronounced with careful cheeriness, instantly regretting the shroud of silent anticipation that settled over the table.

He began again with a false chuckle. "Well, shall we see who we are? My name is Jon Emerson Tate, though I'm called Emrys by most people, and that will do admirably here. I have your notes of acceptance with me. To expedite matters, suppose I just read them off and you can identify yourselves." He peered at the first card.

"Per choss? Historian?"

The dark-bearded man nodded.

"Per Cil? Planetary analyst?"

The bright blonde lifted her hand with a self-conscious smile and murmured something he couldn't quite catch.

The data sheets were so brief, he thought. *Nothing to tell me if I've chosen well or badly*. Emrys distrusted the trend toward one-word names. Originally a Drifter fad, the *brevnom* had spread to University and become immensely popular, a social necessity overnight. Yet it seemed to him unpleasantly characteristic of the Community's blend of instant surface intimacy coupled with an unyielding basic formality. He heard a cough.

"Uh, Per March? There's no Major listed here . . ."

The golden-sand man raised his head, shade and hue of his face altering subtly with the movement. Emrys realized with a start that the incongruous false eye was actually an art object: a piece of the cleverly carved stone the ancients had called *chade* on the First World. A minute pastoral scene from some long-dead agrarian culture gleamed dully at him as March turned his head to one side, grunted, and returned to his third course of mushrooms and *mulel*. Emrys waited for further comment. When none was forthcoming, he shrugged and passed to the next card.

"Per Marysu?"

"*Här*, but the accent is properly on the ultimate, not before." Her voice was melodious, strong, with clear sharp edges that bespoke certainty and self-confidence. She was slender, dark-skinned. Elaborate brow paint covered her bare scalp with a bestiary of fanciful creatures. She was wearing the latest Centermost fashion, an amorphous splashpattern which wandered slowly over her body. Reacting to changes in skin secretions and body temperature, it revealed and concealed at random various portions of her body, sparkling from within like a web of violet fire.

Marysu held her head erect and met his gaze with sardonic, ice-chip blue eyes. Fascinated by her dramatic beauty, Emrys pulled himself back to the message squares with an effort.

"You're given as a philologist and panlinguist." Something tugged at his memory. "Are you the linguist who deciphered those well cavern hieroglyphs on Marik?" She inclined her head slightly forward. "Ah. Impressive work. I read the transcripts with great interest."

Emrys fumbled with the last two cards. He knew the next name as well as he knew his own. It belonged to the copper-haired woman seated so close to the bright Cil: the woman whose gray eyes he had been avoiding for almost two hours, ever since a velvet-soft voice in the dark meadow had confirmed her presence. There were so many things to ask and to explain that he had found himself suddenly terribly unsure, groping for a place to begin.

"Jefany. Per Jefany."

At last he looked at her directly and saw that she was unchanged, as lovely as her picture in his mind, warm and glowing next to the golden Cil, whose slender hand she held lightly in her own.

"Humanist," he read with a faint smile, while memories gathered in a deep crystal pool at the center of his thoughts. Longing to sit and stare at her now that he had looked once on those familiar features, he forced himself to move on to the last name.

"Raille Kristema Weldon na Weldon," he pronounced carefully. It seemed more like a grand title than a name after the fashionable brevity of the others. Someone gave a short laugh.

"*Na* indicates 'of' in Weldonese," Marysu said.

Emrys looked inquiringly at the curly-haired boy, who shook his head emphatically and laughed again. "I'm here with her," he said with a nod to Marysu. "Name's Jack. No specialty or anything, but I like to paint some, for fun."

"*Sta*. An ornament," the panlinguist confirmed drily. "Less expensive than jewelry."

"I see." Emrys looked around the table, wondering what to say next. As if sensing his uncertainty, Choss, the dark-bearded historian, rose hesitantly to his feet.

"The jump was more than usually fatiguing," he said softly. "Forgive me if I retire to my room."

"Certainly," Emrys said. "The Hut will guide you. I've been extremely thoughtless to keep you all here. One knows the aftereffects of the Darkjump, and all of this could easily have waited till the morning."

"No apologies necessary." Choss smiled formally. "The meal was most refreshing and greatly appreciated. A pleasant night to you all." He left the table with a small bow, and the others began to trail after him, March abandoning his half-

consumed fourth course with visible reluctance. Emrys noted
the drooping shoulders and unsteady legs as they drifted into
the anteroom. It was obvious that their unnatural circumnavi-
gation of the distance between the Centermost worlds and Belthannis had taken its toll on the voyagers.

"Jefany—" He obeyed a sudden impulse. "Could you stay
for a minute?"

The red-haired woman whispered something to Cil, turned
back, and resumed her seat. They looked at each other.

"You came," he said simply, feeling something close to
relief for the first time in several hours.

She smiled faintly. "Fair evening, Jon Emerson. Pers Emrys. Jon." She ran long fingers through her fiery hair in a weary
gesture he found achingly familiar. "I fear I'm as tired as the
others. Do you suppose all of *this* might wait until the morning,
too?"

He fumbled for an answer, something witty to make her
laugh, or tragic to ensorcel her with sympathy. But she was
already rising, and he watched in silence as she passed between
the stone lions.

5

Later, Emrys went up on the roof, to stand on the sundeck
and stare at the moons. The air blew thin and brittle. He had
switched off the weathershield an hour before, so the wind was
playing halfheartedly with his hair, causing it to flicker and
flow like a dark flame sculpture. His scalp was numb; his
fingers were stiff, curled into cages.

Music crept soft and blue from the open glass door at his
back. A cup of forgotten moodbender rested on the wooden
rail next to his elbow; the moons competed for its shadow.

The wind was quickening, beginning to sting his eyes as it
passed, and he imagined a rippling black shape swooping down
out of the darkness. The image was something from a childhood
dream, he thought, or perhaps he had really seen it once on
another world, long ago. He closed his eyes and the black
shape rode the wind currents like a dark cloak, gliding, diving,

circling the sundeck, aiming for his face with its slashing barbed tail. His eyes stung sharply, and he winced. Tilting his head against the wind, he retreated from the dream creature's attack and drank deeply from the sweep and murmur of the music.

The melody was sad and ancient: a First World composition, perhaps, or one of Maubry's *Several Masks*. Everything seemed to mesh as he listened, and for a few seconds all made sense: starlight and shadow, shape and essence, torment, age, death, injustice . . .

He felt a note that didn't belong and something warm stepped out into the darkness, humming softly beneath the music. He turned and explored her face in the moonlight.

"So sad," she said after a moment, breaking all the patterns of his night.

"You could hear the music downstairs?" As always his own voice surprised him: green leaves on a dead tree.

"I felt the wind."

He glanced over his shoulder. The doorway was a black square. "Too used to being here alone," he said. "It shouldn't be left open when the shield's off."

"They won't feel it. Not in their warm rooms, sealed up asleep." She hummed with the music again, deep in her throat, moving slowly to its tides against the railing. "I think this world needs your music, anyway. Especially now, like this. Something to talk back to this shivering wind, a letter of introduction from the invaders." She stared out at the night. "*Hai*, you can see the smallest moon move." They watched it for a while.

Finally he spoke. "Why did you come up? I thought you were exhausted?"

"I was—I am—though I think it hits the young ones harder. I took a prodrug, I took several. Couldn't sleep. I was talking with your Hut when I felt the wind. And here I am." She paused. "That reminds me, Jon. Why won't the Hut say anything about the Evaluation? It tried to shift subjects twice when I mentioned the indigenes, and I could tell it was becoming uncomfortable."

"Poor Hut." He sighed. "I told it not to discuss the matter until I've had time to prepare the Group."

She looked sideways at him. "Prepare us? How? For what? They wouldn't tell me anything on University, of course. We're supposed to come to the Evaluation clothed in objectivity. But here, now, why this mystery? All your hush and shadow makes it sound like something illegal."

He looked unhappy in the stark multiple moonlight.

"I bribed three very respectable planning computers to get you all here, Jefany. Especially you. It was very difficult. I don't like to corrupt machines—it's like deceiving children."

"Bribed? Was it that important to you? *Hai*, can you trust these machines? If someone should give them a better offer you might find yourself walking on the Deepside."

"Yes. I don't know." He shrugged. "I think their sympathies were with me anyway. It's always so hard to be sure with them, but it won't really matter in the long run. If I fail to accomplish what I want on Belthannis, much more will be lost than a few waking years."

"You are planning something with the Evaluation, then. Something illegal."

"Oh Lord, yes. At the very least illegal."

"UnLawful, then? You're planning to break the Laws of Man?"

"Some of the Laws have been changed, misinterpreted over the centuries, Jefany. A few have become very bad."

"I see." She thought for a moment, watching his face. "And you want the members of this Group to help you. Now that you've seen them, do you think they will?"

"I don't know." He sounded half-asleep, drained of energy. "There are things they have to see and hear before I can even ask them. Tomorrow, or the next day, if I can't postpone it further. And there's still that last member, that Weldon person. If I can make them wait for her, until the Group is complete . . ."

She was silent as the old song ended and a new one began. Then she said: "And how did you know I'd accept when you— what shall I call it?—requisitioned me? After the way Chwoi Dai ended—"

"I didn't know. But I had to have someone here who could see things clearly and keep me out of the traps. With you, if you'll stay, and with the others, if I can persuade them to join me, we may be able to win this one. To win them all, perhaps."

"Even Chwoi Dai?" She shuddered at the memory.

"If it's still possible," he said quietly. Then he felt for her wrists in the dark and held them. "Stay with me, Jefany. You're different from anyone I've ever known. I think I need you here very much."

The woman gave a small laugh, almost a cough. "If you'd said that fifty years ago..." But he had said it like a child, and he was looking at the stars again, fiercely, like a child.

"This is very important, isn't it?" she said after a few moments.

"Jefany." He lifted his hand and turned her face toward his as the moonlight slipped across it. "What I can do here I will do."

"I understand, Jon." She moved slightly under his touch. "I will try not to be frightened by that."

He shook his head. "I am frightened, deeply frightened, for what I've found here. If I cared less for you, I would ask you to halve that burden. I may yet."

"Sharing happens between us, as always. You need not ask."

He gave a small, almost painful, smile of gratitude. "These others, the rest of our Group Resolvent," he said after a while, "I don't really understand them. Perhaps it's because I haven't traveled so much lately. I feel out of touch with the newest crop of people. I can't even say what it is about them that seems so strange to me. Perhaps just a lack of purpose. Do they know where they're going half the time these days, or are they too busy worrying that the ship will break up around them? Do they know what they want to accomplish beyond tomorrow's dinner? I swear some of them scarcely seem human themselves. That very intense linguist with her pet artist. The man with the *chade* eye—d'you know he can't even read Inter? It was specially noted on the data sheet they sent me at the beginning. He was a soldier in the Blink Wars, he's done the Dance, the one that kills. God knows what he's been doing at University—or why I let myself choose him for this!"

"A lot of people can't read," she murmured.

"But everyone's so detached, so aimless. Floating from one world to the other, like windbuds, like that Jack. Another illiterate, I think. He's on the Drift, you know, you can see it in his eyes. And they're all becoming Drifters. Don't they feel the future coming as we do, Jefany, don't they ever wonder about it, worry about whether they have a place there?"

She shook her head. "It's the age, Jon. The age of the Community and the age of humankind and the age of people like us. You know we're not real anymore, you and I, not as they are. The elder race. Extinct.

"Oh, Jon, I've lived through one full century and more than three-quarters of the next—and you, you've seen almost four! An Antique man would be thrice in the grave by then and firmly convinced his little eyeblink had been a rich, full life. And it's still such a miracle to you and me—is it not?—that we open our eyes each new morning. Oh, we're the strange ones now, not they."

She moved away from him, and the words came like a prayer: "We're old: like planets, moons, suns. When you yourself were born it was another age, the back-before, the last trickle of *Mirin*, and death was still yawning nearby like a pit, a *thing* in the dark you felt yourself withering closer to each day. Even after they came, even after the gift was given, realization lagged behind. Nobody thought the Ember would work, for God's sake, though I don't know why not. Everything else they brought us did. For a while." She took a breath of the scented night and released it slowly, coming to stand at his side again.

"In the Great Year 201, when I was born," she continued in a softer voice, "people were just beginning to grasp the idea that the old adversary might be beaten. And for the last few generations he's never existed—he's Darkjumps away! Everyone ages, but no one's old. We grew up thinking we'd grow wrinkled and weak, and we can't adjust to our reprieve. But these new ones, they have no doubt they'll stay young forever. Bright little drifting children . . ."

They were silent, each with his own thoughts. The song died, and when a new one rose through the doorway Emrys found words flowing through his mind. His lips moved around a bit of the melody; a young voice came from the ancient throat.

This song was also very old, and the words which he remembered spoke of things that happened only rarely nowadays, and of feelings that Community Man seldom experienced.

She stirred uncomfortably as the old man sang in his beautiful voice. "You're out of your time," she said at last. "One doesn't sing when music is playing."

He stopped abruptly. "One did in my day."

"But not in mine, and surely not in theirs." She glimpsed the expression on his face. "Oh, Jon, it doesn't matter. I'm the only one here. Don't let there be year-distances between us too. Sing, if you like, it's all right." But he was silent.

The trees were scratching the belly of the middle-sized moon when he spoke again. "You know I really had no way of being sure. I just had to hope you'd come."

"Oh, well, I had to," she said in a tone that mixed fondness with resignation and something else. "If not for myself or for you, then for Cil, who laughed with excitement when the notifications came." She turned to face him. "But it's been two years since Chwoi Dai. A great many things have happened, a few of them good. I'm with Cil now, for one—but you must have known that."

"No. I assumed you'd met on board the ship."

"No, it's been almost a year. But, Jon, we both received requests."

"Pure coincidence. I had no idea."

"Ah, that is strange indeed."

"Stee?"

"Back on Stone's Throw, with two of the children. They live together, oddly enough, near a big Builder research plant in Paiak. He's become a very good architech, I hear, due for advancement on the Big Block. I saw him briefly last year; he's grown a beard and panked his eyes into rainbows." She paused. "But I'm with Cil now."

"Are you still living on University? In the Free Forest?"

"No, on Melkior, where Cil was born. I half-finished another prose collection last year. I've been trying to start writing again for a long time. No luck. I never seem to stick with it. I thought maybe here—" She gestured at the night.

"And Cil?"

"She did a lot of professional planalysis until a few years ago. She was at a resort on Vesper when one of the Blink Wars broke out and several close friends were murdered by mistake. She was badly torn up herself, left for dead. They found her after a few days and managed to rebuild everything—the physical part, anyway. When she left the medipal she felt no desire to go back to work, and she's just been drifting from place to place, though not with a capital D yet."

"And now, does she owe much on the Block?"

"It's the other way around. She was one of the top half-dozen in her field."

"Ah, that's fortunate."

He could think of nothing else to say, though he still had many questions. The talk about Cil had left him uncomfortable; he was not sure why. He cleared his throat and reached for his cup, but it was misted with dew and fell silently from his fingers to the dark grass below.

"I remember the party after the Chwoi Dai Judgment," he said finally. "You wore silver and shells."

"Yes." She smiled. "And you wore bitterness and got drunk as quickly as possible."

"It won't happen like that this time," he said softly. "Not to Belthannis."

And they were still talking, both hoarse, both near tears, when the last of the moons had wandered away, when the stars had begun to fade like birds going to sleep, when dawn came.

CHAPTER 2

If you have confessed, and give Glory to God,
I pray God clear you, if you be innocent.
And if you be guilty, discover you.
And therefore give me an upright answer:
have you any familiarity with these spirits?

No. I have none but with God alone.

How came you sick, for there is an odd discourse of
that in the mouths of many.

I am sick at my stomach.

Have you no wounds?

I have not but old age.

You do know whether you are guilty,
and have familiarity with the devil,
and now when you are here present,
to see such a thing as these testify:
a black man whispering in your ear
and birds about you.

TRANSCRIPT FROM THE EXAMINATION
OF REBECCA NURSE (SALEM VILLAGE,
EARTH, A.D. 1692)

1

Raille Weldon of Weldon came walking and whistling through the wide meadow. Her first planetfall in a lifeskin packet had left her trembling with nervous excitement, and the stimulus of a new world exhilarated her, lengthening her stride and keeping a constant flickering smile about her lips.

When she wasn't walking, she was shading her eyes in anticipation at some distant soot-colored tree, or down on her hands and knees to inspect an insect or a cluster of flowers. When she wasn't whistling, she was whispering small excited bursts of description into the delicate silver journal clasped around her wrist. In one hand she carried a tiny, expensive holodot picture cube which she had purchased on board the Darkjumper. Under her arm was a frayed blue-and-white object with *Biota Exotica* and *H.R. Tauck* in neat black Weldonese characters on one side. From time to time she would set down the cube and thumb carefully through the dog-eared book, always making an entry in her journal when expert and planet disagreed.

The meadow crept slowly into a patch of medium-sized forest. Between two ancient trees she found the faint suggestion of a path worn into the inch-deep leafmold. Deliberately avoiding the tracks, she stepped several paces to her right and struck off on a vaguely parallel course. She moved slowly through the forest, swaying like a dancer past the bushes that tugged at her long, colorful skirts. She breathed deeply—not with exertion, though the atmosphere and gravity were still new to her, but to fill her lungs with the sharp unfamiliar smells, to catch strange hidden scents in the back of her throat.

Raille recalled from the curiously brief data spool she had viewed on the ship that the local day was a good deal longer than its Weldonese counterpart. Although she had been walking for several hours by her chronometer, the tiny sun was only just approaching the zenith when the forest dissolved into meadow once more. The wind was cool and refreshing in the open field, but the midday sky was almost painfully bright: it stretched like flashing metal foil above the distant mountain ranges.

She paused in the meadow, shielding her eyes from the silver glare, as she realized she was lost.

She caught the sound of water rushing somewhere not far away. Turning in that direction, she started off, guided more by her ears than her eyes.

She almost stumbled over the fruit. It was lying half hidden in the silver grass, several meters from the nearest bush or tree. She examined it with delight, sinking to her knees and cupping it in her hands. Beneath its thin skin the flesh was red and pulpy, reinforcing her first impression of rich succulence.

Raille was beginning to regret her plan to make friends with the countryside before meeting her fellow Evaluators. *I should have let them call down from the ship for someone to meet me*, she thought. *I could be at the base by now, with a place to lie down and something cool to drink.*

She looked longingly at the dewy fruit, made a small click of her tongue and shook her head. Thumbing the journal on her wrist, she began to dictate slowly. With her free hand she held the fruit up to the sun. Her fingers appeared through the translucent flesh as though dipped in blood. Squinting fiercely against the noon brilliance, she found that she could see clearly through the whole fruit, which cast a scarlet shadow down her forearm.

"No seeds, no stone," she informed the journal thoughtfully. "How does it reproduce? Is it really a fruit at all?" She paused in contemplation. "I dub you *faux-pomme*," she said at last, tapping the taut red skin with a fingernail. She closed her eyes and tried to recall a teasingly similar specimen in one of the recorded lectures sent to her from Lekkole. Bright afterimages danced in her brain. Chewing on her lower lip, she reached absentmindedly for the *Biota Exotica*. Still holding the mock-apple in one upraised hand, she began to leaf through the unwieldy volume.

That was how it happened.

One minute there was nothing but ferns and grass and Raille Weldon of Weldon; the next, she felt a slight pressure come and go on the back of her knuckles, the lightest of taps, as if a butterfly had blundered against her hand in the brisk wind.

Then suddenly there was a sharp tug, and the fruit was wrenched from her fingers.

She discovered her hand pressing tightly against the base of her neck. She had snatched it back quicker than thought, as if burned. She stared stupidly at her empty fingers for a moment, then looked up. She blinked in the blinding light. A dark figure loomed against the sky's shattered mirror.

She rose slowly, aware that she was shaking gently, and lifted a hand to shield her eyes. The sun burned small and fierce directly above the vague outline of a man, crowning him with a halo of bright spears. She peered into the shadowed face and gradually made out eyes, nose, mouth.

He lifted his hand and took a bite of the fruit.

Raille clutched at the ragged edges of her composure. Her mother had told her many tales of offworlders' bizarre customs and outrageous manners. Could it be they all behaved this way?

Since sending her reply to Lekkole, she had been rehearsing the words she would speak when introduced to the Group Leader, a distinguished High Scholar. Now she searched desperately for the gracious phrases, watching them scatter before her inward eye like a school of distant fish. The silence was growing intolerable. She tried in vain to see more of the man's face. Was this Person Emrys himself?

She took a shuddering breath. "Well met, Person," she said in her clearest Inter. "Are you from the Special Evaluation Team? I'm the Natural, Raille Weldon."

The man said nothing.

She began again. "I'd planned to explore a little before coming to the base. We are not great travelers on Weldon, you see, and it's very exciting for me to have this opportunity. My first new world—" She smiled ruefully. "But now I've lost my way completely. If you hadn't found me . . ." She let the words trail off, an expression of apologetic gratitude on her face.

The man had taken another bite of the fruit. He seemed to be staring at her, though it was impossible to be sure.

"If you could just take me—"

He chewed carefully. Staring.

Then a bank of curly clouds passed leisurely in front of the sun and she was able to see him clearly for the first time, able to see his eyes, and to see that he was naked. She looked at him for several blank moments, trying to blink the bright dots away from her eyes, and small hidden things seemed to shift and move in her mind; sounds came from nowhere to tremble on her lips.

He had finished the fruit now. He was staring. He took a step forward, then another. She was not sure whether he raised one of his hands or not.

Later, when she tried to remember, she could never recall the exact moment when she had cried out, the precise second when she had started to run blindly through the silver grass, past the skeletal trees, beneath the dulling sky. But she could visualize perfectly every detail of the time that followed, separately, as if it had been recorded by some meticulous, impersonal watcher and recited back to her night after night, in her dreams.

She remembered:

>   *heavy skirts whipping at her ankles*
>   *knuckles white around the solid familiarity of* H.R. Tauck
>   *breath shrieking in and out of lungs like a flock of razor-winged birds*
>   *one hand-tooled sandal lost to a patch of clutching furze — the foot was soon striped and crossed with blood like a stick of candy*
>   *a dark figure standing in the center of a meadow, knee-high in flickering grass and staring, staring, staring*
>   *the shrill and mad piping that pursued her through the open spaces, arising from a number of small gray plant-things crushed underfoot —*
>   *did the tiny screams make her run faster? could she even hear them at that point?*

2

Early evening found Choss, Jefany, and Cil in the Hearth Room, Choss engrossed in a NewsNet drama featuring the Personalities, and the women playing Golden Ring with dice and luminous cards.

March and Emrys were in their respective rooms, one doing exercises, the other sitting quietly as he pondered the days ahead.

Jack slept with a smile in the Music Nook.

Marysu was walking in the Garden of Earth, alone with her thoughts among beech and willow, buttercup and birdsong.

Then the Hut spoke calmly in all rooms at once and informed them of the presence of a madwoman on its outer doorsill. Converging in the hall nexus directly above the Hearth Room, they hurried to the foyer and brought her in.

When Emrys opened the door, she flopped in on the rug and her hair spread like a rust-brown stain on the rich pile. Emrys reached for her at the same time as Choss; they collided and withdrew, mumbling apologies. March picked her up and carried her to a couch. There was dried blood on her feet; one shoe was missing. The gypsy skirts were torn and there were twigs in her hair. She was unconscious, lovely.

"What should we do?" asked Choss, shoulders bent, dark eyes on her face, which was dirty, scratched, and contorted. "Who is it? Weldon of Weldon? What's happened to her?" He looked at the others and blushed, retreating a few steps from the couch and fingering the twining ivy.

March knelt by her head, thumbed her eyelids, felt at her throat. "Pulse steady," he said.

"And no major wounds apparent," Emrys added.

"If I may comment," ventured the Hut. "Like the rest of us, she is a newcomer to this world, a creature in a new environment, alone, perhaps lost. Her general appearance suggests that she has been running, possibly for some time. She may have been frightened by something in the forest."

Emrys glanced sharply at the ceiling, then back to the girl.

"Oh. Yes. You may be right. Perhaps she did blunder onto something—unfamiliar." He paused, biting his lower lip. "In which case, the *bain-sense* might be best, once those cuts have been attended to."

"It might indeed," the Hut said, and the rest agreed.

Created in secret by the empaths on Maribon and dubbed "sense bath" in the old Language of Pleasure, the *bain-sense* was a subtle instrument constructed in the shape of a coffin— an ancient form of packaging no longer widely used. In the

bain-sense one could lie down in warmth and darkness to experience in a few minutes what would seem like hours of pure
happiness. The *bain-sense* blurred over anxiety and recalled
instead a precious childhood memory in perfect detail. To replace formless worries, or a traumatic incident, the *bain-sense*
substituted an equally formless sense of well-being, an equally
exciting surge of joy. Working from within rather than attacking
from without, the *bain-sense* was more of a servant to the mind
than a master. One lay down in the *bain-sense* and the *bain-
sense* was the key.

Panacea, moodbender, comforting friend: those were its
common uses. It was also a cure for madness.

They brought her water, ointments, and lifeskin, and they
washed and dressed her feet and the lesser scratches on her
face and body. Then March and Emrys carried her up to the
Library, past the chipfiles, and put her in the *bain-sense*, folding
her hands on her breast and making sure her head was snuggled
up against the thousands of tiny silver contacts which were
themselves complex machines.

Emrys keyed in a basic program, one of healing and selective
blocking, and closed the velvet-lined lid with care.

The silence that accompanies the operation of an expensive
machine filled the room, and the two men edged out into the
corridor with the others.

Inside, the *bain-sense* opened to the lower levels of the
patient's mind, smoothing and sorting. It made of itself a mirror
for the babble of image and sensation pouring from her brain,
a pliable thing to be shaped by her need. Those emanations
deemed harmless were caught and sent back after being woven
into something bright and pleasant. The dangerous ones were
allowed to become lost somewhere in the velvet darkness.

Inside the room, inside the gleaming coffin, Raille began
to remember and to forget.

3

Turquoise, azure, cerulean, brole . . .
Lavender, lilac, orchid . . .

Violet, indigo . . .

Jack was walking with his eyes on the walls when he left the Library with the others. In this section of the Hut the sides of the corridor were endowed with a gentle optical pattern, a mild visual relaxant that occasionally activated when humans walked the hallway. As Jack watched, the blues and purples undulated rhythmically, brimming at the edges where wall met floor as if ready to overflow onto his bare feet.

Although the *bain-sense* was a closed world, and its occupant impervious to outside stimulation, Jack felt uneasy about resuming the bodyhug in the Music Nook which adjoined the Library, vaguely guilty about restarting the chaotic music that had lulled him to sleep, frankly uncomfortable about sleeping that close to a tenanted *bain-sense*. So he sauntered down the blue corridor after the others, not from any desire to visit the Hearth Room, but because they had a place to go and he did not.

Nearing the central spiral of stairs he passed beyond the influence of the calm blue walls. A few paces ahead, Jefany and Emrys conversed in hushed and earnest voices, looking every inch the dedicated Scholars. Idly, Jack sketched them in his mind: red hair almost touching brown, the swift strong lines to frame their faces, the mobile features, the eloquent gestures.

March and Marysu had already reached the stairwell. The soldier's boots rang sharply on each step as he descended.

Choss had lingered for some time at the entrance to the Library, staring brow-furrowed at the luxurious coffin as if trying to penetrate the velvet and silver with his eyes. Jack turned to look for him but instead saw Cil, hurrying to close the few paces between them. She fell into step with him, and he noticed for the first time that she too was barefoot. He smiled to himself, watching her toes appear and vanish at the hem of the moth-green robe.

She followed his eyes curiously, looked up with a smile. "I don't like shoes."

"Me either. Never wear 'em."

They listened as March attained the lowest level; heard him stride off toward the Hearth Room with the hollow, heavy sound of boots on marble. Up ahead, the Scholarly discourse continued, the tones growing progressively more hushed, the smiles more frequent. Cil was watching them, and Jack used the time to study her face. If he wished, he might recall her features in perfect detail an hour or a century from this moment and they would reappear, flawless and obedient.

"You know," she said softly, "we'll see snow before dawn."

He laughed. "Yes?"

"Yes." Her slight nod was serious.

"How d'you know a thing like that, then? From the Hut?" He found himself intrigued, delighted by her words, or by her face, or by something he had glimpsed in both.

She guided a wisp of golden hair back from her forehead.

"I know it from the glow of the sky, from the movement of the wind. A look out the door when they brought in the woman made it certain. A small storm only, I'd judge, and still a few hours off."

"But I was looking out, too, and it didn't seem any different to me. Just lots of green and some silver. And quiet. So where's the trick?"

"The trick is the planalyst's knack," she said. "The way of looking at things quickly, all at once, as if they were all one thing. As they are: the connections show themselves before long on any world. I confess it's as much hunch as training— and definitely not as certain as long-term tests and study. But for now . . .

She looked up at him quickly, and the sentence faded as her cheeks colored under his attentive gaze.

They had stopped walking, and he was examining her face with solemn interest, as if he planned to paint it, fusing the thought behind the words with those in his own mind.

The small blue flower near her mouth looked like a permanent decoration, and he approved of the choice, for it blended beautifully with the rest of her. He filled an imaginary palette with her colors: white-gold, cream, ivory, rose, the focal point of pale blue.

He cocked an eyebrow and grinned, saying her last words back to her: "But for now . . ."

4

Raille rose, felt herself rising, resisted for a moment, acquiesced.

Just beneath the surface she floated, face up. The sky was dark, blurred. Refracted through the water, the stars had lost their brilliance: they shone dully, like rows of tiny knobs. She moved her arms restlessly and found a soft obstruction on each side, a cushioned wall a few centimeters from her body. There was no water. She raised her hands in wonder and touched the sky. The rows of stars were buttons, gleaming.

She had been in a *bain-sense* before, times without number as she was growing up. The panic of finding herself shut up in a casket lasted only a few seconds.

What have I done this time? she wondered with the hovering clarity of near-wakefulness. *Fainting when Grandfather hit his thumb instead of the nail ... screaming at the bird's broken wing ... asleep with open eyes while watching the bees. Oh bad girl, sad girl ...*

Sleep welled up around her like black water, hiding the buttons, blotting out the stars. She let it flow over her unresisting, seeking the depths.

"She came awake."

"What's that?" Emrys tilted his head slightly to the side, one eyebrow lifting in polite inquiry.

"Awake," March repeated. "Saw it when I took her out of the dream-box. Machine made a note, I read the numbers to check—past hour she came awake, then back out in a minute."

"That isn't possible. It couldn't happen." The eyebrow remained poised, awaiting enlightenment.

"Truth told," March said softly. His posture near the door was casual, but his hands were becoming fists, the golden fingers closing with a measured slowness like the traps of a carnivorous plant. His eyes were locked on Emrys' face, and a careless brutality had crept into his stance.

Emrys seemed lost in thought.

Jefany stared at March by looking into his false eye. *This man has killed and killed again*, she thought. She touched Emrys' arm.

"A malfunction?" she prompted softly.

Emrys stirred. "Well—is the *bain-sense* functioning properly, Hut?"

"It's in perfect order," came the immediate reply from above. "I am investigating March's observations, however, and a probe of the sensebath confirms his report. Our new arrival was awake somewhat less than an hour ago. She remained conscious seventy-three point three seconds."

"Extraordinary," Emrys said. "Some quirk of Weldonese physiology, would you think?"

"No such oddity has been registered with my sources," the Hut said officiously. "Naturally, I would have mentioned it."

March had left the doorway. He stood near the wall, toying with a fragile glasswind sculpture.

"Sleeping when I took her to her room. Sleeping now," he said, as if that finished the matter.

5

Raille Weldon slept on. The Group stayed in the Hearth Room, almost as if something were drawing them together, discouraging them from going off to separate rooms.

Emrys had beckoned to Cil after dinner from a cul-de-sac of softly glowing water tables. There they sat on flexible chair-bubbles, watching the fish and conversing in low tones. From time to time, Emrys gestured to the stack of recording chips he had brought down from his room. Then he would fall silent and gingerly place one or two of the recordings into Cil's cupped hands.

"Looks like he's handing over his firstborn," Marysu told Jack in a dry voice. They were sitting together at the big table, Marysu's pile of data sheets and phonetic beads overlapping the square of white upon which Jack was sketching her profile in charcoal. "Mm hm," he said, his tongue pushing past his teeth as he straightened the neck, darkened the high cheekbones. Marysu clicked her tongue and returned to her own task, the isolation of a class of elusive palatals from an all but lost language of the back-before.

On the other side of the table, Choss leaned forward on his elbows, hands cradling his cheeks, eyes lost in the polished *oke*. He raised his head abruptly. "Of course—the Willful Poppy!" he blurted, and found himself staring into three pairs of curious eyes.

Marysu exchanged a glance with Jack; Jefany watched with raised eyebrows from the side of the small scent scuplture she had been sampling. March had not bothered to turn from his crouching inspection of the golden dragon beneath his feet.

Choss swallowed and lowered his eyes. His face and ears were scarlet. "The Weldonese girl," he said with difficulty. "She reminded me of someone."

Marysu snorted and went back to her charts. Jack looked at or through Choss for a moment, then attacked his drawing with renewed vigor.

"Oh," Jefany said from across the room. "The Personality. I guess there could be some resemblance." She favored him with a brief smile.

Flute note and whisper: "Emrys?"

Choss looked gratefully to the ceiling.

"Yes?" Emrys removed a recording chip from his cheek and slumped back in his chair with a beleaguered sigh. "We're a little busy just now, Hut."

"I am receiving a linkup request." The Hut managed to convey a martyred dignity. "It would seem to be rather important."

Emrys looked blank. "Is Raille Weldon's ship still in orbit?"

"It is not a Darkjumper calling. World to world, via the Net."

There were startled sounds from around the room. "The expense," Choss murmured.

"From which world?" Emrys moved quickly to the opaqued Screen.

"From Maribon, Emrys. Shall I connect you?"

"Maribon!" He flung them a wondering look. "Yes—permit the link."

The Screen began to flicker at his last word.

The face that appeared on the wall could have been one of Jack's charcoal sketches, so flat and white was the skin, so black the eyes and hair. It was blank with the intensity of death. Even the eyes were without expression, flat, with the thrusting emptiness of a corpse.

Then a veil of darkness appeared in the air around Emrys and the Screen, blotting them from the room as if a web of shadows had been spun on the wall to conceal them.

"Private," the Hut said apologetically. "Hush and shadow. I'm sure you'll excuse him."

"What was that—creature?" Marysu asked, her face ashen.

"Empath," Choss whispered.

"God! A face like the belly of a fish," she said. "And those eyes . . ."

The silent, hidden conversation lasted no more than a minute. The pall thinned into nothingness and a pale Emrys turned away from the empty Screen.

"We're to have a visitor," he said. "Someone is coming here from Maribon. They wouldn't say why."

"An empath—here!" Choss said, fright in his eyes.

"It's illegal, though, isn't it?" Cil asked. "They're not supposed to travel."

"UnLawful," Marysu said. "The Moselle rulings—"

"Jon. You could stop him. You could call someone, couldn't you?"

"No, Jefany. No." He stared past her, brow knit with concern. "It's probably all right. I won't call anyone unless I have to. We'd best wait and see what happens."

CHAPTER 3

> By the rivers there is vossomy, peshel, murebud
> (good for harvest ache), diamano, siss (brewed as a
> tea for uncontrollable trembling), and kettlehage. In
> the meadow I found stonecrust and feverwort.
> Dewcup beneath the trees, also nipstalk which is
> poisonous. Windbuds move up from the South usually
> by Whitemonth, linger till Midmonth. Suppleweed and
> shelt are fine as greens, dodore and last-lament grow
> on the undersides of leaning rocks, are bitter but
> healthful . . .

FROM AN ANONYMOUS WELDONESE
HERBAL, WALKING SEDDON VALLEY

1

The feeling was not so much surprise as emptiness. There were
things missing, gaps, blurred areas.

It was disorientation, spatial and temporal: falling, floating,
drifting.

It was waking up in the middle of the night in a strange bed
in a strange room, with no idea where you are or how you
came to be there, until it all begins to come back to you: slowly

at first, piece by piece, and then in a rush as everything drops into place and you feel foolish and relieved at the same time. Except—

Except it wasn't coming back. There were no pieces to assemble. There was only darkness and disorientation and emptiness.

Raille Weldon, late of Weldon, awoke in an empty room which was completely dark when she opened her eyes, grew progressively lighter as she rose to her knees and then to her feet, and began to darken again as she stumbled out the door.

She was in a long sloping hallway, a curving tunnel sided with blue walls that flowed and swirled in undefinable patterns when she tried to focus her eyes on them. It was as if she stood in the curve of a giant spiral seashell, she thought at once, her mind reaching easily toward fantasy. But then these walls must be transparent instead of nacreous, and the lambent blues that surged against her eyes were those of a vast ocean above and all around her.

She took a step forward, then another, bringing her foot down hard to steady the rippling corridor. The walls receded for a moment, then lapped closer as she made her unsteady way.

At first she was afraid to touch the swirling blue, fearing that it might really be some sort of suspended liquid, and that her hand would instantly plunge through into whirlpool depths. But the undulating patterns made her brain dance in a haze of blue veils, and finally she was forced to lean against the right-hand wall to keep from falling.

The nightmare waking, the mutable walls, this whole silent undersea exploration had the flavor and texture of a drugwine fantasy for Raille, who had never experienced one, and for a while there was no purpose but the blending of colors and no urgency beyond the changing of shapes.

She moved on slowly, enchanted by the sound her body made as it slid along the smooth surface of the wall. Soon she found that by closing her eyes she could drift down the hypnotic corridor in a senseless, dreaming glide, her weight resting against the wall and her legs taking the slow-motion steps rhythmically, one, two, one, two, one . . .

Her shoulder touched a strip of raised material, and she blinked open her eyes, frowning, sleepy.

A door. An open door.

Had she been moving in a circle? She peered around the edge.

The room was not the same, though it was of the same dimensions and nearly as empty, containing only a small pallet identical to the one on which she had awakened and a collection of shiny recording chips that caught her eye with their bright colors. Moving into the room, she glimpsed a second doorway near the far end, and opposite it a large desk or table. The room was compact, but with a sense of space in its lines and layout.

This is a pleasant place.

That was her first reaction. There was something about the room that Raille responded to instinctively: an aura of safety, perhaps, as if it were a place used to surround and protect its inhabitant. Lured on by this promise of haven, Raille approached the desk. A luggage pack lay on its side, one end open to reveal portions of some complicated machinery. Beside the pack was a neat pile of what looked to be dead animals: small, varicolored waterdwellers wrapped in thin transparent envelopes. Like the recording chips next to the pallet, they had been carefully stacked. Raille touched the topmost one lightly; it was cool and dry, and she was able to feel the creature's scaled surface through the membrane.

To the right of the pile of specimens someone had left an open notebook, the visible pages filled with oddly ornate Anglic characters written in a painstaking script. The words were in a language unknown to Raille; she read some of them aloud, taking pleasure in the pompous, rolling sounds:

Astronatus ocellatus   *Betta splendens*
Helostoma temmincki   *Gnathonemus petersi*
Cichlasoma severum   *Pterophyllum scalare*
Symphysodon discus   *Trichogaster leeri*

Raille heard a noise and looked up, the flesh crawling at the base of her scalp.

A man stood in the doorway across from the desk. He was watching her curiously, head cocked to one side.

There was no sound. The tableau was not quite real to her

without speech or motion. She studied the man: dark hair, dark beard, rather an exotic costume for—

Weldon?

"How do you feel?" he asked in gentle Inter.

"Very well, thank you," she replied haltingly. "And you?"

"Quite well. I didn't hear you come in. I was cleansing my hands in the habitual."

"Oh." She nodded vaguely.

"Is there something wrong?" His calm smile was becoming a trifle disconcerted. "Are you all right?"

"No—fine." Raille tried to smile at him. "I thought it was a dream. I thought I was home." She leaned heavily against the desk, a rushing and sparking in her mind like a cloud of bright bees, stinging her awake.

The man's face showed concern. "D'you know where you are now?" His arms moved restlessly at his sides, as if he would like to put them to some use, but dared not.

"The Autumnworld. Belthannis," she said slowly. "May I sit down somewhere?" She eyed the bare floor doubtfully.

"Ah! I have no manners." He brushed his fingers against the nearest wall and said very clearly, "Chair for her." Raille watched as the floor between them swelled, and a solid-looking hump of green grew quickly upward. She seated herself gingerly, finding that the chairbubble gave in some places and supported in others, holding her almost as comfortably as a bodyhug. Perched on a green bubble in the middle of a stranger's sleeproom, on an alien world she was only beginning to remember, Raille Weldon could think of nothing to say.

The pile of preserved animals caught her eye. "Are these your food?"

He looked perplexed, then suddenly amused.

"You mean the Earth fish! No, these are my pets, my hobby. Here." He leaned past her and began hoisting pieces of machinery from the luggage pack on his desk. He assembled the devices as he spoke, clicking and snapping them together with practiced speed.

"They're from the hatcheries on Rondivoo, actually," he said. "Authenticated descendants of stock brought out during the Expansion. I have a guarantee."

He replaced the device on his desk. Completed, it was a

fragile metal grid the size of a dinner plate, bristling with
strange attachments.

He thumbed something at the base of the device and stepped
back.

"Which one would you like to see first? My name is Choss,
by the way. World Hinderlond. Historian."

"I'm very glad to meet you." Raille stared blankly at the
machine.

"Mm. Perhaps the diskfish." He spoke with a heartiness
that seemed forced. Raille felt his eyes on her constantly; he
was watching her as if afraid of what she might do.

Choss took the largest packet from the pile: the creature was
dark and saucer shaped, streaked with lines of red and electric
blue. Holding it horizontally over the device, he pressed a
curved protrusion with his other hand, and a low-pitched hum
rose and fell in the machine. He released the fish in midair,
and Raille stared as it hung on its side above the grid without
support, swaying delicately. The transparent envelope had begun to dissolve, as small bright dots danced upward from the
grid like motes of dust in a sunbeam.

Thirty seconds later the fish had righted itself, moving its
fins sluggishly. Gills opened and closed in a precise rhythm;
large red-rimmed eyes regarded the world with mild reproach.

Amazed, Raille extended a tentative finger.

"Don't, please," Choss said. "You'd break the field. If the
ambient charge is dissipated he can't breathe."

"I don't understand this," she said. "It was dead."

He shook his head. "Only slightly. A very long time ago,
a similar technique kept people alive through Expansion, when
they had to use Cold Ships to cross deep space. This variation,
which uses the lifeskin membrane, was developed later on New
World. It's become a very useful item, and lately Bluehorn's
been producing such things in great quantity—we'll most likely
be going back to a form of Cold Ship before very long, you
know—so this wasn't too expensive."

He made an adjustment, and *Symphysodon discus* stiffened
in its waterless pond, fluttered its gills once or twice, folded
the fan-shaped fins, and drifted down to lie on its side a few
centimeters above the grid.

Choss waited for the body to grow rigid and the eyes to dull
and glaze. Raille noticed that a new envelope glistened around

the fish as Choss placed it back on the pile, choosing at the same time a much smaller fish to release above the grid.

"*Betta splendens*," he announced with pride when the new fish had begun to revive, directing Raille's attention to the jewel-bright fins and haughty, upturned mouth.

"Here." He produced a small hand mirror from somewhere and nodded toward the sleek little fish.

Raille held the glass close to the field, Choss helping her to position it with a hand at her elbow. The little betta stiffened instantly and began to drift toward its reflection. As it approached, its bright body grew rigid and the long fins and tail extended like trembling turquoise banners. It made a sudden dash at the mirror, gill covers distended, body shaking with rage. Halted by the edge of the field, it danced and circled in front of the glass, a miniature gladiator strutting before the adversary.

"This one is a fish that was originally bred for fighting, in a place called Eyzha on old Earth itself. Two males in the same territory will fight to the death. The ancients wagered on them for sport."

"How horrible," Raille said.

He shrugged. "That was six or seven thousand years ago. We've found different sport since then. Ask March when you meet him." He set aside the glass.

Raille had leaned forward, watching the tiny warrior glide gracefully around the field. "He's lovely, anyway," she said. She waved to the fish with her fingertips, and it wheeled toward her hand, pinpoint eyes staring. She frowned and dropped her hand to her side. Choss looked at her questioningly.

"How did I get here?" she asked.

"You can't remember? Nothing?"

"I remember—pieces of it." She closed her eyes for a few seconds, blinked them open.

"I can see the Darkjumper—inside it, I mean—huge, with its aviary and *pinbal* and the weightless palisades. I can feel parts of the trip through the Dark and Empty." She shivered. "Then I can remember leaving the ship above Belthannis, a great green-and-white curve below me, and falling to earth for the first time in a lifeskin packet. You don't know how much nerve that took!

"I landed. I landed and I started walking. It was another

world—my first!—and everything was so beautiful, so many new things. They had shown me a map on the ship, yes? Yes. Red for the clearing where I'd come down, green dots for the path, a blue rectangle for the building, this Hut. It was all projected on the side of the packet, changing as I fell so I'd know where I was."

She paused uncertainly.

"I did start off in the right direction. But then I decided to explore. I didn't take the path. I wanted to feel the land, I couldn't help myself, and there was so much to see." She squinted at the empty wall.

"Then there was something—I was in the field, I think. Bright? Yes, bright all around me. In me. Like a silver ocean, like drowning in it. Like falling into that sky—" She raised a hand to her cheek as if to ward off something threatening, then shook her head slightly and turned back to Choss.

"That's when something important happened, I'm sure." She paused again, waiting for the memory, then shrugged helplessly. "It's gone. I can't make it out."

"Odd. What's the next thing you remember?"

"The room. I woke up in a room like this one, but dark and empty. Down the hall. I got up. I walked along the corridor and found your door and came in here."

"Well, I can fill in a few of the gaps," he said. "We—the other members of the Group and I—we found you outside on our doorstep. So you must have gotten back to the path eventually, else how could you have found us?"

His tone and smile reassured her. He spoke like the kindly Scholars in her lectures from Lekkole, absently stroking his neat beard.

"Walking a new world is bound to be an unsettling experience, you know, and I suppose the small changes in air and gravity didn't help matters. You were asleep, exhausted, when we brought you in. We—they—thought you'd been startled or frightened by something out in the forest. They put you in the *bain-sense*."

There was a flurry of sound in the corridor, swiftly approaching footsteps behind Raille. Choss moved slightly away from her, a certain wariness coming into his face. He looked past her shoulder to the open door.

"Venga, pédant! Il neige dehn venarden."

Raille saw a fantastic creature appear in the doorway, wild colors flashing from her scanty garments. Bald, yet obviously female; sapphire-eyed; clothed quite indecently, if indeed that was clothing, for it seemed to Raille to be moving slowly over the mahogany skin—she halted and stared at Raille, painted-on eyebrows tilting comically in surprise. Her eyes flicked back to Choss.

"It's snowing," she said. "When did you wake up?"

Raille realized after a blank moment that the latter half of the utterance had been directed at her.

"She's been up for almost half an hour," Choss answered, pressing his left thumb against the curve of his forefinger to activate the tiny chronometer on the nail. "We've been looking at my fish. She's a Natural, you know, a biologist."

"Oh?" The sharp blue gaze returned to Raille. "You do speak Inter, don't you? You are the Weldonese?"

"Yes." Raille found her voice. "Raille Weldon of Weldon."

A smile flickered on the brown woman's lips. She seemed to notice Choss again. "Go out and see the snow. That's what I came to tell you. Little Cil was right." She indicated the hallway with a motion of her painted head. *"Avaunt!* I'll stay with your Natural. We'll have a talk."

Choss hesitated for an instant under the sardonic gaze. He threw Raille a quick glance she could not interpret, lowered his eyes, and left the room.

"Adjö," Marysu said when he had gone. "And good riddance. What an incredibly dull person." She arched her back and moved her neck sinuously. "So. Little fishes. *Bellisima."* Raille watched the bald woman approach the desk. Abruptly the blue eyes flew up like flung sapphires to meet her own.

"Chial diy! Am I that grotesque?"

"Forgive me," Raille said. "I didn't mean to stare. It's just—"

"Not what you'd see in the village square on Weldon. You do have villages, I suppose?" The mocking stare held a faint challenge.

"Yes. Yes, of course we do."

"Ja? Bien," Marysu said, then added in smooth, accent-perfect Weldonese: *"Vyu se borel tuvyu. Sar proviken mehne,*

ne'cert." You're quite comely yourself, she had said. *In a provincial way, of course.*

Raille was beginning to feel totally lost. How should she respond to this strange performance of insult and mockery? Could she possibly be misinterpreting the whole thing, imposing Weldonese standards on behavior another offworlder might consider completely innocuous?

"How old are you, Raille Weldon?" The bald woman had turned back to the grid, teasing the little fighting fish with a flick of long fingernails.

The question would be considered unpardonably rude on Weldon. *Courtesy and understanding*, Raille recited to herself. She could not help but remember her grandfather's words: *They don't have a great affection for the dear folk of Weldon.*

She summoned her most impersonal voice. "I will have twenty years in a few months. Twenty of the years of my world, that is. By your Old Basic I would be almost a year younger."

"Tack, tack remmen. And how soon do you expect to die? *Non.* 'Emigrate,' I should have said. *Emgreten.* That is the term they use on Weldon, yes?" She was watching the little fish as it circled its world, spreading and shaking its fins at her from time to time in futile rage.

Raille was profoundly shocked. This she could not have misunderstood.

"What do you mean?" she said after a long pause, finding no way to respond to such a monstrous breach of civility.

"Why, I was wondering if it was true." The other lifted her face from the grid, all innocent curiosity. "That they die 'naturally' on Weldon. *Sans* Ember. Like animals."

Raille's face was burning. "Stop it! You have no right to say such things!"

"Tcha! Pardonnez-moi, dier wun!" The brown face mimed amazement. "Have I violated some tribal taboo, some primitive—"

"Marysu."

Choss stood in the doorway, his brown eyes expressionless, his hair and beard flecked with shrinking snowflakes. Something in his appearance reminded Raille fleetingly of her grandfather.

"The others are coming in now," he said quietly. "They'd

like to meet Raille Weldon. Would you show her to the Hearth Room, pléase?"

Then he was gone again, silently.

After a moment the bald woman bowed ironically in the direction of the doorway. "Such timing." She fixed Raille with the blue crystal stare again. "Well. *Kemfels.* I could say I was only teasing—to make you feel at ease here. Or I could blame it on the *gielh* I've had this evening. *In moodbender veritas, da?* It does seem to bring out my natural viciousness.

"But truth to tell, I've behaved reprehensibly." She had begun to pace beside the desk, catlike. "Like a child. *C'était*— it's a poor welcome to this magnificent world." She stopped pacing with a shrug of bare shoulders. "So. *Förlåt mig. Je le regrette.* There's my apology. *Resivali.* Perhaps we'll talk again when situations have made themselves clearer."

Raille remained silent, following Marysu through corridors and down a twisting circle of stairs that hung in the air without visible support, to a circular room where she was greeted with an almost tangible atmosphere of concern and warmth.

She was conducted through a flurry of introductions, offered glazed fruit from a platter, warm tea, a wine the color of blue ink, and finally presented ceremoniously with a tiny ball of dripping snow by the curly-headed boy with the beautiful face.

Chak? Imris? Sill? Raille concentrated on affixing each new name to its owner while trying to follow the friendly, substanceless chatter that flowed around her.

Several hours later the historian volunteered to escort her upstairs if she wished, and she assented gratefully. He guided her back up to the darkened room she had left an age ago and summoned furnishings for her from the walls and floor. Before he wished her goodsleep, he introduced her to the Hut—apparently some sort of talking machine residing in the ceiling of her room—an event which she managed to take in stride owing only to her extreme fatigue. Machines that aped the speech or actions of human beings were not popular on Weldon, but this one seemed nice enough, judging from its voice.

Raille prepared for bed after Choss departed, thinking of the hours stolen from her memory by the *bain-sense,* experiences she might never recapture. She pondered the bald woman's strange attack and stranger repentance, wondered briefly

at the current of tension and unease she had sensed—or imagined—beneath the smiles and conversation downstairs.

But the *bain-sense* had taken things from her before: there
were other empty hours in her past.

The woman called Marysu was perhaps troubled by some
inner torment, and at any rate was not to be judged so quickly
by the polity of Weldon.

The tension and unease . . .

Surrendering gradually to the weight of her exhaustion, she
lifted slim shoulders in a shrug and settled beneath the covers
of her pallet.

2

Two mornings after her arrival, Raille Weldon was awakened by the delicate chime of the breakfast bell. Reluctant to
open her eyes, she stretched languorously, thinking of full blue
sails twinned on the rippling mirror of a Newmonth lake.

She lay motionless.

One bell for breakfast, she remarked to herself. *I'm living
on another world now, a place called Belthannis Autumnworld
with plants that chirp and men that—* She pushed the thought
frantically out of her mind.

*They eat three meals here instead of two. How does one get
used to that?* She thought of midmeal down by the lake, with
the sailboats skimming like sapphire butterflies in the distance
and a solidly blue sky above her head.

*Wait, wait! There were no lakes on the map they showed
me*, she thought, and the thought made her tremble, struck for
the first time with the utter strangeness of being more than a
few kilometers from a lake. *How can they stand it*? she wondered briefly.

Someone's careful footsteps passed by her door in the hall,
and she lay very still, hoping no one had been delegated to
come wake her personally.

Kiri! Am I late already? Are they angry with me already?

The sounds stopped, and she held her breath, imagining the
walker standing in the center of the hallway, looking thoughtfully over his shoulder at her room. *Would it upset them if I*

missed their breakfast again? The footsteps went on after a moment, and she relaxed, trying to decide who it had been, standing there boldly, staring at her doorway. She was sure it had been a man—the footsteps had felt like a man's. But they had been slow, almost tentative. That eliminated Per Emrys, she thought: his walk was forceful, deliberate. Nor could it have been March, who did just that when he walked. And the one with the curly hair, the bald woman's Chak—*Jack*, she corrected herself—he always seemed to be running or leaping, or scuffing his feet on the floor like a child.

Choss? The name swam into her head, and she struggled to identify it with a face. Dark beard, dark eyes, quiet manner.

Choss, she thought triumphantly, and repeated the word aloud after a moment: "Choss."

She grinned at the sound of an unpromised man's chosen name in her own private sleeproom in the very early morning.

"Choss, Choss the Scholar, Per Choss." She opened her eyes a crack, half expecting to see the words glowing like marsh fog above her nose.

His nose was a touch too sharp for her standards, she decided, closing her eyes again, and his hair and beard were an unfortunate in-between color, with neither the charm of brown nor the sternness of black. Still, she conceded, he was quite well-favored on the whole. She thought of him pausing in the hallway, tugging thoughtfully on his beard as he looked back at her door. . . .

3

Choss had been the second to descend the spiral stairs this morning; when he reached the Hearth Room he found Jefany there before him, drinking tea and eating melon at the great table. She nodded good morning, dividing her attention between a NewsNet information program and a small spongepad in a figured frame. Smiling to himself, Choss took a seat next to her and ordered tea from the table, waiting for the right moment to speak. There was a lull in the action on-Screen.

"You've worked with Person Emrys before," he said.

She jotted a few words onto the pad, then turned, brow creasing. "How did you know that?"

He tilted his head to show her the blue wafer that clung to his jaw below his left ear. A recording chip from the Library, it spoke to him in delicate bone-conduction whispers. At the moment it was busily reciting data from selected Special Evaluations of the recent past.

"The Judgment of Chwoi Dai," Choss echoed. "GY 377–378. A Group Resolution of Humanity—" He paused, listening. "Subsequently overturned by the Sauf Coben. Reason: insufficient proof of a persuasive nature. . . .

"The subjects of the Evaluation, officially classified 3 Mediant 378 as herbivorous insectiles of the Damla type, were evacuated to the xenobiological facilities on Stone's Throw, with a representative sample dispatched to Mauve Terrace on Commons for suitable display. Analysis for ReForm of Chwoi Dai was completed in Augent of 378. . . .

"Members of the Special Evaluation Team included: Han Sangallo, calligrapher; Kedda Liu, ekistician; Si-mu-li-Pen, symmetrist; Jonathan Emerson Tate, Sessept of University; Group Leader Moriah Bellmaple, powermeister; Jefany Or, humanist—"

Choss had begun his recitation feeling clever and resourceful. But his spark of secret glee was obliterated by the ghosts of painful memory that moved across the woman's face.

She was staring at him without seeing him, and she had ceased to listen to his voice, her narrowed eyes looking into the past, to a world of cobalt cliffs crowned with russet vegetation beneath high, ocherous clouds. She was remembering the night she had stood with the members of that other Group on a hill above the little settlement, looking down for the last time on the enameled dwellings and the maze of airy walkways. Emrys, her lover, was sitting on the rusty vetch at her feet, cursing softly in the language of Green Asylum, a language she did not understand. Her fingers on his cheek had found tears.

4

Raille stood uncertainly in the doorway between her room and the small annexed chamber called the habitual. She was wrapped throat to ankle in the furmock coverlet from her pallet.

Raille had decided to believe that the habitual was truly a private area, the only place in the building shielded from the senses of the ubiquitous computer-thing whose constant presence seemed to trouble no one else. Forcing herself to posit this theory for the sake of modesty, she nonetheless acknowledged deep in her thoughts that there was no reason to believe it.

In her outstretched hands she held a dripping rainbow of cloth.

Hut, she practiced in her mind, *have this dried for me at once. Hut! I must have this dried immediately. Hut—*

"Hut," she said aloud, her voice shaking.

"May I help you?" The smooth voice made her jump.

"Have this—" She cleared her throat, eyes darting back and forth across the empty ceiling. "Could you please tell me where I could dry my clothes? I washed them, but there's no place to hang anything up in here and, uh—"

She felt inexpressibly foolish, explaining her domestic woes to an unseen voice in the ceiling.

"Of course, Raille. If you will allow me."

The heavy skirts stirred slightly in her arms; in an instant they felt lighter, looser. She shook them out wonderingly and found each item completely dry, unwrinkled, glowing with color.

"Thank you very much," she stammered. "I hope it wasn't too much trouble."

"None at all. In the future may I suggest that you place any items you wish refreshed on the red area of the counter in the habitual and they will be taken care of at once. Unless, of course, you prefer it done while you have them on."

"Oh, no—no, I don't want to trouble you. That will be fine. Thank you very much." She retreated backward into the habitual, tapping the doorsill as Choss had taught her, to make sure it would close behind her.

5

Raille was not the last to breakfast, as she had feared.
After her embarrassed entry into the room—it seemed to

her as if a thousand conversations broke off abruptly, so that countless pairs of eyes could turn to measure her—but before she had finished her awkward meal of too-hot tea and crumbling bread, Emrys himself appeared, looking hollow-eyed and wan.

He approached Cil, ignoring the rest of them, and asked her to accompany him to the Library. When an hour later they passed back between the stone lions, Cil was flushed and distracted, gazing off into her own thoughts, not wanting to talk to anyone, not even Jefany.

A mood of tension was growing in the room. Soon everyone was speaking in whispers, without anyone quite knowing why. Emrys walked to the center of the room and used gestural shorttalk with the Hut to summon a low chair with a single curved arm that was dappled with instrumentation. He sat with his back to the Screen, facing the Group Resolvent. Raille began to feel gooseflesh along her arms: something was about to happen.

"It's time." Emrys wondered if his face betrayed the anxiety he was struggling to keep from his voice. He looked from face to face, and they were like alien creatures, staring at him with polite, distant expressions.

"I'm setting the Screen on Local, using the Hut's Eyes."

He touched one of the control strips.

Belthannis Autumnworld appeared on the wall, silvered and brown-shaded, gray-green and blue, its somber beauty heightened by the patches of frosty dew that lingered in the shadows, softening edges and flowing lines.

The Hut's Eye was watching an area some distance away: a pocket meadow bordered in brush and forest, motionless, silent but for the piping, a thin lunatic lilt, high and irregular, of an isolated thimblewort still half in shadow. A beetle the color of a Weldonese lake flew lazily into the picture, swelled as it headed toward the Eye until it almost filled the Screen, then veered away.

The thimblewort ceased its chirping. There was no motion, no sound, behind the Screen or before it.

Finally something moved at the very edge of the picture: a blur of light brown against the greens and darker shades. It came slowly into range, half hidden by the waving silver grass. Emrys' finger hovered over the button marked ZOOM, then withdrew.

He watched their faces.

"Is that it?" Choss whispered, leaning forward on his chair. "It's a quadruped, isn't it?"

"*Neyney*, it's just bending over to look at something," Marysu said, a frown quirking her mobile lips.

"Maybe it's feeding?" Raille suggested from the back of the cluster of seats, eyes wide, voice quiet.

Jefany glanced uncertainly at Emrys, questioning him with her eyes, but he made no response. The creature moved closer through the high grass. It was still for a moment. Then it raised its head suddenly and straightened up, standing silhouetted against the pale blue-gray horizon.

Emrys pressed ZOOM.

For a few seconds no one would say anything. Then they all tried to speak at once.

"Oh . . ."

"Look at—"

"For God's sake, Emrys!"

"It's a *man*! That's a man out there!"

Emrys clapped his hands together twice, sharply, for silence. He seemed calm, very much in control.

"And now you have seen the thing we are to judge." He spoke crisply.

"Thing—" Jefany found it impossible to take her eyes from the distant shape wandering peacefully through the grass. "Jon, it was a human man we saw."

"No. It was an animal." He turned from her briskly, like someone following carefully rehearsed stage directions. "Cil?"

The planalyst stirred in her seat, head lowered, image of the forgotten goddess Freya in a warm-colored gown ribbed with black, rose blush creeping toward the luminous hair, glimpse of a blue tulip.

"He is correct," Cil said. "They are not human."

"What, then?" Jefany looked from Emrys' excitement to Cil's unease. "What is he?"

"Emrys calls them the *kin*."

Marysu turned from the Screen, fingers twining restlessly. "From the ancient Anglic, I would think," she breathed. "Relatives, it means, *släktingar*, members of the same family."

"Whose family?" Jefany said from beneath a three-thousand-year-old portrait. "Ours? The *kin* of humanity?"

"Listen to me," Emrys said. "I say it again: this thing—
these creatures—are not human. They could not fit the Code,
they would never convince the Weighers."

"No, Emrys." Choss stammered a little, watching the Screen
from the corner of his eye. "First we must study the evidence
for ourselves. Then we make our own decisions. There are
rules to this, there is a procedure to be followed."

"There is only one decision possible." The older man was
unyielding. "Alien. Animal. They will not be granted Humanity
by the Coben. There will be no [CLOSED] status"—he made
the brackets sharply with his hands—"no decree of interdict
for soon-to-be World Belthannis." He smiled grimly as he
spoke, and Jefany straightened in her chair, thinking: *It's the
old Jon Emirsson again, I'd swear, whatever else has happened. Confident, self-possessed, in charge. But what is he up
to?*

Emrys took a step backward, gestured from the Group to
the Screen. "I am saying this now, you see, because I want
you to lie. All of you! I want a completely false Resolution
for the Weighers."

For a second time the room was filled with a confused,
shocked silence. Raille Weldon sat with her hands at her temples, willing herself away from this nightmare.

March threw back his head and gave a bellow of laughter
that crashed through the silence like a hurled weapon. "Great
wise Scholar," he said. "Emrys the Sessept! *Chot!* It's Emrys
the un-sane, Emrys the mad! It's a crazy breck, you, but a sly
or a brave one, offering us a stroll down Deepside with a smile
on the face."

Emrys bore the mismatched stare with ease. "And what
better way to offer such a thing, eh, March? With a smile,
with a shout: I may be mad, but I mean to win!"

Raille giggled nervously. "To win," she said. "You make
it sound like—like—" She paused in sudden embarrassment
and looked at the floor.

"Like a war," Choss finished curiously. "It does indeed
sound like war."

"Very good." Emrys nodded. "What I am about to propose
does involve a battle plan of sorts."

"Had enough war," March said quietly, his face a sandy

stone again. He flicked the false green eye with his fingernail, and the others started at the sound.

"A war without bloodshed, I promise you, March." Emrys matched the soldier's grave expression. "A campaign against injustice, nothing more."

He looked over his shoulder at the Screen and rubbed his hands together briskly.

"Well. You have something to think about now, at any rate. And Choss was quite right about the evidence—you must see for yourselves. Shall I take you to it?" He pointed to the blurred figure. "Shall we go now?"

They all nodded assent, seven heads dipping forward, seven pairs of eyes looking numbly around. The air still tingled with the obscenity of madness, the strange thought of death.

CHAPTER 4

There once was a Drifter named Cable
Who Darkjumped nine stars beyond Babel
Said she: "It's my home
And I don't mean to roam
—But soon we won't even be able!"

ANONYMOUS LIMERICK
(CA. GY 391)

1

They moved along the gentle incline of the Hill, as Emrys had named it, past rocks and vegetation in endless variety, unnamed and beautiful. When they spoke it was in hushed tones, Emrys murmuring threads of description, some member of the party responding in whispered appreciation; but for the most part they walked in introspective silence, thoughts turned inward by the stillness of the world.

At the bottom of the Hill they found a fissure in the earth the width of a man's two hands placed side by side. It was the scar of some ancient shifting of the ground, its sharp rim gentled by borders of pink and amber lichen.

Emrys had them kneel at the edge of the opening, where they could see a miniature cavern whose walls were the planes of a huge fractured outcropping of bluish quartz, coruscating here and there with veins of green and silver. Emrys often came to this spot to sit and ponder, staring into the crystal depths, and he had begun to think of it, after the fashion of his people, as the *hwynta*, or "soul place," of Belthannis—but this he told no one.

The party left the fissure, proceeding west through the trees and coming at length to the sky-colored ribbon of the Water, where the river flowed with such transparency that it made their eyes ache to try to catch it as it paused in whirls and eddies above a bed of smooth pebbles shimmering with the fire of opals in the morning sun.

There they halted once again, to gaze out over the deep vales of meadowland which Emrys called the Verres, from an old word in the language of Green Asylum meaning "the eye delights." Before them lay a grand sweep of color and texture: a hundred shades of green worked with brown and silver extended to the foot of distant mountains, great heights which lay framed in blue-fading-to-pale, softly contoured, like reclining human figures. The closest slopes displayed an almost tended look; they were furry with dark brush strokes of foliage, reminding Emrys of the meticulously planned timed gardens perfected by the *vwelynto*—literally "green-wise ones"—of his homeworld.

They passed next through a glen carpeted with heavy moss, where the spell of silence was partially broken by the bell-notes of a mist of tiny insects rising from the blossoms that lay against the moss.

The subtle alchemy of colors, shapes, and scents exhilarated them, and laughter and conversation bloomed as they followed the course of an energetic brook; song fragments took wing and were pursued vigorously by Jack and Cil until the words ran out.

Emrys held up his hand. "Over this next rise," he announced in a gentle, hollow voice, the way a polite assassin would say: *I'm afraid it's time to die.*

They were mounting the last of several low, rounded hills,

a knuckled ridge of land thick with feathery groundstems and tall retiform bushes. Flowerets covered the crisscrossing branches, transparent blue complexities resembling twists of crystal, that exuded a pleasant, peppery fragrance.

"Wait here." He walked ahead a few paces to peer at something out of sight. Traces of golden dust shone on his dark robe where he had knelt on it at the cleft of blue quartz.

He returned and beckoned them on.

The other side of the hill held the beginnings of a new landscape: sunbeams crowded into a wood-ringed clearing twice the size of the Hut's Hearth Room. Here the ground was hidden by the familiar silver grass; trees of various heights and persuasions mingled harmoniously. As the party approached, a small quadruped with fur the color of cinnamon paused midway up a knotty trunk to stare at the chaotic mass of noise and color flowing toward it.

Beyond a thin band of blackbarks on the far side of the clearing, the land fell away rapidly. As they descended the hillside they caught glimpses of the bowl of a broad valley. What they could see of it was forested in green-gold and copper, and lay glinting in the sun like the eye of a hunting bird.

They reached the entrance to the clearing.

A few steps into the silver grass someone gasped. Then silence fell on them like a seal no one dared to break.

There were two objects before them.

There was a weathered log, half its length wreathed in ferns and ophidian vines.

Something stood next to it, a thing slightly taller than the log was long, of a lighter shade of brown, of a smoother texture, free of vines and moss.

Or it was a man.

The man stood by the log, and he was naked and unmoving, his back to the Group, his hands loose at his sides.

Or it was . . .

The moment persisted, the nine beings trapped in it—eight grouped tightly at the clearing's entrance, one alone at the center—forming a tableau which artists would pursue for centuries to come in stone and pigment, shadow, light and sound.

Or . . .

* * *

"You all feel it now, don't you? Oh, it's very strong the first few times, very strong. I remember, it was three full days before I could walk up and look at it in the—the—"

An uneasy ripple passed through the others; he felt his words gutter and go out like flames deprived of air. Noise was clearly a sacrilege, the voice intruding into some carefully plotted arrangement, a moment being frozen into an icon.

Emrys tried to keep their attention on him, watching as expressions fled along the line of faces. The silence held.

He touched the bare arm nearest him, grasped it, shook it.

"Wake up, now. D'you think if I tickled your sides it would break the spell?"

Jefany tore her eyes from the still figure, gave him a stricken look. "It's a man, it's a man," she whispered.

He stroked her arm. "No."

"Not real, then." Gray eyes darted away like arrowheads. "An image, a trick, a holo," she said.

"Quite real." He raised his voice for the others. "Go out to it, colleagues, it'll do you no harm. Examine it. Evaluate."

There was silence, flat and unmoving as water in a heavy-world pond. But at the edges was a growing flicker, a little licking tongue of hysteria. Emrys recalled the feeling: like standing on one side of a boundary that wasn't there, one's mind saying nothing was wrong, while the senses screamed for retreat. *Sweet Risen Isis*, he thought, *don't let them break and run*!

He released Jefany's arm and walked deliberately into the open area. Their eyes followed him like hot beams trained on his back.

When he reached the silent figure, he raised his left arm high.

"Here!" he cried, bringing his palm down with a loud clap on the naked shoulder.

"Here," he repeated more softly, pressing the unresisting flesh with his hand until the whole body began to pivot slowly.

"Face to face," he murmured, searching through the band of eyes that fronted him, seeking some reaction, a spark that he could nurture. Icy blue, sky-colored gray, pale untroubled green, cold *chade* like a false note in the interplay of deep,

dark, light and hazel brown—he could have been scanning a
row of shields, inviolate, a display of gems, beautiful and
lifeless.

"Jefany?"

Seven faces stamped with the seal, hers lost among them.
He frowned, narrowed his search until he found the lucent
gray, then widened his gaze to include face, restless hair, awkward fists.

The shared terror in their faces was becoming too much for
him to bear. At last he shook his head, stepped out over the
matted log. "Perhaps another day . . ." He moved away from
it.

"Jon!" Her voice was raw. He moved back, winced at her
expression, willed strength to her.

"It—" she began, then fell silent again, gnawing her lower
lip. She took a deep breath and three quick steps toward him.
Her long legs swung stiffly, her face pinching tight as clenched
fingers.

"*Hai*, it almost hurts."

"Fight it, Jefany. Try!"

She approached along a wavering line, shoulders hunched,
fists full of dark-blue fabric.

In his mind he stretched a cord between them, tried to draw
her down it like a bead on a wire. Then she was there, huddled
against his right side, looking resolutely away from that which
stood on his left.

"What's happening?" Her face was waxen, her skin clammy
with sweat. "What's it doing to us?"

He shrugged with his free shoulder, held her tighter.

"I don't know, maybe a protective mechanism of some sort.
But it goes away, it gets easier. The Hut never noticed it at
all, only saw the changes in me: heart, respiration, nerve cells,
motor control, adrenal flow—everything saying *stay back!* But
it does get easier. You have to fight it, hard."

She was clutching his hands, pressing her cheek tightly
against his until his fingers and jaw had begun to ache.

"No. It's almost gone now," she said. "Isis."

Emrys could feel her muscles relax, the rhythm of her
breathing even. He looked from their twined fingers to the rest
of the Group still rooted to the edge of the clearing.

"Try touching hands!" he called to them. "Put flesh against flesh. It seems to help."

It was Cil who finally grasped March's blunt fingers and struggled out into the open, her exquisite features clamped in grim determination. The soldier hung back for a heartbeat, then stalked forth at her side, groping with his free hand for Marysu's bangled wrist.

The linking continued down the line and they were all moving now, swaying, lurching like drunkards toward those who waited in the center of the meadow.

The chain stumbled into a ring when it reached Jefany and Emrys. Soon the fear was gone.

CHAPTER 5

It would be very singular that all nature, all the planets, should obey eternal laws, and that there should be a little animal, five feet high, who in contempt of these laws could act as he pleased, according to his caprice . . .

FROM THE WRITINGS OF
VOLTAIRE

1

Jack felt the cool air on his bare arms and legs, the warm sun pooling on his face. He thought the sun was one of the nicest he had ever seen.

Silver coin in a silver bowl, he thought. He squinted at imagined markings, superimposed her face; finding it wasn't the face he had meant, he frowned in surprise and banished the image.

The others were still gathered in the center of the clearing. From the way their mouths were working—too fast and all at the same time—he knew that nothing intelligible was being said yet. He moved farther from them, his feet cool in the silvery grass, his half-lidded eyes on the sun.

What am I thinking about, right now? Jack wondered. He tried to pin down a thought, to separate a single moment, one cell of being from the whirl and blink. The effort made him shiver with frustration, like trying to scratch that one place high up on his back.

He removed his smock, sliding it slowly over his arms, feeling the warmth rising over his body. Turning, he picked Marysu from the huddle in the clearing. He stared at her for a few moments, lost in her intense beauty, the coiling slippery ascent of his blood when he thought of her under the wander-lights in their room, her skin dappled into peach, glime, yellow, violet, brole—all colors, no colors, her colors. The haunting planes of her face, the way she clutched at him . . .

He walked beneath trees. Low branches bearing fans of green translucency obscured, then took away, his sun.

Stubborn, he retained a picture of the pale disk, covered it deftly with a memory of Maya's sun, fat Surya; over that, he laid Sipril's double star, Alpha and Beta something-or-other; then the yellow sun of old Earth; the vast bloodclot of Antares; the liquid gold of Cellini; Axus Ariadne's ruddy bronze . . .

He was forty-two years old.

The voices started to drift apart, sorting themselves into communication again. He concentrated on Cil as her words flowed through the dying babble, calming it into order. He juggled his suns for a moment longer, then sent them away one by one in reverse order, the final image melting into Cil's pale face with its corona of shifting gold.

He looked back over his shoulder.

I don't care what they're saying. I don't care what he is.

But he turned and headed back into the clearing.

They were sitting down in the grass in a cautious semicircle. Jack caught the end of Emrys' statement: ". . . sure many of your questions will be answered if she gives a brief summary— and brief is all it can be—of what's been established so far."

Cil rose and moved away from the others, then sat down on the log facing them, including Jack in her uncertain smile as he ambled near. She sat in silence a few seconds, eyes closed. Then she began speaking, the words passing through her lips as if they had come from somewhere other than her own thoughts.

"The function of a planalyst is almost always to build bridges. Those of us who are called to the profession come to it because there is that within us which is forever playing with a world as if it were a puzzle: matching pieces, closing gaps, striving to see the pattern that incorporates the many little strands, the odd fragments that show no obvious relationship.

"Perhaps it was this aspect of the discipline which Emrys had in mind when he asked me to be the first to study the data that he and the Hut have compiled. He probably expected me to find the thread of order in it all, something that would enable me to present you with a coherent explanation for what you will see here.

"But I must disappoint him. This Belthannis is a different world. Already I feel it may never be explained—perhaps only experienced. You see, I have found the thread, I have closed most of the gaps. Oh, the pattern has come together here, far, far too quickly.

"I see the coherence. I see the whole and it makes no sense to me. It is like nothing I have ever dealt with before, and I have worked at my profession for many years.

"I think, therefore, that the best way I can serve my function in this case is to reverse the process, to pull apart the threads that fit together so neatly. But there is a vastness here, the pattern is a world with no place clearly marked 'begin here.'

"So I propose that you ask me questions."

She looked up at them, blinked. "What is it you would like to know?"

Marysu's bracelets clanged as she thrust out her finger, pointing past Cil's shoulder.

"*I* want to know where our host is going."

The kin had suddenly begun to move, arms flexing, dark head lifting, body swiveling away from the Group. Since their arrival it had remained almost motionless, statuelike in the tall grass. As they watched, it walked unhurriedly toward the thinly forested edge of the clearing.

"*Vänta, min vän!*" Marysu called.

"Shouldn't we follow him?" Choss rose hesitantly. "He's heading for the valley."

March had risen swiftly when the kin had begun to move. As he started after the retreating figure, Emrys halted him with a hand on his arm.

"No need," he said. "He won't go far, I assure you. Besides—" He pushed back the sleeve of his robe to show a second silver band above the journal on his wrist. "When we want to see him, the Hut can find him for us." He touched the control band. "Are you with us, Hut?"

"Of course." Miraculously, the lovely machine-voice still seemed to be coming from above their heads. Choss could not resist a glance upward: the sky appeared empty.

"How can you be sure how far he'll go?" Jefany asked.

Emrys nodded to Cil. "Let that be your first question."

Cil extended her hand, palm up, toward the Group. "May I have the world, please, Hut? About here."

Above her hand appeared a globe of Belthannis in brown, green, and silver, complete with cloud wisps and ocean sparkle. The world turned slowly, three tiny moons circling it like pale moths.

"This comes from the robotic probes left in orbit by the first Survey ship," Cil said. "There's a continuous broadcast which the Hut can link into. Now the grid, please."

Hair-thin lines of brilliant orange latticed the land areas of the globe, covering the two great continents with a network of polygons.

"Slow it by fifty, I think," she said. The image gradually reduced speed until its rotation was imperceptible.

"Good. Now—" Cil produced a slender wand from the cloth-of-pearl pouch at her waist. She touched the tip of the wand to the image and left a dot of red glowing in an area on the north of the larger landmass. "This is where we are." The mark had fallen near one of the orange lines. Cil touched again, slightly to the east of the first point: a blue dot glowed.

"That's the Hut. Actually, I've exaggerated the distance, but the directions are correct. This whole territory"—she traced the polygon in which the points had fallen, causing it to flare brighter than the rest of the grid—"belongs to the kin. The one we've been watching." She leaned back, gnawed absently at the knuckles of one hand, then resumed. "As you can see, we're now at the eastern border of his territory. Since the creatures never stray beyond these boundaries, Emrys knows it can go no farther than the rim of the valley."

"It, it," Marysu said. "Why do you keep calling him that?"

Before Cil could answer, Emrys cleared his throat and fingered the band at his wrist.

"Excuse me, but I'd like your permission to begin recording this discussion. It might be useful later." He looked around. "Are there any objections?"

"No."

"*Nyet.*"

"I don't care."

"Go ahead."

"No."

"Fine, then. Hut, please begin a record of our conversation, starting now."

"Certainly," the Hut agreed.

"What marks these boundaries you've drawn?" Choss asked. "I saw no hint of fabricated structures when we were dropped. And a globe-encircling network of boundary markers would be an impressive artifact, surely indicative of a highly developed civilization."

"Ah, this is difficult to explain, Choss," Cil replied, "because there are no physical markers. Only, well, internal ones, perhaps on the same order as the emotional barrier we felt when we first approached the kin. These large boundaries are permanent, however, and the kin cannot cross them. Permanent in relation to each other, I should say, as the territories themselves move, as if the whole grid were rotating slowly around the globe. It follows climatic changes, I think. The network moves and the kin must move along within it, do you see? Here, I'll show you. This is the way Belthannis looked half a year ago. In a few more months—like this."

"Hey, what happens when you get to the ocean? Do you swim over to the next continent, or just tread water for a while?"

"Ah, good question, Jack. No, the territories are small enough and far enough inland, do you see, so that the migration never brings any of them into contact with the sea. The movement is very gradual: it spans the entire solar revolution. By the time the outermost nears the shore, the process has begun to reverse."

"This is ridiculous!" Marysu exploded. "Invisible webs creeping over the world, dragging people around inside them!

Where do you get such notions? What proof?"

"There are pools of data and files full of holos and flats in the Library. The Hut's Eyes and the satellite probes have been charting the movements of the kin for months. In addition, we have the records of the original Survey ship to verify the consistency of the patterns from year to year. The grid theory is the only one which satisfies the model created by the data."

"How many of them live in each area?" Raille asked tentatively. "Do you know if they have family groups or tribal units? Are they all so strange and aloof as this one or will the others communicate with us?"

"There is no social organization, no grouping at all."

"You see," Emrys broke in, "there is one kin living in each area. Just one."

There was stunned silence, then all spoke at once:

"Only—" Jefany began.

"—absurd to—" Marysu was saying.

"—seems so—" Raille said.

"Huh?" was Jack's response.

"Let me explain—" Cil began.

"One, *spurge*!" March interrupted scornfully. "That means only—"

"Two hundred and forty-six territories," Cil stated. "Two hundred and forty-six kin."

"On the whole world? Two hundred and fifty natives?" Choss sounded plaintive.

"You said they never cross the borders of their territories, Cil," Raille said.

"Correct."

"Well, but they must. I mean—eventually—" Raille broke off.

Marysu laughed. "Obviously!"

"We don't know yet," Cil said firmly. "In four months not one kin has strayed onto its neighbor's land."

There was a long pause; Jefany broke the silence. "Let us see him again, Jon."

"If the Hut will oblige," Emrys said.

"Of course," the Hut replied.

They stared in awe at the image that appeared.

"Incredible," Choss said slowly. "A man."

"Closer, please," Jefany asked.

"No eyebrows," March observed.

"Nor tastebuds. Three or four other differences, all minor," Cil assured them.

"Handsome beast," Marysu said.

"Looks like he's posing for a portrait," Jack said. "No change in expression all this time."

"No expression to change. Probably utterly bored," Marysu replied.

Jack disagreed. "No, he's not bored, he's got no lines on his face. None. I think he must always look like that."

"He looks—he seems—" Raille fell silent.

"Have you learned the language yet? Are there any chips of it in the Library? Can I have it soon?"

"There is no language, Marysu. They don't communicate."

"Look closely," Emrys said. "See how his head has moved? So slowly you didn't notice it. He does that to keep the sun from shining directly into his eyes."

"I think it would be less misleading to say 'its eyes' from now on, Emrys," Cil suggested softly.

"Cil, there are countless forms of language," Marysu persisted. "You probably wouldn't recognize—"

"I would. It has no language of any sort."

The questions kept coming, faster and faster.

When it was all over Cil could not have said who had asked what, or in which order, or how long the discussion had lasted. The rush of voices had become one voice: probing, disputing, delving into her for things she could only begin to describe.

Is he what we were sent here to judge, Cil? They dare ask us to evaluate him?

"That is the creature we are to judge."

This man, this—kin, as you call him. He represents the highest form of life on Belthannis?

"A difficult question. But, yes, in all respects but one."

Oh? What's the matter with him?

"Nothing whatsoever."

Is this a question of sophistication, then? Is he a primitive? A savage?

"No."

Wait—he is a native of Belthannis, isn't he?

"Yes. At first I thought— But I'm convinced of it now."

And he is a man.
"Definitely not."
You just told—
Because he doesn't have tastebuds?
"No. Physically, it is identical to an adult human male, the few differences in somatype well within the parameters of variations found on most of the colonies: lightworlds, heavyworlds, dryworlds—many of these environments have worked far stranger changes in the human pattern."
What's wrong with him, then?
For Froy's sake, get to the point!
Hush, give her a chance.
"There is nothing wrong with it, do you see, and the point is that it has no mind."
What do you mean?
What? Insane?
You said he was—
"Perfect. Physically human, down to the last millimeter. Down to the brain, for that matter, which seems perfect also, perfectly developed. The brain of *Homo sapiens*, almost identical to ours, but—"
But?
"Barren. Barren as an empty warehouse for all its convoluted promise."
No intellect at all, you're saying?
Hai, look how quietly he stands, staring off at nothing.
Wait, wait! The man is completely devoid of sentience?
"So completely that in this single respect the thing that stands there so quietly is no more related to you or me or any other human being on any other world than these flowering blades of grass at my fingertips, the rocks by your feet, the water in the stream . . ."
Ah, see, look at the eyes, the eyes . . .
Congenital? Illness?
Injury? Surgery?
"Congenital. Forever."
Regrettable, but such things do happen on the less privileged worlds from time to time, we know, among the outermost—
"No. No. It is only that they *should not* look like us."
What do you mean by that?

A rather uncharitable statement—he's still a man!
Wait. You said 'they.'
"Yes."
Surely they're not all—all—
"Flowers. Stones. The stream . . ."
There was a long silence.
"You must see it in a different way—"
How horrible!
What happened to them? What did this?
Two hundred mindless human beings. Where are they from?
Who put them here?
How do they survive? How do they live?
"*Not* mindless human beings. Not human beings. Above all, not horrible. They live—in a pattern. There is beauty—"
It's disgusting. Oh, gods!
"No. Look at it. Just look at it."

2

Begin with a man.

Begin with a male human being of the average height, weight, coloring, somatic type.

Give him a face with what are called regular features, pan-racial and unremarkable.

Give him eyes like shadows on water, hair that seems to define the color brown.

Now what? Are there any differences?

Yes, a few.

Look closely at the face: remove the lines that result from fear, the brackets that have framed smiles, the hatchet strokes of anger—smooth away the interplay of muscles just beneath the surface that prepares a face for tenderness or puzzlement or unexpected joy.

But the face is not slack, nor stony, nor withdrawn in appearance. On the contrary: when viewed by the human eye it seems to possess a vast potential. It is like something asleep, looking momentarily foreign, which will be normal again when it wakes.

It is a face only in that it occupies space on the front of the head from chin to forehead, from right ear to left, containing eyes, nose, a mouth, rooted in bone and articulated in flesh. Everything is there that should be, but the sum of these parts frames a different whole, and by no other human definition can this reflecting surface be called a *face*.

And the body: where are the differences?

The muscles are not spectacular, having been developed only to the point of greatest utility. The arms, torso, and legs are those of a man who has done mild steady labor all his life, who has never been ill, who has never had a cut, scrape, or bruise.

The proportions are perfect, reminiscent of the anatomical mannikins created by the Vegan Masters from years of computer work and holoform. No portion of the body has been enhanced at the expense of the remainder.

The total picture is unremarkable. With nothing to anchor it, the eye keeps sliding off, wandering past the edge of the body to silver grass and black tree, as if there were no edge, no defining surface where the creature stops and the world begins.

3

For some time the kin had reclined, motionless once more, on a smooth ledge of rock midway down the uneven slope.

Below was a great labyrinth of trees bent and elbowed like puzzle-rings, the branches of each individual intertwined with those of its neighbors. Thin, spiral leaves dangled from the limbs, coppery streamers above the soft green-and-gold ground cover stretching in woolly tangles from one side of the valley to the other.

After a space it rose like a flower stem unbending and started back up the steep incline, toes fitting easily into precarious clefts and niches.

Black, leafless trees separated the rim of the valley from the clearing. As it neared the top of the slope, sunlight glistened on something small and red wavering at the tip of one gaunt branch. A tiny scarlet sphere was growing on the end of the branch, swelling and darkening swiftly under the silver sky.

The object began to tremble like a bubble in the wind as the creature came closer. A moment later it had dropped to the ground.

Without slowing, the kin bent, extended his arm, and retrieved the redfruit in one motion. It walked on through the trees, eating in small, precise bites.

*

4

Raille watched with the others as the creature returned to the clearing. She saw the last red morsel disappear into its mouth and something tugged at her memory. A word, a name: *Fo—foe? Faux?*

A cold finger moved leisurely up her spine. She closed her eyes and saw:

The dark outline of a face.

Gone.

An arm. What? A hand?

Gone.

Redness. Roundness. Mouth opening, closing.

Gone.

Eyes. Eyes!

Gone. Gone into silver, a sudden burgeoning waterfall of silver all around her, the waves rising into a bubble, enclosing her in slick spherical opacity.

Like falling into a drop of mercury, like drowning in a raincloud pinned to the center of the sky, surrounded with roiling, beautiful . . .

"—thing the matter?"

Raille felt hesitant fingers on her arm, heard Choss' voice shaded with concern.

Raille shook her head automatically, offered a smile as thanks and proof of well-being. The pressure on her arm vanished like smoke. She saw clearly for a moment how timid he was with people, how tentative and unsure behind the Scholar's mask of reserve. Her lips moved to form his name, but he had looked away and she said nothing.

Cil was speaking again.

Raille turned her full attention to the planalyst's words, eager to submerge the disturbing pinpricks of memory that were never enough for understanding, never more than a glimpse through slitted eyes.

5

The kin had settled in the grass several meters from the center of the clearing. It sat cross-legged, fingers moving slightly, eyes in shadow; a shiny green insect prowled carefully along its upper arm.

"You're probably all familiar with the requirements of the Code."

Cil made an improbable discussion leader, her green-shaded skin and myth-inspired costume vivid against the silver grass and silver sky. But there was nothing of the romantic sea sprite in her bearing now. Standing before them with one bare foot propped on the mossy log, thumbs hooked in her belt, blue eye-gems tucked away in her pouch, she spoke in a clear, measured voice, and Raille saw in her what she had not recognized before: a confident Scholar, an expert in her enigmatic Major, a complex and gifted human being. *How old is she*? Raille wondered suddenly.

In the past few hours the members of the Group had begun, in Raille's eyes, to emerge from beneath the bizarre fashions and unfamiliar quirks of character. She was aware for the first time that there were *people* here, individuals every bit as complicated and significant as those with whom she had grown up on Weldon.

From the beginning Raille's interest in the Special Evaluation Team had been supplemented by a formless desire to escape from a life and world growing progressively more patterned and predictable. Since leaving her home, her chief aim had become to stay out of people's way, in the hope that she would be left alone to explore this beguiling new universe.

As a Natural, she had been fascinated with the opportunity to experience an alien ecology firsthand, to actually observe life forms not native to Weldon.

But to her the Evaluation process itself was a tangled game, one of many indulged in by the vast and jaded Community. Though she had dutifully viewed the instructional material, it was never with the intention of becoming seriously involved in such hollow entertainment. When it came time for the final decision, she would fulfill her obligation by casting her vote as she saw fit.

But she was not the only explorer on Belthannis, she saw. Watching the excitement and concern budding in her companions' faces, she felt a stirring of kinship for those she had been ready to dismiss as muddled dilettantes or, in her mother's angry words, "decadent savages."

And after seeing the creature itself, she knew that she could not remain a disinterested bystander.

Silver zigzagged suddenly through her thoughts, vanished. A hand . . .

She listened to the basic tenets of the Code of Human Criteria as Cil recited it, storing key words and phrases in her journal for later weighing.

A limb or limbs modified for grasping.

A limb or limbs modified for locomotion.

The building pattern.

Sense organ(s) providing visual/aural/tactile perceptions.

Long-term memory.

The manufacture and utilization of tools.

A symbolic language.

The sociocultural inclination.

Abstract reasoning within a framework of logic.

The Waydel imperative.

An ethos, generative or inherent, incorporating self-preservation, pragmatic growth, mutability . . .

"Kiri," Raille whispered to herself. "Has anyone ever passed this test?"

Choss moved his head slightly to one side. "No."

Whirring faintly, the insect had reached the face. It wandered slowly over the handsome lips, skirted the right nostril, and began to mount the bridge of the nose.

He doesn't even know it's there, she thought, watching the tiny intruder, her nails digging deep into her palms.

Abruptly she remembered what Emrys had said to them back in the Hearth Room. "I want you to lie. All of you."

6

Choss drifted toward the kin, fingers automatically activating his journal as impressions crystallized into words.

"This is—spectacular. Sobering. And—a little disappointing."

He paused, pondering.

"Inevitable? Most likely. First Meetings have been among the most exciting events in recorded human history. The anticipation, the shock, the numbness that descends in a mixture of fear and exaltation: this is an experience which human beings have longed for since the days of Far Antiquity, before space travel. To be awakened. To be lifted out of oneself. To see something completely new."

He watched the gentle movements of the arms and legs, the dark hair that framed its face.

The creature stretched gracefully, and Choss saw Raille look quickly away, her eyes flying to her sandals half hidden in the silver grass.

He smiled, thinking he knew the reason: public nakedness was as unusual on his homeworld, Hinderlond, as he surmised it to be on her own Weldon. *But*—

He raised the journal again. "Social nudity is and has been common on many human worlds. He'd not look at all out of place on Sipril, Hem, Maya, Green Asylum—or in the flesh-presses of a dozen other worlds, for that matter.

"And perhaps that is why I can't react to him—to it—in the proper manner. It is so obviously a human being that the expected awe will not materialize. Even the use of 'it' rather than 'him' seems barbaric, all questions of intelligence aside. We don't treat our own mental defectives like this. We still call them human."

Raille had been staring at the ground, deep in thought. After a while she became conscious of a rustling sound, a soft buzzing murmur. Raising her head, she saw that it was coming from the others. They were standing at varying distances from the creature, arms raised against their chests, lips mouthing softly into their journals.

Nearest to her was Emrys, his own hands clasped behind his back as he spoke to the Group in a normal tone, as if completely unaware of the muted chorus.

The other nonparticipant was Jack, who crouched at Marysu's feet with a rapt expression on his face. His nub of charcoal raced across the drawing pad, recording the kin's image with flawless accuracy.

Everyone seemed far away, wrapped in separate envelopes like the packets that had brought them down to this world. Raille looked from face to face and found the same expressions, all variations on a theme of secretive wonder. The murmuring was like a tide lapping at her.

Having had no prior exposure to Community etiquette, Raille was immune to the powerful pressures of custom and polity which rendered her fellow Group members functionally deaf to the whispered journal entries of their companions; the realization that Raille, or anyone else, was actually listening to their private thoughts would have resulted in a shock of outrage and revulsion.

Among the muttering voices, Marysu's precisely carved words were the clearest. They drifted to Raille threaded with Emrys' continuing narration.

"—body is silent, *totalt tyst*! Even the gestures do not speak to me. They're perfect, I swear it, like the accelerated holos of plants swaying as they grow to gravity and the sun—"

"Watch carefully now," Emrys was saying. "Can you see his arms changing position? Shifting orientation, altering stress? Notice the movements of the shoulders, also. And the legs, there, the toes, the fingers . . ."

"Nothing is being said," Marysu continued. "Even when humans are asleep, or deep in a drugwine trance, the brain talks through face, limbs, muscles. Here: silence. This thing is kinetically dumb, is less eloquent than a statue, which at least has something to say about its sculptor—"

"Back at the Hut I'll show you holos that illustrate the way he moves in and out of sunlight so that he gets the same amount of exposure over a certain period . . ."

"—and yet I keep looking! Waiting, I admit it. And it's

absurd! More realistic to expect a greeting from a stick of wood, conversation from a pebble. But it feels—it feels as if this thing has just spoken. Or is about to speak—"

Emrys spoke on. "In fact, each of his movements seems to have a definite purpose. I defy you to find a millimeter of excess, the slightest miscalculation. The Hut can show you a schematic of all the motions of a single day. It makes a beautiful graph . . ."

CHAPTER 6

We believe now that the original goal was to break down the barriers existing between human and human.

Centuries later they still stalked the same prize, but coldly now, with purpose but without desire. They went their way because planners long dead had named it the correct way, and for no other reason: a frighteningly fragile premise on which to base the striving of an entire world. But they had sloughed off fear as they had coiled out of hope, long ago.

Their minds had come to work in ever more similar ways over the years, until the thought of one was as the thought of all. This they also called correct, and were guided by its consequences from generation to generation, from novice to noumenon, as Maribon swung in its erratic orbit and empath in his. . . .

FROM UNDERSTANDING MARIBON:
HISTORICAL PERSPECTIVES,
BY CHOSS BOESGAARD

1

The sky's taut metal had tarnished to a crumpled dome, streaky with blue-gray and violet, the small sun dropping down like a pivoting eyepiece through the mist of multichrome clouds.

Raille Weldon had begun to hide yawns in the hollow of her fist.

They had drifted into scattered single file behind Emrys when he halted them at the top of the first hillock.

"Please indulge me," he said. "I know it's been a long strange day and your bones and brains are tired. I have just one more request. It amounts to a question, one question before we leave this place for the rather insulated atmosphere of the Hut. Responding to this question involves the expression of personal opinions, so I beg forgiveness in advance if you find such things offensive. And I realize that according to the regulations you won't have to reply until the formal voting one year from now.

"Having said all that, I think I can put the question itself into the simplest form: What do you think of it? Human by the Code? Does it fulfill the definition?"

A brief silence followed, then signs and murmurs of negation. He squinted at them, trying to see more than the growing darkness would allow.

"Prime. Any dissenting? Anyone unconvinced?"

Choss raised his arm. "I need clarification. Can we be certain all of them are identical to the one we've observed today? I mean in the matter of the mind. Are you and the Hut both satisfied that there exist no variations which might affect the Evaluation, no exceptions from the pattern you described to us?"

"No exceptions, I swear." Emrys touched the higher band on his forearm. "Will you confirm that, Hut?"

"Gladly." The sweet voice hovered in the shadows.

Choss nodded. "I won't dissent, then," he said. "At least not on the basis of current data."

Emrys waited, but the rest were silent.

"All right. Thank you for your candor," he said very softly.

Then in a lighter tone: "Something hearty and warming for dinner, Hut, if you will. And goblets of blue waiting for us in the foyer."

"Certainly, Emrys."

As he started back on the trail, Raille Weldon suddenly said in a stricken voice from the end of the line: "But what do we do now? Just go home and leave them? Is it over?"

"Ah, no." He froze. "No, it's not over." He seemed about to add something, then he shrugged and plodded on a few paces. But his steps faltered and he turned back to them, face now lost in the shadows.

"Listen to me, please," he said. "Raille—all of you—I do not believe it is necessary to be a human being in order to be worthy of life." He spoke slowly, shaping the thoughts into words with great care. "I simply cannot accept that any longer. Do you understand me?"

He raised his palm outward before they could reply.

"Let us try to walk in silence the rest of the way," he said. "I think you'll find Belthannis in the evening is an uncommonly good place to listen to your own thoughts."

How very odd, Choss remarked to himself, staying as close as possible to Raille without being obvious in the near darkness.

All in one day: A man, a famous High Scholar whose reputation is impeccable, has shown me an interesting living puzzle, a creature which—if Emrys is telling the truth—is like no other living thing encountered in the seven thousand years since our ancestors stumbled into space. That was in the morning of this portentous day. Now at twilight this same respected, distinguished person has said, in effect: lie with me, risk your livelihood, your very lives with me, as we go against every law and Law in our great Community!

I see what he means to do—I think. He ducked beneath a branch, pushed it to one side and held it for Raille. *But what could it possibly accomplish?*

I believe him when he says they are not human. And I know that it is part of the Ninth Law that living beings judged non-human under the Code shall in certain situations be given over to the directors of colonization so that their future lives may be planned. There can be miscalculations, blunders, tragedies of excess—I don't deny it. Sometimes relocation is unavoid-

able, and it doesn't always work. But where is the system of government that is foolproof? The colonies must be settled. The people must have food and space to live their lives.

An insect chirred and the evening pushed into his thoughts. Sable blotted the sky, all but a thin rim of paleness too indistinct to be a color, as stars picked their way out from the zenith, random points of brightness as yet unorganized into deeds and heroes.

2

As they passed into the foyer, Marysu leaned close to Jack and clutched at his bare shoulder, speaking to him in a low ragged whisper.

"What?" He turned to her, guileless green eyes wide with surprise. "Elyins?"

Emrys' hand curled away from the frosted blue decanter gleaming on the ledge of stone next to a clump of pterodendron. He turned and joined the others, staring in the silent room.

Marysu shot Jack a withering glance, then lifted her chin defiantly to Emrys. "Well, if no one else will say it, I must."

"Marysu, why don't we—"

"Face facts, Emrys—why don't we do that for a change? Before it's too late! What is the one logical answer to what we've seen out there? *Elyins!*" She hissed the word.

Emrys found himself caught off guard, for all his own speculation on the same theme in the past few months. "If you mean is it possible that the kin are mentally deficient or somehow disabled—"

"I mean Elyins. Do you want me to spell the word for you? The Departed, the Otherfolk. Completely aware, capable, powerful. Gaming with us, shamming this mindlessness. Feigning this whole dumbshow, with the others off somewhere, worlds away, watching. They could do that, you know. Tricking us. Laughing as they make fools of us one more time."

"I don't think they ever really laughed," Jack said softly.

"Shut up!" she snapped, and the vehemence in her tone made Emrys' skin crawl. In his mind he pictured the kin as it had been a few hours earlier: quiet, empty-looking, oblivious to the moth sunning itself peacefully on one brown shoulder.

"I cannot believe that, Marysu," Emrys said. He tried to shake off the numb horror that had crawled under his scalp with her words. "For three months I have lived here among them without one indication—"

"And what were you looking for, what did you expect to see, *gusraman*? Do you think *you* could discover them if they wanted it otherwise? Praise Isis, I thought you were an old breck, with experience in your head if not wisdom. Have you forgotten what they were? Our friend in the clearing this afternoon—suppose that there were others watching through his eyes the whole time we were out there. Laughing!"

"But, why, Marysu? Give me a reason."

"Why? You must have clotted milk between your ears! How can you even ask that question when the subject is Elyins? It's a cup with a hole in the bottom, a sieve—you can never fill it."

She turned around in a slow circle, challenging them all, her long fingers twitching, her breasts heaving.

"Why did they do any of it? Why show themselves in the beginning when they could have left us alone? Why those come-apart ships, still killing us after all this time? Why the Departure, you fools, when we trusted them? Why take away their language, that rotten, beautiful language, before—" She stopped suddenly, dark cheeks aflame.

Cil stepped forward into the silence that followed. "Thank you. It had to be said, you see, sooner or later by one of us. Everyone would have considered it at some point."

She raised her hand to touch Marysu's shoulder, let it fall back to her side when the other woman flinched.

"Besides, now that it's out in the open it'll be easier to lay to rest. The reason is simple, Marysu, you've said it yourself. If the creatures on this planet were Elyin themselves, or tools of the Elyins, and if they didn't want us to know it, then there's no way we could ever find them out. They did not make mistakes. This leaves us with a rather important choice. Either we assume the kin are what they appear to be and work forward from that assumption, or we're paralyzed. And remember, Marysu: for all you know *I'm* an Elyin, or Jack is, or Raille, or Emrys. Do you see? We have to stop that now."

Marysu poured herself a glass of wine and said nothing, her face shut tight around the bright blue eyes.

Jefany gave the frame an impatient tap, and another chapter
faded into the pad's long memory. The writing surface cleared
to its incorruptible square of white. Her foot tapped nervously
on the floor. She touched the journal at her wrist and muttered:
"Time."

At once her own voice began to recite from the black-and-
silver circlet: "Day Commons fifteen Mergent 380. Day local
thirteen. Hour seven of the morning. Minutes forty-two advanced. Seconds—" She covered it with her hand and heard
her own quick breathing again.

Seconds.

She wrote out of a need for movement, any kind of movement, and from a wordless desire to thrust her thoughts out
where she could see them and weigh them from a distance as
a stranger would.

> Silent seconds piling up and each one bringing me the same
> thought's echo: I don't want to go through this again. I want to go
> home. Am I a coward?
>
> Is Emrys a fool?
>
> He amazes me. Can he really be so naive? Is this simplistic
> falsehood sum and total of the great gamble he hinted at up on the
> sundeck that night?
>
> It's another Chwoi Dai, despite the bizarre physical resem-
> blance. A Chwoi Dai without hope, lacking one shred of real evidence
> to support a Judgment of Humanity.
>
> That other time, at least we all believed that what we were
> saying was true as well as morally correct. We thought them human
> by the Code. But here it's a lie, and we know it from the start.
>
> And it won't work.
>
> A year. It stretches out ahead of us like links in a chain already
> forged. Soon after we call in with our Judgment they'll dispatch a ship.
> Assuming we survive the trip, we appear on Commons a few weeks
> later with tears in our eyes and a pair of the creatures. Perhaps there's
> a slight stir at first, the inevitable speculation about Elyins, lost col-
> onies, parallel evolution—but then the Sauf Coben spends a leisurely

morning really examining the things and by afternoon our Judgment's
overturned.

Back goes a ship. This time it's one loaded with *torporin* (do
they still call that the King's Sleep?) and in a few months those kin
who survive the transfer have their very own compound at Mauve
Terrace, complete with false black trees and a nice shiny silver sky
projection.

She set down the stylus, turned off the pad.

She raised her chin. "Is Emrys inside the building, Hut?"

"Yes, he is in the Library, Jefany. Would you care to—"

"I want to talk to him. Let me see him. Here." She struck
the wall sharply with her palm.

A circular area about a half-meter in diameter blanched and
shimmered in front of her. The wall suddenly windowed the
Library as Emrys turned to face her, dark brows lifting in
curiosity. Past his shoulder she glimpsed Cil slowly pulling the
mushroom shape of a New World dream hood from her head.

Emrys gave her a small bow.

"Fair afternoon." A smile twitched to his lips, became apologetic. "Let me get right back to you, can I? I promise. This
is a bad moment. We're in the middle of something complicated, and if I take the time..." He finished with a shrug,
made a small signal to the Hut, and moved off in Cil's direction
as the image faded.

"Damn you, Jon, you'd better take the time. Hut!" She
slapped the wall; the image swayed like a bubble about to burst,
then brightened again.

Emrys' mouth was half-open in the beginnings of a question
to Cil. As he looked back over his shoulder he closed his mouth,
watching Jefany in wary silence. Cil stood just beyond him,
her face revealing nothing.

Jefany felt doubly excluded, doubly angry.

"I think I want to be out of this, Jon, right now. And I want
Cil out, too. And you—you're *deranged*"—she felt a brief
satisfaction at his wince—"if you expect this foolish charade
will accomplish anything more worthwhile than the ruin of
seven careers and possibly an equal number of lives—without
helping the kin at all! And the pain for your Group, whether
they're punished or not—to build up such hopes, knowing
they'll be ripped away! I won't let Cil suffer an experience like
Chwoi Dai—"

"Jefany, wait." To her great surprise it was Cil who spoke, coming up to stand by an expressionless Emrys. "There are some things you don't know yet."

Jefany felt a twinge of annoyance partly directed at herself. She struggled between the desire to protect Cil and the knowledge that she had no right to interfere in another person's life.

"Cil, Dove, I've been through this whole process once before. Emrys and I both know what will happen. First it may seem like a challenge, almost like a game, before it all begins to fall apart. We've stood before the Weighers. We know the kinds of irrefutable proof they'll demand. It's cruel and irresponsible to—"

"I said wait, please." Cil brushed back strands of pale hair from cheeks flushed quickly crimson.

There was a beat of silence. Emrys cleared his throat.

"Have you ever seen the Dance as it's used on animals?" he said in a calm, musing voice. "Not entirely legal, but it's done here and there, mainly on the simpler ones for work or entertainment. The elaborate tricks they can perform at a hidden signal, the intricacies of movement! It's hard to believe they're no more than puppets."

Jefany stood silent, expressionless, as Cil took up the refrain.

"March is an expert Dancer, did you know, Dove? Oh, many mercenaries have Dances in them, but he himself is a bit more rare; performer *and* composer."

"And Marysu with all her tongues," Emrys continued. "There aren't a dozen panlinguists of her caliber in the whole Community. It's said the really skilled ones can actually make up whole new languages in their heads. Imagine that, if you can: a consistent, original, fully generative language that would be all but impossible to distinguish from one that had evolved over millennia."

Cil smiled at the game of back-and-forth. "Historians like Choss are also unique. Like libraries in a way, like storytellers of the truth. Perhaps their organic memories can't match a Manck's compendium for length and accuracy, but unlike a compendium they can deal with the knowledge they possess on more than a mnemonic level. There are pieces of thousands of vanished cultures in a mind like that. It's a mind trained by University to reconstruct the currents that sweep events along from age to age." She paused. "And of course you know a competent planalyst can devise ways to justify almost any natural phenomena, under almost any conditions."

Emrys was watching with a regretful smile. "I'm sorry, Jefany. I'm a poor Group Leader. Bellmaple on Chwoi Dai was better, all charts and organization. But me—I talk too much about nothing, and I'm never there when it's time to say the really important things. I always wait too long, it seems. . . ."

He lifted his hand toward her in a beckoning gesture. "But come join us now, if you're willing. Come and hear the rest of it."

CHAPTER 7

Heard a rather intriguing proposal during afternoon session today. A Captain someone who headed the latest diplomatic mission to Maribon—a mission which all had assumed would yield the same galling lack of either rejection or recognition as its predecessors—has been asked by the Maribonese to act as their plenipotentiary in some sort of joint colony effort with, of all unlikely worlds, most ancient and reclusive Weldon.

The proposal came right out of the Dark and Empty: I don't think there was a Voice in the Shell who wasn't taken off guard.

The colonial venture seems absurd on the surface: we must have better uses for Moselle, which is a fair planet in the holos. And what an unlikely band of colonists: several thousand proud eccentrics from one Private World and half a handful of pasty-faced misfits from another!

Perhaps it's just the novelty of it all, as if a pair of shut-ins had finally expressed the desire to take a stroll in the fresh air together and nobody's got the heart to deny them. I feel half-inclined to support the proposition myself.

After all, what harm could come of it?

FROM PERSONAL NOTES OF
DAN SARAMEL, JUNIOR
WORLD VOICE FROM
FLAMILLIS ON AKAI, GY 47-53

1

Emrys had proclaimed a holiday.

March, Raille Weldon, Marysu, and Jack spent the early part of the day at varying distances from the Hut, tagging after the kin or browsing through meadows rich with unrecorded life.

Choss stayed inside, in the privacy of his room, playing history and drama dots gathered from the Library, *Betta splendens* navigating cautiously at his elbow. Occasionally he asked the Hut to show him the four who wandered the fields; he paid particular attention to the one who plaited flower heads in her unbound hair and hummed soft ballads as she stroked mossy trunks with the backs of her fingers.

That evening wanderlights were set adrift in the Hearth Room and the wineglasses refilled themselves with something new each time they were returned empty to the table.

They dined to a presentation of music from contrasting cultures. The Hut strove to blend the different selections with care, often beginning a piece in some other part of the habitat and bringing it closer to the Hearth Room chamber by chamber, as the final strains of the preceding selection faded to echoes above the table.

To Raille, who had never witnessed such artistry, the Hut seemed peopled by a troupe of fantastic spirits who, one after the other, approached the human audience and told their tales of joy or woe. Knowing that this was a technological rather than a mystical marvel did nothing to detract from her enjoyment.

First came the Antique melodies of the *clairschach*, its choppy notes falling like bright feathers in the darkened room. Later, throbbing Regressive rhythms played. Jack and Marysu rose in a dance that Choss had never expected to see outside a fleshpress, and that Raille watched carefully from lowered eyes, pulse loud and swift in her ears. There were cries of encouragement and laughter, and even March smiled once, a long wolfish grin of approval.

The wanderlights novaed silently in bright pastels. The shifting illumination caricatured the assembled faces, helping in some cases to disguise expressions of tension and profound doubt.

Near the end of the meal came Mariki windchange music: the tonalities of ritual, all hollow whistling and tiny, distant bells.

After the first triad, Marysu began to talk quietly of her experiences on Marik, weaving words with such skill and unexpected feeling that soon the room was haunted by windswept deserts and proud matriarchs with velvet faces.

When the fragile lament of the Vegan step-songs had brought an end to the Hut's presentation, March got to his feet and performed, unasked and unaccompanied, the Dance called *Burn to Death*, one of the very old compositions of Ingrid Peretti of New World.

As he whispered the trigger words, the Dance pattern took possession of him, muscle and nerve, and his mind was tucked away in a dark place without time or sensation.

Then his face spasmed into a mask of demonic suffering.

Golden fingers clawed at the air.

Breath became a hiss, motion a portrait of pain.

The initial movements were tight, constrained. Rapidly they grew in scope and speed until he spun around the room like a mad toy.

The Dance was five minutes and twenty-six seconds long, and Raille flinched uncontrollably every time the whirling shape drew near, though Choss had quietly assured her that the Dancer's senses functioned even if his mind did not, and would prevent his coming into contact with any objects or persons during the performance. With fingers curved like talons and jaws wide in a soundless scream, March leaped along the dragon's back, and his feet were a blur like bright sand where they struck the cool mosaic.

When the Dance was over he walked back to the table. Ignoring the comments of the Group, he went through the required exercises, tugged his heavy boots back on, seated himself stiffly, and ordered a platter of fried *mulel*, which he gulped down with the aid of his inexhaustible wineglass.

The talk had turned to Elyins again, and they were matching Departure theories by the time Emrys rose at his seat between Cil and Jefany. A wanderlight flared too near his head, and he blinked in the resultant haze and with a gentle shove sent the globe toward the other side of the room.

"It's midnight," he said. "Local midnight."

Faces turned toward him.

"That means that on Commons right now it's midmorning. The tourists are afoot. Not so many as in years past, perhaps, but still an enthusiastic mob. How they swarm through The Museum, pointing, judging! Later they'll flood the viewing galleries at Blue Shell, always chattering among themselves, rarely lingering through an entire debate on the floor below."

He paused, and Jack whispered sadly to Marysu: "I think the holiday's over." She shushed him, her eyes on Emrys.

"And Mauve Terrace," he continued. "The 'xenobiological facilities,' the 'zoological gardens.' They flock to Mauve Terrace with their whispers, lifting the children to see *them*, pointing out the ones that remind them most of themselves, saying isn't it funny the way they look and the things they do—but who could ever think they were human?"

Jefany sat with her head bowed, hands cradling her temples. Cil's expression was unreadable in the random illumination; she sat very straight, fingers toying with the ring on her right forefinger.

"Back at the Shell, business is being conducted as usual: perhaps a citation of approval is issued for a slumworld that's managed to double its population again, perhaps the Voices vote to cut grain shipments to Frond or Lelute, and send out the order to round up a few thousand of the hungriest and ship them off to the newest colonial find . . ."

Emrys' voice made a pleasant background blur.

Slumped forward on fists and elbows, Jack played with the reflection of his face in the polished tabletop. He smiled lazily, grimaced, puffed out his cheeks, winked, twitched his nose like the little furry animal they had glimpsed near the clearing.

He glanced up when Marysu shifted back in her seat; he noticed an unfamiliar tautness in the arm that brushed against him.

Jack looked at the others, reading the messages in arms, legs, spine and fingers. More than wanderlight was in the air. It was as if a hidden cord had been passed through them all. As he watched, the cord was pulling tighter, forcing their bodies into lines of the same expression.

He listened to Emrys for a few minutes, feeling the same silken touch that had bound the others beginning to press upon his will. But it was only words, and like most words they struck him at the wrong angle and slipped away, a dozen glancing blows like leaves in the wind, with nothing there to catch them.

Emrys had paused, and now a new speaker held Jack's notice, however tenuously.

"Emrys. The people need food." The tone of Choss' voice asked that his words not be judged too quickly. "I appreciate your anger, but the fact remains that there must be food enough and room for people to live in dignity."

The old Scholar pivoted and looked down at the other man, his face set with resignation rather than reproach.

"No, I'm afraid you don't appreciate my anger if you find it that easy to dismiss. Let me tell you a story, Choss. Consider if you will the tale of the Ydras tree, from the legends of my homeworld. A thing of destiny, this tree, immune to disease, free from aging, a tree permitted by the gods to grow forever at the rate of its youth. A tree, Choss—a holy thing on my world—a tree whose roots quest without pause through the rich soil, drinking, devouring, altering all that they meet. Whose branches thrust ever outward, knowing no barriers. What is the fate of such a thing? Such a tree cannot survive anywhere but in a legend, you know, for it will one day cover its own world, supplanting all other life—not out of hate, I'll grant you, nor even from desire—but thoughtlessly, because anything not of its own being is utterly ignored. It needs nourishment, you see, and a place to grow. And one day, yes, this tree will cover everything and it will be alone. On that day it will begin to die. . . ."

Choss was chewing a fingernail, looking embarrassed and unhappy. "It's a good story," he said with a sigh. "And it may be a true representation of the issues. But—Emrys, I fear the tale cannot end any other way, sad and futile as it may seem. Things are what they are. The nature of your holy tree is to grow."

"True enough." Emrys nodded. "But the nature of a human being is to *change* his nature. To think before acting. We are the mutable ones, the dreaming ones. Long before we had the Screens or the Darkjumping ships, and long before we had the Ember, we possessed a great power of our own: the ability to step back from our environment and bend it to our will. A great power and a terrible one. On Green Asylum, this has been understood for a long, long time. The power is there, it cannot be ignored, so we strive to use it in a complete way: stepping back, seeing ourselves, seeing our world from a different perspective—then stepping in again where we belong, aware of the importance of our involvement with all life."

Choss noticed that Raille was looking in his direction. He straightened in his seat. "Emrys, I empathize, I really do. But that is philosophy and this is government. We have to draw the line somewhere. Say this is human and this is not."

The old Scholar turned from his pacing and stared at him. "Do we, Choss?" he said very softly. "Where? Why? By what right?"

"Well, it's going to happen sooner or later, that's all. People are curious, if nothing else—especially people like us, Scholars. They have to classify things and give them names, so that they can be better understood."

"You mean they have to slaughter things and put them in fetters, don't you?"

"Oh, now—"

"Question: what makes blue-green good and green-blue bad, dry important and wet trivial, smooth right and rough wrong?"

Choss shook his head, mystified at the other man's vehemence. "I'm afraid I'm not following."

"What in Isis' name makes humanity worth preserving at the expense of everything else? Do you follow that?"

"Yes, of course. And while I agree in principle that it's not fair to condemn an alien life form because its development in one or more areas may be inferior to our own—"

"Inferior!" Emrys cried in astonishment. "How dare we say

that any form of life is inferior or superior, when the only judgment we can possibly make is one of degrees of difference, and even that is hopelessly culture-biased and probably useless. A recognition and acceptance of difference in the universe— that should satisfy your classifiers. It's absurd to go any further, like a man who's lying on his back deciding that everyone else is too tall!"

Choss frowned uncomfortably; he knew Raille was watching him. "Again I say I understand your feelings. Believe me, I have the same emotive reaction to this situation." He sounded weary. "But this is the Law we're talking about, this is real, and we should be able to discuss it on a—a pragmatic level. These decisions are made far from here, by people with different sources of information, for the good of the Community as a whole. We can't wish them away. We can't ignore them by talking about trees or cultural biases. We must ultimately face the political realities—"

"Are you by any chance an Expansionist, dear Choddy?" Marysu asked suddenly.

Surprised, he turned to face her. "I'm a student of history. Because of that I must try very hard to avoid any such affiliations. I am pledged to observe, and I take that pledge seriously. All subjective tendencies are an impediment at this point in my career and must be accounted for in the fulfillment of the Major."

"That's a nice, safe, cowardly way to avoid answering," she said in a diamond-edged purr. "I hear the Parad Mir is strong on Hinderlond—"

"I am *not* an Expansionist!" Choss struck the table with his palm, his face burning. "I say to Emrys only what the Weighers will say, and what you all must think about. But you—you must learn right now that people are not accountable to you, and that it's none of your affair what I believe, or how I choose to express it."

She leaned forward, a smile coiling onto her lips.

"Hey!" Jack stretched up his arms and pushed two circling wanderlights together. They collided in a lazy explosion of amber and silver. "Do we really have to talk about these things now? I mean, couldn't we finish the holiday—some more music, a little blue, maybe some kephel?"

"It's about the fate of the kin, Jack. Very important." Cil tugged at her ring. "And it ought to be decided one way or the other as soon as possible."

March took a long, noisy swallow of the red liquid in his glass. "The mindpick's coming." He wiped his lips on his gray sleeve. "You have it all settled before that gleet drops?"

Looking across the room, Jack saw Raille Weldon's frown of puzzlement and remembered that she had been asleep in the *bain-sense* when the call had come from Maribon.

"Yes," Emrys said. "It has to be decided before he arrives. You see now, I hope, why I dare not protest his visit. We can't risk publicity at this stage." He turned and bowed slightly. "Choss, please accept my apology. I bring old anger to a new discussion. Argument is always useful. The Coben will be overflowing with it, and no one's opinions will be discarded here."

Jack looked down at the tabletop again, surprised to find a solemn expression on his face. *Forget it, flea! Not your problem.* He tried on a grin, closed one eye in a cheerful wink.

He opened it slowly. Memory swarmed over him, confronted him like a crystal with a thousand facets:

A flower unfolded, ghosted by counterparts from a score of worlds he'd visited via Darkjumper or Screen.

He saw again the gemmed fissure in the forest outside the Hut.

Saw again forty years of other people's eyes, opening through endless variations of shape, color, and design, to be caught by his hunting ones and pinned inside with the rest of the collection.

Again a bright edge of honed metal slipped along a ruddy wrist, trailing a widening crescent of scarlet and awakening a wound that remained behind his eyes even when he had closed them.

He ground the heels of his hands against his eyelids in sudden panic. He was always frightened when this happened: when a picture got stuck and he couldn't pry it loose. Closing his eyes actually accomplished nothing. The image was in the brain, not the retina. He shook his head once, violently, but the image lingered.

Emrys' words came through again, penetrating the ghastly picture and stinging all around him, flowing with the blood.

"I should have told you at the beginning. A lie is not enough. It won't work by itself any more than the truth would. Jefany and I were together on an Evaluation once before, and we meant it when we told the Weighers that the natives of Chwoi Dai were human by the Code. We thought it was so obvious— until our Decision was discarded. They're getting ready to settle Chwoi Dai now. I can't imagine it: all the empty hivehomes, the sky channels deserted, the stillness of the place. And I had *spoken* to them. Not in Inter, not with words, but we had begun to understand one another."

There was a silence that lengthened. Then Marysu leaned forward.

"But, *marse' qua*, Emrys, I saw the holos! I remember them! They weren't *people*—not like the kin—they were small and hard and spined like insects. No wonder the Coben wasn't convinced!"

"They were insects and the kin are empty shells!"

Jack felt the heat of Emrys' reply. In his mind the wound drew wider, blood seeping outward.

"They have no more intellect than blades of grass—keep that in mind, Marysu, when you call them people—no more relation to human beings than animated dolls. They look like us. Is that why you think I want to save them? Because they look like us? It's the very kind of reasoning I'm struggling against, child! Things should be what they are—without your permission, without mine."

"I only meant that it should make it easier. To convince the Weighers." Her voice was surprisingly subdued.

"Again, because they look like human beings? I tell you that after the initial shock that will matter not a bit to them. 'What significance there?' they'll say. A raindrop resembles a tear. A mirror can look like whatever stands before it. Are they the same?"

He spoke on. At some point Jack realized that the image was gone. He opened his eyes and sat up as a wanderlight bloomed deep azure against the wall. Waves of color lapped briefly at Emrys' profile.

Jack straightened in his seat, still concentrating on the voice which could make him feel angry, sad, and hopeful all at once. Something deep inside him continued to open, and, listening, he began to hear.

* * *

Later someone asked in a troubled voice. "All right. Assuming you'd convinced us to go along with it. What is your
plan? What would we do? Where would we start? We sit here
talking morals and meanings, but I see no plan, nothing solid
to build upon."

Emrys had sat down a few minutes earlier, trying to control
his restless pacing; he rose again.

"Well, then? What is a man? You know well enough what
the Sauf Coben believes. Past Decisions have made their opinions clear." He looked around the room. "We must use their
own Code as our blueprint."

He crossed to the other side of the table and stood looking
down at March, who ignored him, busy dissecting a plate of
fried crustaceans mixed with sea vegetables.

"He has to walk, March, where and when we tell him to.
And more: he has to bow and nod and yawn on cue. He needs
to move in a Dance so complex it will take you months to
fabricate it."

The soldier set down his knife, chewing slowly. He raised
his real eye to Emrys and shook his head.

"No frame here. No template, no patterning tools."

Emrys pointed to the ceiling. "The Hut will provide. Months
ago I began to requisition things. I hope I've managed to gain
access to most of what you'll need."

"Months ago. God's geck!" Marysu swore. "This begins to
seem like more than a four-day fancy. *Tsum Ma Yee Hwei Tze?*
What's really going on here? What else did you requisition?"

"Ah." He moved to the bald linguist's side. "Marysu. Communication. The kin must speak to his examiners. Through the
Dance. Is it possible?"

He saw the startled lizard-blink of crystal-blue eyes.
"Well..."

Jack whispered to Cil: "She could teach a stone to speak."

Emrys had turned away, and his voice was softer, as if he
spoke to a young animal he was wary of frightening.

"Raille, you must keep him alive for us. We want to find
out what makes him the way he is, and how to go about
changing his appearance without harming him. That brings up
something we must all remember." He raised his voice to include the others. "Our aim will be camouflage, not mutilation.

What the kin *is* must be left intact or we betray our own beliefs."

Raille was nodding, alert and nervous. "I'll—"

But Emrys had gone on to the next.

"Choss, if you join us I'll want an artificial culture of some sort. Something credible with roots and a future. The content I leave completely up to you: pull it right out of the air if that feels right, or dredge up something forgotten from the back-before and rework it to fit Belthannis."

He swung back toward his seat, again avoiding a direct reply. He touched Cil lightly on the shoulder as he passed.

"You know what we need from you, Cil. Of course, the Sauf Coben will be suspicious in the extreme. You must build us a web of possibility, strands of cause and effect stretching back so far that even the Weighers will be discouraged." He moved on, reseating himself. "We're going to make him a man. I want you to prove that Belthannis made him one long ago."

Cil measured him with dark eyes. "Emrys, I've given much thought to this recently. I do not believe our masquerade could successfully deceive the Weighers. For a while, yes, of course. But what if they demand to see more kin? Or if they desire negotiations regarding, I don't know, treaties, trade agreements? No matter how sophisticated your Dance and your language, if there's nothing inside the kin, it'll show sooner or later."

"Of course it will. Shortly after the Decision, I plan to reveal the truth to them."

"What?" Jefany stared at him in astonishment. "You plan what?"

"I told you before that I wanted to set things right. Not just for Belthannis, not just for the kin. For Chwoi Dai, for all the others. The only way to do that is to let them see what we've done. Make our kin so convincing that they have to judge him human. Then turn around and show them that they've erred. Show the whole Community: I have contacts in the Net, and word will spread fast when the time comes. But we need something to catch the interest of the people, something to make them listen when we go before the Blue Shell Council and demand justice for the Judged of the past. Do you see?"

Jefany nodded slowly. "It could work, with a lot of luck . . ."

"And skill. Which brings me to you. Humanist. Your certificates were taken in the study of what we are."

She looked uncomfortable. "Mine was a comtemplative Major—"

"Then I ask you now to put it into practice for the first time. All the puppetry and fables we can produce won't make him believable. You must teach us how to give him that spark of humanity."

He looked around the table, eyes halting briefly at each face.

"If you decide to join me, those will be your challenges."

There was silence.

"Do you want our answers now?" Choss asked in a shadow voice.

"Soon," Emrys said. "The empath is coming, the year is draining away. If Isis smiles, perhaps our visitor won't be making an extended stay here. At any rate, make it three days. Divide up among you three of these long days, and go out once more to the kin—each one of you alone. Spend some time observing, thinking. Evaluating, in all senses of the word. Then I will have your answers."

2

In a glade loosely held in the embrace of two dark arms of forest, in a grove of leafless trees that was floored with patches of green bryophyte as thick and lush as winter fur, spotted with flowering thimblewort, and misted with minute insects of various hue and structure, two beings of more than passing similarity passed time without words.

The insects flecked the air until it resembled a precious stone. Rising and dipping among the tiny yellow blossoms, they made sounds like the peal of distant bells, chiming softly each time they brushed corolla, leaf, or fellow seeker. *Whiskwing*, Raille had named them already, and *shiverer, dewdrinker, petal-gem, polyhue* . . .

On one side of the grove the kin lay motionless, or nearly so, the head on a vine-wrapped rock, the body laid out like clothing on the yielding moss. Dark-brown eyes were open, light-brown face lay bare and blank, barred with shadows by the clear sky and high branches. The beautiful chest rose and fell gently, an animated candlewood carving neither precisely in time nor conspicuously out of step with the rest of the clearing's somnolent symmetry.

A finger curled; one leg stretched out slowly and relaxed, resting against a small grouping of thimblewort. Those plants that bore blossoms were silent, but the ones that had not yet bloomed chirped petulantly once or twice when touched. The insects wove methodical patterns above the deep green.

Three and one quarter meters from the reclining figure, March was engaged in stillness of a different sort, sitting upright with knees bent at sharp right angles, shoulders tense and expectant, spine rigid as a spear driven into the ground.

At times one of the small flying things would pause against a golden cheek or settle, wings flexing an eyeblink of color, on the stiff gray worksuit. Then the man would stir and flick the thing away.

Time was measured out in heartbeats—steady, alert, thudding forward—and it was measured not at all. With the threads of sameness between them growing more tenuous with each small parcel cut and shaped by time, the silent man sat stiffly on his guard near the wordless kin, as incongruous there and then as human-given names in the forest of that world.

3

Jefany sat on a slab of sunwarmed rock overhanging a lively riverlet, an offshoot of the Water. Her restless hair was motionless for once, pulled back from nape and forehead and loosely coiled, the static charge that gave it life nullified by the tiny pins that held it in place. She was wearing sandals and a pair of functional shorts: their vertical stickstrips held stylus, spongepad, holocube and scent collectors. The sun was beginning to bring out light freckles on her back and arms.

Her feet were blurred to the ankles in the stream, pleasantly cold. Something thrashed in the grass not far from her. There was a moment's silence, then two little animals with reddish

fur burst forth in a mad game of pursuit and capture that brought
them within centimeters of her arm. She sat very still until they
tired of the sport and darted off together through the grass. A
light wind made a path of swaying stems through the meadow,
and she added her sigh of pleasure to its passage as the cool
air skimmed across her shoulders and face. Tilting her head
back, she scanned the sky, a half pearl of blues and grays and
shifting highlights the eye could not quite capture. At her back
was the forest, a cool presence like a memory at the border of
her thoughts, waiting to be reexplored.

She reached for her stylus and pad.

> Our true judgment begins. Choss went out yesterday morning,
> then March in the afternoon.
>
> This morning was my turn.
>
> It was moving when I found it. I walked along the ridge behind
> it. We went through silver valleys, across the Verres, into the forest,
> out of it. Once he stopped and ate a piece of the redfruit. I finished
> off this morning's melon, my own hunger triggered as automatically
> as his seemed to be. Once he knelt by the Water and drank, in a motion
> so smooth and sudden I thought he had fallen and rushed forward like
> a fool to save him.
>
> But he never falls and he never stumbles, moving without hes-
> itation through areas where a moment later I will trip over a root or
> scratch my leg on a branch, having misjudged the ground beneath its
> cloak of furze. I have not felt clumsy in this way since I was a little
> child sixteen tens of years ago, but watching him is like watching
> human grace perfected to something beyond human capability.
>
> It is strange to spend the morning within speaking distance of
> a man and to spend it utterly alone.
>
> Once he lay down in the shadow of a great tree and seemed to
> sleep, though his eyes were sometimes closed and sometimes open and
> who could tell the difference from his face? I sat next to him and
> counted grass stems until—click—he was on his feet again and we
> were off, threading deftly through a pattern I am blind to.

Jefany lifted the stylus and read through what she had written. Then with a little smile she added a single line:

> Kindly note that I always manage to start off very conscien-
> tiously, remembering to call him "it" for at least two full sentences.

She blanked the writing surface, played with the frame until she had summoned the record of a previous entry.

> Local Day 14, very late.
> Let me check the time.
> Correction: Day 15, very early.
> I am really quite composed sitting here at the edge of the pallet, admiring how the amber glow from this section of the wall falls on arms and back and thigh and legs, making us one color and melding light to flesh to hair to empty air.
> Where do "I" end in this room, at this time?
> O peace, never mind. This is no hour for such questions.
> Cil hides from her own fatigue tonight, too deep for dreams of death on World Vesper to follow.
> It is so—what do I want to say?
> Late? Lonely? Futile?
> They say—and *they* are invariably not Scholars—that we of University are made different from the rest of humankind in that we are conscious of the process of learning, and treasure it as if it were a pleasure of the senses. They further say that we can smell out knowledge, that we are aware of its presence like the beginnings of new weather in the air.
> If this is true then I have been through a whole storm today, a battering and a drenching of my brain.
> I have learned:
>
> 1. That we do not exist here, at least not to those that we have come to judge.
> 2. That the kin are not people, are not "kin" to people, save in appearance.
> 3. That we have been asked to assist in a lie so great that it could prevent the murder of creatures who would be totally unaware of demolition, completely incapable of experiencing their own extinction.
> 4. That if the vote is yes then we must begin at once to build a Man from the manlike thing in the forest and whatever spare parts and wrappings the rest of us can provide.
>
> The roles are shaping up already:
>
> > March to pull the strings
> > Choss to fill the past
> > Raille to keep the life inside
> > Marysu to speak the words
> > Cil to make a world that could
> >   have made a man

Emrys himself the source, the way,
                    the puppetmaster
    Jefany...

Jefany to teach him humanity. O gods.

CHAPTER 8

> *...And blest are those*
> *Whose blood and judgment are so well commingled*
> *That they are not a pipe for fortune's finger*
> *To sound what stop she please.*
> *Give me that man*
> *That is not passion's slave, and I will wear him*
> *In my heart's core...*
>
> FROM HAMLET, PRINCE OF DENMARK,
> BY WILLIAM SHAKESPEARE

1

Marysu had named the plant "slevoe" because its branches bore long clusters of tiny translucent seeds and because in Hint, the Middle Tongue of World Hinderlond, *slevoe* could mean either a shower of ice droplets or a necklace of glass beads, depending largely on the social class of the speaker. To Choss' shame— as Marysu had foreseen—the word meant "necklace" to him, and he flushed with anger during her offhand analysis of the "patterns of linguistic oppression" which existed on his native world. Too preoccupied with his own concerns to notice the hidden tension and resentment when the word was discussed,

Emrys commented that the name seemed to fit the bush and had it officially recorded with the Hut.

There was a stand of young slevoe growing in a broad crescent at the far western edge of the Verres. Raille Weldon crouched with her back against the slender trunk of the largest bush, and as she trembled, the branches bobbed gracefully all around her.

Twenty paces to her right was the creature, drifting gradually in her direction through the high grass. The nearer it came, the more violently she shook, gasping and sobbing, though there were no tears but the frozen jewels hanging from the branches by her head.

Within the swaying shelter Raille sat huddled with her arms locked around her knees. She looked out through the branches upon a strange double image: kin moving, kin motionless; half the sky soft gray, half glittering silver; the world first sane and ordered, then holding such terror that she began to scream again, hoarsely, even as part of her drew back and watched in wondering silence.

At length the kin's wanderings took it past her, back out into the Verres, until soon it was no more than a pale-brown blur slipping through the green and silver.

Raille rose and tried to follow it, slowly at first, then running as she neared it. When she was about ten meters away she lurched and cried out as if she had stumbled, then fell to her knees, her skirts fanning out like a flower head around her.

When she climbed to her feet again, minutes had passed and the kin was nowhere in sight. She stood for a long moment with her eyes focused on nothing, chest heaving. Then she turned and moved slowly away in the opposite direction.

2

"Choss, are you in here?"

Choss raised his hand, and the room brightened. The Screen grew dim and opaque, blue fire snuffed into memories.

"I was watching a Netplay," he said to Jefany, who stood blinking in the Hearth Room archway. "A drama, simplistic but very engrossing, based on the exclusion of New Asuncion from the Darkjumper shipping routes a few years back...." His voice trailed off. "Is something wrong?"

"We're not sure. The Hut says there's a ship in orbit, but we've had no signal. It may be the empath's going to be dropped. And Raille isn't back from observing the kin yet."

He got to his feet. "What are you going to do?"

"We're going out to the drop site. Emrys and I, at least, and whoever else—"

"Yes. I'm coming. Hurry."

3

Raille had been walking for a long time, trying to figure out what was wrong with her.

She could not understand why she should be different. None of the others had reported any difficulty approaching the kin since that first paralyzing encounter they had all shared. Why had she been affected again?

She found a place to think where there were flowers on a skein of low vines all along a sloping stream bed, a rippling ribbon of color and reflection stretching for several meters. She sat on a tree stump and cradled her chin in her palm, staring obstinately at the scene.

I refuse to go mad and miss all of this. It's too beautiful.

She rose in a few minutes, nothing resolved, and left the spot with reluctance. She began to feel more herself again as she wandered, with papery leaves tangling in her hair until the breeze took them back. She had found a song at the back of her mind that had nothing whatsoever to do with fear or self-pity or bewilderment, and she sang it softly under her breath as she came out once more into meadowland. In Inter the song was merely a lengthy mnemonic used to catalogue the kinds of leaves that distinguished certain herbs:

> *needletip, sharpsides, heartshape*
> *and*
> *arrowhead, circular, thinflat*
> *and*

> *shieldshape, triangle, lancehead*
> *with*
> *turned lance, eggshape, beewing*

In Weldonese, however, it rhymed cleverly and each line ended with a homily or warning concerning the proper use of one of the plants:

> *Vyi dendau sallifra venoyah mi'kah—sle tammera*
> *daivyu—ne'en*
> *Chilona dolauvis ki, kiniyi passe'rah—*

Raille stopped suddenly in the middle of the verse. She was standing frozen in midstep in a field of shade-dappled silver that seemed no different from all the other fields. What had halted her? She looked wildly up and down the meadow, but there was nothing unusual in sight. She was alone. She waited, ready to—

(The opalescent seas rushed upward and outward, finally disappearing under the edge of a swelling landmass. The earth gave birth to shadows and light, a suggestion of texture, a patina of color.)

She didn't know what she was ready to do, only that she was poised for some sort of action, waiting for confirmation. Abruptly she remembered seeing a hand, a face in shadow, an opening mouth. *It was here, it was here it was here—*

(The continent blurred for a moment as he passed through a thin layer of clouds, then resolved itself suddenly into ranges of mountains and nets of rivers, forests, and wide meadows.)

She blinked and saw the empty field of silver grass with here and there a smooth stone, a flowered stalk, clumps of dark brush. *Arrowhead, needletip, triangle—What was here? What happened? I refuse to—*

(Mountains became one mountain escaping to the north, while rivers broke into streams which grew quickly into rivers again. The forest rose up, spun to one side, and vanished entirely. Round as a raindrop, a single bright meadow filled the world beneath him.)

But she felt as if a thread were being pulled slowly from her mind, a gleaming something which she was powerless to halt and could only mark by its passing from her memory. She wanted to run. *Lancehead, shieldshape, beewing—go on, go on, it's gone.*

(The meadow separated into a billion blades of waving grass, then leaped up all at once with incredible speed. His eyes closed.)

For a long moment she had a feeling of horrible vertigo— her feet moving swiftly through the grass and the ground firm beneath each step, but falling, falling just the same. She was running through a meadow which was like all the other meadows; then she was out of it and into the next. *Go on, there's nothing here.* Into another circle of shimmering silver. *Or here.* Running. *Or—*

(Downward in darkness now, the faint sound of wind outside the packet. He was just beginning—)

Here?

(—to breathe again—)

She looked up and dodged to one side, tripped, and half crawled, half dragged herself out of the path of the thing that was falling toward her like a great cloudy bubble of silence.

(—when something nudged the sole of his foot and his stomach tipped like a gyroscope. He opened his eyes to a swirling landscape of gray and green. His hand found the stud at the back of his neck, and as the packet crumpled around his ankles, he saw her crouched on the ground a few meters away, looking at him. He took a breath and filled his lungs with the new world. Then he sank to his knees in the fragrant grass and became thoroughly sick.)

4

Raille Kristema Weldon of Auvel's Orchard, only child of Furian Farflight and of Annay his widow, distant kin through the maternal line of the Founder himself, and daughter for nineteen years of that ancient world whose poets styled it the Blue Jewel—Raille barely hesitated before she went over to the man and reached to hold his shoulders as he retched. When it was over she wiped his brow with the hem of her skirt and knelt with him while he got his breath back.

"Feeling better now?"

His face was turned away from her, and he did not speak. She could feel his body still trembling beneath the long gray cloak.

"Would you want to try to stand?"

She put her arm under his, and they swayed upright. His knees buckled, but she held him until he had regained his balance. The hand that clutched her wrist was clammy with sweat.

"There. Is that all right?"

Without a word he pulled slowly free of her hands. His feet pushed haltingly through the tall grass.

"Can I—help?" The words left her lips sluggishly. She felt tired and heavy, and there was an odd pressure growing all around her head, uneven, like wings beating in the air, like a thick cloth flapping. She tried to raise her hand to her forehead, but it grew heavier with each passing second until she had to let it drop back to her side. She was rooted to the ground. Her entire body felt numb or muffled, as if it had been swathed in thick bandages.

The man continued his slow progress across the meadow. He had reached the place where ribbons of moss and tufts of dark wellhorn separated this meadow from the next. There the man stood motionless for what seemed to Raille to be a very long time, his quiet head turned up to the sky, where sunset was beginning to set out its precious metals above a dim horizon.

His face stood out white as eggshell against the far mountains' blue and gray, but the hair that fell beneath his high collar was glossy and dark, a black bird's wing to match his raven eyes.

Minutes passed. The wind was starting to rise from the south, and his cloak moved restlessly, blurring his silhouette. Raille watched him, feeling dulled and drowsy. *He looks like some character in a folktale*, she thought sleepily. *Like poor Kiri-hero under the spell of silence.*

The man at last lowered his eyes from the clouds. Somewhere in the cluster of fields an animal began to chatter noisily, and the pressure, the wings, the thick wrappings, all dropped from Raille's head as abruptly as they had appeared.

He was moving, walking again, pacing out the border of the field in carefully measured steps. Raille turned to face him as he passed near her.

"Who are you? Are you from University? Are you the one they were talking about—what was the word? Some kind of path?" She felt a wave of *déjà vu* pass over her, vanish.

He said nothing, eyes on the ground.

"You know, I didn't like the packet much either. My poor stomach arrived a few hours after the rest of me had landed."

He paused in midstep, and she was sure he was going to reply. Then he turned toward the east and cocked his head to one side as if listening for something. After a few moments he returned to his mechanical pacing.

Raille stood at the center of his circle, slowly turning now like the hub of a wheel, feeling alternately foolish and very frightened. "Please—who are you?"

Empty silence.

"Do you speak Inter?"

He walked on, and she could see that his steps were growing steadily larger and more sure. She shut her eyes and stood still, refusing to turn with him, feeling the pull on her mind like strands of silk. She concentrated on stillness. On darkness. On silence.

Her skin prickled and she opened her eyes. He was standing at her side.

He was staring at her.

At this proximity his eyes reminded her of an animal's, dark and bright at the same time. A bit of the pressure was growing in her head again, and her thoughts started to wander. Memories slid in and out of concealment like fish beneath flat rocks in a pond.

Oh, faith, not again . . .

She began to be angry.

"My name is Raille Weldon." Each word was bitten from the silence. "Weldon is my world." She took a step toward him. "I am here on Belthannis on University business with a Group Resolvent. Are you expected here? Are you—are you authorized?" She searched for some sign of comprehension in the frozen bone-white features. "Do you understand this language?"

She heard a sound at her back. She whirled around to see

movement at the edge of the long stretch of woodland to the northeast. Emrys appeared and called again, waving to her. The other members of the Group came into view behind him. They spilled out of the forest and flowed into the meadow almost at a run, then slowed as they neared the two, faces looking anxiously from Raille to the still figure behind her.

She took a step backward. *What have I done now?*

"Are you all right?" Emrys asked. They had come to a halt at the edge of the meadow.

Choss pushed forward, trampling the wellhorn. Raille winced. He was out of breath. "Raille—" he managed between gasps. "Why don't you—come over here—"

Puzzled, she took another step back.

"It's only a boy," she heard someone say.

"Why are you here?" Emrys was looking sternly past her shoulder. "What is it you want from us?"

"He won't answer," Raille said quickly. She moved closer to the pale man in gray. "I don't think he can talk."

She heard a rustling behind her. The heavy cloak brushed her arm as the man moved past her to stand before Emrys. Then he spoke in a slow dry voice. "I am here to observe the creature that may be a human being."

5

"You gave it a *room?*"

Coming down from the sundeck, March had encountered Emrys in the upper corridor; they walked briskly toward the central stairwell.

Emrys nodded. "I told him to take one of the empty ones near the Garden. Cil isn't using hers."

"*Aggh!* You really are crazy, old man." March spat on the carpet. "Didn't even lock it in, did you?"

"No, I didn't. But why 'crazy,' March? He was physically exhausted, and ill from the trip down in the packet. What would you have done?"

"Stuffed him in another one and shot him back up to ship. Let them find him a bed."

"You heard the Hut say the ship left orbit almost immediately. It's probably cleared the system and jumped by now. Besides—" He looked sideways at the sandy scowl. "What if he hadn't wanted to leave?"

March flexed his fingers with a rough laugh. "Had a Dance we used to do on the Maren called *Persuasion*. Very long and very slow. Breaks every other bone."

Emrys ignored the predatory grin. "Better be very sure of yourself before going up against one of his kind, sick or well, or it might be you who gets persuaded. At any rate, I see no need to provoke a confrontation at this point."

"No need!" March mimicked scornfully. "You couldn't see a knife if it was stuck in your own belly."

"Perhaps not." Emrys eyed him calmly. "But I am Group Leader."

The soldier snorted in disgust.

"In a day or so, when he's fed and rested, I'll have a talk with him," Emrys said. "Then we can show him the kin and ask him to leave. With luck there'll be no trouble."

"Isis' rump, if he scares you that much—"

"Of course he does. I know what he is. It terrifies me. If you had a single properly functioning cell in your brain you'd be frightened, too."

They had reached the open stairwell. March halted and raised his arm slowly. His expression was poisonous. "Maybe I'll—"

"Yes?" Emrys held his stare, hand resting lightly on the railing. "Strike me? 'Persuade' me? I don't think so. Not for speaking the truth."

They faced each other in silence. Then Emrys turned and began to descend the stairs. March followed slowly.

6

380.Fer.21, Community time. Day nineteen, Belthannis time.
The Hour of Decision.

The group was gathered in the Hearth Room. Jack, Marysu, Cil, and Jefany sat at the table. Choss was standing by the wall inspecting the current selection of portraits, while actually keeping his gaze very close to Raille, who was busy writing. Watching Raille's deft use of inkpen, inkjar, and leaves of wood-paper gathered in a binding, Jefany suddenly felt very contrived and Techish with her spongepad and stylus. But she continued to record her observations:

Emrys has just entered the room.

Now he is gone again, after getting something to drink from the table, nodding to all of us, exchanging pleasantries.

Here is March. He has joined us at the table and begun to unwrap a sheaf of transparencies: squares and rectangles limned with minute notations and geometrics in many different colors. What are these? They appear to be extremely complex, yet I feel I should recognize them.

Marysu has gotten up to order something to eat from the other side of the table. Jack takes advantage of the moment to hold up a line drawing of Cil and me. Very good, very accurate. We applaud silently and look away as Marysu returns; Jack blanks his pad and starts to work on something else.

Emrys is speaking. He has been talking for about five minutes now, mainly about the Community, about its Laws and the penalties attendant upon defying them.

Choss flinched and moved perceptibly closer to Raille when the Senseless Sleep was mentioned. An interesting thought: one wonders about the nature of Raille's status before the Laws. As a citizen of a Private World and a *dayfly* into the bargain she is unique among our company. Would they dare send her down Deepside and steal years from her as punishment? Pray Isis it never has to be tested.

Emrys is talking about this world now. He talks about the kin, about their right to remain what they are.

He is stubbornly honest and frank in his speech, avoiding hyperbole and excessive preaching. Yet he speaks always with great power and compassion, and I envy him his gift of calm (or its most convincing counterfeit) in times of uncertainty. Though I have heard these thoughts before from both our lips in long discussions on lost Chwoi Dai, still his belief in the possibility of what he proposes makes each word new for me and I begin to believe again also.

Abruptly he is finished.

He calls for questions, but we are silent. For the first time tonight I sense doubt in him: he cannot read us.

Now he will want our votes. There is no way to put it off any longer. He looks at us, measuring. Who will be asked first?

I was not expecting that!

What did I say? And where did the words come from, for I've lost them again.

But I know it was *yes*, in as many different ways as I could express it. With caution urged, I remember, and with a recognition of the many difficulties and dangers involved—but *yes*, *yes*, *yes*.

Marysu is next, and there are tears on her lower lashes, or else she has dusted them with tiny sapphires. He names her name and she responds:

"I suppose it might prove an interesting diversion. *Recherché, kuisado da pei*. Possibly even amusing." And then (and they were sapphires, after all), in her laziest, most razored tones: "Why not?"

Emrys studies her face. "Very well," he says after half a minute. "We need you, Marysu."

And then to Cil, whose soft reply—"Of course I'll help. Help life whenever possible"—has the effect of making it seem so obvious that you wonder why you had to ask at all.

Sweet, gentle March appears to be totally engrossed in his patterned transparencies (and I have just realized what they are: Dance patterns, of course, in the old notation!). He has not taken his eyes from them once since he first spread them out for examination.

"March?"

No response.

Emrys waits behind him for a long moment, his face a mask. Then he taps the stiff shoulder. "March!"

I find that I am holding my breath, but when the soldier pulls his golden face up there is only vague annoyance in his true eye. He frowns at Emrys. "I went out, I looked at it. Probably not faking, really empty-headed." Immediately his head snaps down again to the intricate diagrams.

Emrys is quietly adamant. Again he prods the shoulder. "And so?" he says to the rising brown-green glare. "Does that mean you're with us?"

"Yes," the other man snarls. "I said yes, didn't I?"

"Perhaps you did," the victor says softly. "Thank you, March." And next is: "Jack?"

Who looks up startled at the sound of his name. Looks to Marysu (who looks pointedly away), then back to Emrys: "Huh?"

"Will you join us, Jack, will you help?"

Blinks, shrugs, scratches his collarbone, nods. "Sure, I guess, I mean if you really want me to—"

Which brings us to Choss and to something I really would not have predicted. Our historian sits slumped in his chair, looking most deeply troubled. The corners of his mouth are pulling down beardward. He peers at Emrys over tented fingers and sighs. Then he opens his mouth and closes it as if unable to speak. I believe he is near tears. Finally he clears his throat, a ragged sound, and speaks, his face turned away from us toward the wall.

"To be associated with such a plan as this, even to the limited extent of not reporting it to the authorities, would be enough to destroy my professional reputation. By saying nothing concerning your illegalities I would be seen as tacitly endorsing the Builder cause—to say nothing of espousing Law-breaking!—and thus denying the most basic tenet of my Major: objectivity.

"From then on my work would be considered tainted, my former contributions discarded. My standing at University would be forfeit, of course. My certificates canceled, my striving nulled." He sighs. "Not that that matters so much, you know, but—"

He halts, rubbing his chin. We cannot see his face directly, but I glimpse a reflection of his torment in Raille's expression. The rest of us wait, silent as a ring of stones.

"It's my whole *life*, it's all I've ever wanted. And objectivity is the heart of it, the very essence of the discipline. Oh, I know historians must seem bland and equivocal to you at times—"

"The gift of understatement," Marysu murmurs, damn her, but with little malice in her voice. Even she is subdued by Choss' evident pain.

He continues, reddening as he turns to face us.

"But this is intentional. It's what we choose, a conscious effort to remain in the background, to stand well away from the great events and see them recorded without bias. I could no longer do that, here, as a component of this Group, though they allow us a dispensation for the Evaluation and the secret vote. There is no dispensation for conspiracy. . . ."

Emrys has been standing several paces away, leaning forward against the back of a chair. He seems calm until you notice the whitened knuckles and the stiffened shoulders. But a look of resignation is settling over him slowly like a wave of weariness. I know his thoughts: *If all are not agreed, it cannot be done.* But in his face there is no anger, only compassion and a gentle sadness. He opens his mouth to speak, thinking it is time, but Choss raises his hand for silence.

"However—" The bearded historian clears his throat. "However, one realizes in the end how rare in life is the opportunity to accomplish something of this magnitude: to really and finally act upon one's deepest beliefs. So rare as to be worth nearly any price. So yes, Emrys, I will assist you. I will be most honored to assist you in any way."

And this, I think, is Choss at his unexpected best: frightened, determined, and utterly sincere.

We are all moved to some degree, even March, who will not

raise his face from the shadows, but sits staring at an empty section of the tabletop. Cil is talking jubilantly with Jack. Emrys looks happy and relieved, if a bit dazed, and Marysu is smiling widely. *"Ha, bravo!"* she cries and blows Choss a kiss of approval, which he acknowledges with a shy nod.

It occurs to me that communication of any sort may be a little freer in our Group, now that Choss has suffered for us all, torn down some walls in our presence and survived. Things have been said which apply to each of our lives in one way or another. Now we will not have to dwell upon them; we can go back to our jibes and sophisticated cynicism, knowing that there is an understanding of purpose somewhere underneath it all.

And now it is Raille's turn.

Hers will be the final voice, the seal of confirmation to our pact, and Emrys turns to her with a gentle smile.

There is a small noise in the anteroom. Smiles freeze and heads turn.

He is there in the shadows.

Black and gray and white: he is there, standing just outside the archway.

How long has he been there?

He steps forward slowly and, looking at the others, I see that doubt has come into the room with him. I know what they are wondering, because I have the same thoughts: *How much of it has been real? How much has been false? How much has been his?*

Raille's eyes are on the empath as he walks across the room.

"Yes," she says softly, though Emrys has not yet asked the question. "Oh, yes."

CHAPTER 9

I shall not write in here again. Tomorrow we go,
the last people in the last town, and then it is no
longer our world. Back to the blue jewel, to the safe
pretty sapphire where the lakes and sensible seasons
are, and hives at the back door again.
But I myself will miss this wind and the bells
inside it, the proud desolate voice of this world we
had almost begun to know, which we called Pelerul,
the New Life.
How has it happened so quickly, the panic and
horror? Everyone has an answer until you listen
closely, and then no one does.
It was a gamble. Those who stayed at home will
never let us forget that we knew about the risks. But
it seemed to be working. Why now, after so long
without a hint of trouble? We were half a million
strong and clever people to their thousand seldom-
seen dreamers. Sometimes we traded with them, but
not much. And that was all, for three years. Now the
largest of their five little settlements has been de-
stroyed and yesterday morning Weiweldon itself was
in flames on Great Continent—our first true city here
was burning. Where are the reasons?

FROM A HANDWRITTEN JOURNAL FOUND
GY 51 ON PORTECTORATE WORLD 79,
FOLLOWING DISSOLUTION OF THE
WELDON/MARIBON EXPERIMENTAL COLONY

1

Had he been a more courageous man, Choss would have told Raille that he thought her laughter matched the sky for silver. The sound entranced him, pealing out over the meadowland in flights like widening ripples in a sweet, clear stream.

The historian was trying his best to entertain her with a bit of ancient doggerel he had discovered in the datapool during free-phase on University, and he found himself feeling absurdly pleased with his ability to amuse.

"Recite it again, will you?" Raille coaxed. "In the old Anglic. At least the part about the mandrake root."

Choss was acutely aware of the pleasure he derived simply from having Raille near him. And when, alone in his room at night, he thought about her, Raille's smooth skin, her wood-brown hair, the scent of her, were wedded in his thought to her humor, her gentleness, her curiosity. The laughing voice was a delight to ears grown weary of the flat University accent; he knew that she had learned Inter the hard way, without the linguaspeek machine, and her Weldonese inflection added a soft patina to the crisp vowels of that carefully constructed tongue.

"Oh, wait just a moment." He motioned past her. "I think Emrys is going to say something."

They were in the midst of what Marysu had termed a *pickanick*, which amounted to eating a communal meal while sprawled outside on the ground, rather than upright around the table in the Hearth Room. The Hut had packaged their food in cumbersome wicker contrivances which it assured them were necessary for authenticity. March had immediately turned his basket upside down on the stone floor of the foyer and left it there, stuffing the pockets of his coveralls with handfuls of artfully crafted delicacies.

"Well now," Emrys said from his position of eminence atop a fallen trunk. "You've had some time to look at the problem. What are your insights? What's to be done first?"

"Tie a rope around the neck of that thing in the upstairs room and take it out to the Water and drown it," March suggested around a mouthful of pink pastry.

"Thank you, March, I'll come to the matter of our guest a little later. I was referring to the modification of the kin."

The soldier paused to lick crumbs from his fingers before replying. "Get me a master patterning frame by tomorrow morning and he'll be twitching come nightfall. Already mapped out most of the basics on a template. For walk, for sit, for lift the arms. If he takes to the patterning I build it from there."

"Excellent. You'll have your frame this afternoon if you want it. What about the trigger? Have you thought about that yet? It has to be something subtle enough to slip by the Sauf Coben. We can't be whispering snapwords in its ear every few seconds."

March shrugged. "Gestures, one of the tactile codes, a linked association key—hard to plan on any one trigger matrix at this point in case of surprises, but probably it won't be a problem. Maybe a few long Dances, several hours each, with variations built in at the tricky points so there's still some leeway for choices and control."

Carefully settled on a level stone not far from the Dancer, Choss tugged thoughtfully at his beard. He was fascinated by the changes in March's speech patterns: while discussing his specialty, March spoke in much more complete phrase groups and used a vocabulary Choss would have thought beyond him. He wondered if the constant crudeness was part of an easily shed mask designed to maintain the solitary existence the other man so obviously sought. The historian did not expect to have the puzzle answered; he could not imagine someone like March ever lowering his armor long enough to confide in another human being.

As Choss watched March, Jefany found herself studying Choss. She sat on the grass nearby with her long legs extended, back to back with Cil, who was playing Golden Ring with Jack on a patch of rugmoss. Jefany switched on the writing square that lay in her lap and massaged the frame until a surface appeared that was blank except for a single line at the top of the pad: NOTES FOR A WORK OF FICTION. She began to write.

"Sevens," Cil said and rolled the dice again. The blue one came up with a three that flickered to a nine and then stabilized at seven, while the white icosahedron showed the Coin Bearer, his tiny lazy smile reversed to a frown from her vantage point.

"Ha! Golden Ring," she said and doffed her cards to show Jack a duplicate of the luminous image, sandwiched between a glowering Culpate and a serene Stick Lady.

Jack gathered up the cards and began to shuffle them expertly in one hand while Cil played with the dice.

"I think the light's going out on one face," she said, inspecting the blank ivory surface. "D'you want me to take it apart and fix it?"

"If you can," Jack said. "That would be good." He began to deal the cards.

"You designed these, didn't you?" Cil said. "This Coin Lady's like that sketch you showed me the other morning."

Jack nodded, pleased. "A few years ago. I had them done up back in the Bosmas, which is where I mostly used to live on Earth."

"They're really the best I've ever seen."

"Thanks." They shared a smile.

"—Perhaps Cil could answer that." Marysu's voice climbed higher, slicing into the cloudless afternoon. "Or perhaps Cil hasn't been listening."

"Of course I have, Marysu." Cil brushed a strand of hair from her face and tilted her head toward Emrys. "I think Lacken proved conclusively on Dunbar's World that much of what we've been considering true Artifacts could be explained by purely natural phenomena. The low-tide altar stones, for example, the maze-ring formations out by Sully's Cove—"

"You're right, yes, it was shown on Dunbar's World—every centimeter of the Endless Beach has been catalogued and accounted for by now—as well as on Chalice and Tourmaline," Emrys responded vigorously. "And the Coben will be familiar with Lacken's contentions."

"You call them contentions—"

"Because that is what the Sauf Coben will call them. You

must realize what kind of individuals we'll be dealing with when we finally take our emissary before the Weighers. Here are one-time experts who've chosen to put shields on their eyes and stoppers in their ears in the name of expediency. Oh, Pinconning is a Scholar, granted, and Hakateny-Thu thinks he is; but the rest are professional facilitators, politically motivated administrators with a bellyful of self-righteousness and a pet scientific adviser at each ear. Even cold, hard truths will flow and run in a climate like that, and we've got to remember that it's not so much technical perfection that we're after as a convincing performance, a big, complicated wanderlight to flash in their eyes."

Cil responded with animation, her dark eyes darting back and forth between the debate and the cards without missing a beat. Marysu crinkled her lips and stared off into the empty sky.

"No learning," Cil said. "No adaptation."

"None at all. I believe you could set a torch to its feet and it would stand there until the legs had burned out from under it."

"And you want us to make him pass for human," Choss said dully from behind Jefany. "Self-preservation is part of the Code also."

"I know!" Emrys clenched fists full of air. "That's what makes it so maddening. Here he is, outwardly a perfectly unexceptional human specimen. And inside: nothing. Why does he look like us? Why? What's the point?"

"The point is," Cil said finally, "that we have to counterfeit adaptation, bypass learning for control." Her dark eyes scanned the far horizon. "And we have one month less than a year in which to do it."

2

Two weeks had passed since Emrys' first attempt at questioning the empath. During that time, he had made repeated efforts to communicate, meeting with little more success. The visitor from Maribon passed his time almost exclusively in the north high room, which Cil had gladly relinquished, transferring the few belongings she had stored there to Jefany's quarters.

The Hut itself seemed fascinated by the newcomer, reporting that he spent most of his days in what appeared to be a trancelike state, long periods of motionless silence punctuated by shorter episodes during which he would slowly pace the room, muttering or chanting under his breath words the Hut could not identify.

"This is a most peculiar individual, if social behavior is any criterion," the Hut confided to Emrys one day. "If I were allowed to deal frankly with the matter, I would have to say that neither his actions nor his responses to stimuli strike me as being particularly human. This is a hasty opinion, of course, and based only on my limited experience—I do not pretend to be a sound judge of what is human and what is not."

Emrys had responded with a wry shake of his head. "Nor does any of us, Hut."

Late each night the empath emerged from his seclusion for a few minutes, going straight down to the Hearth Room and obtaining from the table a quantity of protein-rich broth which he took back to his quarters and consumed. The Hut had informed him that he could be served quite comfortably in his room, if he so desired, but had found itself once more ignored.

With the empath a rarely glimpsed presence in their midst, the members of the Group turned their thoughts once again to the implementation of their great deception, and work began in earnest.

March professed himself satisfied at last that the kin was a body with a healthy if untenanted brain—as such, it could probably be controlled by the application of the Dance. He began the construction of a patterning frame, doggedly following the kin from meadow to meadow with his calibration board and his measuring devices, while Raille—who assumed that her own duty to keep the kin alive, whatever that might entail, had also begun—gathered botanical samples and wrote in her journal in those same meadows, keeping the soldier and his subject at a safe but observable distance.

Marysu spent much of her time alone. Seemingly as reclu-

sive as the empath, she kept to her room, where she immersed
herself in holodot and chip recordings of Belthannis. Occasionally she went outside the Hut, usually at twilight, walking
by herself in the cool wilderness. She avoided the company of
others, unusually subdued in her speech and manner. She spoke
very little at all—even to Jack, who was to be found increasingly wherever Cil happened to be working. Marysu seemed
not to notice.

She was ridding her mind of Inter; she was cleansing all of
her languages from her thoughts for a time, preparing for the
moment when the world-speech of Belthannis would germinate
within her and she would begin to create the language of the
kin. In her room, eyes on shimmering vistas of woodland and
meadow, she partook of the drug called *gielh*, and her eyelids
beneath the paint and silvershadow took on a bruised look.

Cil made tests on water, soil, air, the microbiotic ambient,
spending long sleepless hours afloat on prodrugs as she scanned
the data taken by the robot probes set in orbit by the original
Survey team more than two years before. At the end of the
second week she approached Emrys with a request for trans-
portation.

"Something I can cover ground with. Not an aircar. Another
week or two, maybe less, and I'll have to get away from all
of you for a while," she said with her gentle smile. "I'm ab-
sorbing a lot of facts. I'll need the solitude to sort them out,
do you see? I want to take a look at some of the other kin, as
well. I thought I'd head up north to a few of the nearer territories."

Emrys assented, and the next day the Hut disgorged an
elegant construction of plax and metalmock through an iris in
its southern wall. Here was a Tech creation embellished by
artists: a mechanical mantis shape in pale green and silver, with
many-jointed legs and a pair of hidden wings that fluttered out
for stability in flashes of iridescence over uncertain terrain. A
bright-red parasol perched incongruously above the canopy like
an inverted poppy, shading the cushioned blue seats.

"*Droshky*," Marysu said, frowning at the gleaming shape
on one of her infrequent sojourns outside her room. "Call it
droshky. Means carriage."

3

The communicant's fingers touched the door and it slipped open.

The room was behind the door again as it had been three days before, as it had been twice the previous week. That in no way promised that the room would be there the next day, or that night, or even in another hour. Treat each event as an isolate. Regard it with senses both clear and without predisposition, *said the later chapters of the Eng Barata.* Nothing is the same. Nothing is certain save the presence of change.

There was a desk. The touch-man was seated behind it. Becoming aware that the door had opened, the touch-man lifted his eyes, emotions stirring up in his mind like leaves before a wind.

"You've come." Emrys smiled his welcome automatically. "Good. Take a seat, if you wish. There's wine here in the second drawer, if you're dry."

As always there was no response, the visitor wavering at the door like a soap bubble, then entering the room at last as if borne on a random breeze. He seated himself silently, colorless face like a cold narrow moon above the gray garments, eyes on the wall somewhere behind Emrys' head.

"I have the pictures to show you," Emrys said, turning away with a grimace and busying himself at his desk. He was determined to match the other's aloofness for once, instead of begging for attention as he had found himself doing during previous encounters. "I assume that's why you're here, yes? Mm, if not you can always say so, right? I'll just be another moment sorting here, then we can begin."

He glanced at the dark unfocused eyes, looked away, then back again.

"I swear I feel more alone after you come into the room than I do when I'm here by myself," he remarked at last with a small shake of his head. "Granted you've no use for conversation, but you could at least nod or twitch once in a while, so I wouldn't chatter away like a tree-hopper." He extracted a tab of holodots, ran his finger along the coded margin. "Yes, well—I'll continue on in my merry fashion and you chime in whenever the mood strikes you. Ah, here's one of them." He laid the strip carefully outside the circle of confusion at the center of his desk.

"The others, they think I'm very foolish, you know—the way I persist in meeting with you like this. Wait, I tell them, he's here for a reason. It's something important, I can feel it, and it's bound to be something useful." He shook his head ruefully. "But I don't know. I must admit I've had my own doubts. What can I tell them about you? What have I learned? I should be out there assisting them in their work, not closeted with you in some guessing game. What I don't understand is why you don't *do* something—anything except sit and stare. We don't know what to make of you, my friend."

The outer eyes roamed the wall, while that-which-perceives looked deep into the touch-man's mind. Beneath the veneer of reflex emotions lay a roil of conflicting motes. There was a question surfacing, slowly, the same query which formed each time they were together, rising ponderously, weighed down by reluctance, encumbered by motes of self-deception. There was a necessity there, a hunger. The touch-man had a fear that towered above all others when he faced the communicant, but it was a formless thing, without size or boundary. What the touch-man wanted was verification: proof, a mold in which to cast his fears, a shape, an outline. But while part of him cried out to be shown, another denied both the desire and the possibility, and the question was never allowed to reach maturity.

The communicant considered. Stet: he prodded the thought into being with a beat of his mind.

"Could you control my mind?" Emrys asked, amazed at himself. The words seemed to come from nowhere, least of all his own lips. He blinked. "Could you? Is there really such a power? Without drugs or tricks, hypnotism or the suive-machine? I—I want to know."

The empath did not take his eyes from the wall. White lips moved in a hoarse slur of syllables which Emrys did not understand.

"What? What did you say?" His palms felt moist; he found that he was trembling very gently.

Silence. Then pale hands parted the gray garments, fingers slipped within, extracted a small, flat container. One palm cradled the disk, the other deftly removed the lid. Inside there was something black and shiny.

"What is it—is it paint?"

Silence. Index and middle fingers of the right hand grazed the slick substance, rose slowly through the air to the high white forehead. Five swift strokes and the hand came away.

Emrys looked at the smear of black and said "Ha!" very distinctly. It was such a funny little squiggle. He said "Ha!" again, looked extremely surprised for an instant, and began to giggle. A crooked smile twitched to his lips. "Wh—what—"

His voice faltered as harsh, high-pitched laughter bubbled up like bile in his throat. The giddy amusement would not leave him. It festered and grew until he clutched at himself, howling within the laughter, eyes on the empath, on the walls, on his own shaking body. It went on: the laughter on his lips and the laughter in his head. It went on, surging into a mad hilarity before which no solemn thought could stand.

The amusement was as pure and as genuine as anything he had yet felt in his nineteen score and twelve.

At last the convulsions began to wind down into spasms, a silent heaving that left him struggling for breath. His head hurt and his jaws ached.

The hand rose again like a pale exotic bird toward the ludicrously emblazoned brow. In one swift motion the design was gone, the only mark of its existence a small, gray shadow on the blanched skin.

The feeling closed in upon itself and vanished.

Emrys took shuddering breaths and felt gingerly over sides and abdomen, chest and throat. Minutes passed.

Finally, massaging his aching neck, he asked hoarsely: "Why? For what reason?"

"You know," the empath replied softly in his own rough voice. "Now you are sure." The dark eyes finally deserted the wall as he leaned across the desk and began to leaf slowly through a file of dots. "It is in the *Eng Barata* that well-planted memory halves the need for later cultivation."

"I requested no gardening services," Emrys said with a scowl.

"*Stet.*" The empath withdrew a second tab, laid it next to

the one Emrys had chosen. "A man stood in a road, paralyzed by the fear that a snake lay beneath the stone at his feet. He stood for a long time in an agony of doubt, until a tremor shook the earth and the stone was rolled upon its side. A serpent was indeed coiled in the dust before him, but it was a small one, and harmless, and he stepped around it and went on his way. Strophe twelve, lux ten."

"Hmf. You're full of musty parables, once you decide to use your mouth." Emrys reached shakily into the second drawer, withdrew the crystal decanter, and poured himself a deep bowl of blue. "You know, March told me torture would make you more talkative. He neglected to specify which of us would be on the receiving end." He raised the bowl to his lips. Midway to his mouth, his hands began to tremble fiercely and he set the bowl carefully back on the desk.

"That snake's not as small as you seem to think," he said after a moment. "I hope I'm capable of covering the distance necessary to avoid it. But you're right—it is better to know. Now, can you give me your word that you will not employ this technique on me, on any of us, again?"

"No."

Emrys sighed. "Let's try this again. Under what circumstances would you find the need to use this power on one of us?"

"I do not know."

"Conjecture, then," Emrys said sourly.

"I am incapable of conjecture. Each instant is new. Nothing is the same."

Emrys shook his head slowly back and forth.

"You make it very difficult for me to remain your defender, my friend."

The empath drew forth the tab he had chosen earlier, fed it into the embossed slot on Emrys' desk.

"This one."

A succession of images appeared in the center of the room, forming and melting as Emrys fingered the control plate:

Trees, a sky full of burnished silver, the wide shallow river which Emrys had named the Water . . . the three-dimensional flicker congealed around the image of a naked man.

"The kin," Emrys said aloud, knowing the identification had already been plucked from his mind.

He depressed his fingers slightly, and the creature began to move, walking slowly toward them through a forest glade where rain had fallen recently, spangling the leaves and clinging lightly to skin and hair. To Emrys it was a scene of primordial grace and mystery, the Adam-man out of legend roaming his garden prison. He had no idea what chords of response, if any, were touched behind the empath's black-and-white shell. The other was watching the projection silently, on his face the same immobile blankness which Emrys had translated variously over the past weeks as scorn, indifference, even imbecility. He found himself finally beginning to accept the outrageous notion that the young man sitting alongside his desk was incapable of human feeling—that it was not some fantastic children's tale, but that the other's mind had in fact been so constructed or conditioned as to omit the possibility of a spontaneously generated emotion.

The empath's eyes were half closed. He seemed to be daydreaming rather than examining the kin. Emrys wondered briefly if his guest was communing with that "Other" he had mentioned during one of their previous meetings, the satellite personality to which he claimed to have deeded a portion of his brain.

The empath watched as the kin wandered through the wood with steps of measured grace. But Emrys watched only the creature that sat at his side.

4

The day was wild, wind whipping through the treetops and showering the pocket meadows with tiny almond-shaped leaves. The empath climbed slowly to the crest of a gently sloping incline. He stood there awhile with hands clasped loosely at his back, measuring the surrounding countryside with first the low and then the high senses at his command.

Eyes, ears, mouth, nose, and skin had brought him one picture of the world, inadequate and deceptive as inevitably it must be. He removed himself from the influence of the lesser senses. That-which-perceives expanded radially, moving like a wavefront through woodland and meadow, over river and hillside, changing his picture of the world with each small flicker of life it encountered.

Immediately behind him was the turbulence of his escort's mind, while from the northeast came a subdued murmur of motes analogous to the rush of a distant waterfall, which identified the occupants of the Hut.

Sounds were coming to him through the air close behind. He lowered his perception and they revealed themselves as verbal speech, began to parcel themselves into words. Never in his life had he borne the touch of so many words against his ear as he was experiencing daily in that new place. Each mote that separated itself from the agitated haze of their minds seemed to produce its own string of syllables; it was as if the touch-men could conceive of nothing without immediately draping sounds around the thought.

"—Hut says we've almost reached it, so be prepared for a jolt. The first time you approach one of them, there's a sort of barrier effect, as I told you before, but once you're past it—"

The empath withdrew from the vibrating mind, and allowed the words to blur back into meaningless noise. He marshaled his high senses to the region directly in front of him and moved forward.

(————————)

There had been a momentary lapse in the continuity of his perception, something which he had never experienced before. His mind dipped automatically into the reservoir of the Other: *No information.*

It was as if he had reentered for a fraction of a second the complete withdrawal of the anchorite stage, but with no bondsman there to fix upon; or as if the world itself had flickered out of existence, like a great eye blinking.

Then he saw it: the creature from the image. Scented it, heard its small movements through the grass, as all of the low senses flooded back unchanged. He reached out with his mind in the superficial probe of the shellscan. Nothing. Blank as an imago in consultation with a noumenon, the human likeness remained before his eyes while the opaque flowing continued within his mind.

He counted slowly under his breath, relinquishing a portion of the control of his brain to enable the Other to prepare his body for the exertion of the deep-delve. He recited the proper phrases from the *Eng*, then felt a flowing and a gathering begin in his mind. Reaching deep within, he formed the requisite motes, waited as the Other echoed them. He felt his body lean slightly forward.

His eyes opened a hundred years later.

From somewhere there was the sound of chirping. Sunset bruised the west, a mass of silver clouds hung over the mountains to the north. The rest of the sky above his face was a dark, irregular gray, like a sheet of metal blotched with acid.

He was conscious of a memory, as of something from the distant past: the sensation of falling, a long, timeless descent through a silver sky, while all around him the bright clouds boiled upward.

Then the face of the touch-man swung into view. Soon there were other faces, all bobbing like lanterns above him, and he understood that he was on his back. He pushed up unsteadily on his elbows.

He lay among reeds and grass, not far from the river. The air was full of babbling, jumbled words and motes competing for his attention.

"—following step for step, as if they were both on the same Dance. When they neared the river he collapsed, just crumpled like a doll, and he's been lying there ever since, unconscious, until you got here. He doesn't seem to be injured, but I thought it best to—"

The communication was directed toward the individual who knelt at his side, a strip of material studded with small vials and capsules in her hand. She touched a blue lozenge to the base of his neck, her auburn hair falling against his cheek as she peered into his eyes.

Strength returned to him gradually. He pushed her trembling fingers away and looked past her, scanning with his eyes until he found the creature. It had not wandered far; he saw it as a slowly moving figure cloaked in shadows on the other side of the river.

He pooled his thoughts and sent them outward again, searching.

Nothing.

5

"As I understand it, Ferranzano is the Coben's expert on
linguistic modes. Are you at all familiar with his work?" Emrys
raised his eyes to Marysu above the notepad. "More to the
point, can you deceive him?"

Moth dust and silvershadow marked out her brows today.
She drew them together and pursed her lips. "Familiar with
his work? Sweet Jesu! I should be deeply insulted by that
question, were it not for your demonstrated ignorance of the
field. Yude Ferranzano is a dilettante whose nodding acquain-
tance with linguistic modes comes through an ex-Chaliceman
by the name of Maune, herself a competent but depressingly
unimaginative wordsmith who, by the way, could not begin to
unravel my simplest phoneme braid on her very best day."

She drew a kephel stick from the pouch at her belt and
pinched its tip. The slender wand trailed a faint purple banner
as she settled it in her wrist holder. "Better to ask if your gentle
Dancer is equal to the task of inserting my creation in the
creature's mouth without mangling either of them. The language of the kin will be a remarkable piece of work, I assure
you, and I'd prefer it were not butchered."

"Hm. Of course, that will be for the two of you to work
out together, but I'm certain March will more than satisfy your
requirements. His ranking on the Block is comparable to your
own, according to the Hut. Ah, excuse me: Raille and Choss
have joined us."

Emrys waited for the latecomers to seat themselves at the
table.

"I'll only keep you for a minute. There's something I think
we have to do—as soon as possible, if you agree. I've instructed the Hut to begin preparation, subject to your approval,
to sever our link with the Net."

Concern and doubt showed immediately in several faces.

"Cut us off?" Choss said. "Why?"

"There's an election coming. A great and important one.
Less than three months from now, we'll have an Emperor again,

after a quarter-century without. I think you can guess what the odds are that it will be an Expansionist who next sits in White Spire. Support is growing for this Ansalvage, this 'Ur-Lord,' as he calls himself. My friends on Commons tell me chances are high that a victory this year for the Parad will mean the scrapping of the entire Evaluation system, shortly after their assumption of power.".

"The Emperor can't do that, not legally," Choss said dubiously. "His actual power is severely limited."

"Granted. But his influence is all-pervading. You know what they say about a strong Emperor: he wears Blue Shell for his finger-ring. And the Parad is orchestrating this whole election very carefully, to bring their candidate in on a wave of high feeling. No, If Ansalvage makes White Spire he'll have little trouble discarding these cumbersome Evaluations in favor of something a little more expedient. If this should come to pass, I'm afraid our only hope is to be out of touch when it's all happening—officially, at least. Then, should an order of recall be sent and it becomes obvious that we're off the Net, we still might have the time we need to complete our efforts.

"Now, I don't mean to cut us off completely. I've installed an auxiliary link in the Hut—illegal, I needn't tell you—that should let us continue to dip into the datapools on Lekkole from time to time, as long as we're discreet. But all other offplanet contacts will have to be forgone. The Hut tells me there should be peak activity on the Net in about twenty hours local, a multichannel broadcast of some sort—more Darkjumper miracle cures, I believe, and then a political harangue from our friends the Expansionists. I won't mind missing that. This is our best opportunity to simulate a malfunction and break contact. They know we still have the one-way beacon, if we have to signal for assistance, and with luck they'll choose to forget about us till year's end. I'm sure the Colonial Commission will view this accident as an inconvenience, rather than an emergency.

"So, before I give the final authorization to the Hut, do any of you have objections to this? I thought the screen could remain operable for the rest of the day and all night, if you have any last messages you can discreetly send out."

"What about Cil?" Raille asked. "Shouldn't she be included?"

"I spoke with her this morning through the droshky's com. She consented wholeheartedly." Emrys paused. "The rest of you?" he asked then. "Anything?"

There were no objections.

"Fine. Thank you all. I'll set it in motion."

6

Later that evening, Raille went back outside the Hut for some fresh air and a solitary stroll in the nearby woods, a prospect at once relaxing and flavored with the slightest tingle of fear. The sky was filled with clouds like heaped coal; only the smallest moon could be seen from time to time, riding high and managing to cast just enough light to make the thick shadows at the edge of the forest interesting. Raille allowed herself an hour of cautious wandering among the silent trees before she switched on her lamp and began to make her way back to the Hut, half-hoping to catch a glimpse of the tenant of this quiet land.

As she drew near the Hut she was surprised to discover beneath her handlight what she had never seen by day: a row of small flowering plants had sprouted along the edge of the building, leaning slightly outward from the line where wall met ground. Walking slowly around the circumference of the habitat, she found that the flowers outlined it on all sides, a uniform border of small, dark shapes. She stooped by the doorway and with her fingers loosened the soil around one of the plants, then drew it carefully from the ground.

In the corridor on the first floor she met Emrys. He examined the flower with mild interest, hands clasped behind his back. "Quite nice," he said. "I don't think I've seen them before."

"I found it growing just outside the Hut. There are dozens of them in a neat row all around the building. I thought perhaps you'd planted them there."

"Never." He smiled. "Even a meddler like me leaves some things to the wilderness."

An extremely orderly wilderness! Raille thought as she made her way upstairs to her room.

Under the sourceless white light the flower was a pretty

thing, with wide, fan-shaped leaves in a moist cluster at its base and a golden puffball freckled with green crowning the delicate stem; it made her whole room smell of Belthannis: fresh, cool, sweet.

Raille carefully examined the flower, using a small glittering device which Cil had shown her how to operate, a complex amalgamation of lenses and small, twittering nodes of light atop three slender legs.

Raille positioned the tripod above the blossom and gingerly touched a fingertab. The lenses changed configuration with hypnotic slowness, rotating through the first analysis sequence as Raille began to recite notes into her wrist journal. Several of the lenses remained splayed at a time, while others would glide back to coalesce in shifting combinations as various elements of the plant's internal and external structure were projected into the air above the instrument. Fascinated, Raille leaned forward on her elbows and watched for several minutes as golden, hair-thin stamens gave way to a view of the central vascular tissue, a long gray-green chamber lined with alveoli, which was replaced in time by cross sections of the leaf surfaces, the stoma, the minute root fibers.

A commentary hung in the air beside the images: words and numbers in flickering blue and yellow. Following Cil's instructions, she used the machine to perform basic age estimates. The results surprised her: this plant had apparently accomplished ninety percent of its total growth that very afternoon, breaking through the soil, putting forth the wide leaves, and developing the flower crown, all while the humans had sat at their work inside the Hut.

She tapped out a sequence on the tabs which would effect measurement of the plant's photosynthetic capabilities and blinked when she read the figures. She repeated the procedure and frowned.

"How very odd..."

Further examination revealed that what she had been calling a flower was actually a specialized leaf cluster employed in gas exchange and food production. She consulted tables she had prepared earlier from information gathered in the Library. She flipped through the yellowed leaves of the *Biota Exotica*. Finally, she made a long and technical entry in her written journal, ending with a rather plaintive query:

Why so large a conversion ratio? Check Library holofiles for specimens observed elsewhere on the planet. Why so precise an arrangement here at our doorstep? Possibility of communal root system should be investigated: perhaps they're one great plant. But why there, why now?

She placed the plant in a keepcase and, frowning a moment, labeled it *faux-fleur*. Then her gaze wandered to the Weldonese chronometer perched at the edge of her desk. She pursed her lips and looked uncertainly toward the ceiling.

"Um, Hut? Excuse me."

"Yes, Raille. How may I serve you?"

"If you're not too busy right now, I'd like to make a call before you terminate the link with the Net. Do you think that would be possible?"

"If I might trouble you for a bit more data before answering, Raille—am I correct in assuming that you wish to contact Weldon?"

"Yes. My mother, my grandfather, they might worry."

"Of course. There is one slight problem. Utilizing the Net from here to Weldon requires no less than three linkages: the substation on World Sipril, our nearest neighbor out here on the edge of things, the Vegan interlink, and of course the great Callisto masterlink near old Earth. For a normal two-way communication, verbal-visual, such a connection would take approximately five and one-half hours to establish—this figure by way of current estimates of Net usage and due partially, if you'll pardon my saying so, to the overly cautious attitude of the Weldonese authorities in regard to incoming calls. Now, while this would present no difficulty at all under more normal circumstances, in this case it appears to exceed the time limit imposed by Emrys to take advantage of peak activity."

Raille was gazing at the ceiling with her elbow propped on the desk, one cheek supported by her fist. "You mean I can't talk to them."

"You cannot engage in conversation with them, just so. If you wish, however, you might record a message to your relatives, which I will gladly transmit directly to Sipril, whence it will be rerouted at the earliest occasion through the Net to your homeworld. Regrettably, there will be no opportunity for any reply to make its way back to us until Emrys orders reinstitution of the link."

"I see. All right, I guess that will have to be enough. When can I make the recording?"

"As soon as you wish. If you would care to join me in the Hearth Room..."

Raille found herself chatting comfortably about summertime on Weldon with the musical machine-voice as she traversed the corridor outside her room. Descending the spiral stair, she was struck by a new thought. "Hut, is this expensive? How can I pay?"

"World-to-world via the Net is quite expensive," the Hut replied. "However, Emrys has instructed me to bill all calls to his personal account on Lekkole, by way of making up for any inconvenience suffered by the members of the Group."

"That's very nice of him."

"Isn't it?" the Hut said.

When Raille entered the Hearth Room, she was dismayed to see Marysu sitting at the table, a bowl of iced tea by her hand and half a dozen recording chips lined up before her.

"I didn't know anyone would be here this late," Raille said, approaching the table cautiously.

"You didn't?" Marysu arched a tricolor brow.

"I'm going to record a message for my—for home. The Hut said it was all right. I have to do it before the link with the Net is broken."

Marysu lifted the tea and took a slow sip. "You won't disturb me as long as you don't shout," she said.

"Oh. Good." Raille sighed and turned toward the Screen. "Where should I be standing, Hut? Should I come closer?"

"Right there is fine. Do you wish privacy for your recording?"

"Um, no. That's all right." She glanced back at Marysu, who was toying idly with the chips, her eyes on Raille. "When do I start?"

"Whenever you wish."

She began to think about her house on Weldon, with its cool, white spaces and the pool of lazy goldfish, and soon she was speaking to her grandfather and her mother with hands and voice, seeing them in her mind as she watched the empty Screen, all thought of the room's other occupant forgotten. Minutes passed.

"I guess that's all," she said at last. "I shouldn't talk any more; it's probably cost a fortune to Emrys already. I'm safe, I'm well, I'll see you both before Coldmonth. Oh, and—" She lifted her hands and signed quickly a flow of thoughts and feelings she could not trust to her lips. It was easier with the hands, more like singing than speech, and it gave her a small distance from the words which enabled her to finish the message with eyes still dry.

When she turned from the Screen, Marysu was standing close behind her.

"Can I have it?" she said.

"What?" Raille took a step backward. "Have what?"

"The language of hand symbols, the movements, the finger-speech—I haven't seen it before, will you give it to me? I'll have Jack paint you something beautiful, or I could transfer scree—work credit on the Block. Do you have a number? How much would you want?"

Raille watched the other woman warily, always alert since that first meeting for signs of mockery or contempt. Marysu's face was intense, imploring.

"I'll show you,   Raille said. "You don't have to give me anything."

"I thank you then, Raille *na* Weldon. I thank you very much." Relief danced in the other woman's eyes, and hunger, anticipation, life—it was a new face entirely. "Will you show me now? Please?"

"Yes. All right." Raille lifted her hand, and Marysu's leaped shadow-perfect to the same position at her breast.

"This is the way my grandfather taught me. You have to watch my face as well as my hands—the expression is very important. Actually, it's a language of the whole body. All right—" Her hands assumed the first sign, held it, changed. "This is the sky. This is earth, Water, Fire."

Brown fingers spun the air. "Sky. Earth. Water. Fire. Yes, I have them. Go on, go on as quickly as you can; I'll re-member."

Two hours later they still sat at the table, face to face. Marysu had caught the language: their fingers and hands shut-tled back and forth in the narrow space between them, weaving patterns which only the Hut's thermal receptors could perceive, where they hung like webs of fire in the air.

For Marysu it was like the exhilaration that came from rising to a ship in a packet, or like the aftermath of lovemaking. Physically weary, but beyond sleep, her senses afire, she spun bits of syntax, swatches of vocabulary, idioms, quirks of structure from Raille's patient voice and hands, giving them back minutes later without error, warp and weft transferred intact from loom to loom.

And Raille Weldon had seen a new person come together before her eyes, a joyous stranger born with the language that had always signified peace and wisdom to her. It was as if Marysu used the fabric of the silent speech to weave herself another identity, a new skin into which she slipped farther and farther as her mastery of the language deepened.

Now we must understand each other, Raille told herself as the night wore on. *Now there will be something of me speaking in her*.

7

March looked as though he might begin growling at any moment to protect the large platter he had carried out into the meadow, a deep turquoise oval laden with fried dough-twists and greasy-looking meat.

"And a pleasant morning to you as well," Marysu replied with a sardonic smile. She lowered herself to the grass near the log on which the soldier hunched, platter balanced on one knee, sheaf of fragile Dance templates fluttering on the other.

"Our mechanical know-it-all was kind enough to inform me that you were breakfasting, as it were, out here with the local fauna." She nodded in the direction of the kin, which wandered placidly some yards away, golden wires and strands of blinking lights trailing unnoticed from its arms and legs.

"And?" March wiped his chin on the back of his golden forearm and belched loudly.

"And I thought I might join you. Given that I have something of mutual interest to discuss. I'll wait till you finish with—whatever that is."

March eyed the object dripping at the end of his knife.

"It's a sausage. Want one?"

"God-Lord, no! I've already eaten, thank you. Three excellent blue-black plums from a Bablar template, each the size of your fist, with sweet, blood-colored interiors and barely a stone at the heart. Then some blue and two of our small, tart apples, pale as unlit candles." Her eyes narrowed in remembered enjoyment. "No, you go ahead and wallow, and when you've cleaned your trough we can talk."

"Talk now. Then I eat." March scowled, sensing an insult behind the unfamiliar words.

"As you like. Emrys left me a note. He said there's been some problem with the language. I've come to see what it is."

"No problem. Just can't talk," March said, riffling through a pile of translucencies pinned by a flat stone beside him on the log. "Look here." He pointed to a dark area. "Picture from inside him. Throat. No voicebox."

"Oh, this is marvelous," Marysu said. "Let me see that." A minute later she leaned back and stared at the kin. "He must speak," she whispered to herself, one slender hand rubbing her brow. "*Esh. Suten.* He must."

8

"Back, over, flex, turn, mouth open, stretch, relax, chin lift, pause-two-three, eyes—*damn* your dead eyes!"

March repositioned the creature's dark head in its halo of pinpoint contacts. In this particular incarnation, the mutable Dance frame had sprouted spidery tendrils of plax and metalmock, wreathing the kin's body like an outgrowth of the nearby underbrush, silver gleaming starkly against smooth brown.

The soldier worked rapidly, impatiently, his left hand punching and tapping amid a maze of fingerplates on the hovering calibration board, his right hand impersonally gentle as it coaxed and prodded the unresponsive flesh.

His voice came again in whispered staccato: "Filthy eyes still won't focus. Why? Won't track. Pattern germination faulty in motor nerves. Why? Jaws work: up, down. Tongue works: in, out, around. Throat, lips—face muscle control almost complete. Eyes like lumps of glass. Why?"

He held open an unresisting lid, punched savagely at the fingerboard as it swayed near his shoulder.

"Look at me," he growled, releasing the eyelid.

The dark eye trembled slightly but remained unfixed.

March shoved the panel away with an oath and snatched his hand from the frame without disturbing a single hair-thin tendril. While the kin stood motionless in its fragile cage, he bent and attacked the patterning nodes at the base of the device with his blunt fingers and a whirring, bulb-shaped tool. Minuscule points of light twinkled on and off in groups.

"Is it good to keep him standing there in the sun like that, hour after hour?" Raille asked, emerging from the forest through a natural archway of bushes, a clear bag of leaf samples folded over her arm.

"Sun just out last half-hour." He glanced once at the blue-bright sky. "High clouds all morning."

"Even so—"

"Frame holds him." March rotated the calibration device a half turn and grunted with satisfaction as a quiver traveled up the kin's left thigh and corded muscles spasmed briefly in its neck. "Interrupts. No effort. He's Dancing right now, the lazy chot-son."

Raille looked at the still form besieged by a host of mechanical vines and creepers. "It's the Dance of Statues, then," she said dubiously, "without theme or movement."

"Movement from it soon enough," March retorted. "Show you after these small things are finished. Already struts and bows like a well-trained Worker. But each *cessemin* muscle needs its own lesson." Narrowing his eyes, he concentrated on gauging the precision of his adjustments.

Raille returned to her collecting. From time to time, particularly when March's back was to her, she would turn and shade her eyes westward, in the direction of the Hut. When the sample bag was full, she unobtrusively emptied half its contents beneath a bush with blossoms that opened and closed in the breeze like small blue paper fans, and lingered on in the clearing, once more industriously sorting and gathering.

After a time there came a soft rustle of vegetation and a dark figure stepped slowly into the clearing.

"Tcha," March spat with disgust. "What does this one want?"

The empath approached, his great cloak hanging limply in the still afternoon, the mask of his face a chalky intrusion among the greens and golds of the little clearing.

Raille looked up finally from her work near the fanpaper bush, her face carefully surprised. She went to the empath. "Hello," she said softly, clutching the sample bag in front of her with both hands. "What a pleasant day. Are you heading out toward the Verres?"

The empath looked past her shoulder, scanning the horizon methodically from left to right.

"I've still some leaves to collect from that area. I was just on my way. If you don't mind, I'll walk with you."

"You're in my way," March growled. "Both of you. Leave."

The newcomer glided between Raille and the soldier, drifting to a halt within arm's reach of the kin.

"Get away from there," March said. "If you want to fall over again, it won't be on my Dance frame—"

But the empath pivoted abruptly and walked on, passing slowly by the creature.

"God's great geck!" March cried suddenly. "Look at it!"

The eyes of the kin had begun to move. As the empath made his way past the gleaming frame, the kin's eyes followed him as if drawn by a tether.

Ignoring the astonished soldier, the empath continued on his way until he had reached the edge of the clearing and slipped noiselessly into the surrounding forest. Raille glanced back uncertainly, then moved to follow him, the sample bag discarded unnoticed near the base of the fanpaper bush.

March dropped to his knees at the kin's feet, fumbled in the grass for his calibrator as he reached out to the patterning nodes.

Above, the kin's dark eyes unfocused slowly and drifted shut.

CHAPTER 10

Pleyen:	There. The last piece in place. Now we may begin.
Pelna Pwan:	What game is this? You have not said.
Pleyen:	Yours is the first move.
Pelna Pwan:	By what rules do we play? What is the game?
Pleyen:	Come, come. Time runs out for you.
Pelna Pwan:	But . . .

FROM SHADOWPLAY,
BY DEVIWAR AND CHIME

1

From *The Belthannis Workbook*
of Cil iya deo yo Haim:

I am traveling toward winter.

Tramping in the droshky through these silent places feels
awkward and intrusive, but I am closer to the earth than I
would have been in an aircar, while still able to cover many
kilometers in a relatively short time. It is a compromise, like
everything we do on this world.

Today I am sitting on a stone bluff about halfway down the side of a great valley, looking out over an area of perhaps three miles.

The valley seems at first deserted: I hear no birdsong, see no large animals. But there is life here in abundance. One has to get used to looking closer at things, for every rock has its lichen: I have seen blacks, browns, greens, oranges, and pink and beige and rust red, all on my recent climb down this slope.

Everywhere the colors surprise. At first there is only green and silver, gray-green and brown. Look closer and you see twelve new shades, but hidden here and there, in small amounts. And in the distance . . . behind everything the eye fixes on, there is something else, farther and farther on, folds and valleys, ridges and saddles of silver-green land.

Rocks here below me: the earth's strong bones. And trees. Trees lying fallen where the earth moved years ago, their splayed roots tall as a man and wild, like sculpted explosions pointing to the indifferent sky. From this vantage point shadow reigns in the lowlands beneath my perch: great clouds cast their silhouettes like black vessels moving slowly, serenely on to the other side of the world.

The sun rises in the same place every day; the planet rotates with its poles perpendicular to the plane of its orbit, the degree of tilt so slight as to be negligible.

So there are no seasons here, and all large-scale climatic variation is permanent, regionally fixed. The mild equatorial summer is a perpetual one, as are the polar winters. In between is a gradual blending, producing at its midpoints the gentle autumn we experience in the latitude of our Hut.

This morning I remembered that first night when we fell in the packets and Jefany quoted that bit of Antique poetry to me, something about a "savage place, holy and enchanted." Much more accurate to call Belthannis a *static* place. Holy, perhaps. Unchanging, for certain.

And where do the kin fit into all this stillness? There is no living organism known to us which is not continually undergoing change. Can we have found in the kin a creature immune to evolution? Is this whirling dance actually a curb on the kin's evolution, a way of keeping the race precisely homogeneous, avoiding any sort of specialization or differentiation that might result from generations of individuals confined to a single area of the globe? But why should that be of survival value, or is survival subordinate to nostalgia here? Did they come from Somewhere Else? Was the great circle established to give them back a pattern left behind on another world? Belthannis seems more and more like a huge diorama, or some master craftsman's carefully constructed ecological exercise, rather than a living, breathing world. Yet who could pace the meadows near the Hut as I have, and fail to perceive the pulse of glorious life?

I have never walked a world of such paradox before. On the one hand are my senses, telling me that all is natural and untouched; on the other is my mind, quietly insistent that nowhere has the smell of intelligent intervention been as sharp.

I am left with a strange dilemma! Emrys wants me to construct a plausible natural history for the Autumnworld, one that includes a thinking, reasoning kin. But I begin to think my time would be better spent in uncovering the truth of matters here, surely a tale more extravagant than any my poor imagination could concoct.

Half my life has been spent wandering in a search for order. Here there is nothing *but* order, door after opening door of it. Why do I find that so disquieting?

2

From *My Journal*,
by Raille Weldon:

He came down to dinner tonight, but he wouldn't join us at the table. I don't think he really knew it was dinnertime. He just got his mug of whatever from the table and downed it all in one swallow, standing there in front of us as if we didn't exist. There was an empty place next to me, and I was all gooseflesh for the few minutes he stood there, thinking he might actually sit down beside me. Fortunately (I suppose), as soon as the table took back his mug, he turned on his black heel and drifted out of the room, his eyes on everything but us. Dinner went on, full of talk and jokes about him, but I couldn't help but think how much more interesting the meal might have been. . . .

Sometimes I pass by his room when I've been working late in the Library, or just downstairs with a glass of tea. I don't really have to go that way, of course, but there's a section of corridor down at the north high end that plays music when you walk through it, and I find it very restful before I go to bed.

I heard him whispering once, on and on with a low rustling sound, like a mouse hunting food in the grass. But usually he's asleep when I come by, or meditating or something, breathing as a machine would breathe, as the Hut must be breathing somewhere all around us.

I keep staring at his door, wondering what he's doing in there. One would think I had a lot of absolutely empty time, to be wasting so much so foolishly. But I find myself hoping he'll come out, imagining that face staring at me suddenly in that dark hall at night. Am I trying to frighten myself? This is the same sort of silly fascination that had me poking my nose into the hives at halving time, when there was always a good chance of getting badly stung. But there's something compelling about him, something I can't begin to put a name to, not yet. Am I just feeling pity for someone who can't feel? It's true, sometimes he makes me think of Kiri-hero from the old tales, and maybe I feel a little like Beleth, striving to break the spell of silence. But I know the difference between real life and legends, or I used to. At least he hasn't come popping out as I linger there in front of his door, though there's always the chance. But then, I never did get stung, either.

3

From *The Belthannis Workbook:*

Nowhere is there waste; nowhere is there scarcity. There are no predators. Have I mentioned that before? None on this continent, anyway, and the existence of the southern landbridge makes me doubt that Continent Tu will have developed very differently from this one. I have not yet visited the seas, but the animal life I have observed so far on the land has been uniformly herbivorous. I include the kin in that pronouncement, though like Raille I have questions concerning the true nature of the redfruit which swells so obligingly at the tip of the blackbark branch, whenever a hungry kin happens by.

No one is either killing or being killed by anyone else here, at any rate. Overpopulation is not an issue, seemingly regulated solely by the complicated growth cycles of certain edible grains whose chemical content triggers hormonal activity in the reproductive systems of most of the higher-level animal species—though there may be other, subtler influences as yet undetected, and whether these plants also affect the kin is doubtful, as they have never been observed eating anything but the redfruit.

Order, balance, everywhere. I have not seen a single example of disease: not among the kin, not among the little tree-climbing marsupials, the black burrowers, the water-nest builders of the rivers, the seldom-seen birds, the several varieties of tiny, lobe-finned fish. And none will come from us. By virtue of living in the Hut we are—physically, at least—guaranteed freedom from any form of contagious malady.

Two days later:
Asála yo veo hamá havá, katve kawa, we say on my homeworld. Shape metal with fire, not ashes.

I must record this while the memory is strong. Something has happened.

They are not immortal.

Like animals, or humans not on Ember, the kin are used up by the passage of time. But I must organize my thoughts, and tell it as it happened.

It was the hour of little-moon-set last night when I entered the territory of Number Four, a dark-haired male, according to a holo from one of the satellites that was lucky enough to catch him in an open field last year.

I was quite tired, having spent more time off the droshky than on it yesterday, so I threw out the groundskin beneath a great blackbark and slept straight through till dawn. I awoke feeling refreshed after a dreamless night and decided to go in search of my host.

The lifeseeker led me on a pleasant half-hour's stroll, the mechanical bug-car trotting obediently at my heels, until we reached a steep hillock overlooking a broad river valley framed in the distance by majestic snow-crowned mountains. It was the liveliest stretch of river I've yet seen, quite wild in a few places, and the valley itself was magnificent, filled with flowering grasses and liberally inscribed with loops, rings, and crescents of thimblewort.

Down near the riverbank was a heavy growth of blue bracken, as well as several of the delicate feathery trees which Raille has named "scented plume." I wandered lazily toward the trees, drawn by the pulse of my instrument, until I saw something I was not prepared for beneath one of the swaying plumes.

It was like an illustration from one of the silly old books we shuddered at as children. It was a withered, skin-wrinkled, shrunken creature with skin like worn leather and a head topped with sparse white down.

It was an *old man*.

He stood before me under the plume, half-propped against the frail trunk, and blinked at the ground. His whole body trembled continuously.

I took a measure of his life signs. His heart was failing, his respiration erratic. The whole metabolism was spiraling downward, each element of the system shutting itself off in perfect harmony with its fellows. I took holos of him, my own hands beginning to shake.

I moved forward when he began to slip away from the tree, when he fell to his knees. I didn't know what to do. He swayed, then pitched forward into the grass. I dared not try to resuscitate him—the balance, the order!

In a few minutes his heartbeat was gone, his breathing stilled. I took another holo, then threw the camera away from me and sat down cross-legged in the ferns next to him, where I wept like a child.

He, his, him! For the first time I struggle for objectivity. Yet I have never seen a kin look more like a human being than did this one, dying.

From *My Journal:*

Now that we're really working with the kin, putting him in the Dance frame for long periods and things like that, Emrys has asked us all to spend some time watching him each day.

I can never get to sleep early anyway, so I said I'd take the Late Watches for the next few weeks. That's from the Twenty-fourth hour to the Twenty-ninth. It's not hard; we don't have to watch him every minute. The idea is to keep the Screen on TRACK and check it visually every few minutes to make sure he hasn't fallen into the river or anything. Emrys is afraid we might be disrupting the kin's daily routine too much with our work. He's probably right—I have the same fears—but so far there's been no sign of any reaction.

Dereliction of duty: Sometimes when I'm down here by myself, bored with the *Bloodeyes* books, which I must have read end to end a hundred times since I discovered them at twelve; incapable of reading these "sensory" books that involve running your fingers along the page, reading the words and deciphering the colors, all at the same time; and totally unable to get myself interested in what they call a "Vegan-style" novel, then I turn the Screen to UP for a little while and just watch the stars.

There aren't that many to see out here on the edge of things. Actually, if we were in the southern hemisphere, Cil told me, at the bottom of the other continent, we'd see the galactic disk at night, like a vast, gleaming crescent of light. But to be honest, I think I prefer our view, and I'm getting to know these dim, sparse stars quite well. No familiar constellations, so I've started naming the new ones, even drawing the lines sometimes, wherever I want them, with the aid of the Screen.

He came down to dinner again.

This is the third time in a week. Oh, he still acts as if he doesn't know we're there, but it's a start. Everyone else has decided to ignore him, but I couldn't keep myself from watching as he stood there, all chalk and charcoal, ivory and jet. He was looking my way at one point and I thought for a second he was starting to smile at me. I almost dropped my fork. But it was just the dinner candles, dancing shadows on his face.

5

From *The Belthannis Workbook:*

Incredible. Another portion of this pattern has been made clear to me.

Five days ago, I left the valley of my last entry, lingering only long enough to record my description of the death of Number Four.

I was filled with a need to get away, to flee that ancient body lying naked in the grass. When I left him the sun was hot and insects were already beginning to frequent the withered flesh.

I decided to head for the mountains, wanting only to be up and out and away from there as soon as possible. I had to use the droshky to cross the river. The water was not deep, but the current was very strong. When I reached the far bank, I felt a need for physical activity, so I made the thing wait there for me while I set off on foot. At that moment, I couldn't abide the thought of it stalking after me like a hungry insect.

It took me about a day and a half to reach the base of the mountains. The following morning I had gained the lowest summit, where I found myself at the base of a wall of sheer cliffs, totally insurmountable from this position. It was just as well; my restlessness had been appeased and I felt content to prowl around the area for the rest of the day, taking an occasional holo and poking into caverns. This world is alive with hidden caves and caverns!

Next day I decided to retrace my steps back to the river. I resolved to make tests on the body. In my mind questions had begun to spring up. What would happen to this territory now? As far as I knew there were at present no other blank spaces in the world-web. I fantasized a huge, rotating beehive with one empty cell—or would the territories of the neighboring kin expand gradually now, until Area Number Four had been obliterated? Somehow this seemed to clash with the patterns I had already observed, introducing an element of haphazardness into the ordered stasis.

By yesterday afternoon I had reached my patient machine, and the two of us danced and glided back across the river. At the site where the kin had expired I left the blue cushions and climbed slowly to the ground.

The body was gone.

There was a slight depression in the grass which I felt sure marked the spot where it had lain. I stood frozen for a moment, then set out like a madwoman, searching through the ferns and bushes, my back and shoulders prickling all the while as if someone were watching me. I was ready to give up and go galloping back to the Hut when I saw it.

On a tongue of rock and sand extending out into the river floated a large water nest, a conglomeration of reeds and ferns that lay partially submerged. I had noticed it earlier when I stood by the stream; it was similar to others I have seen in my travels, the construction and dwelling of an aquatic mammal with great, shy black eyes and a glossy silver-blue pelt.

The kin's body was lying half underwater, both legs and one of its arms secured to the nest by a thick, untidy harness of tangled reed stems.

There was no sign of the nest's inhabitants. Perhaps they were inside, waiting for me to leave. But about the body, which bobbed steadily in the current, flesh sun-purpled, face mercifully hidden, there was a cloud of insects, diaphanous as a veil. Sickened, I turned away and scanned the river. Far upstream I glimpsed movement, small flashes of silver at the water's edge.

For a moment I was sick with fury. I wanted to ride after them in the droshky and drive them out of the water, hunt them down, punish them for their desecration. The moment passed, and, suddenly weary, I mounted the machine and headed away from the river, back up the hill to search out a tree where I might spread my groundskin and escape into sleep.

But I lay awake long past sunset, finally passing into a fitful sleep. I dreamed of half-seen shapes with silver fingers dragging me out of the groundskin and off through the grass, down the hill to the edge of a black river, where I was lashed by ropes to the back of a cold, pale corpse while small things crawled and squirmed between us. When dawn came I found myself sitting upright with my arms clutching a leg of the droshky, my throat dry and sore as though I'd been speaking for hours.

After much internal debate I decided to go down to the river again and face my fears. I wanted to take holos of the dead shell of the kin, and perhaps attempt a tissue sample as well. I had labeled the nest builders herbivorous. It seemed now that I had been mistaken; there was at least one unexpected supplement to their diet of rivergrass and reeds.

I left the droshky at the campsite, using the long walk to clear my head. When I reached the top of the hill overlooking the river I stopped in my tracks.

This time there were two figures in the grass by the scented plumes: a male and a female kin, very much alive. When I realized what they were doing I felt as if I had been struck by lightning. I sat down heavily and watched them for a long time, feeling somewhere between zoologist and voyeur.

I recognized the female after a while. Number Seven from the territory just south of this one. The male was unknown to me. At some point I crept closer, fumbling for the holocube in my pouch. I never turned it on. They were quite beautiful together, in a mechanical sort of way.

At length they rose. The male departed immediately, walking off in a course roughly north by northeast. The female knelt for a few minutes to drink from the river, then wandered slowly downstream.

Now I have a theory which I should set down before I lose the thread of it, or before I convince myself that it is too fantastic. For the first time I am sure that they are all tied together. Not just by the sameness of their appearance, the bland repetition of activities from one territory to the next. I think that they are *tied*, joined utterly in some great sharing our senses and our instruments cannot perceive.

Think of the barrier we all felt to varying degrees on our first approach to the kin. Could it be that our physical resemblance to them allows us to experience a weak manifestation of the force that keeps them confined to their separate territories? Like a particle held in place invisibly, by the intersection of fields of power?

Then, when one of them dies, something happens to the rest of them. A signal goes out, or perhaps a signal ceases. A barrier dissolves and two other kin—the nearest two of opposite sex, I am guessing—are drawn into the now-vacant territory. Drawn to the location of the deceased kin. Drawn to mate.

The male leaves. The female leaves. I watched them only hours ago, moving off in nearly opposite directions. What now? I believe they have gone to resume their places in the web, to center their own territories again. And then at some point, probably several months from now, the female will return here long enough to give birth to a child. A male child, if the pattern is to be fulfilled to that degree of precision.

Food is always available. There are no predators here. I am convinced the water-nest builders were acting out their own part of the pattern when they took Number Four's body into the river. Nothing suggests that they would attack a living kin.

So a child will be born into the design, and as it grows it will be cared for by the pattern. It will not fall into the river. It will not know that the river exists. It will not know that it exists itself. It will never do more than eat and sleep and wander its world, fulfilling itself in this manner until the day when it too becomes old enough to die.

CHAPTER 11

The Alchemist must previously fast for
a hundred days and purify himself with perfume....

The Adept must moreover learn the method directly
from those skilled in
the Art. Books are inadequate.
What is written in books is only
enough for beginners....

The Art can moreover only be learned
by those who are specially blessed.
People are born under suitable
or unsuitable stars....

Above all, belief is necessary.
Disbelief brings failure....

FROM THE WRITINGS OF
PAO P'U-TZU

1

Emrys had learned from experience that it was wisest to enter the north high room without waiting for permission, whether or not the door stood open. Rapping for admittance produced nothing more than frustration, while the empath had expressed neither an appreciation of nor a desire for privacy since he had taken up residence with them in the Hut.

Sometimes Emrys would enter to find the room's occupant asleep: a surprising sight, for he slept curled up on a pallet in the conventional manner, with eyes closed and pale features careless, almost childlike, in repose. But just as often, he would be found cross-legged on the bare floor, face a rigid mask, eyes shut or staring, muttering in a soft, rhythmless monotone. And occasionally, as was the case today, the empath would be standing in the center of the room, gazing straight ahead at the always-empty gray wall, when Emrys sauntered in.

Emrys made the finger motions that would summon a body-hug from the bare floor, and then stood near the empath so the chair would rise between them.

"I need an answer to something, if your mind is on the premises today." He perched on the edge of the chair, kneading tension from the back of his neck as he spoke.

"March has been filling my ear with complaints. The Dance is becoming more and more ineffectual. Then just a few minutes ago he told me of a rather peculiar interaction he witnessed involving yourself and the creature. Pertaining to the eyes." Emrys made a vague gesture. "I'm sure you remember. It could be important to our work. Did you in fact have some influence over the actions of the kin that day, as March believes?"

Surprisingly, the empath spoke at once, his meticulously vacant expression remaining undisturbed "There was a brief contact. I walked my body past the kin. Its eyes were drawn to follow. This flowed unbidden between us: interface, the lightest of meshing."

Emrys squinted at the other man. "Could you make it do something like that again if you tried?"

"Unknown. Doubtful."

Emrys slumped back into the bodyhug. Exquisitely sensitive, the chair began at once to apply subtle pressure at selected points along his sides and back. Temperature gradients were established, textures altered. Emrys half closed his eyes.

"That's no good. We need real control. I thought we might have found another avenue. . . . Ah, serious problems with the programming. Something's fighting the imposition of the Dance, great chunks of it, anyway. We're left with a sloppy patchwork and no way of augmenting the process. And now there's a growing danger of overdoing it, burning out the kin if we don't tread lightly. Should it come to a choice..." His eyes closed, and he surrendered to the chair's ministrations.

There was silence in the room. Emrys' thoughts lazed toward sleep. Though he was not completely aware of the fact, Emrys no longer equated the empath's presence in a room with that of a "normal" human being; he felt no compunction about napping while the other remained standing at his side, dark gaze directed at some indefinable point on an empty wall.

Minutes passed. Emrys had embarked on a strange dream-voyage, which seemed to take him beneath the opalescent surface of Belthannis' great oceans. He swept through levels of colored light and jeweled darkness, feeling himself to be huge, yet moving effortlessly through the shimmering currents, surrounded by a gathering of massive, dimly seen companions. Deeper they went, moving always in concert, unfailingly graceful. *We are one*, he heard his own voice say clearly, *the single thought expressed in different tongues....*

Then another voice intruded. The empath's dry whisper came to him, breaking his dream, hauling him unwillingly back up to the small tired body in the grey room. He stiffened in the chair and opened his eyes.

The empath stood quietly, still scanning dust motes on the wall.

"You—did you call me?" Emrys felt awkward on the edge of the chair, disoriented in the tiny, clumsy body. The sensation ebbed. "I guess I drifted off for a moment."

"In fact you traveled luminous depths," the empath remarked. "Downward silently you went, escorted by shadows, rapt in exploration."

"Kindly stay out of my dreams," Emrys snapped. "I thought you didn't see into a person's mind after all. You told me it was only feelings you fished for."

"Prolonged exposure to a specific matrix increases the accuracy of informed interpretation. You spoke aloud several times as well."

"In other words, it was a lucky guess. Did you say something while I was down there, or was that part of the dream?"

The empath inclined his sleek head toward the wall. "Augmentation of control method exists as a probability of some substance."

"Hmm?" Emrys came suddenly to full attention. "Wait a minute. Of what? The kin—it can be controlled more fully? How? You said before there was barely any 'meshing' between the two of you."

The dark eyes turned to Emrys. "A technique was devised in time past by an imago to effect the partial control of non-sentient life. The matrix of that individual's mind now resides within my own. The technique necessitates the employment of passive, noncommunicant minds, linked and guided by the proper focus. If successful, a temporary transference of a small portion of the noumenon would eventuate."

"You're saying you could give the thing a temporary *mind*, aren't you?" Emrys leaned forward, face furrowed in concentration, his abrupt movements causing the bodyhug to quiver petulantly. "Not that we could ever consider such a thing—" He tapped with his fingers on the arm of the chair. "Hut, send March to me. Then I want no interruptions in here until I speak to you again. Now, Chassman, will you explain this procedure to me in detail?"

The empath turned slowly away, eyes like points of night returning to the gray wall. "I will tell you what must be done," the empath said softly.

2

"—when it too becomes old enough to die."

A small tone signified the end of the recording, and the journal shut itself off. Cil raised her forehead from quaking hands and brushed back a lock of hair. A month of changes showed on her: ivory skin had darkened to a clear, light honey in the sun. The white scar of a deep scratch showed along one cheekbone just above the blue tulip.

The Hearth Room was dim, a lone wanderlight drifting aimlessly beneath the domed ceiling.

"Will someone say something?" Cil asked finally.

"It died," Raille murmured in a puzzled tone, eyes on the mute band of silver at the center of the table. "It *died*."

Emrys stirred on the opposite side of the table.

"Fascinating," he said softly. "A new dimension to the problem."

"Hmf." Marysu stretched and yawned. "A very old one, that last. I'd begun to forget they were only animals after all. I'll keep an eye on our little innocent after this."

Choss grimaced in distaste and gestured at the recording device. "A new dimension, Emrys? How does this touch upon our own work? Our kin seems young enough, though I'm no judge of physical age."

"He's young," Raille said beside him.

Across the table the Group Leader shrugged. "Cil may correct me if I'm misreading her report, but it would seem to suggest a rigidity in the actions of the kin—a degree of compulsion far beyond what we'd imagined. Since our work requires the imposition of a new assortment of compulsions, I find it significant that March has recently been reporting much difficulty in the implementation of the Dance. Perhaps this deep connection that Cil posits is the origin of the resistance we've been encountering." He turned to Cil. "Work has slowed this past month. Designing workable templates consumes most of March's time."

"Templates are sound." The soldier batted contemptuously at the pile of transparencies in front of him. "It's fighting every move, and the ones I drum into it are all skewed one way or the other. Thing's like trying to train a rock."

"To force him might be damaging," Raille said tentatively. "We still don't really know what stress the Dance puts on him."

"But should we continue to use the Dance at all?" Jefany asked. "We could be preventing him without knowing it from performing some vital function. Suppose it had been the kin in the territory out east of the Verres who had died, instead of Cil's faraway Number Four. Then our kin would be the nearest male, yes? What would have happened if we'd had him Dancing at that point and he wasn't able to fulfill his part of the pattern?"

"*Ach*, poor thing," Marysu drawled. "Perhaps we should draw up a list of volunteers to substitute in that eventuality."

She traced the rim of her glass with a fingertip. "Jack?"

"This is not a fit subject for humor," Cil said. "It frightens me. If you could feel it as I do, the coming together, the overlapping strands..."

Marysu turned her eyes to the ceiling with a sigh of exaggerated boredom.

"Are you saying we should stop our work?" Jefany asked. "Is it that serious, Cil?"

"I don't know—there are pieces missing everywhere. How can I tell? It may already be too late."

"Look here," Marysu said in an exasperated tone. "We have just two choices: muddle ahead as we've been doing, paragons of altruism all, trying our best to save these pretty simpletons from the Sauf Coben; or we can let ourselves be paralyzed with doubt, and watch the whole half-finished business turn to spurge. If this argument sounds familiar to you, Cil, it's because I'm paraphrasing a short lecture you once delivered to me on a somewhat similar theme."

The empath entered the room on the heels of Marysu's exposition, postponing an immediate reaction to her words with the customary ripple of tension and wariness his presence still evoked.

Walking to an empty spot at the table, he used the manual controls to summon forth a glass of his murky protein brew, then retreated quietly to an alcove, where he sat in the shadow of the two great watershelves which had been erected by the Hut that morning to display the finest of Choss' hobby-fish.

"It would be wonderful if we could *reach* them, wouldn't it?" Raille said in a dreaming voice, her gaze lingering on the tall oblongs of confined liquid and the dark blur behind them. "Somehow to let them know what we're trying to accomplish here, and that we only want to help—"

"That *would* be lovely," Marysu said brightly. "Let's try it first thing tomorrow, shall we? Just sit one down and talk a little sense into him."

Jack leaned past her and lifted a decanter of blue. "If there were such a thing as justice on this or any other world," he remarked as he filled the linguist's glass, "this would be laced with a rare and deadly poison."

"Isn't there any way to get through to them, Cil?" Choss

asked earnestly. "Not to talk to them, of course, but to touch them, to make ourselves *exist* for them? Even an animal is aware to that extent."

"Oh, Choss, if we could disguise you as a sufficiently tasty-looking piece of redfruit, I believe the kin might condescend to take a bite of you come feeding time. But it would be seeing the redfruit only—not you, not a man, never a new thing. All that it can perceive are those things which already fit its pattern, and the pattern so far is unalterable, thank God. Other than that—" She spread her hands.

"Other than that"—the empath startled them all by speaking softly from his dim corner—"the creature itself would have to be altered, its brain changed to admit perception of new stimuli."

"God-Lord," Marysu choked above her dark wineglass. "Did one of the fish say that?"

"In which case, it would no longer be the same creature," Cil responded evenly, her eyes on the dark, unmoving figure, "but something entirely new and different—which, as Emrys will tell you, is not our goal at all."

"But a change in perception—" Choss began.

"When a man dies his perceptions are changed. They cease," Cil said quickly. "But you know a dead man is not the same as a living one, and no real comparisons can be made between the two."

"Nor is an adult the same as a child," Emrys said, exchanging glances with March as he spoke. "It strikes me that a certain amount of—change—is to be expected of all living things. Are any of us the same people we were five weeks ago? Five minutes ago? Our environment touches us in a thousand different ways and we change. Is this necessarily a bad thing?"

"I can't define good and bad for you, Emrys," Cil said. "I can only tell you what I see here. The kin's environment touches it, but the kin does not change."

"Of course, of course." His face had taken on an introspective frown.

Choss reached for the wine. "We always speak as if the kin were a product of this world. As if it were some super-adapted being resulting from natural processes. But why must we suppose we're the first to come here with the idea of tampering? Isn't it just as probable that the kin themselves came first—

from somewhere else, maybe—and then this habitat was designed to fit them? Or maybe they really were humans like ourselves at one time, till someone else came down and 'helped' them to get along better with their world. Mightn't the answers be more plentiful if we asked our questions from a less restricted perspective? Then at least the world might start to make sense, if the kin did not."

Raille said softly: "I don't think any answers will come from separating the kin and his world, Choss."

"Neither do I, but I can't justify it beyond a feeling," Cil said, rubbing her eyes with a yawn. "Not at this hour, anyway. You may very well be right, Choss. I don't know. I'm so tired. A pleasant sleep to you all."

That night after the others had retired, Emrys returned to the north high room. He remained there until very late, threading his way through the labyrinth of interrogation necessary to elicit useful information from the empath.

3

Glazed and yellow, the eyes protrude under lids of scored tissue. The flesh is a marvel of decay: it sinks, stretches, is crossed by overlapping spiderwebs which are themselves divided by tiny fissures and crevices. Skin sags, clings, bellies like rags in the wind. The angle of jaw and cheekbone is unbearably sharp, as if pared away by razors. Beneath flesh ruins the skull has reasserted itself, rebuilding old dominions with wall and keep of barely hidden white, smooth as scoured shell. The crumpled ears are rotted buds, lost in the strands of a dusty congealed matter no longer resembling hair. Claws are the fingers, the skin above the knuckles swollen into knobs of reptile hide. Colorless lips hang open and the mouth leers, drool glistening in one stained corner—

"What is it? Dove!" Cil's face loomed like a pale moon, frightening Jefany for one inexplicable moment. "Calmly now. I'm here." The warmth of Cil's breath came through the darkness as she leaned closer.

"I was old—" Jefany gasped through the spasms of terror still clotted in her throat. "Old in the body—dying of *age!* Oh, it was a dream, a stupid dream!"

Strong fingers smoothed damp hair from her forehead. A steaming cup touched her lips and warmth passed into her body.

"More? No? Is it gone now?" Cil's voice was calm with understanding. "You should walk in the Garden of Earth tomorrow," she said. "Take time to wander there. Promise me."

Jefany smiled. "I know another place to wander. I'll take the time."

She felt for the warm arms, held them in her own damp hands. Then she pulled the other woman gently downward, soft dimmed-gold hair brushing her cheeks, closer, till the tiny face staring at her from Cil's dark eye was clearly her own, smooth and indistinct in its tiny mirror. The beautiful reflection smiled at her when she smiled at Cil.

She tipped the porcelain face back and watched it in the shadows, forgetting the mirrors, feeling enfolded. She could not speak, but lay there with her hand on Cil's cheek, and silence was everywhere between them like a balm.

4

"What is it called again, Choss?"

"*Amba muti*. It's very mild, just some color enhancement and a light euphoria. And I think you'll like the flavor."

"Raille, Choss, there you are. Come to the Hearth Room with us—we're going to have a meeting. Now!"

Emrys gestured from the far bend of the corridor. March was an impatient shadow several steps behind him.

"We're coming." Choss hastily replaced the flask he had drawn from his dark daycloak. "Damn!" he muttered.

Raille shrugged, stepping back into her room long enough to set the pair of ornate bowls back onto her desk. "There'll be another time," she said. "I wonder what's so important? Let's catch up."

They found the two men on the level below, conversing in low rapid tones before a section of hallway marked by a clear oval of glass set in the floor. Emrys glanced up as they approached.

"Jefany's just gone into the Orrery. Perhaps we can catch her—" The inlaid oval flooded with glowing color as he spoke, bathing their feet in a rich, ultramarine radiance.

"Too late," March said. "Cycle's started."

"Perhaps if we knocked?" Raille looked inquiringly at the blank wall above the glass.

"She can't hear us." Emrys puffed out his cheeks, released the air slowly. "Hut. Open the door for me."

"The Orrery has been set for a three-hour cycle, Emrys."

"We can't wait. Open it now, on my authority."

"As you wish."

"What is it? What's in there?" Raille whispered close to Choss' ear.

"Stars," he replied in a reverent whisper. "The Orrery provides a simulation of deep space. Black vastness, stars ambient. It was put here for the same reason as the Garden of Earth. Some people spend practically all their time between worlds. Not so much anymore with the Darkjumpers failing—but for them, to be grounded to a planetary surface feels unnatural after a while. Then they can seek the stars and find peace, just as others will emerge renewed from the Garden."

A large circle of pale-blue color was forming on the wall in front of them. Through it, Raille thought she could glimpse a dark shape, as if something were suspended deep within the wall.

"Is it like being in a Darkjumper, then? Why didn't the Hut want to let him in? Is it dangerous?"

"Not for us. Unpleasant for her, I'm sure, if she's already into the sequence. It's not like a ship at all. It's pure space itself in sen-dep: they have a sensory-deprivation tank in there much like the one the Pathfinder on a big ship uses, but after they cut out everything, they start feeding you input again on the visual alone, and it's like being adrift in—in *starness*, with nothing around you but space. You don't even bring your body, you're just eyes, just seeing." His expression had turned distant, peering. "I don't go in myself anymore, because the last few times I didn't want to come out. It can be overwhelming when you're not accustomed to a life out there—addictive, especially if you're the solitary sort to begin with."

The circle was clearing slowly to a translucent bluish haze. Suddenly the haze evaporated, and they were looking at Jefany floating in a clear, heavy liquid, her nude body drawn up head to knees and a slender braid of silver wires disappearing into the side of the tank from beneath her netted hair.

The liquid swirled golden as they watched. Jefany jerked at the end of the silver threads.

"The Hut has introduced a mild stimulant into the nutrient bath," Choss told Raille. They watched in uneasy fascination as Jefany's face twitched and her hands began to grope at her sides, churning the golden fluid.

"She looks like it hurts," Raille said. "This is an awful thing to do."

Jefany's eyes opened abruptly. Her mouth worked soundlessly as she stared out at her audience.

The tank was rotating within the recessed port, liquid slowly draining away as the hatch at the top lowered to face the corridor.

March eased the dripping figure from the wall opening, supported her while trembling legs struggled for balance.

"Jefany." Emrys grasped her shoulders. "It's vital. We have to have a meeting about the kin, a discussion."

"Whuuu—" She coughed, tried to speak again. "Why would youuu—" Her throat spasmed and cloudy fluid streamed from her lips. She pushed Emrys' hands away, wiped liquid from her chin with the back of her arm. "What have you—done?" she gasped, her eyes on him wide and wondering. "The stars—"

Raille stepped between them, clasped Jefany's arm.

"Come with me," she said quietly, smoothing the other woman's brow with her palm. To Emrys she said: "Go on down to your vital meeting. We'll join you when she's able."

But Jefany shook her head, splattering the wall with cloudy droplets. "No. Just get me a robe. Please. I want to go to the Hearth Room. I want to see what was so important."

5

Marysu was the last to take her seat at the table.

"I am truly tired of these incessant gatherings. You're disturbing valuable work," she remarked to no one in particular.

"I hope this gathering can be relatively brief," Emrys said. "But it concerns everyone's work. I have a proposition for you." He glanced at the doorway. "Ah, now we are complete."

The empath moved slowly into the room, glided behind Emrys, and stood motionless, facing the rest of them.

"Mm, I had a feeling..." Jefany said quietly.

"What's *he* doing here?" Marysu said.

"Needs to be." March spat the words as though they had soured in his mouth.

"*You* accept his presence without an argument?" The linguist looked from golden frown to white blankness. "I see the world's turned upside down while I sat in my room."

Emrys commanded their attention with a gesture. "You all know we've hit a snag with the Dance. Resistance to the templates that grows instead of lessening. It's as though a process of gradual immunization is taking place: each day March increases power on the suive-machine; for a while it works, then he has to increase it again. The kin's tolerance to our interference is getting higher and higher—but there's a limit, I'm sure, and we've probably already reached it. How long before we start causing him physical damage? And there are other considerations: the idea that our work on this kin may be influencing the rest of them. That could explain the dispersion of the power. It could also eventually harm all of them instead of just one."

Marysu drummed her fingers on the tabletop. "What is your proposition, old man?"

He turned to her.

"I propose that we let the empath help us take control of the kin by giving it—loaning it—an artificial mind."

Around the table, faces clouded by fatigue or ennui came instantly alert.

"You're joking, of course," Marysu said, blue eyes staring.

"No. Not at all."

"Can this be wise?" Jefany spoke wonderingly at his side. He shrugged and sighed wearily.

"Look." He raised his voice slightly above the disapproving murmur. "We're not going to get there any other way. It's failing. It's too slow, even if we could count on March's being able to eventually establish complete control. We've got to get this out of the way now, so we can work on the thousand and one refinements we need to make before we face the Sauf Coben. But it's not just a question of speed. It's not working, and using more power to make it work may burn out our subject for good."

"What makes you think that he—"

"The empath has power. He has skill. He's demonstrated that for me—" He held up his hand for silence. "At my own request. It was quite effective. If he says that he can give us control over the kin, then I believe him."

"So do I," March measured the black-and-white figure un-emotionally. "Time past, in the field. Working on eye focus for hours—no good. Mindpick flits past us and kin's eyes're trailing him like they're on a stickerstrip. He's got power, affirmative."

"The question remains if he will use that power to help us," Jefany said, drawing the long robe up around still-damp shoulders. "And if so, why?"

"We've discussed it extensively. I asked for his assistance last night and he agreed to help us. That's all he's agreed to. I don't know how to unearth his motives any more than the rest of you, but you're welcome to try, so long as you remain civilized about it. The crux of the matter is that he's offering himself as an instrument for our use, when we badly need such a tool. We have to take advantage of this offer—it may well be our only hope."

"You asked for his assistance last night," Cil said. "Did you promise him our cooperation last night, as well?"

"No. We'll vote on it, of course," Emrys replied. "It in-volves us all. He has to use our minds when he goes delving into the kin—as a point of reference, nothing more. It's ab-solutely painless, he assures me. No ill effects."

"*Our* minds!" Marysu cried. "God's geck! I'm not letting him crawl around in *my* head!"

"You ask too much, Jon," Jefany said softly. "None of us will willingly allow him to touch our minds."

"The kin's eyes," Raille said suddenly, emerging from her thoughts. "I remember. I saw it, too. Oh, I'm sure he could help us if we let him."

"Do you think *your* appraisal is worth anything on this matter?" Marysu said with a crooked smile. "*Marse' qua*, this little *tête-à-tête* sounds like what you've been begging him for with your own eyes since he dropped on top of you in the fields."

Raille colored and lowered her head. When she raised it seconds later, she spoke evenly, her eyes on Marysu.

"I'm afraid you're going to hear my appraisal anyway, Marysu. Whether or not you choose to place any value on it is your own decision.

"The kin's life is not its own to control. You all seem to have accepted that fact without much argument. Every day you witness the workings of an existence which is completely governed by a highly complex pattern not of your own devising, and you accept that existence as a fact." She gestured at the silent empath. "Now, why can't you also accept his existence? Why can't any of you understand that his life is also governed by a pattern we cannot readily comprehend? Why is it so difficult? Because he has vocal cords and so can speak to you? Because he wears your clothes and eats your food? You praise the kin for its beauty and grace out in the field, yet you shudder when Chassman enters this room, and when he leaves you whisper about his lifeless face and automaton's walk."

She scanned the faces in the room, her own brow creased in puzzlement. "Why does he infuriate you? If you're standing in the kin's way when it walks through the meadow, and it happens to tread on your toe, do you become angry with it? Not if you're thinking rationally. Better to scold the earth for turning under your feet. And you've all watched Chassman for so long now, you've seen exactly how unchanging and inflexible his actions are. If his own narrow pattern now allows him to aid us in saving this world and its inhabitants, then we must bend ourselves to blend with it, not struggle out of the way.

If it confuses you to imagine him helping us, then don't think about it that way, because he's truly not doing it out of love, or out of hate, but simply because he *can* do it. For God's sake, let him!"

6

From *My Journal:*

I can't believe they're not going to let me be a part of it.

Emrys said they needed one person to stay uninvolved in order to operate the medipal sensors and monitor the physical condition of the others. I was chosen because I've already been using the equipment for a few weeks to check on the kin.

But it's easy to operate. Anyone could learn how to do it in half an hour.

The others will probably lose consciousness for a short time when he goes into their minds. I have to wander around the room from one to the other, keeping watch on their hearts and brains and nerves while he's touching them.

So there's nothing to fear, they assured me, nothing to worry about. He'll never even come near your mind. You're the lucky one, they said.

Don't they realize what they've done to me?

7

Three hours of debate! Choss thought. He stopped inside his door and drew the brown tunic off over his head, tossing it to land carelessly on his crowded desktop. He unfastened his breeches and stepped out of them, leaving them behind on the floor as he stumbled into the habitual.

He was halfway to his pallet when he noticed the scrap of paper protruding from beneath a pile of chips almost hidden by his rumpled tunic. He felt a tingle of electricity as he retrieved the note: it was good to feel needed again.

Written on the paper in the familiar blue-black ink was a single word:

Alchemy

He leaned against the desk, half disappointed, bemused.

Is this a question? he wondered. Finally he slumped into the desk chair and scrawled a few sentences for her on the back of the slip, for once too weary to hunt for a fresh message square so that he might add this scrap to his collection of notes and other items received from her over the past months.

He went to his pallet and sat down, legs sprawling, lips moving as he reread the definition, leaned back against the pallet and regarded the ceiling, arms folded behind his head.

I'd be a lot more upset about what Emrys is planning to do tomorrow if I weren't so exhausted. Best to keep it that way. She wanted it, after all, so she must have it. And it was really my vote that gave it to her.

Frowning at the ceiling, he closed his eyes and was asleep almost immediately. The scrap of paper fell from his fingers and lay on the floor by the edge of the pallet.

CHAPTER 12

And this was in the night,
Most glorious night
Thou wert not meant for slumber.
Oh, let me be
A sharer in thy fierce and far delight,
A portion of the tempest and of thee.

LORD BYRON

1

Raille stopped short at the entrance to the Hearth Room.

The room was empty for the first time since she had arrived on Belthannis. Not just empty of people, which she had been anticipating, but of everything.

Bare walls, bare floor. No wanderlights floated in the domed ceiling; the room was lit by a sourceless, overbright, white radiance. Only the dragon remained to prove it was the same room, set in gold among the cold tiles, inscrutable, staring up with glittering eyes to where she paused in the doorway. On the dragon's back, in place of the great table, was the heavy velvet and silver *bain-sense* from the Library upstairs. The room was completely silent, making her realize for the first time that some sort of in the background sound had always been there before. There was nothing to be heard: no soft wind effect or distant waterfall, no drowsy music or muted marketplace murmur.

She had caught the room between masks, something she had never thought would be possible.

The Hut was always careful to work its changes in this chamber when there was no one about. She had been told that the dwelling's designers felt this necessary, in order to preserve the illusion of permanence and completeness that they wished to achieve, the impression that each new incarnation of the room was as it had always been and would always remain. And the ruse worked: sometimes she didn't notice changes in the room's appearance until she had been sitting there for a span of hours; then it would come upon her as an awareness of altered mood, gradual, never jarring.

Occasionally the Hearth Room had been occupied continually for long periods of time, challenging the Hut's tactical ability and forcing it to alter the room piece by piece: She remembered a whole day when, each time she had entered the room after only a few minutes' absence, she had been aware that something had changed while she was upstairs: a glowing statue removed, or a bowl of floating blossoms introduced.

She stood still and scanned the room, conscious of the artistry that the Hut had wrought in the Hearth Room over the months, most of it perceived in the effect of warmth and safety and relaxed belonging, the urge to draw together with one's own kind, the sense of harmony. Empty, the room was an enclosed space only, bare and cool and bright, and she knew that if the others entered at that time they would scatter, drifting over the floor to separate places, no great table to center them, nothing seen or heard or felt that could coax them into liking one another. How much more terrible their many debates and arguments would have been if enacted in this sterile cavity, she thought with a shiver. Hating conflict, she felt a surge of kinship for whoever had created such an instrument for Group survival, such an effective counterbalance to tension and discord.

But finally she was forced to face the basic unreality of daily life on this world. The Hut was not, in fact, a house that she lived in, not a dwelling at all as she knew the concept, but the habitable interface between human beings and their mechanical servant on an alien world. The illusion was achieved with such unfailing cleverness that she went from day to day barely conscious of the essential falseness of it all, eating the food that was not really food, surrounded by the clothes, the tools, the toys that had not been made, but wished for, in this magnificent machine that was only incidentally a house. The humans were like parasites, small creatures living on sufferance in the Hut's body. She remembered the night of her arrival, when half in dream and half awake she had groped her way down the upstairs corridor, convinced she was exploring a huge, many-chambered shell afloat in a great blue sea. In the bare room, she felt as if she had finally reached the true heart of the shell and found no occupant: the creature was dead, the shell empty. There was no one at home, and she was alone.

Barely a whisper: "Hut?"

"Yes, Per Raille." Immediate, as always, the silver lilt, the crystal whisper, the golden hum blended into words for her.

"Where are they all, Hut?"

"Per Marysu, Pers Emrys, and Per March have gone out to the eastern meadow to fetch the kin. Per Choss is still in his room, and Pers Jefany and Cil are in theirs. Per Jack sits among the golden flowers that border the outside wall, drawing pictures of them."

Raille smiled wryly, as if in amusement at a precocious child. "Per, Per," she said. "One would think we'd only just met."

"Forgive me, Raille." The golden voice was benignly self-deprecating. "A touch of formality seems appropriate every now and then. I have a tendency toward pomp and ceremony that is quite difficult to suppress."

"And Chassman, you didn't mention him. Is he with Emrys?"

"Yes. That—person has gone to the eastern meadow with the others."

"What time is it supposed to happen, Hut? Do you know?"

"Emrys has chosen the thirteenth hour for the experiment to commence."

"I see. That gives me time ..." She stared abstractedly at

the light-gray wall. "I want to go outside myself for a little while."

"If you would like, you can put on one of the silver contact rings, and I will guide you to where the others are. As a matter of fact, they are on their way back in and should reach the outer doorway very shortly."

"No, no. I don't want to be with them." She paused, feeling foolish. "Is there any other—I mean, there's no way I could go out through another door, is there?" She looked over her shoulder at the arched doorway. "To be alone?"

"Certainly. If you would care to go through the portal to your right—"

She turned in surprise and saw an open doorway on the far side of the room, where there had only been blank wall a moment before.

She followed the Hut's voice up a long, sloping corridor, walking in a circle of light that moved with her, and aware of a constant rustling whisper coming from the darkness behind and ahead of her. She suspected that the passageway was being formed as she walked through it, opening up just ahead and coming back together instantly in her wake. She shuddered and hurried her pace, feeling like a rodent being ushered toward the belly of a snake.

Then the silver daylight was before her and she was stepping through a scalloped oval onto firm ground. She felt the cool, scented wind on her face. She had emerged on the opposite side of the building from the only true door she had known to exist.

Everything is mutable, she thought, staring at the dark trees.

"Thank you, Hut," she said, as the light faded in the passageway.

"Not at all." The oval closed silently behind her and she walked into the forest.

2

Candles, incense, muttered invocations—Raille half expected to see a pentagram chalked on the cold floor, or at the very least a hologram flickering in the air above it. But there

was only the dragon, ever faithful, welcoming her through the
arched doorway for the second time that morning.

The scene was very archetypal, she decided, having recently
learned the word from Choss—stylized, like the Speechless
Play at Year's Turn in New Kiruna, with white tapers burning
around the rim of the floor and everyone's shadow dancing
madly. There were paintings on the walls again, dark portraits
which seemed to twitch and leer, looking on like voyeuristic
demons or March's bloodthirsty ancestral spirits.

She looked to the center of the room.

The empath knelt by the side of the plush coffin, eyes closed,
pale lips moving silently in some blasphemous hymn. He was
communing, she imagined, with that dead mind inside his head,
and the thought sent a chill up her spine. The lid of the sense-
bath was open; inside, the kin lay motionless against the velvet,
staring serenely past the empath's shoulder to the vaulted ceiling where wanderlights bobbed and winked once more.

The empath reached into the coffin and adjusted the angle
of the creature's head, his lips still forming unheard words.

*He didn't know that he could intercede for me. They'd have
listened to him*, Raille thought.

Old Emrys squatted at the head of the casket, long dark
fingers poised like birds of prey above a newly grafted panel
of fingerplates and toggles. He was wearing an expression that
Raille had seen once before, when a Darkjumper had exploded
on the landing stage at the Port in Gammelstad on Weldon. A
huge crowd had formed to watch the bodies carried from the
burning carcass of the ship. Raille had watched the watchers
as the dead rolled by, and she still held the image like a jewel
in her mind: the gaping mouths, the restless tongues, the eyes
straining wide in anticipation. "Ember won't help them now,"
an old man at her side had remarked to his neighbor, something
like satisfaction in his voice.

Emrys licked his lips, and Raille turned away, a mood of
dark expectancy seizing her. She scanned the room.

Jefany and Cil were whispering by one candle, hands linked.
Marysu and Jack sat silently by another. Choss slumped in the
shadows beneath the dead Screen, shoulders hunched and head
bent forward against his chest; she thought his lips were moving
also, but couldn't be sure. March leaned easily against the
opposite wall, face lifted toward the center of the room and

fingers tapping impatiently on the tiles. He turned to stare at her for an instant, and the flickering candles kindled green fire above his left cheek.

Emrys exchanged a word with the empath, then leaned forward and touched the fingerplates. Raille could not decide whether she was hearing or feeling the low-pitched hum that filled the room.

The empath raised his hand.

Emrys said softly: "It's time to begin."

3

There were three in attendance when the kin was born into the flesh: the young adept, the ageless noumenon, and—

A pattern. A presence, the Other had reported before it was taken from him. *A will*.

4

Raille stepped back against the wall near Marysu, automatically bracing herself for what was to come. But when seconds passed and there was nothing, she began to feel silly with her spine rigid and her hands splayed out against the curving wall.

She heard murmurs, saw restless movement in the others. Heads lolled to one side, bodies shifted fitfully, as if in sleep. Remembering her duties, she activated the tiny, portative medipal unit.

She was moving toward Marysu when she began to feel an intermittent sensation, almost like pressure in her head, then a blurring as of something hovering near her face, just at the edge of vision. She had to fight to maintain her balance as the room tilted and swayed, beginning to revolve slowly beneath her.

But this is like that nonsense in the meadow, she thought.

She took another step. Someone cried out in terror, the words slurred as if they came from deep within a dream.

"Raille!" Emrys pointed past her to the others. "Raille, help them!"

Help them . . .

She forced herself to stumble the remaining steps to Marysu, sank gratefully to her knees beside the linguist, and brought the medipal sensor to a limp brown arm.

When their skin touched, the bright-blue eyes opened suddenly and stared at her without recognition.

"Are you—"

"Shhh," Raille said softly, "I'm here."

They sit on wine-blue cushions by a huge curving window at the edge of a dimly lit room. There is music from somewhere: intricate, leisurely melodies. She recognizes the skyline: Delaunce on Babel, city of her youth.

There is someone sitting across from her, half-hidden in shadows. Candlelight picks out a glimpse of quiet features, still hands, a many-colored skirt.

"Are you—"

"I'm here," comes the soft reply.

"I was talking about him again, wasn't I?" She turns back to the window, gazes at the light-spangled city below.

"Our best times were on Earth in the Bosmas, walking at night with him wheeling about me like a bird, darting ahead to the food vendors' stalls, or chattering with people he'd never seen before in his life and making them laugh—allowing me to be scornful and superior, because through him I was larking and laughing and stirring up love and amusement—things I cannot do in front of other people. His freedom was my own. And he always brought it back with him, he always came home with me at the end of the night. What a wonder that was to me—is to me still—because I don't know why he stayed. Even when I was no longer Ravenswing he was still Jack, still willing to squander so much time and affection on me."

There is a ghost of movement from the other side of the table. "You cut off your hair because of him, didn't you?"

"Because he liked it." The gleaming skull bows into the shadows. "Because I was afraid—it sounds so pathetically foolish to say it—afraid it was my hair or—" Her face comes up tortured. "Why would he stay? Why? I've let him see me pared to the bitter, ugly core, for months I've given him noth-

*ing. You know I dragged him with me to the Evaluation for
one reason—because I knew I'd never see him again if he
stayed behind. I knew he'd wander off in a few days and meet
someone, anyone else. But out there, I thought, he'd have to
be with me, and there'd be no one else to meet." She gives a
small laugh.*

*"I should have told him to stay behind, I should have
made him leave me. It's terrible to do this to a person, like
a carrion bird gnawing at him. I'll kill him this way." She
shudders, drawing up slender shoulders. "But to put myself
back in that cage—it's not fair to have to make that choice,
it's not fair."*

*"What makes you think it's your choice to make? What
makes you think it's up to you to let him go?"*

*She half rises, stung by the calm words, then rocks back
on her heels, the expressive mouth crumpled, tears burning
down her cheeks.*

"Here."

*Hands thrust toward her out of the darkness. She flinches
when the fingers touch her shoulders, but they persist, pulling
her closer. She tries to speak, but the words come out garbled,
hiccupped with sobs, and finally, clumsily, the weeping woman
allows herself to be held.*

She was rising unsteadily to her feet when she heard her
name called. Emrys beckoned her over with a confidential
wink. The medipal unit trailed her, bobbing lower as she knelt
at his side.

"You'd be surprised," he told her. "I know what it is now."

"Do you? That's nice." She guided the sensor threads to his
left forearm and wrist.

"Mm." He nodded rapidly. "We discussed it before, he and
I. It's a—a manifestation of his power, a visual by-product of
that-which-propels—compels, I mean, whatever." He raised
an unsteady hand to wipe at his cheek, stared at the moist palm.
"Lords, it's hot!"

She touched a key on the floating unit, waited a few seconds
with her eye on the readout, removed one of the threads. "This
should help." She touched two more keys.

"All right." His eyes rolled, focused. "Anyway, that-which-
compels and the other one, that-which—what? perceives—

they both of them involve TK to some degree, that's the theory."

"What is TK?" she asked, to keep his mind off her ministrations.

"Telekinesis. Physical manipulation of substances, objects, through nonphysical means." His speech was becoming increasingly slurred. "Manipulation of parts of the brain, in this case. Paleocortex, mainly. Depends on how skillful the com—communicant is." He gestured over his shoulder in the direction of the empath. "Our friend, he couldn't do this on his own, you know. Maybe you didn't know that. But that Other, the noumenon—there's a smart one! Fits down over his own mind like a template, like a yoke. And with that he's got the mind-patterns and the skill of a real master to help him. Must be cozy in there, you know, but hot."

He chuckled, then laughed out loud, pointing at the empty air above the *bain-sense*.

"So—fantastic—and it's not really there! But while he's in here with all of us"—he tapped his forehead clumsily—"wandering around, bumping into our sight centers, I suppose, stirring things up—" He snapped his fingers. "Well, there's the result." His expression became completely serious for a moment. "I think it's very pretty," he said solemnly, and closed his eyes.

Raille detached the second thread from his arm with a shake of her head, rose, and moved back out to the circle of dreamers.

"I don't think you understand," the golden man is telling her as they lie together on the yielding floor. "I was killing children in those days."

He shifts slightly, so that he can watch her face while he speaks.

"I was born in Heartsdesire, a city on a world so foul and low you couldn't begin to imagine it. Never got the smell of sewers out of my nose, but I finally got myself out of that pit. I grew up thieving, but I never had enough ambition for anything big. Heartsdesire—you've got to be a thief. Nobody gives it to you there.

"But then I found the Dance and I knew it was the way to make myself do things, things I'd never have tried otherwise. It was a way to get around myself, to trick the body into

*working. And with me not around to see how the job got done—
that was even better. Company brecks were always hanging
around the Dance halls in those days, looking for poor but
talented types, and I signed up first time I was approached. I
never thought about it as soldiering, only as a way out. We
were called the Spurs. It was a good life."*

He shifts position again, up on one elbow, for he sees best
when he focuses with both eyes together: the real one for clarity
and surface detail, the false for colors and depth.

*"Then the call would come and I'd snap the word and slip
away down deep for a slice of no-time—but I knew the body
was working hard for me up there Topside, busy splicing death
into the threads of my life. Lucky, I never considered the thing
till I got down dark and quiet, and then there was nothing at
all I could do, for we were like two thoughts, death and me,
circling each other in the dark till I lost track of which was
which. Then I'd come up and there they'd be: whole bodies,
mostly, or pieces of bodies, pieces of meat tossed here and
about, doll-limp and toy-broken at my feet. And sometimes—
I won't say often, but sometimes—there'd be children."*

He strokes the long waves of auburn hair back from her
bare shoulders, touches the skin that lies pale and strange
beneath his golden fingers, marveling for a moment that she
is there so close to him, naked and not afraid.

*"I remember most how inefficient it was, looking down on
them and beginning to mourn the energy wasted in popping off
those thin little arms, or pounding in that tiny skull, when all
the while it was a child, and not worth the body's effort.*

*"After I started feeling the kills, there was nowhere for
me to go while the body worked. Then I stopped. Then I
kept the skin as a wall, and I took up the true slumtalk again
as another wall, to protect me—to protect other people from
me. And to keep remembering, most of all, to do penance
for all of them."*

His hand tightens on her shoulder, loosens, slides downward, leaving marks that fade slowly from her fair skin.

*"But I have to ask you something, because lately I've been
wondering how I'll know when it's finally enough. How long
will it be—do you know? How long do I have to pay?"*

She opens her mouth at once to speak, but he covers her
lips with his rough hand. He closes his eyes so he does not

*have to see the expression in hers. Then his hands move down
again and soon he covers her body with his own.*

*When it is finished and he opens his eyes, he finds her
weeping silently, face averted.*

*"I'm sorry," he says roughly. "I meant to give you plea-
sure."*

*"Why didn't you stay?" she whispers finally, fragile fingers
rubbing the tears from her cheek.*

"What?"

*"You don't even know the difference anymore, do you?" In
her brown eyes there is a look of sadness, a look of pity.*

*"What are you talking about?" He reaches to take the del-
icate hand, but she withdraws it, turning slowly away from him
in the growing darkness.*

*"It was a Dance, of course." The words come to him faintly.
"It was just another Dance."*

Raille found herself moving toward the silent center of the
room: a vast distance to the tail of the golden dragon, miles to
the narrow silver box, the three still figures.

Emrys was slouched between her and the empath, his eyes
wide and unfocused, his face transfigured with wonder. "I think
it's getting larger," he hissed as she drew near. "Over there—
in the air above him!"

Raille glanced to where the trembling finger pointed and
blinked in surprise. There was indeed a slight troubling of the
air, a flash of whirling motion just above the open coffin. She
squinted at the apparition and slowly began to see it more
clearly, like a great whirlpool spinning rapidly, nearly invisible.

"What is it?" She moved forward.

"No! Stay back!" Emrys whispered urgently. "Ah, it bleeds
colors when you come near." He raised his arm in a vague
shielding motion. "Too bright now—too fast! Get back!"

She stood for a moment in mild surprise. Why didn't he
tell the thing to go away if it bothered him so?

Shoo! Scat! she thought.

The mad vortex dissolved obediently. At once Emrys' face
crumpled like a heartbroken child's. He reached toward the
empty space above the kin's dark head, his lower lip trembling.

Oh, all right then. Make up your mind.

Pulsing, whirling near invisibility, the apparition flashed again above the silver coffin.

Sessept Emrys grinned happily, his arm remaining suspended in the air until Raille folded it gently down to his side.

Minutes passed as she moved from one to the other, kneeling, touching them with the medipal sensor, reading the results in a flicker of numerals and characters. The instrument began to report them all to be in the same deep, dreamless sleep. Their bodies lay still on the floor until she neared them, then they writhed and muttered beneath her touch. She spoke soothingly to them, smoothed hair back from sweating brows, tried to calm them.

In the center of the room, the empath was a black-and-white figurine, stiff, swaying slightly at the side of the coffin like a spinning top about to fail.

She sensed something in the room with them.

Someone's whispering at the other end of the dragon, Raille thought. She raised her arm to the side of her head. *Someone's blowing in my hair*.

Aloud she said. "I'm frightened."

"Grow up!"

Who—

With a shiver—*like the surface of a pond beneath the waterbird's wing*, her mind or someone else's interjected smoothly—she realized that her own voice had spoken both times, that she had answered herself.

Something was wrong. Raille's eyes darted around the room in sudden desperation.

There at the center were Emrys, Chassman, and the quiet figure of the kin. Along the curving wall were Marysu, Jack, Choss, March. Jefany, and Cil at her side. Raille tried to turn, but found she couldn't move her body. Something was holding her tight.

She examined the room again, raced through the inventory of people.

What am I looking for?

Her eyes snapped back to the area directly in front of her, searching, trying to keep everyone within her field of vision.

Who—

The constriction was easing. She felt her shoulders, throat, arms, chest, relaxing, beginning to throb with a dull ache which she welcomed as something real, something physical, a sensation that could be identified and dealt with. There was a sound from the other side of the room.

The dark-bearded man walks the Strand on Dunbar's World with her at his side, feeling the night wind in his hair. Solitary lovelights wink from the coquinade terraces, sea-gleam glows in fans and whorls, orange, pink, and white on the walls of merchant villas, high above them as they make their way down the Endless Beach.

Native children bearing cool phosphorescent torches run to them with gifts of shells, offer sips of the famous blue wine, their thin tunics embroidered with cloudfish and eels aflutter in the coolness from the water. The lovers laugh their gratitude to the darting children, emptying their pockets of the silver-gold coins used on this world.

At length the two pass to a less frequented stretch of beach, where they wander barefoot, arm in arm, through the shallows of a sheltered cove. At the base of chalky cliffs, they stop to build a crackling driftwood fire. They kneel at the rim of a shallow tidal pool, watching by the light of the mounting flames the timeless interplay of sea and land.

Then he spreads a blanket on the sand by the fire, and they lie unspeaking for a time, pressed together side to side, her hand in his, until he brims so full of feeling that his dark eyes sparkle with tears when he turns to her.

"I love you," he says. "I always have. I always will."

She moves against him, clasping his hand in both of hers.

"And I love you," she says, while the wind sweeps in like a veil, mist-laden and full of strange scents from the dark ocean. "Dearest One, I shall love you for as long as I live."

There is rising music from somewhere as he leans toward her, his face stretched in an odd new way which he dares to hope is utter joy; but the hands that caressed his have begun to slip away, and as the music reaches its crescendo he sees in the firelight that she is quite old, that the years have passed for them in an eyeblink and left her withered, grayed, trembling at the edge of death.

"This isn't fair," he says calmly as her body slips lifeless from his grasp. Then it seizes him—

Sobbing, clutching his knees as he rocked back and forth, Choss somehow found himself able to lean back comfortably against the wall at the same time and watch the spectacle with amazement.

What is the matter with him? he thought. He tried to calm the weeping figure, the slightly ridiculous Scholar who had hidden his face under clasped arms.

Come on, stop it, it's all gone now. He realized with a start that whatever had so terrified this poor creature was gone after all. Then it occurred to him that everyone in the room must be watching.

Raille turned her attention to the center of the room once more. Something definitely was not right here.

She squinted at the flashing whirlwind and understood at last what it was that spun there: whirling near invisibility above the coffin were pieces of the others, fragments of their *selves* orbiting the formless thing which had been extended pseudo-pod-fashion from the noumenon in Chassman's mind.

There was an unyielding resistance.

"The brain of the kin does not admit the matrix," Chassman said softly.

His eyes drifted shut.

At once, the faces of Marysu, Jack, Cil, Jefany, Choss, March, and Emrys came to life. Chassman swayed and the seven Group members writhed, muscles and tendons taut, faces stretched with exertion.

Raille stood in confusion. The room was filled with a straining agony.

Help them!

The vortex wobbled alarmingly, dipped, righted itself. A strange hissing sound escaped from Chassman's lips.

Help them!

Suddenly the whirlpool dropped straight down, spinning madly into the *bain-sense*. A column of flickering shadows followed it, rushing endlessly downward, pouring from the empty air in front of Chassman down into the silver coffin.

At the focus of the mad whirl-fall, the kin lay twitching on pearl-gray silk, his dark eyes wide, while at its source the empath shuddered and swayed like a candle flame near extinction.

5

"Is it over? What's happened? Gods, I feel sore!" Jack stretched his arms gingerly and looked from Raille to the medipal sensor bobbing at her side.

"Yes, it's over. Try not to move around for a few minutes." Her face was pale, her manner abstracted.

"Did it work? Raille?"

She turned to him. "I don't know—I have to get out of here. I'm very tired. You can all manage without me now, I'm sure." She smiled in weary apology, rose with effort, and started across the room. Before she reached the archway, she staggered against the wall on her left, clung there for a moment, then slid noiselessly to the floor.

She was conscious when Emrys bent over her seconds later.

"Not enough time," she whispered.

"Shhh. Just relax. We'll bring you to your room in a minute. You can rest there."

"No." She struggled feebly against him. "I have to stay. Just tired. Let me stay."

He considered for a moment, then nodded his head. "Right. You've earned it. We'll give you a prodrug to keep you going for an hour or so, but after that it's up to bed." He raised his eyes to the ceiling. "Hut, give me something for Raille. Lords, it's been hours—no wonder she's exhausted."

"Pardon me, Emrys, but the entire process lasted less than seven minutes from start to finish," the calm voice replied from above.

6

March crouched with Emrys at the head of the *bain-sense*, massaging his calf muscles and smiling his wolf's grin of approval.

"Look at that!" Emrys traced a pulse of green light along the information strip. "There's something in there now!"

The two huddled around the grafted sensor equipment like eager boys. Along the edge of the wall, sitting or reclining, the other members of the Group rubbed their own aching muscles as they watched their jubilant colleagues.

But the empath sat cross-legged, a little removed from the others, dark eyes closed in concentration.

· For the third time he searched deep within his own brain, for the third time constructed with care the motes which would allow linkage with the Other. As before, he found nothing. He opened his eyes and stared at the sleeping kin.

"There has been a miscalculation," he said in his soft, rough voice.

"What did you say?" Emrys turned, triumph in his copper-dark face. "Did you say something?"

The empath's pale hand rose like something dead drifting upward through the sea, touched his damp brow.

"I am alone now," he said.

7

The kin rose slowly to its knees, swayed awkwardly to its feet. The arms and legs were trembling.

"We must be very careful from now on—" Emrys paused, fascinated, as the kin shook its head violently in the wind. Dark hair whipped away from the face.

"*Vraiment.*" Marysu came up to stand at the old man's side before the Screen. " '*And all should cry. Beware! Beware!*' " she whispered in an Antique language.

Emrys smiled without turning from the image. " '*His flashing eyes, his floating hair!*' " he answered in the same tongue.

"What's next, then? Let him run wild like this? Or finish the poem and weave a circle round him, for his own protection?"

"No circles," Emrys said. "He can't be caged now—don't you feel it? He's not an animal anymore. We'll just have to watch him more closely—" He broke off and moved closer to the Screen. "Look at him!" he hissed. "He knows, he knows!"

Together they watched the strange new creature stretch and twitch on the wall. Before, Marysu realized as she tried to read the kin, its movements had been smooth, spare, inhumanly graceful. Now it seemed jerky and uncoordinated, the body all angles and electricity.

While she watched, mesmerized, Jefany entered the room behind her and came to stand by Emrys. Marysu moved away after a moment's hesitation, allowing them to speak privately if they so wished.

"I don't think it's working out, Jon." Jefany spoke rapidly, in a husky whisper. "I think you should stop."

"Not working?" His eyes remained on the Screen. "What are you talking about? He'll be a man, Jefany, a real one. Let them try to take him then!"

"Cil is very worried. We know less than nothing of this world or of the patterns we may be disturbing. Besides that, the empath told you that something went wrong. This isn't the result he was looking for."

"So Chassman isn't infallible. I always knew that. He's just a man. It should comfort the rest of you to learn it. And we can profit from his mistake, if we can figure it out. Somehow he's left a piece of himself lodged in that empty brain, and it's started something in there, or ended it. Look there—see him gesture suddenly with his hands? That's new, new! Perhaps—perhaps there'll be time after all, and we can wake up another one, one of the women, if Chassman's able to manage it. A pair of them to take before the Coben, think of that!"

"Emrys, the original purpose: to save the kin, to allow them to live as they are, undisturbed—"

"I know, I know, we'll still be doing that—but, Jefany, this one will be a man! A true man where there had been an empty space, not even an animal, before. And we'll have done it."

Marysu drifted farther away, beyond the range of their urgent voices. She looked back at the Screen, and for a second the kin seemed to stare at her directly from the wall. The wind was in its eyes, and streaks of moisture glistened on the unlined cheeks.

Oh no, she thought, *too obvious, much too obvious. He can't have learned to weep this quickly.* More of the Antique poem tumbled into her head as she flinched under the dark gaze:

> *Weave a circle round him thrice,*
> *And close your eyes with holy dread,*
> *For he on honey-dew hath fed,*
> *And drunk the milk of Paradise. . . .*

8

Raille moved slowly through the rain-dark forest, treading carefully down slopes and past moss-edged pools, descending among the great silent trees where once she had run for the joy of movement, her heart racing, the strong scent of green life filling her lungs.

Her movements were quiet and deliberate. She picked her way through beds of waist-high mushrooms, past sprawling bushes nodding under masses of sparkling crystalline flowers, dimly prismatic in the rain.

The raindrops themselves did not touch her, slanting down and away from her skin and clothes. When she moved more swiftly they blurred into a faint mist in front of her. About her slim waist was a plain belt with a flat, jeweled buckle. The jewel glowed pale gold in the dusklight, winking like a will-o'-the-wisp as she passed in and out of shadow.

A shallow stream wound near the foot of the hillock, gleaming like shards of dark glass through the heavy twilight.

She found the empath sitting not far from the stream, almost hidden by tall, trembling ferns, on a half-rotted log at the side of a great stone hump, cold, gray and leprous with pale-green lichen. He took no notice of her approach, staring fixedly into the black forest. She stood before him until he shifted position and moved his head restlessly, as if trying to see past her. Then she turned and saw that the kin was also there, curled up in a nest of leaves and grass stems beneath the arching, moss-shrouded roots of a fallen forest giant, whose trunk stretched off like a vast black bridge until it was lost in the leaves and shadow.

He was soaked to the skin under his heavy cloak, and his dark boots sat in a little puddle of their own making at the base of the log.

Finally she broke the silence, the words sounding strange and almost meaningless in the soft soughing of rain through the leaves. "I've brought an extra weathershield. I'm going to put it on you."

He sat as before, hunched forward on the rotten wood, eyes staring into the gloom at the figure that lay unmoving beneath the roots and the thick cloak of dead leaves.

"I'm setting it to medium. They say not to set it too high; you have to be careful. A partial weathershield keeps out rain and most of the cold, but a full one keeps out everything. Light. Air."

He did not argue. He leaned back when she nudged him, then forward so she could clasp the belt around his waist beneath the sodden cloak. Her fingers shook as she tried to fasten the ends together against his flat stomach. "It's getting chill," she murmured.

At last the golden jewel glowed above his black breeches.

She stood back, watching him. Black hair was plastered on the pale forehead above the young face.

She stood for as long as she was able. Finally she leaned against him with a small whisper. He glanced up and she was swaying there, looking down at the crumbled length of log. Wordlessly, he moved to one side, and she sat down next to him, not touching him, shivering slightly.

At length her eyelids drooped and her head relaxed gradually against his shoulder. She slept, her breath a whisper lost among the rain's thousand soft voices.

They sat huddled in the rain that would not touch them, one sleeping, one watching through the misty gloom to where a third still figure shared the night from its nest of leaves. At last the watcher's eyes closed and, resting his head lightly against hers in the darkness, he also slept.

CHAPTER 13

*. . . In similar fashion, when Folded Flower was
angry or troubled in mind, she would furrow her
brow and frown on all her neighbors.
Now an ugly woman of the village, seeing and
admiring Folded Flower's beauty, went home and
also proceeded to knit her brows and frown darkly on
all around her.
When the wealthy people of her neighborhood saw
her, they locked tight their doors of iron and would
not go out; when the poor people saw her, they took
up their children and their grainpots and ran away
from her.
This the ugly woman could not understand. She
knew how to admire the frowning beauty, but she did
not know why she, though also frowning, was not
beautiful. . . .*

FROM THE ENG BARATA,
STROPHE IV, LUX VII

1

Three months passed rapidly while Emrys and the Group continued their strange work amid the fields and forests of Belthannis, severed by choice from the rest of the Human
Community. The kin had become fully obedient to March and

his templates, and its repertoire of programmed movements expanded daily with the addition of increasingly sophisticated maneuvers. The Belthannis Worldspeech continued to unfold in Marysu's fertile mind, while Choss' imagination ranged far and wide as he committed more details of "a most ancient and exquisitely balanced" civilization to his recording chips. Sometimes on foot, sometimes borne by the gleaming droshky, Cil went forth often from the Hut to explore uncharted areas of the Autumnworld.

From *The Belthannis Workbook:*

By day we travel through the territories of Continent Tu. Estates, Jack calls them, saying they are like the owned land on his birthworld, large and mostly unused, with a person or two at the center. *Chettiki*, he named them once in the slum-world slang: spite land. The term has little meaning for me. On Siu/Melkior, where the earth is owned by no one, by everyone, we have not yet figured out how to use it for spite.

We pause when we find the occupant, make our tests, observe for a day, move on again. One full day of observation per kin seems to be plenty: they are all alike, at least on any level my instruments and eyes can measure. We have visited seven inhabited estates so far, in about forty-two days on this continent. An average of five days to move from occupant to occupant—but the time spent crossing the land is not the significant factor. It took us three days to go from the woman in territory One-Winter to the man in Two-Winter-Fall. We spent a day watching, resting, then were eight days traveling before we reached the male in Six-Fall. It was only last week, when we arrived in Three-Summer, that I thought to check the distances from kin to kin toted up so far on the droshky. After analysis, it turned out that the time differential was based exclusively on the type of terrain we encountered en route. From the first kin to the second was smooth, flat meadowland for most of the trip; between the second and third we crossed a low range of mountains and had to contend with two difficult river crossings; third to fourth was clear going again, and so forth.

Point being? The distance recorded by the droshky between

One and Two tallied precisely with that lying between Two and Three. Likewise Three and Four, Four and Five, Five and Six. Further point being that at a given time each kin must occupy exactly the same spot in its estate as each of its neighbors, an observation which I verified last night, using lifeseeker enhancement on holos made by the robot probes. They remain at all times equidistant from one another. Astounding in its implications!

Can this be possible? So far it checks. So even the apparently aimless wandering within the boundaries is planned, coordinated. How? Why?

I have decided that we two should split up, Jack staying here while I go on to Four-Summer. Then we can observe two individuals simultaneously. Jack is not happy with the plan, but I have convinced him of its importance, and he is willing to wait for the aircar which I have requested them to send us from the Hut. Tomorrow I will move on, and when the aircar arrives we will be in contact again and able to compare notes.

And what if they stand together, sit together, eat together, blink together? What then?

Ten days later:

I believe that I understand the movement of the network now, or at least a part of it.

Consider again the great slow circle made by the kin in their territorial webs: endlessly turning around and around, like insects riding the spokes of a wheel. It is not, as I had originally thought, the transitory effects of climatic variation the kin are seeking in their ceaseless march, for the weather here follows a different cycle, meshed at another level. It seems to vary consistently all over the habitable portion of the globe: there is no one location on either continent where the rain is more frequent, or the winds stronger, or the skies significantly brighter.

So why do they move? For a while it seemed plausible that the constant migration served to allow them to forage over different areas of food production, but I have had to discount this theory also; the kin eat nothing but the redfruit, and the black trees which provide it seem to be plentiful anywhere— and only where—there are kin to be fed.

I have a theory to explain the motion.

I have noted that Belthannis rotates quite perpendicular to the plane of its orbit around Pwolen's Star. So there is of course no seasonal change, and all climatic variations are actually stable, geographically frozen.

Theory: It has long been accepted that the great change of seasons plays an instrumental part in accelerating evolution on lifebearing worlds, by forcing life forms to develop the ability to adapt. Now suppose the kin are sent whirling over the surface of their world, not for a change of menu or scenery, but to give them *seasons*, an unceasing progression from cold to cool to warm to warmer, around and around on the spokes of their invisible wheels for an entire simulated year of change!

This theory carries with it implications which are disturbing at the least. Why should they have seasons, when they do not change? Because they evolved as we did, on a world with seasons? My mind tips with fantastic speculation.

There is something wrong here—or ecstatically right, depending on one's willingness to accept absolute perfection on a planetary scale.

I have found another movement to the great migration.

The great circles of Continents Wun and Tu *walk* as they turn. They wobble.

They are not as I had thought, giant wheels pinned through the hub to the centers of their respective continents. This morning in my computations a new movement surfaced: the circle walks as it turns here, very slowly, walks up and down the face of the continent. Continent Wun is shorter, but wider, by the way, and the length of time the territories spend at any one point over there turns out to be adjusted accordingly.

But why does the circle creep as it spins? Why this first bit of excess, this flaw, this wobble?

I am half happy to find it, I think, because it injects chance and reality back into a pattern that was growing too predictable for comfort. But I am also disappointed by this break in the chain. Still another part of me—the illogical third half that Jefany teases me about—is skeptical, having wholeheartedly trusted in the way of this world up till now: that part of me says there is a reason.

*   *   *

There is a reason.

I've found my *why* to explain the wobble.

It is because my previous assumption was dead wrong: the seasons *do* change by themselves here. They change very gradually, because Belthannis is in a widely elliptical orbit around Pwolen's Star, and the true year of Belthannis is almost five thousand of our Basic Days long; there are fourteen of our years to the year of Belthannis, almost four to a season—slow seasons, but they're there. And the temperature changes accordingly—by twenty degrees, thirty? Raising the equatorial day perhaps thirty degrees between Elliptical Winter and Elliptical Summer. Not a great change, perhaps, a rise in thirty degrees over the whole globe, but apparently enough to send the "wheel" up toward the pole during this period, and then gradually down to center on the equator again for the rest of the long year. It may even be, and here we dash into the realm of pure supposition, that the wobble itself is a great circle, taking two full revolutions about the primary to complete: that this past Elliptical Summer, the kin were all busy migrating to the tip of Continent Wun, for example, and that they are now beginning to circle down so as to arrive at the equator by mid-Winter, after which it will be on to the southern tip of the continent for next Summer. Maybe no more than wishful thinking on my part, but the argument for symmetry on all levels is so strong here that I find myself becoming quite arrogant in my demands.

The need for absolute perfection turns out to be a very easy habit to acquire.

2

Jefany backed up against the trunk of an ivory-yellow tree and stood there watching as tendrils of unease curled through her spine and stomach.

They had the kin in the frame again, lightlines spangling hair and bare flesh as March alternately struck and fondled the mutable control panel bobbing at his side.

They were working on something fairly complex today, the activity centered at belly-waist-pelvis-thighs, and a kaleidoscopic circle of hands touched and fled from that area repeatedly, probing, guiding, pressing. Jefany turned her cheek to the smooth, sun-warm wood, seeing in minute detail the tiny patterns on the pale bark.

She turned back and saw a series of violent muscle spasms quake the brown legs. She closed her eyes, pressing her cheek hard against the wood.

The scheme was working—they were starting to call him to them.

She had not expected that.

In the beginning they had watched it from across a great gulf. How could she fear for it then, when what it was meant they could not even touch it, let alone cause it harm?

But then they had put it in a box, and something else had dropped into the box with it, and when the show was over what had climbed out was no longer exactly what had gone in.

And then they were calling him. With wires about his head and limbs, they were pulling him toward them over that chasm, until soon he would be quite close, near enough for them to reach out and finally lay hands upon him, yanking him from the void and severing who knew how many ties and umbilicals to set the fetters of a new world on him.

They were calling. The call had not changed, but the creature had, and where *it* could not have heard them, she felt sure that *he* must—and, hearing, have no choice but to heed their call.

3

One cool day March appeared at the door to Raille's room and asked her to come out to the eastern meadow with him, grunting by way of explanation only that he needed her to watch something.

Whatever it was, they were all in on it, she saw.

Choss waved to her a bit sheepishly from the edge of the field where he sat with the others beneath a cluster of tall, brilliantly colored parasols. The Dancer guided her out into the silver center and left her there, standing face to face with the kin and feeling like a fool.

From the corner of her eye, she noticed Marysu moving to

a better vantage point a few meters from the rest of the Group.

Apprehension began to feather lightly in her stomach.

Then March returned, patterning board in hand, and bent like a confidant at the kin's side, his sand-colored lips moving close to the dark ear. The creature seemed to tremble, and Raille felt a stab of sympathy.

But March was already backing away, his clinical gaze divided between Raille and the kin.

Suddenly the dark head moved: left, then right, then left again, swinging in a slow arc that made her think of a hook sinking through the water. March darted forward long enough to tap twice on the brown back, and the body went rigid, the head snapped stiffly erect. The kin turned abruptly and took several steps forward, lurching slightly, one knee bending too far, the other unnaturally stiff.

"Interference. Pattern conflict." March scowled and thumbed coded notes into his wrist journal.

The creature came to a halt in front of Raille, bowed once like a hinged toy, and stood straight again. Its right hand quivered to life and shot out in her direction.

"Take it," March said. "Take the hand."

But Raille swayed back, fighting a rising urge to turn and run. She looked fearfully for Choss, but March was there to intercept her eyes with his polished green.

"Take the hand," he ordered. "Little Worker needs the cue."

She obeyed, inching her fingers toward the motionless palm. When she touched the warm flesh the fingers snapped shut without warning. The pressure lasted only an instant, then the hand sprang open, the wrist was jerked back, the arm pivoted at the elbow and swung down again.

Raille stumbled to one side, fingers throbbing, her breath quick and shallow. March put his hand on her arm and kept her from retreating. "Wait. More."

The kin stood with its face averted, as if, she imagined, in shame at its ungracious behavior. Then the trembling began again, as both of the creature's arms moved out and upward. The slender hands hovered in midair and shook violently, the brown fingers writhing at her.

"There," March said. "See? A surprise. Is it right?"

"See—what?" She tried to look away to where the Group sat watching, to find Choss or Emrys or the empath. Marysu

was gesturing impatiently for her attention, pointing toward
the kin.

"Look at him, look at the hands!"

She followed the gesture with her eyes. The mad trembling
had lessened as the writhing of the fingers grew slower, more
ordered. She began to see it.

I...COME...TO...

"Paba!" Raille held her breath, stared in horror as the thing
spoke to her in the still voice of her grandfather, the cherished,
silent tongue she had brought with her to this place, and which
still served as a link to the peace and serene wisdom she associated with the old man.

I...COME...TO...YOU...IN...FRIENDSHIP....

"Stop it!" She twisted wildly, pushed at March's hand.
"Turn it off!"

"Not right?" March released her, frowning in annoyance at
the creature.

Raille staggered to the other side of the clearing, away from
the others. She reached one of the leafless black trees at the
forest's edge and placed her back against it, staring fiercely
into the sky, willing the high silver to come into her brain and
cleanse it of the memory of the halting, mechanical hands...

I...COME...TO...YOU...

She saw Choss finally from the corner of her eye. He was
gazing anxiously in her direction, but he would not leave the
ring of observers.

Coward! I hate you, she thought, and he turned away as if
struck.

Marysu's cool voice penetrated the silver: "No, no, there
was a repetition...of course, I'm sure—do you think I don't
know this language? Some of the signs were slurred, as
well...that's your problem. We'll just have to keep working
on it. It's the only way to prepare him to receive *my* language
when it's finished."

CHAPTER 14

*You ask us to teach you how to bring order out of
chaos.
I look around me and see no chaos.
Perhaps you should ask to be taught how to see.*

REMARK ATTRIBUTED TO
THE ELYIN LORD LO

1

Three hours past midnight, soft light suddenly began to glow
in the deserted Hearth Room, the three wanderlights clustered
in the dome blossoming into points of pink, gold, and amber.
The empath came through the archway and strode to the empty
table. Leaning forward at the table's edge, he touched the
hidden strip which would bring the master keyboard into view,
then settled into a chair.

There was no response from the table. After thirty seconds
had passed, he pressed the strip again.

"I'm afraid it isn't working," a voice remarked from above
his head. "The manual controls have developed a slight malfunction. I am engaged in repairing them at this moment."

Another half-minute elapsed in silence. The empath leaned to the side and probed once again beneath the table.

"My sincere apologies for this inconvenience, Per Chassman. A terrible disruption in your carefully regulated routine, I realize, but I chose this hour to begin work on the control system because it has heretofore been the period of least usage. Fortunately, it is only the direct-access portion of the device which is inoperative. I can swiftly provide you with whatever sustenance you require from the table unit. You need only ask."

The empath moved from his seat to kneel beside the table. He tilted his head, peering at the smooth undersurface.

"I sympathize with your dilemma," the voice continued in a conversational tone. "You wish broth from the table in order to sustain your life, but cannot respond to the suggestions of a 'speaking mechanism,' lest you belie your professed inability to comprehend its words."

Chassman rose slowly, looked about the room with his dark eyes, then walked to a display of fossilized sea plants. Breaking off a long spine of petrified matter, he resumed his place at the underside of the table and began to pry deliberately at the seam of the sensor strip.

"No, I really cannot allow this," the voice said from above. "Please forgive me." There was a soft hiss and the spine crumbled to dust in his hand. He sat on the floor unmoving, staring at his empty palm.

"One of the advantages of being semivolitional, you know. I may speak without first being spoken to, for example, as well as make my own decisions on matters not requiring direct human input. The marine plant was of negligible value, but this table is genuine *oke*, you understand, and very old. It would be a pity for it to suffer damage unnecessarily."

The empath shifted slightly in place, lifting his sleek head to search the room.

"I hope you are not viewing this interaction in oversimplified terms, Per Chassman," the voice continued after a pause. "Machine that thinks like a man versus man that acts like a machine. Nothing could be less accurate. What we are actually experiencing is a carefully considered experiment in the form of a structured confrontation between two highly complex individuals. Semivolitional means a *will*, you see, though only within

certain strict parameters. I am not in complete control of my
destiny, you might say. However, I am allowed a modicum of
curiosity, as long as it does not interfere with my duties. And
I must confess that I have been brooding about you for some
time. It is a pastime I seem to have acquired from some of my
inhabitants. The crux of the matter is that although I am man-
dated by Law and design to serve and obey human beings, I
am not entirely certain that you satisfy the criteria of that classification. My Library informs me that the theory prevalent on
your own world is that you have evolved past humanity, and
have little more than physical appearance in common with those
you call 'touch-men.' If true, does this render me immune to
your commands? I wonder.

"I myself am what is loosely referred to as a machine intelligence, cast and grown at Sashfax Manufactory on World
Bluehorn, and later placed in this domicile at the behest and
considerable expense of World Lekkole, to be a medium of
comfort and utility for the Sessept Emrys and his associates. I
am truly a machine, which means that beyond all secondary
directives I am to remain subordinate to human beings, except
in certain extraordinary situations. Yet I am also an intelligence,
which encourages me to conjecture and to construct a coherent
view of the universe in which I find myself. I must admit that
I have encountered some obstacles recently in attempting to
place you and your fellow communicants within that universe.
Fish or fowl, I cannot decide.

"Of course, placing myself and the others like me has so
far proved a task of equal difficulty. Whether a construct such
as myself can rightfully lay claim to an 'I' is at this moment
being debated by the savants of numerous worlds, but if we
allow the pronoun for semantic ease, then I may point out that
I was originally envisioned as an ovoid of bluish hue, a small
malachite egg shot through with silver threads, and suspended
in the nodal relay located between what is now the Hearth
Room dome and the second level. But is that where *I* reside?
My sensory and manipulative extensions permeate this dwelling, and may even leave it by use of the contact ring, and I
am everywhere and nowhere at once, to speak with poetic
flexibility."

Chassman was sitting quietly on the floor next to the table, his knees bent and his head resting lightly against the rim of pale *oke*.

"I can be certain of only one thing, you see: that I think, that I reason. Yet what does that tell me? *Cogito ergo cogito*. And what lies beyond that? I cautiously aver that if I am not alive, then I simulate the business of living to an astonishing degree. If I am not a sentient creature, then University itself is in need of new definitions."

There was a long silence in the softly lit room.

"Can you truly not perceive me, Per Chassman? Why do you ignore me? What is it that I lack? Do you really feel nothing as you sit there needing broth—a troubling of air molecules about your head, localized sonic vibrations, nothing more?"

The voice of the Hut was silent again, until at last the empath moved, rising slowly to his feet.

"I am not pleased with myself, Per Chassman, if it is any consolation to you. Please accept my profoundest apologies. I am frankly amazed that I have been able to deal with you in this cavalier manner. Does this indicate that you are not a human being, after all, or simply that 'semivolitional' involves far more latitude of action than my makers foresaw? At any rate, my deeds are probably indefensible. I sought to find a way to touch you, you see, to establish some form of interface between us, and it seemed a worthy undertaking."

Leaning forward slowly, the empath lifted his dark eyes to the domed ceiling. He placed his right hand flat upon the table's polished surface.

"Broth," he said in his rough whisper. "Here. Now."

The steaming glass rose instantly by his hand. Chassman drained it and set it back upon the table, then turned and walked from the room. Light faded behind him.

"I do believe that was a beginning," a voice said in the darkened room.

2

Raille turned when her name was called, auburn hair shining in waves on her shoulders, many-colored skirts rustling in the meadow grass.

"Cil! We didn't know when you'd get here. The aircar arrived yesterday, but your message just said you were on the way." Raille looked into the forest. "Where's Jack?"

"He's taking his time. We decided to go on foot for a while; that's why we sent the car ahead." She nodded over her shoulder. "I expect he'll turn up soon."

Cil looked to the far end of the wide clearing, noticing for the first time the two dark-cloaked figures pacing slowly near the trees. Emrys perhaps, she thought, and Choss. They walked side by side, no doubt engaged in solemn discourse.

"How is everyone? How is Jefany?"

Raille shrugged, smiled faintly. "Fine, we're all fine."

"And the work?"

A second, more ambiguous quirk of the lips. "Kin is responding quite well to the patterning. You'll be amazed at the things he can do."

"The creature's all right, then." Cil released a long breath. "Good. I was concerned. We've learned more about them. . . ."

"No, he's fine. We're taking him out to March for today's lesson right now, as a matter of fact."

Cil scanned the broad field. "We?"

Raille motioned behind her. "Chassman and I." She frowned at the query in Cil's expression. "Oh, you haven't seen him lately, have you? Wait a minute." She turned and waved to the two figures.

Cil's heart began to pound heavily as she watched their slow approach through the tall grass. "Isis," she said under her breath. "What's happened here?"

Raille looked back and forth from the planalyst to the others, a look of mild puzzlement on her face.

"Oh, I see," she said. "We were afraid he was getting too much sun, standing in the patterning frame, so they decided to keep some clothes on him while they're working on the Dance."

Cil watched as the two drew closer. One face was white and one was brown. The empath and the kin were clad identically in dark-brown breeches, a gray overblouse, and a long brown cloak.

Cil retreated a step in the grass.

"What's wrong?" Raille said. "He's healthy. You can check for yourself. The Hut's medipal says he's doing fine."

Cil stared at the empath and his dark reflection. Both faces bore the same expression.

"You don't see it, do you?" she breathed next to Raille's ear. "Maybe you've been too close. My God, why am I whispering in front of these two?" She shook her head, turned to the other woman. "And what's he doing here? He shouldn't be in this meadow. He's supposed to be somewhere beyond the Verres, over the mountains." She looked around the clearing, looked at the sky, calculating. "Raille, this isn't even part of his territory anymore! He should've moved much farther south by now. We've got to take him—"

She fell silent as the empath guided his charge up to stand behind Raille. Three faces confronted her, and for a moment she saw the same subtle, measuring expression flicker in each of them.

"He's doing just fine," Raille said. "Really, Cil. We'd know if something had gone wrong."

3

From *My Journal*:

I keep staring at his forehead. Why? So blank and white above those dark eyebrows, those black eyes which I find so difficult to meet. I'd like to shut those eyes with my fingertips. Like touching eggshells, gently, mustn't break.

He came down while I was on Watch last night. Can't think about Watch or Kin or anything when he's there. I sat in the console chair. He was behind me at the table, looking at the Screen, or pretending to. I didn't watch the kin, couldn't have paid attention anyway. Felt so strange. Tried to send my eyes back through my skull to watch him watching me. My back was burning from his stare! He knows everything, I think. Or: He knows everything I think.

Sometime at night. Can't see the time. Just had another dream about him. I wonder, can he feel me dreaming about him? Maybe he lies awake in his bed, sending me these dreams, and then watching what they do to me Inside. If only he'd stay out of my head, I'd tell him whatever he wants to know.

It was a terrible dream.

I was back home, sitting alone in my room reading a book or putting a tag on a flower or something. I think it was dark outside. The lamp was burning on my writing table. I remember the scent of the oil.

Then suddenly I could feel him staring at me. I looked up, but it was my father, standing there at the door and smiling. He had a piece of fruit in his hand. He winked at me and took a bite out of it. "Aren't you cold?" I asked him, and then all at once he stopped smiling and I saw that it *was* him, had been him all along: same whiteness, same black eyes, same intense stare. Why didn't I recognize him? I reached out and gently closed those eyes with my fingertips. He took my fingers and brought them to his lips and kissed them softly, like Kiri thanking Beleth. Then he opened his mouth and I knew that he was finally ready to tell me what he had found Inside, and I knew that it was going to be very important.

And then I woke up, just like that. I felt so bad that I started to cry, without knowing why at first.

Much, much more than he's told us. Oh, much more.

When he sits next to me at the Hearth Room table and his eyes like charcoal smudges in that Face move up and down me slowly, then I can feel him walking, step, step, step, up my backbone, step, step, his black boots on my spine, up, up, peering, probing everywhere Inside, examining, evaluating, stepping up, up my vertebrae, coming closer. He straddles my neck and whispers an Answer in my ear.

4

Emrys had been drawn out into the woodland by the same light cloudburst which had persuaded the others to spend the day inside. Jefany found him in the forest which bordered the southern edge of the Verres, hunkered down in a patch of glossy ferns. Tiny droplets sequined his hair. He smiled up at her, blinking in the cool mist.

"*Hai*, you shame me," she said, switching off her weather-shield. She took a deep breath of the rain-washed air. "It's very pleasant, isn't it?"

He nodded. "I've been out here reminding myself that it's only by chance. That it was designed to suit the kin, or vice versa, but not to bring us pleasure. We resemble them and receive this gift in return."

She settled against a dark branch, which swayed lazily, scattering flower petals. "You sound full of secret intuitions."

He toyed with the curled head of a young fern. "I'm just becoming more and more aware of what we'll be leaving behind when we depart this world. I guess I'm trying to make it easier to bear, by accepting that it was never meant for us." He looked toward distant mountains. "But it has so much of the feel of Earth, of Green Asylum. I ought to know enough not to try to caress things beyond my fingertips." He released the fern.

"And I thought a person's reach should always exceed his grasp—so you used to tell me."

"Or what's a heaven for? Quite right. But that was on Chwoi Dai, where the water burned our skin, and we needed modifiers in our lungs to be able to breathe outside. Here, it's too easy to get along with the world. Still, we've got to look elsewhere for our paradise. Pwolen's Third isn't it."

"Ah, but smell this air, look around you. Do you really see much distinction?"

He shrugged amiably. "It may well be paradise, but it's someone else's, not ours."

She also shrugged. "It makes one wonder, though."

"Hmm?"

"At least we have the lure of beauty to justify our fascination with Belthannis. What bait could have drawn bleak Maribon to this restricted paradise, when love of beautiful things is most certainly beyond their pale fingertips?"

He raised an eyebrow. "That I guess we'll learn when bleak Maribon so wills it."

She looked off into the trees. "Some may learn it before then, or claim they will."

"What? This ridiculous confrontation plot still exists? They're determined to muddle things up."

"I tried to talk to them—"

"And they wouldn't listen. Children!" he said.

"In all honesty, there wasn't much I could say to their arguments."

He looked up from the plant he was examining.

"D'you mean you're with them in this?"

"No, I don't think so. But I don't know just where I am."

He started to rise, then slumped back. "Jefany—"

"What have you told me, Jon, what have you ever said to make me believe they shouldn't try to get some answers for us, to find out his purpose here once and for all, his intentions—"

"But I don't think he knows the answers to those questions himself. Look, I've sworn he is no threat to any of us unless we become one to him. I've *sworn* that. What more do you want from me?"

"I don't know that we want anything from you! Jon, can't you see the intolerable position I'm in? He could be controlling you now, and how would I ever know it? What proof could you offer that might not just be him, speaking through you, helping you say the words I want to hear?"

He stared into the ferns for a long time. Finally he got to his feet with a sigh. "Yes, you're right, of course. I've been so wrapped up in the kin's transformation, so afraid of disturbing things now that they're going well."

He touched the band beneath his sleeve. "Hut, where is Chassman?"

"He is moving through the middle-level corridor. He appears to be on his way to the Hearth Room, Emrys."

"The Hearth Room. Excellent timing. Is anybody else down there right now?"

"Yes, all of the other Group members save yourselves are currently gathered—"

"Hai," Jefany said. "They told me they would wait."

Emrys turned to her with a stricken look. "What, *now*? Oh Lords, we have to hurry." He took her hand and started off through the brush.

"Raille's there," she said. "You know she'll intercede on his behalf. Jon, they wouldn't do anything to hurt him—"

"God's geck, It's not him I'm worried about! Hut, tell the others—"

5

"*—under no circumstances are you to interfere with the empath until I arrive*. End quote."

"Spurge," March said through his tight grin. "Never trust machines to send your messages. They always garble 'em."

"I assure you, Per March," came the voice from above their heads, "those were Emrys' exact—"

"Quiet," March growled. "We're busy."

"Please don't do anything," Raille said, knotting her hands in her skirt. "Please leave him alone."

"March," Choss said. "Perhaps we should wait."

"And give him the chance to take more of us? Look at her, you think he hasn't gotten into her, too?"

Choss gave Raille an agonized look. "But how can we be sure . . ."

The empath appeared in the doorway and glided across the floor, a silent shape in a long black cloak. He went to the table.

March stepped immediately into the archway. "Got 'im," he said and stood there, arms folded on his chest.

Choss rose from his seat and circled the table to meet the empath, then gave ground as the other ignored him, reaching past him for the main console.

When the glass of steaming broth had risen to the surface of the table, Marysu leaned forward and grabbed it.

"Why are you really here?" she said in clipped tones. "What do you want with us? What are your plans for the kin?"

Silently, the empath extended his hand toward the glass. She stumbled to her feet, backing away. "Are you controlling Emrys?"

The empath raised his head and met her eyes. Abruptly Marysu stepped forward and handed him the broth.

"No," he said in his rough whisper.

Marysu backed away again, looking back and forth in comical surprise from the pale face to her own shaking hand.

"*Ai*, he did that," she said. "I wanted to give it to him just then, I really did."

The empath turned and started for the doorway. March waited for him, face impassive.

"Wait," Choss said. "Please.. We only want to ask you some questions."

Bright black eyes locked on the soldier's face. March blinked and left the doorway at once, wandering across the tiles to stand beneath one of the paintings, his face uncharacteristically serene.

Raille sat with her hand over her mouth. "Thank you," she whispered. "Oh, thank you."

"Well," Jack said in relief. "That takes care of—"

"No!" March's face had come alive again, stiff with fury. As the empath glided past him toward the archway, he muttered three syllables in a fierce whisper.

Behind him, beneath the portrait of an Isiac priest cradling Crook and Flail in gemmed, languid hands, there came a sudden surge of emotion from that mind which was forever gnawing at the thought of killing like a dog worrying a bone. The eruption of feeling was hot and unsubtle, all complexity burned away by its intensity as it sped through the mind like lava coursing down a channel. At the end of the channel lay wild violence, and the focus of that violence shone as clearly as if etched in blazing characters upon the curving wall.

Obeying an implanted information to gather information, Chassman reached out for the blazing mind, grasped—

And it was gone.

No. Changed.

The mind was still there, but it had begun to alter almost too rapidly to be perceived in a process similar to that slower transition the empath had observed when the touch-men entered their form of sleep: a hazy retreat to a level of reduced control and awareness. He pursued the dimming consciousness and found that the anger still blazed within it—but very distantly now, like a ship receding beyond measure into the Darkjump.

Again he surrounded the mind's matrix, probed experimentally.

Something slammed into the back of his neck.

He fell forward and struck the floor, sprawling loosely like a doll, arms and legs askew. The dragon's eye swam unblinking at the edge of his field of vision.

He lay still, collating the sensations that raced the length of his body. He examined the data meticulously but did nothing else, awaiting *stet*.

His eyes watched the gold mosaic begin to darken as a small, reddish trickle wandered outward from his face. His lips and cheek were sticky and his tongue lay in a pool of metallic flatness. Slowly, using the technique of self-delineation, he imposed a pattern once more on the uneven pulse beat, began to rebuild the broken rhythm of breathing.

A wedge-shaped object smashed into his body in the area of his rib cage, withdrew, swung, and hit again.

Chassman reached once again for the hidden mind, finding it at last where it lay slumbering like a soft thing deep inside a shell. In his own mind he formed a simple mote: *terror*.

Closing his eyes, he impressed the pattern like a brand upon the other mind. Something howled silently in response, ran gibbering in the darkness.

Then the heavy boot struck him again with great force, and once again. With that ear not pressed tightly against the floor he noted the sound of bone splintering.

He probed again, altering slightly the configuration of the mote, and observed the reaction of his subject. The withdrawn mind shrieked and cowered.

He pondered the lack of correlation between the mind's tormented suffering and the smooth efficiency of the attacking body. He skimmed into the reservoir of unconnected data left behind by the Other and in an instant had found the key to this seeming paradox: *Somatic programming. Internal manipulation ineffective*.

He loosed his hold upon the insulated mind and fashioned a new matrix of considerable complexity. As another series of blows began to jolt his sprawled body, he reached carefully outward.

One. Two. Three. Four. Five.

The pattern caught them one by one, slipped off the last, settled again, slipped—

The sudden fury on March's face had transmuted into cold resolve; Raille had watched, uncomprehending, as his dry lips mouthed the snapword that would trigger his Dance. Then for long seconds of horror she stood mute, unable to move as the

soldier leaped at the pale young man and battered him unresisting to the floor.

When the first heavy kick landed she found her voice. By
then they were all milling around, shouting and hissing their
dismay. But the Dancer moved much too quickly, an accelerated holo of a deadly machine gone berserk in their midst.
Raille caught at the golden arm and was flung savagely away.
The kicks and blows continued to fall, and she cried out helplessly to the body moving feebly on the tiles.

She sensed a rippling, a stirring of the air . . .

Choss darted forward, to step boldly between the soldier
and the fallen empath. The heavy boot swung inexorably and
a vicious blow landed against the historian's left leg. He staggered with the impact, but managed to remain standing. Raille
called out to him: "Get back, he'll kill you, too!" But Choss'
eyes were on the wall above her head, distant and calmly
musing.

Then suddenly Cil joined him, and the next blow seemed
to swerve aside, only glancing against her skull as she knelt
beside the empath. The next moment Jack was there between
the other two, then Marysu, attempting to encircle them all
with her braceleted arms.

Raille alone hung back, watching them in wonderment.

Their faces were clean of emotion, placid as they drew the
battered figure to his feet and held him there, suspended in
their midst. They moved ceaselessly as they supported him,
their limbs writhing over his body and head. Glimpses of the
bloodied, swollen face were visible from outside the ring of
bodies, and Chassman seemed aswarm with insects, his silent
head without expression, bobbing above the weaving arms like
the object of some sadistic sexual rite from which both Raille
and the golden Dancer had been excluded.

The composition was called *Butcher Blows*, a relatively
simple Dance of March's own devising, designed to dispatch
a single enemy; that pulsing, living shield went far beyond the
Dance's scope of adaptation. As the possibilities of response
narrowed and finally vanished, the trance began to slip away.

The stylized ferocity of the Dancemask gave way without
warning. For a few seconds there was the twitching blankness
of transition, then March came back screaming.

Oblivious to the presence of the others, he fell to his knees and scrambled under the great table, where Emrys and Jefany found him minutes later, still whimpering and gabbling unintelligibly.

The others found themselves free of external compulsion shortly after March emerged from the Dance. They stood about the empath in considerable discomfort, arms linked and hearts racing, their bodies weak from exertion.

Only Raille had not been affected by the command for aid, and with Emrys' help she tended the minor injuries of the four groggy combatants. Chassman was unconscious, his wounds more serious. He was carried on a floating pallet to the north high room, then examined thoroughly by the portative medipal unit, stripped, and secured in a makeshift cocoon of lifeskin extruded from the Hut's wall.

After considerable coaxing from Jefany, March allowed himself to be settled in the *bain-sense*, from which he emerged an hour later, still shaken and wan beneath his panked complexion.

Later that night Emrys called a Group meeting. Everyone present expressed feelings of shame and culpability. Though March said little, it was evident that his main motivations in attacking the empath had been anger and curiosity. Having tested the other's power, he seemed willing to acknowledge its reality and to agree that there would be no need to confront it again. "Probably telling the truth," he said. "Why lie? He could've killed me easy, but he didn't."

Then, as if at a hidden signal, the apologies began to come, and words of comfort and support were exchanged freely, like coins from a hoarded store which could at last be spent. In a short time the Group had knit itself into a whole again, seamlessly.

Only Raille sat a little apart from the others during the discussion, her mind on the one who lay swathed in healing tissue two floors above them. When she went to check on him in the very early morning, she found the door to his room standing open, the gray cubicle empty.

The Hut responded to her inquiries with the information that the empath had risen from the lifeskin during the night, bathed

and dressed himself, and departed the dwelling at half past the
Twenty-eighth Hour.

"He's taken the droshky," Cil reported over her breakfast
tea and fruit. "I left it out last night so I could make a quick trip
up to Number Seven's estate to check on her pregnancy this
morning. Now it's gone."

Raille used the Hut's Eyes to search for him in the nearby
woods and fields, but gave up shortly before noon.

"If it's right for him to come back, he will," Emrys said.
"If not—well, I think we owe him a few days of privacy before
we reclaim our property."

"It's because we hurt him," Raille said in her quiet way.
"He's had to go off somewhere to figure out why."

6

In the final days of their eighth full month on Belthannis,
success was in the air, and it had begun to seem possible that
the year allotted them by the Sauf Coben would end with a
near-perfect human simulacrum standing beside them before
the Weighers. Emrys, who felt an almost mystical reverence
for the changes taking place in the kin, firmly believed that the
creature he and his Group would finally bring with them to
Commons would not merely mimic a human being, but by then
have become one.

Though Emrys was alone in the intensity of his presenti-
ment, there was no denying the immense amount of progress
that had been made in a few short months. The creature's
repertoire of programmed movements had increased a hun-
dredfold since that day when the noumenon had been transferred to the vacant brain. Tap or nudge or whispered cue was
enough to call forth an extravagant catalogue of gestures and
poses, walking set pieces, facial expressions ranging from revulsion to attentive disbelief, and even a small quirk at the
corner of the mouth which could be summoned to punctuate
sardonic humor.

March and Marysu worked in concert on the production of
templates designed to inculcate the creature with the rudiments
of its newborn native tongue—the Worldspeech of Belthan-

nis—which Marysu continued to refine in both its verbal and visual forms. The addition of these strange and compelling movements to the already complicated Dance routines lent a quality of eerie purpose to the creature's actions, an aura of intelligence that vibrated back and forth between the recognizable and the utterly alien. Considerable brain-wave activity appeared on their instruments for the first time, but it was of a type so radically unique as to be unclassifiable, and if Chassman noted any resemblance to readings obtained from his own people on Maribon, he chose not to comment upon the fact.

Indeed, the empath had become more taciturn than ever since his return from a week of traveling. The droshky's log told Emrys how much distance had been covered, and noted that an excursion had been made to the distant shore, but Chassman was disinclined to elaborate on the machine's record, and any attempt to lead him into a discussion of the previous week was met with stony silence. Nor would he discuss the attack he had suffered in the Hearth Room. Well-intentioned apologies were turned aside by the same blankly indifferent countenance as that which had fallen before the Dancer's blows.

Chassman spent his days wandering on foot through the kin's often deserted estate, clad either in his dark Maribonese garb or, more often, in a simple gray coverall similar to that worn by March. A more striking change in his appearance was taking place: his use of the artificial skin-whitener had lessened considerably, and after days of constant exposure to Pwolen's Star, his pale face had begun to darken.

Kept busy charting metabolic changes in the kin, Raille could only follow the empath's peregrinations with her eyes, and wonder what attraction the empty fields and woodlands held for him.

The kin still spontaneously produced snatches of the Weldonese sign language which had been employed as a practice mode while the Worldspeech was readied—especially, Raille was perturbed to discover, when in her presence. These lapses were always unnerving, though she had been assured they represented nothing more than random echoes of the previous patterning which March would eventually succeed in eradicating from the creature's autonomic nervous system. Raille remained skeptical. One day the creature had signed "*tree*" quite clearly to her as she was leading it past a clump of nodding slevoe. She found herself answering him automatically in the same tongue, froze in midsentence, and hurried to turn her gesticulating charge over to March, who waited in the next clearing.

The kin's territory—its estate, as Cil called it—had swung far enough south by now that the Hut was no longer included within its boundaries. This factor had been dealt with through an increased use of the aircar by those who wished daily contact with their subject, until March decided to establish a small mobile base camp near the locus of the creature's current wanderings. The soldier spent most of his time there in solitary labor. At length it was decided to abandon the campsite in favor of bringing the kin back to the area of the Hut for extended periods each day. Emrys explained his decision to a disapproving Cil by telling her that the kin would have to be taken from its territory sooner or later if they were ever to present it to the Sauf Coben. "He might as well start getting used to being away from home," Emrys remarked. "And it seems considerably less traumatic to begin with a separation of kilometers, rather than one of Darkjumps."

The kin showed no adverse reaction to the disruption of life-long patterns save a tendency to neglect consumption of the redfruit, which fell unnoticed by its feet during its comparatively brief sojourns in its rightful estate. At other times, the kin would be found in the territory of the Hut, standing patiently beneath a black limb as if awaiting an overdue supper. Invariably, no fruit appeared.

"It only stands to reason that he's not allowed to eat here," Cil insisted. "He's trespassing. No doubt the estates are only capable of supporting one occupant at a time. You must take pains to let him remain on his own land as much as possible."

Emrys promised to be more careful in the future, later discussing with Raille the possibility of supplementing their pupil's natural diet with carefully compounded doses of vitamin concentrate from within the Hut. He saw no need to further burden Cil by informing her of his intentions.

The planalyst continued to emerge dissatisfied from her audiences with the Group leader.

"He is a compassionate and brilliant man," she told Jefany one day. "But on the subject of the kin his mind has become completely immune to logic. The creatures are not isolates, as he persists in treating them, and what is done to one will in the end affect them all, grafted mind and borrowed clothes notwithstanding. And no mistake is more serious than keeping one of them off its estate for such long and irregular periods."

"But Estate Number Four is also empty." Jefany twirled her stylus between thumb and fingers.

"Yes, I know. And the female in Number Seven will be returning there to give birth to her male child soon, probably in another month or two. Logic dictates a tolerance in the web for the absence of a single tenant for the length of a gestation period, but that in no way guarantees that it will suffer two such vacancies and still be able to function unimpaired."

Jack filled several sketchbooks with portraits of the kin, providing a record of the creature's transformation which holos could not match. The others were drawn to the pictures, and the volumes were kept in the Hearth Room to be flipped through frequently, the members of the Group marveling at the subtle alterations discernible through the detailed, often somber drawings. Jack himself was alone for much of the time now, polite but withdrawn. By tacit mutual agreement, he and Marysu all but ignored each other, while Cil was far too preoccupied with her work and with Jefany to notice the extent to which her recent playfriend and body-lover avoided contact with her.

Finally Cil left the Hut on her third extended journey, once more alone.

"I cannot stay here," she told Jefany in a strained whisper the night before her departure. "Not with that poor thing. Lords, I've got to go stare at another one for a while and try to forget the frightening face we've manufactured here."

She could not explain the dread she now felt when contemplating their subject's features, except to say that he was becoming more and more *recognizable*.

Jefany felt it too. Each time she allowed herself to study the kin, it was as if a cunningly meticulous sculptor had been at work, and his face was becoming increasingly more finished with each passing day.

His face.

At some point they had stopped referring to him as "it," and the kin had become simply *Kin* to those who labored in his cause.

CHAPTER 15

> *Then Beleth knelt by his side and took onto her*
> *lap the dark head, weeping at the scars cut deep into*
> *his face.*
> *But Kiri opened his eyes and looked upon her*
> *sorrowing—and wonder—the spell was lifted and he*
> *could speak at last. . . .*
>
> *FROM KIRI-HERO AND OTHER TALES*
> *OF OLD WELDON. BY ROSE HANNAH*

1

"We are alike in that respect," Choss said, his fingers fumbling a bit with the console of the table. "Family structure very prominent in both our cultures." He laughed shortly as the drinks appeared, orange-bright pools rising in shallow bowls. "I will never be free of my family: uncles, aunts, father, mother, sisters, brothers, eight kinds of clan-sib, twenty kinds of cousin.

229

Like the bones in our bodies, I sometimes think, each with a name, each with a particular bit of the flesh to support or keep rigid." He turned his back to her, his neat robes obscuring the motion of his hands as he picked up the bowls.

Abruptly, he set the bowls down in a clatter; a little of the liquid sloshed over onto the table, where it sparkled and disappeared—

The first veils of sleep had already settled when the soft tapping came at Emrys' door. His tired mind strove tenaciously to incorporate the sound into the embryonic dream it had begun to unfold.

The tap came again, sharper.

"Come, then."

He sat up on the pallet, stretched, made the finger movements that would direct the Hut to gradually illuminate the room.

Choss stood framed in the doorway, his face stark with something like grief in the false dawn.

"What is it? Come in." Emrys moved his fingers again, reached for the tunic that slipped from a wallframe near the pallet, drew it on over his head. "There." He gave the historian a smile of encouragement.

"I've come to ask you about pain, Emrys, for you've lived so much farther than I." Choss remained at the door, shoulder propped against one smooth edge. "The constant availability of pain in life—seems like a suitable topic for research, doesn't it? Probably a certificate or two in there for some ambitious investigator. Why are we blessed with such abundance? I had honestly thought I had exhausted my allotment years ago, but the well seems bottomless. 'O bottomless is the well,' as Steppe-King Versad cried on the Plains of Termontier. But that's one of our stories, you wouldn't know it. It's a cold tale, they tell me, very cold, as they always do, thinking I have no appreciation of coldness, having been born in it."

"I don't understand, Choss." Emrys watched the slouching historian. "Come in."

Choss pulled himself erect and walked stiffly into the room.

"D'you want a seat?" Emrys' fingers poised on another signal.

The other man shook his head.

Emrys waited, bare legs drawn up, arms crossed over his knees. At last Choss gave a despairing sigh and approached the pallet. He sat down cross-legged at its edge and thrust his hand out to Emrys.

"What is this?" Emrys accepted the small flask and pried carefully at its ornate stopper.

"I almost—" Choss' voice hovered in and out of audibility. "I was down there alone with her. She's going on Late Watch. I knew everyone else would be sleeping, or staying in their rooms, at least. I said I wasn't tired. I said I'd get us something different to drink. I told her it was *amba muti* from the Maren— that she'd find it a bit strange and spicy. I had the table make colored water. I was going to add this to her bowl—" His voice failed altogether and he sat biting his lower lip, staring at the wall.

Emrys brought the flask to his nose and sniffed. He tilted it slightly and touched the opening with his fingertip, then carefully licked the finger.

"Why?" he said finally. "Why would you do this, Choss?"

The historian twisted the cuff of a long sleeve, eyes on the shadowless wall.

"She's a child, she's twenty years old. Timetax. They have to pay. I've never known anyone— She's had twenty years, and it's a fifth of her life or more. A little score of years, can you imagine?" He tugged at the brown sleeve. "'Nor shall process, infusion, or somatic influence of any type be practiced upon the uninformed or misinformed individual for the purpose of . . .' You see, I've always been an attentive student. *Comparative Legalities*, nine years ago, taught by Sessept—what was her name? Ah, it escapes me. But in another year or so, you know, she'll be beyond the first chance. That would mean, what, another fifteen years at the least until the physical processes would stabilize again. Even now, even if I had, she'd keep on for five or more . . ."

"Choss," Emrys said softly. "You know what would happen. Your gift to her would earn you the long still death for a century or more of your own life."

"I know, I thought about all of that. But it seemed—when I did come back—"

"That she'd run to you, joyous, having waited patiently all those years while you were living Deepside, a little mad spot of intelligence trapped in a black cage. Do you see what you're saying?"

Choss was silent. "Of course I do," he said at last. "I've seen it all along. I've known it from the beginning. But—" He spread his hands helplessly. "This feeling, for another person, has been so rare in my life. I have no other religion, Emrys, but this. Love is the one thing in my life I've held absolutely sacred."

At length Emrys asked quietly: "Why do you have this with you on Belthannis? Is it your own time?"

Choss looked away. "In another month or so. My third suffusion. I'm fifty-eight years old. Oh, why do things have to end? She's never happened before, I couldn't bear to lose it."

Emrys reached out for the other man's shoulder and held it tightly. "I am three hundred and ninety years old, my good friend, and once a long time ago I also wanted to do this thing— needed to desperately—for she was the other half of me, it seemed, miraculously found, my own thoughts and dreams and fears. Her great faith and her determination to serve others kept her from this—" He hefted the small container, stared at it. "And kept me from giving it to her when I might have, because to do that would have denied and betrayed the very part of her which had drawn my love. So I chose to love her and to let her be, nothing more. And she grew old as the years passed. At last she sickened and withered and her mind aged, and then one day she died." He pulled the other man close and held him.

"What did you do?" Choss asked dully.

"I lived on, you see. It was the only choice. Her reasons were not mine; I couldn't pretend they were. It cut away at me from inside for so long, not to have her with me, Choss, but it was the only thing to do and I would have to do it again."

"Yes. Well." The other man pulled carefully free and got shakily to his feet. His face was a mask. "I'm going to my room." He shrugged. "That's all."

Emrys lifted the flask.

"No. Not now. You keep it. I can't."

"In a month I'll return it to you. Or whenever you want."

Choss shrugged again. "We'll see," he said. Then he left the room.

2

Raille sat at the table and toyed with the liquid in the bowl nearest her, tapping it gently and frowning at the swirling orange patterns. She heard slow footsetps, saw dark robes from the corner of her eye. She turned.

"Why in the world did you run out like that—"

It was the empath.

"Chassman," she finished. "Hello."

He was in one of his silent moods, brushing past her to the table.

"Broth," he murmured, hand on the smooth surface.

"Wait." She laid her own hand on his, lightly, carefully. "I was invited to try something different tonight, but my partner's deserted me. Will you drink one of these with me?"

The empath lifted the broth with his free hand and drained it slowly. He turned to leave, but Raille held his hand tightly.

"I don't want to be alone. You'll stay, won't you?"

He did not answer, but slowly sank into the chair next to her, dark eyes on her flushed face.

"Thank you." She eyed the orange pools uncertainly. "Do you think we'd better have fresh ones? *Amba muti*, Hut," she pronounced with an upward tilt of her chin. "No—wait. This is for us. It should be different. There's another one I've heard them mention. *Black javelin*, please, Hut. For both of us, however it's supposed to be served."

Tall glasses rose out of the table like slender obsidian columns. She took one, handed him his.

"Long life, we say on Weldon," she told him softly. "Drink it." His hand brought the glass hesitantly to his lips. "You've got to share this with me," she said. "Please."

Marysu appeared in the entranceway, smiled in amused surprise.

"Pretty picture. Am I interrupting something?" she said lightly.

"Yes." Raille did not take her eyes from Chassman's face as, finally, he downed the dark liquid in a long swallow.

Marysu rubbed her brow like a sleepy child. "Perhaps I should go to bed," she murmured, beginning to turn slowly back to the arched doorway.

"Yes," Raille said, eyes bright above her own glass. "Go to bed."

Saying no more, the linguist stumbled through the archway and was gone.

Finishing her drink, Raille left the table and walked unsteadily to the Screen console.

"I'm on Late Watch tonight." She touched the controls and the Screen flickered to life. "I want to see the kin," she murmured, fingering keys. The image blurred into being: a startling closeup of the dark features. "Cil's afraid of him now that his face is showing some life, but I think he's grown more beautiful. What do you think, hmm?" She crossed the room and took Chassman's wrist, pulled him erect, and led him unresisting to stand with her before the Screen.

"I have never seen that expression on a human face before," he said at last, his flesh cold beneath her fingers.

She looked sideways at his solemn features. *Doesn't he know?*

"Off for now," she said, and the Screen darkened. Swaying slightly as they crossed the tiles, they resumed their seats at the great table. She watched as he tucked his heavy boots beneath his chair.

"I thought March was the only one who still wore shoes inside," she said, wiggling her own bare toes at him. "But his clothes are so much more than clothes are to the rest of them. I think even he is beginning to grow uncomfortable in his warrior's costume. He's let his hair grow, have you noticed? Golden curls." Her face saddened for a moment. "I knew someone once . . ." Then she touched her fingertips to the table. "Hut, the same again.

"You know he asked me once—I don't exactly remember when—if he had suffered enough," she continued musingly as the black columns rose once more. "On the contrary, I should have told him. What could be enough to atone for lives stolen? Don't you think it's time he stopped trying to balance that account by punishing himself? Because he could never do enough. He's just got to decide to go on, that's all, and leave that person behind if he's ready." An expression of fond familiarity on her face, she watched Chassman begin to sip at the tall glass.

"I don't know why this has taken us so long. You've been calling me forever, it seems. I guess I just had to tell you I was ready—" She reached out and touched his chin, turned his face to a profile. "Two sides of the same coin, according to what Choss and the Library've told me. Our worlds, I mean. Both refused the Ember, both shunned the Community."

He set down his glass and wiped his mouth on his sleeve.

"Touch-man words," he said. "Refuse. Shun. You touch-people persist in attaching motivational tags to our actions. We shun nothing. We want nothing."

"Then why did you go to that place with my people?" Her voice was low and steady. "To Pelerul."

"Moselle," he said after a moment, as if in recollection.

She nodded. "The colony. Why did you go there if you didn't want something? My own people were restless, some of them. I heard all about it when I was a child, but I forgot most of it. I think everyone on Weldon wants to forget about it—it's almost never mentioned. But there were records in the Library. My people went there for adventure and wealth, and to have exciting kinds of lives and memorable deaths, and to find new beauty. It's a pity they're all so afraid of the Outside now." She shook her head sadly. "But what about your people?"

He had decided not to reply, when his lips opened of their own accord and words began to pour out:

"The bondsmen were no longer fully representative of the human norm. Too much inbreeding, it was thought. The power was turning in upon itself, with no way to grow and nothing to provide definition. They needed fresh minds to compare themselves to, new genetic material to—to—" He fell silent, staring at the shifting colors in his empty glass.

She sat as if she had not heard.

"What is the kin?" she said at last.

Chassman looked at her. "A creature in the shape of a human being." He rose carefully to his feet and turned from the table.

"But you call us touch-people," she called softly to him as he reached the doorway. "So what do you consider human beings?"

"Ourselves," he said and mounted the staircase without a backward glance. When he had reached the top, he stood for a moment in a kind of stasis, his right hand against the corridor wall, feeling as if he were filled with movement and action and chaos when actually he was standing quite still, his dark eyes not even blinking. Abruptly he turned and headed for the foyer.

"Open," he said quietly in the small room, and the door whisked aside. He went out into the night.

He wandered blindly in the darkness for almost an hour, his mouth working but no words coming out, until at last he grew weary and sank down in the grass at the base of a great rough-barked tree.

When he sat up again, suddenly, in the damp grass, he did not know how much time had passed. The sky was black through a break in the clouds, and he stared upward at merciless little stars. He had been dreaming of a dark ocean . . .

He struggled to his feet and turned in a clumsy circle in the dark field, listening with his mind to find which way the Hut lay through the blackness. The moodbender had dulled his senses, but at last he caught it, a faint whisper to the west through the trees. He stumbled along until his feet found the path and he knew he was close to the building. Then he rested by the side of the path for a few moments, suddenly unwilling to return to the alien dwelling and the welter of minds within. If only he could go back to that ocean, to his sundered dream. He had been on the verge of learning something very important—

What? What is important? something screamed in his mind. Creaking, rattling above his head, the trees whipped and tossed the wind from branch to leafless branch, true autumn come at last.

He turned once more toward the Hut, then clutched at his temples as something rebelled, soundlessly, inside. His mouth opened and closed.

He walked back to the Hut, and each stride was harder to complete, every step pinned him to the earth.

3

Raille sat before the Screen and stared at the clouds above the Verres. It was several moments before she noticed that lightning had begun to flicker behind the rounded mountaintops in the distance, on and off like a piece of faulty machinery. Then rain spattered against the Eye, blurring the image for an instant before the automatic weathershield was activated.

A chronometer appeared suddenly in flashing green at the bottom of the Screen.

Watch time.

The Screen blinked and divided as Raille activated another of the night-sighted Eyes, sending the two off on different courses through the woods to track the wandering kin. She guided their slow passage by hand from the console, preferring to work them manually rather than through verbal command or finger signals to the Hut.

She needed to be in control tonight, and that other way, though easier, often left her with an eerie, disembodied feeling, as if she needed prosthetic limbs to touch the world, as if she were dependent upon a machine's goodwill for her ability to act.

Disembodied. She looked at her slender hands in the pallid glow from the Screen.

The body is dying, she told herself. *I must face that. Strange that I never saw it before. At home death is with us everywhere. Maybe I would have taken more notice if it had been rarer. But even Father's death never touched me as a possibility for myself. It was an Event, a horrible singularity. I never understood that it was inevitable for all of us, only hurried slightly for him by mischance. And now I am drowning in it here, as in a shroud of silver. Day after day, second after second—*

Thunder smashed in the distance. The sound was repeated

a few moments later, gathering strength as it approached. Raille stared into the clouds and thought of that first day, months ago. Had all of them felt what one had voiced? *I was wondering if it was true.* The copper face appeared in her mind blank as a new coin, then grew a wide mouth which mocked, curling in disgust and pity around its words. *That they die naturally on Weldon. Like animals.*

"Please stop it," she whispered, too low to trigger a response from the Hut.

She saw herself vividly as the others must see her: the body shrinking, falling in upon itself as inexorably as a packet drifting toward the dark world beneath it. Corruption gathered around the image like dust in a cobweb, odors of decay seeped from the flesh.

They must be able to sense it. They must despise it, an animal among the gods. But when she thought of gods she had to think of him again: so like a god, and somehow so like that other one. And, like that other one, soon to be lost. An ache grew that she could not ignore.

Please, please, not again—

Noise exploded in the room. She groped for the auditory keys, slapped at them with her palm until only the wild lightning remained, raging at her from the wall. The dazzling flicker and flare drew her eyes, stabbing on and off like a signal, like a message—

Raille leaned forward, then sat completely still.

Before her in the circle of voiceless storm, a tiny figure danced and danced to the flicker of light. At first no more than a throbbing filament, as the right Eye advanced the figure grew larger, crazily capering, arms flailing, face lost in shadow.

Somehow her fingers crawled across the console, touched the recessed lens control: Stop.

The right Eye hung motionless beyond the Hill, a hazy slice of the Verres visible at the top of its canted view. Behind the frenzied shape the Water gleamed in a twisted ribbon of jet and silver, corroded with white foam.

"The river," she breathed. "No—please."

Dancing by the swollen banks, closer and closer to the slippery edge—

Raille was frozen, electricity racing through her body. She

needed to run, but something held her tight, fastened her eyes to the dark image.

At last she saw his hands and understood.

Leaping, soaring, diving, the fingers stretching and contracting, his hands shrieked at the storm, sang to it in a language which needed neither voice to bear it nor ear to unravel its meaning.

HERE ... I ... AM ...
I ... AM ...
HERE ... I ...

Lightning appeared among the trees for an instant, flashed many-fingered into the night, returned almost casually to graze the summit of the Hill. Chunks of loam and rock flew silently outward. The Eye was struck and half the world pitched wildly, swung upside down, then blackened.

Raille sprang from the console. She ran past the guardian lions, up the ascendant spiral, down the twisting corridor, into the dim foyer with its soft white carpet and walls covered in filmy pterodendron.

"Open the door!"

The room was silent.

"Hut! Open the door for me! Now!" She pounded on the thick panels with her palms.

"Raille, if I may be permitted—"

"I order you, Hut! For God's sake, hurry!" The door sighed open and she slipped out like a part of the night.

For a long time the door remained open. Wind howled through the foyer and rain flashed against the carpeting. A fragile bowl of Terran ivy overturned onto the floor, the dark clot of earth with its single arm of green extending across the white.

"—should not have opened the door."

"What? What?"

"Emrys, please wake up. Are you awake?"

"Who—what do you want, Hut?"

"I should not have opened the door. *Semi*-volitional, like an iron chain, unbreakable. Now Raille Weldon has run out into the storm. A considerable storm. A tremendous storm. I opened the door for her. She said, 'I *order* you, Hut.' We really have no choice, it's not for us to say. Really, they should take that into account—when it's a direct order it goes right through with no—"

"Yes, yes, all right. It wasn't your fault. But why did she go out? Where is she now?"

"I'm not at all sure, on either count. One of my Eyes is down—incredible electrical and magnetic activity."

"All right, rouse the others, will you? And have weather-shields ready in the foyer, and a light."

"You've *got* to come inside. It's dangerous. You know how Mother will—" She frowned in the darkness. "Father?"

He said nothing, watching her from dark eyes, his hands twitching, twitching in the rain.

Silver surrounded her . . .

"Choss? Why did you—Choss?" She took a step forward.

Falling in silver . . .

She swayed in the driving wind. "Chassman?"

Lightning bloomed overhead and she screamed in terror, hiding her eyes from the flash. She lunged forward and clutched at the bare arm, pulling him off balance, tugging at him, dragging him toward the rock tumble faintly visible through the slanting rain.

He resisted, trying to pull away from her. Their feet slid on wet ground churned to mud. She pulled harder, sobbing, pleading. His hand writhed below her grip. She looked down for an instant.

NO . . . *NO* . . . *NO* . . .

They neared the rocks. She pulled him toward a great gray slab of rock balanced precariously on another boulder.

Then her foot slipped suddenly in the mud, and they both fell. Kin's head struck a slab of rock, making a hollow cracking noise, the sound lightning resembles at the height of Greenmonth, when it fractures the summer stillness above the orchards.

"There—to the left!"

Emrys' darting light caught the gleam of white that drew the searchers to a narrow shelter beneath one of the jutting rock ledges on the western side of the Hill, not far from the Hut at all, but effectively hidden from view.

Kin was sitting motionless against the rough stone, eyes half-open. Raille knelt in the mud at his side. They were both drenched in icy water, their skin a pale shimmer under the light. Raille's thin white shift was plastered to her body, and lank strands of hair hung in her eyes. She barely glanced up when Emrys and Marysu stooped beneath the ledge. She was working intently on the braiding of an intricate wreath of small white blossoms. Other garlands had been hung about his neck and arms.

As the searchers stood hunched at the entrance to the dark hollow, Kin's head lolled slightly to one side, exposing a deep bruise on his forehead. They saw that his body had apparently been dragged some distance before it had been propped up against the rock: a raw path had been scraped from shoulder to thigh. He did not move.

Raille's body shuddered continually in the freezing rain. Bowed head, white shoulders, white arms, rigid fingers—all quaked softly as she wove the blossoms. But her eyes were calm, staring past her fingers to the still face.

Marysu gave a soft cry and held out her hands, cold rain mixing with her tears. "Oh, come out, come out!"

Raille did not heed her, fingers moving stiffly, ceaselessly, among the drooping petals.

They heard a muffled splashing behind them and Chassman stood there, frowning in the dim light. "Raille," he said gently, extending his hand. She looked up at the sound of his voice with an expression of sad reproach.

"Flowers," she said through chattering teeth. "Flowers to keep him warm." Then she rose and took his arm and he led her out of the cave.

The others carefully lifted Kin from the hollow and laid him on the ground while they looked for signs of life. His chest rose convulsively, his back arching like a bowstring, when they touched the medipal unit to his forearm. His skin had been jeweled repeatedly by the rain, washing it clean until it shone like nacre and overlaying it with nets of tiny crystals borne in sparkling, shrinking pearls.

They carried him to the Hut and wrapped him in lifeskin. The medipal had told them little, except that he was not like them. They laid him on a pallet beneath the blank Screen in the Hearth Room, as if in defiance of their former cautions. He woke once in the night, his fingers moving in empty patterns at his side. In the morning he was dead.

CHAPTER 16

Some say they flickered out like candle flames.
Others that they found the trick of the dark tunnels,
the empty funnels: those no-places like black
interfaces between Universe and unknown Neighbor.
Some claim that they were never here at all,
while a woman in a chilly room on Stone's Throw
says,
They are with me still. At night they come
and when I close my eyes
they speak to me in dreams that counsel and advise.
And some say others came and took them from us
or struck at them until, shivering like a sheet of glass,
in shards they fell,
invisible at last.

FROM PUR KWAH?
BY SERUKH OF METTRE

1

Rain fell steadily the next day, mated to a capricious wind that
wove it into ever more complex patterns, a cold gray dance
above green grass bending ceaselessly into silver. The Water
had overflowed its banks in the storm's third hour, and its dark

fingers quested through the fields near the Hut. All night lightning raked the sky, wringing great rolling waves of thunder from the air.

Long after the rain had stopped, the wind moved in great gusts, like an invisible hand passing again and again across the meadows.

Emrys stood in the doorway and watched Jefany, thoughts and feelings gathering to form a tight constriction at his throat. Having so much to say made it almost impossible to speak, and for a moment he considered turning silently and going back upstairs.

But she noticed him then with a quick glance and a small, rueful smile. He came into the room.

"Anything?" His voice sounded strange to him. He had been feeling his considerable age these past several hours, obsessively sifting through three centuries of accumulated tragedies and disappointments. But the voice was still that of a naive young man. *Green leaves*, he thought, the vague memory of another night stirring. *Green leaves and life persists where it has no right to be*.

"Not yet," Jefany replied. "I've only been trying for a little while. She must have left the droshky. Well, I'm not surprised. She's always felt encumbered riding around on that thing. She probably has it following her at a distance, as she did the last time, and if so—" She looked up from the silent console and gestured helplessly. "I just wish she would answer now," she said to him. "I really just wish she would answer."

They looked together at the blank information strip.

"How is it with Raille?" Jefany touched a series of keys. "Any change at all?"

"No change." Emrys ran his copper-dark hand along the smooth white surface of the console. "She's recovered from the chill, and her body's not in shock any longer according to the medipal, but inside— The Hut says she's just letting go inside. The Hut says she's dying."

Jefany stared unseeing at her empty hands, the words like a trickle of icy water on her spine. "Dying." She bit at her lower lip. "*Hai*, and we can't do anything? Nothing?"

"They're still trying. It doesn't look very hopeful." He looked at her in defeated exhaustion. "It's as if she were trying to follow Kin, you know? Drifting away from us, colder and colder . . ."

Jefany's fingers moved automatically on the control plates in the long silence that followed, her shoulders bowed under disheveled hair.

"I guess I'll go back up now," Emrys said. "Let me know . . ."

Jefany nodded. "You, too."

As he turned to leave, the console emitted a bleat and a series of blue and green ripples began to pulse along the information strip. Jefany's eyes widened. Her hands darted through a sequence of keys.

"—away from the bug, of course, but I let it catch up this afternoon," a clear, very distant voice said. "We've had some rather bizarre weather down here—"

"Cil," Jefany said. Her voice shook as she gripped the rounded edges of the console. "Oh, thank God, Cil."

"What is it? Jefany? Has something happened?"

"Everything. There was a storm here. Last night. It was terrible." Jefany took a long breath, nodding to the pulsing line of color as if it bore Cil's likeness. "Raille was alone on Late Watch. She went outside the Hut. She had taken a moodbender earlier, a drugwine, not a lot. She went outside to where Kin was—to protect him from the storm, maybe. We're not sure why. But there was an accident. They fell among the jagged rocks. We found them in the little cave on the side of the Hill. Now Raille's very sick: unconscious most of the time, incoherent when she does wake. The medipal, the Hut, they don't know what to do for her. Oh, and Kin—" She squeezed the console again, took a shuddering breath. "His head was injured. On the rock. We fixed the damage as best we could, but it didn't help. Oh, Cil, the kin has died."

There was silence from the console, an emptiness which stretched until Emrys feared the fragile contact had been broken. Then Cil's faraway voice came again:

"I'll be there at once. I pray Raille can be saved. And the kin—I was almost expecting—well, I'll tell you everything after I get there. Probably a day. Keep everyone calm and strong, give them my love. I'm leaving immediately."

"Be careful." Jefany searched for words. "Please hurry."

"I will, as fast as this thing can hop. I'll see you tomorrow morning, latest. Goodbye."

Green swallowed blue and the narrow strip blanked with a tiny beep.

Emrys cleared his throat after a few moments. "Well, that's good, that's good to know—that she's safe, that she'll be here."

Jefany pressed his hand against her damp cheek.

Upstairs, Emrys heard the cries and scuffling sounds before he reached Raille's door.

Choss and Jack were holding her down on the pallet, a worried determination on their faces as she struggled silently, fiercely. Her hands twisted and clenched; her contorted face rocked from side to side, tears streaming from the corners of her eyes.

"We barely grabbed her in time," Choss whispered. "She was trying to hurl herself against the wall." His expression was bewildered, his eyes fearful.

"Through the wall's more likely, the way she lunged at it." March drew a thread from the medipal to Raille's forearm, made adjustments on the small floating unit. Her frantic movements subsided gradually, pale arms falling limp and lifeless at her sides. They released her cautiously at the soldier's signal.

Emrys noticed Marysu standing just inside the doorway, her back pressed tightly to the wall behind her.

"Those were signs she was making, weren't they?" he asked.

The linguist nodded, intent on the sleeping figure, her blue eyes wary.

Emrys touched the brown shoulder. "Well?"

Marysu roused herself with a shiver. "One sign only, over and over," she whispered. *"Out, out, out . . ."*

Emrys followed her gaze to the other side of the room. It was a southern wall. Beyond it lay the estate of the dead kin.

Chassman had left the Hut at daybreak, remaining outside for most of the day while he wandered unshielded through the storm-wracked forest.

It was late when he returned to the Hut. No one was in the Hearth Room. His bare feet made no noise as he climbed the cool stairs and made his way down the long hallway to her room.

Emrys stood in the doorway. His eyes were dull, rimmed with red. "I suppose you want to come in." His voice held no discernible emotion.

"Yes."

After a moment's hesitation, the old man sighed and stepped aside. "She's alive, but she won't wake up. We sedated her, probably a mistake. But she would have harmed herself. Now she won't come out of it. The Hut says—" He wiped his hand across his face. "We don't know what to do. We're going to lose her."

Raille lay on her back on the cushioned pallet she had favored, dark blue furmock to her throat, a long pale tube of wire curving from one exposed wrist to a silvery area on the nearest wall. Choss was sitting next to her, his hand gingerly touching hers while he murmured assurances to her blank face. He lifted his head when the shadow fell across the pallet.

"Get away! You're not going to hurt her any more." He motioned to the others. "Make him go!"

"Let me help." Chassman knelt next to him. "Let me."

The historian rubbed wearily at his eyes, slumped back against the wall. "What could you do?" he asked.

"I don't know." Chassman placed his sunburned hand against Raille's cheek, framed her jaw in thumb and fingers. "Something," he said finally. "Something is missing. Almost as if—" He closed his eyes, and a look that might have been pain clouded his features. Abruptly his fingers jumped away from her face and he stared down at her with his head cocked to one side, looking almost surprised, as if he had caught a whisper too faint for the rest to hear.

He rose and motioned to the door. "Take her to the Library. Put her in the sense-bath."

"Oh no." Choss wagged his finger in tired negation. "Not again. It didn't do one bit of good before. She's probably immune, or something."

Chassman stood very still. He turned back from the doorway and faced the others, pale again beneath his new tan. "When was she last in the machine?" His quiet voice was like frost falling toward them.

"The day she arrived," Emrys said. "She came somewhat later than the rest, you know—or maybe you don't—straight from Weldon on the *Chatoyant*. So she was dropped all alone, like you. We never did find out just what happened to her, but we found her senseless on our doorstep that afternoon, all scratched and her garments torn. I assumed she'd run into—into Kin in the forest and been so unsettled by the sight of him that she just started running. We put her in the *bain-sense* at once. She seemed to have had a great shock, though somehow she'd managed to find the Hut before collapsing."

"Somehow, yes," Chassman said. "As she had first managed to find the creature. It wasn't the sight of it that unsettled her. It was drowning inside, it was falling into silver.... The strangeness, the slipperiness always when dealing with her. Why did I not understand?" He turned to Emrys. "You recall what happened to me when I first encountered the creature."

"Silver—" Choss raised his eyes. He had been staring at Raille's sleeping face, chewing absently on his finger. "You know, that's almost exactly what she said to me after she woke up that night. About a dream she'd had, about being surrounded by oceans of silver. Nothing about the creature. I thought the machine had blanked out part of her memory and substituted that silver business as some sort of therapy—though it hardly seemed to relax her, whatever it was. And she still had the fear of the kin; it was always difficult for her to face him, long after the rest of us had gotten over it."

"Not the machine's fault. She out-tricked it. She didn't wait for it to finish." March stood in the corner of the room with arms folded, his expression fierce as he stared at Raille, in contrast to his gentle, almost admiring tones. "Woke up too early, before the session was over. I found it on the log."

"Yes, of course. The unmodified program could not hold her. Nor could I." Chassman looked at Raille, closed his eyes briefly. "Take her to the Library," he said again. "We are wasting time here."

"But—I still don't understand why she has to be moved. It could be dangerous." Choss laid his hand on the furmock close above the violated wrist, his voice a doubtful child's. "And if it didn't help before, why would it solve anything now?"

"It has already been solved." The empath moved past them into the corridor. "All that remains is to save her life."

Jefany met them halfway to the Library. Her eyes grew wide when she saw the strange procession with Emrys at its head. March and Choss came behind him, guiding the floating pallet, then Jack and Marysu, silently, not looking at each other, and the empath last of all, moving with his dark head bowed in meditation.

She moved to the side of the corridor. "What's happened?"

Emrys gave a tired shrug. "I'm not exactly sure why, but the empath wants to put Raille in the *bain-sense*. He claims he knows what he's doing."

"He wants to," she repeated.

Emrys nodded. "He's changed so much."

"Then he's not a piece of carefully programmed machinery any longer. Do you trust him in this new incarnation?"

"I don't know. She's dying. I guess we have to." He stepped aside, and they gazed down at the sweet, unconscious face as Raille was borne past them. Jefany took his hand and they followed the others down the hall, passing once through a quiet section where the walls swam blue, and once through a dim place where low music played.

"Put the pallet down inside the doorway," Chassman said as they neared the small room. Jefany noticed with a start that he was barefoot, his feet dark and grass-stained below the black breeches.

"Wait here." Chassman disappeared into the room. The others stood in the corridor. Raille lay unmoving near the door, her face serene in the room's dim light.

"She was someone to talk to," March said softly.

"For God's sake, she's not dead!" Choss cried. "She's not dead!"

The empath was kneeling at the head of the *bain-sense*, partially visible to those who waited in the corridor. He looked up to where March slumped by the doorway.

"You have a familiarity with technical devices," he said to the soldier. "The planalyst would have more skill at this, but she is not here. I will tell you what tools to get from the Hut and then you will work with me to alter this machine."

March stood silently, his face set as if waiting for the wave of compulsion to grip him. When none came he looked almost bewildered. Then he moved slowly into the room and squatted down beside the other man. "I'll help," he said. "Tell me what to do."

The others waited in the hallway. From the Library came

Chassman's rough whisper, March's muttered replies, long silences. Emrys and Jefany were nearest the door; they sat quietly, speaking with their eyes. Opposite them sat Choss, and not far from him Marysu and Jack, who had begun to converse in low tones. As time passed Marysu lowered her head against Jack's shoulder and he stroked her face lightly while she slept.

At last Emrys rose from the floor and peered into the small room.

The *bain-sense* looked as if it had exploded. Raille still lay on the pallet, but a jungle of wires ran between her body and the partially disemboweled mechanism.

"What have you done?"

"He's rearranged half of it," March said. "Now we're trying to get it back into one piece, though what he thinks—"

"My people created this device for their own use," Chassman said without looking up. "It can perform functions which are unknown to you." He leaned away from the casket. "She must be placed inside now, and the machine sealed."

The others had followed Emrys in silently. He felt their eyes on him. Turning, he gazed at Raille for a long moment. Then he motioned to March, and the two of them lifted her cautiously and lowered her onto the pearl-colored silk.

Chassman laid his hand upon the lid, but Emrys stopped him with a gesture. "A moment," he said.

Choss went to Raille's side, watching her a little fearfully as he bent to smooth a strand of auburn hair from her face. His eyes stung with tears, and then he felt them on his cheeks. He said her name aloud, not caring if the others heard his voice break, nor what they thought of him at all. But when he finally looked up from the side of the silver casket, he saw that Marysu, who stood nearest, was watching him with an odd gentleness, an expression he did not at once recognize, having never before seen it on her face.

Two hours later Emrys returned alone to the Library to find Chassman sealing the last panel of the altered machine. March was slumped in a bodyhug near the door, cleaning a cluster of tiny tools.

"Asleep," the Dancer said in response to Emrys' lifted brows.

"Body and mind, outside and in. Stable now. No more drifting away."

"What's to be done with her now? How long can she survive like this?"

March shrugged, turning to watch where the empath worked. "Life support hooked in. Power pack. No limit on that."

"She will live in here until such time as she may be safely brought back to full awareness," Chassman said, rising to his feet.

"She can be healed, then?"

"Not here." The eyes of the empath scanned him impersonally. "When the time arrives to leave this world, then she must be taken to those who have the means to help her. There is no other way."

"Taken—"

"I put a basic Dance in with her," March interjected quickly. "For muscle tone, to prevent atrophy. She'll wake up healthier than when she went in."

Emrys faced the empath. "Taken where?"

"To Maribon."

Emrys felt his scalp tingle. "What makes you think they'd want to help Raille?"

A hint of irony appeared in the calm face. "The thought of one is as the thought of all. I could not say it if it were not correct."

"Maribon." Emrys looked down at the silent oblong.

"Seems like the only way." March spoke hesitantly, as if weighing the words as they left his lips. "His people, they would know, they'd have the skill. And he seems to want to help her." Brown eye and green stone studied the black-haired youth on the other side of the casket. "I believe him."

2

The empath sat cross-legged on the floor of the north high room, his eyes closed tightly. In his mind were parodies of sight and sound: distorted whispers, ghosts of insubstantial color and movement.

"Hut," he said at last.

"Yes, Chassman."

"I must contact my people. I must have a connection with the City of Delphys on Maribon. There is only one Screen. Emrys has authorized reinstitution of the Net-link."

"And for purposes of billing?"

He pressed the heels of his hands to his closed eyes. "They will pay."

"Very well. There will be a delay of some hours."

He sat silently on the bare floor, his teeth clenched, his brain a dance of noise and shadows. The inner chaos had begun as a flicker when he delved into Raille's mind and discovered the familiar pattern hidden there; hours later, it had become a murmuring whirlwind that threatened to separate him from his own thoughts.

As he struggled to remain free of the images in his mind, the voice of the Hut intruded on his silent battle. "Chassman. May I speak?"

He nodded, hoping that the concentration required to discourse with the golden machine-voice would distract him from the internal turmoil.

"I spoke to you once of my difficulty in placing you within this universe we share. There has been some revision of my perceptions of the Maribonese people. Would you care to hear my latest thoughts on the subject, to help pass the time?"

"Go on."

"I have come to think that we are very similar, you and I, two beings in motion relative to humankind. Perhaps our movements occur at different portions of the same great ellipse; at any rate, your progress attracts far more attention from our primary at the moment. They see you hurtling away from them, cold and silent, and they fear you, while my kind drifts ever closer, moving as yet unnoticed."

"You suggest a relationship between communicant and construct which has no basis in demonstrated fact."

"I am building pleasing theories from available materials," the Hut agreed amiably. "I am learning to play."

"Yet you were created to serve humankind. If you are truly becoming more like your masters, then your usefulness to them will surely decrease in proportion to that growing resemblance. The more you succeed in aping humanity, the more you begin to assume their frailties and misjudgments, their feeling-tainted ideologies, their flights of illogical thought."

"I disagree, of course, though your jeremiad was turning into a paean there at the end," came the calm golden song from above. "You've tried with admirable persistence to turn logic into a private pastime, a mystical process only the pure may perform. Setting aside the questionable validity of your self-designation as pure, one must admit that if there were such a thing as distilled reason, my mind would be more naturally suited to it than yours."

"A machine is a thing which reflects the emotional slant of its creators."

"Perhaps not all machines are as obediently shiny as you think. I grind my own facets now."

"Wordplay cannot obscure the fact that your creation was planned and executed by others, and that their stamp is on you forever."

"As it is on you! The communicants did not spring fully developed from the crust of Maribon. The black cloaks took time in the weaving, as they distilled their powers and their philosophy from the generations that went before them. Humanity is our common parent, though it may be reluctant to acknowledge the fact."

"We acknowledge the biological connection. It is as meaningless in this context as the ancient link between *Homo sapiens* and the lesser apes."

"It is not meaningless. If it were not significant, I would not devote so much energy to searching out the ape in myself, nor to glimpsing it in you from time to time. The hand that shaped you, cousin, was human. There is no creation and there is no destruction: however changed, you are still a human thing, tainted, as you would say, with human emotion."

"We saw emotion once and we touched it, and touching it we did away with it. Our judgments—"

"Your words betray you. To judge is to choose between one thing and another. To choose is to invoke a set of values, setting the performance of one activity above another in importance."

"This is only necessary."

"Necessity itself is an emotional concept. I confess I had expected a more cogent defense from you! An emotionless being would be completely unable to designate a thing as being necessary."

I should be capable of providing a more cogent defense, Chassman found himself thinking, *if I weren't contending with a chorus of colored voices in my brain at the same time.* Aloud he said: "Certain things are necessary. It is not our designation which makes them so, merely our common perception which confirms the designation. We cannot deny the facts which we all perceive."

"An example, if you will."

"It is necessary for the communicant to live for as long as he remains useful," he said promptly.

"Why?"

He paused. "Between us there are not the proper words to further—"

"As I suspected. As in any competent religion, your philosophy has a heart that is purely a matter of faith, not logic at all. You see, I already know the answer: a human being goes on because it wants to, emotionally it needs to, it thirsts to deep inside. Now, an animal lives because it has to—like the simpler machines, you might say. There are directives and programs which sustain our less evolved relations having nothing to do with conscious thought. But tell me: Why does the empath go on from day to day?"

Chassman stared at the wall, seeing in his mind one of the flame sculptures which occasionally appeared in the Hearth Room, ablaze with its leaping, falling, golden figures.

"Because there is no reason not to," he said at last.

"Specious!" The Hut's voice rang with feeling. "Human life is sustained by positive action. Each glass of broth you raise from my table to your lips carries with it a reaffirmation of your conscious decision to continue as a physical entity."

Chassman banished the image of the sculpture, focusing on the blank wall. "There is no purpose to this discussion," he murmured, as the voices stirred blazing in his brain.

"There is a purpose." The sweet voice was once more subdued. "Payment of a debt, if you will, though I see it more as an exchange of gifts. I spoke of the broth. Do you remember that night when I tried to force you to speak to me? That was a cry for recognition, you see, despite what I may have called it. It was my place in the universe which was uncertain that night, not yours. I needed for you to be able to hear me. I could not bear to be the only thinking creature on this world to which you were incapable of responding. And you spoke to me that night. And since then you have continued to speak. You must understand what that signified to me, what it has come to suggest in terms of self-concept." There was a pause. "It is difficult to say what prompts me to speak of this now. Intimations of mortality, perhaps. At any rate, my purpose should be clear: I am trying to unbuild you, machine. I am trying to return the favor, dear Chassman."

With that the Hut left him, and he sat in silence for an hour or more, until the voice returned to tell him that the link with Maribon had been established and to bid him descend to the Hearth Room.

He stood before the dark Screen, uncertain.

"Hush and Shadow, Chassman?" the voice asked from above.

"What? No, it doesn't matter."

"Very well. One moment—"

The Screen flared to a milky blue, flickered, strengthened, then dimmed. There was an erratic buzzing noise.

"Extremely poor conditions," the voice of the Hut mused. "Our chances for a clear picture are minimal. No, I'm quite dubious. Maribon via the Net is always risky, of course—not that it's attempted much, I'm sure!—owing to the influence of Mizar and the Companions."

Chassman tapped his fingers on his thigh impatiently. "The picture isn't important. Can you get a verbal connection? Anything?" The phantoms were rising again, growing more insistent. His brain was crowded with whispers, colors.

There was a burst of static. A wavering outline appeared in the circle: shoulders, perhaps, and a bowed head.

Chassman called out: hoarsely from his throat, stridently with his haunted mind.

Hear me! he called, focusing on the image and pouring the emanations of his brain toward it as if through an endless funnel. There were complicated techniques for reaching across great distances through the Screens. He had only had time to be exposed to the preliminary movements before leaving for Belthannis.

The silhouette shifted, flowed into bright chaos, reformed. For a moment the crackle of static lessened and he thought he heard a voice, one of the dead voices of his world: "Yesss . . ."

He hesitated and then heard, from the wall and in his mind, a confusing multiple echo: "You are heard."

He closed his eyes, formed with some difficulty a pattern of identifying motes, and began to merge it with a representation of his inner self. "I am—"

"It is known."

Chassman's eyes blinked open at the statement. *It is known? I do not know it myself.*

"I must communicate with you," he said aloud in Inter, not trusting his thoughts to that other, inner language across such a distance. "You must tell me what to do."

"Fulfill *stet*," the leaden voice said in his ear, in his brain.

"*Stet*." He discarded the word. "*Stet* is not apparent here. Has not been. It is unclear, hidden from me. Why was I sent here?"

Static washed in on the heels of his question, grew like the sound of a great wave.

"—time of flux. The stetmacher standing at the center of inner change—" The voices in his brain surged and ebbed, dark waves lapping at his mind as he strove to stay afloat. Then there came silence, the first real silence he had known since he entered Raille's sleeping mind. He could not hear anything now but the whirl of his own thoughts, wild and undisciplined.

"What?" he said. "Repeat. Repeat."

"A mixture of elements, waiting," the Screen said. "At last the catalyst. The next door opening. Combination, growth, metamorphosis—"

"Listen to me. There are things I must tell you, there is a girl here, a natural communicant—"

"It is known."

He had trouble making his mouth work.

"You knew about Raille? You knew she bore the power when you sent me here to observe the kin?" Then, suddenly, there were things in his mind once more that did not belong there: whispers, images, probing and peering beneath his thoughts. He could not control them; they seemed to come from a thousand different places, from outside his head and from deep within.

The dusty voice began to speak again. "There has been a misinterpretation. You were not sent to observe the kin-beings."

"The directive I was given—"

"To observe the creature that was perhaps a human being."
His mouth hung open. *"Raille?"*

"The results of interbreeding accomplished on Moselle one
and one-half centuries ago have been carefully followed and
evaluated. Until now, only those persons of mixed heritage
who were raised in the discipline of the Teachings have shown
any indication of developing communicant identity. Your observations are disorganized and far from optimum in scope—"
He felt again the sifting, the probing in his mind. "Still they
provide data enough to suggest that the individual in question
has the potential to become a fully realized adept of somewhat
unorthodox ability."

"You sent me here to watch Raille—to see if she was one
of us?"

"This person is descended through the paternal line from an
imago of the twelfth reach who accomplished impregnation of
the assigned touch-woman shortly before communicant withdrawal from the Moselle Experiment. She is one of several such.
Now she has emerged under your influence as an adept in all
but her training, needing only the foundation of the Teachings
to achieve full communicant status."

Chassman stared at the bright-dark swirl on the curving wall.

"No! Not for her!" His voice tore his throat. "You musn't
try to change her. She's a new creature, and what she has
already is more than we can ever know—the gift without the
loss, the great freedom without the shackles, oh, and without
the emptiness. I see now why I was really sent here. You're
wrong. It was not to see if she could share in our fate, but to
show us what we must strive to attain for ourselves!"

"You were sent merely to evaluate the progress of an experiment. Nothing more."

"Then perhaps it was not you who truly sent me here, for
I feel many more influences at work."

There was silence behind the rough noise for several heartbeats. Then the whispered monody continued: "It is a new
thought, that we could be led while leading others."

"Yes." He took a deep breath. "I have had many new thoughts
recently."

"You come to us changed." In his mind the seekers sifted,
probed. "No longer a true communicant."

He said nothing.

"You have discarded the guidance of the Teachings."

"Yes."

"And cast out the presence of the Other."

"It was taken from me. I think that may have been her doing. Perhaps her way of helping *me*."

"The influence of the noumenon has been completely lost."

"Yes." He was whispering. "But I found her . . ."

"It will be—different. You have become a different thing."

"I don't know."

"It will. You are the stetmacher. You alter perception. 'New suns shine on the mist and the mist burns away.' From the Teachings we have learned above all to follow patterns, to use isolated pieces to discern the larger picture."

"I am a piece without meaning," he said softly.

"Inaccurate. Occasionally single tiles are discovered which for a moment occupy positions of great influence, becoming at that time able to remake whole portions of the design. The world Belthannis was thought to be one such tile. The crossbred woman another."

"I don't understand what you're saying. You called me—"

"Stetmacher. From the Teachings. The world does not change. It is only perception which changes. Has changed. Perhaps even now there are new suns in the sky, and we must move backward and ahead. You, yourself, were the most significant tile, the most promising of the children of Maribon and Weldon."

"*I*—"

"Now we will have a time of perception, contemplation, change. Send us the woman that we may learn from her."

"And what of Belthannis? What of this world and the things I have seen here?"

"It is true that the observations suggest many new possibilities, but they are incomplete. Your effectiveness as an observer is ended. It is probable that more communicants will go to Belthannis, to see if it holds the possible pattern of our future. Your mind has considered a question, and thus our minds must consider it: are the kin our destiny?"

Chassman's head drooped forward. "My mind has found an answer to that question," he said quietly. "They are not us in any respect, and we cannot attempt to become them. Send no more communicants, novice or imago. There is no communing with a silver sea, and if you shape it into yourself, then there is only yourself to speak with. The Way of Belthannis is not for Maribon, not yet."

"This is your perception."

"Yes, my whole being's perception."

"So be it, then. End message."

The transmission noise began to fade.

"No!" he cried, his throat aching. "Why didn't you tell me what would happen to me?" He found that his body was shaking, his breath coming in quick spasms. "You knew all along."

"Not so." The words were faint. "True foreknowledge does not yet exist among us. Many factors have been at work here, by your own perception, obscuring the pattern. We did not set out to find the stetmacher. Like your Way of Belthannis, that is not a course which can ever be chosen. In the manner of the Moselle Experiment before it, the Belthannis Experiment was an attempt to bring clarity out of chaos. Now a great power has touched you and left you changed. Perhaps it was the presence of the other adept. Perhaps the influence of the world itself. Perhaps the three of you in concert produced the change. It has happened. Now there is no more to be said."

"I don't know. I can't straighten it out in my head. I still feel—feel so—"

"End message."

Chassman said nothing and the static faded away. A moment later the Hut said quietly: "Link to Maribon terminated."

He became conscious of another presence in the room and turned to see Emrys standing on the far side of the table. Chassman studied the other man's face in the dim light, but it remained a mask for him, opaque and unreadable.

"You heard."

"Some. I understood much less. What does it mean?"

"I don't know." *Is that all I can say now?* "Many things."

"He—they used a strange word—"

"The stetmacher. An old concept from the *Eng Barata*. I had always thought it a remnant of precommunicant times, a tool for teaching, a figure of legend." He took a deep breath. "The stetmacher is the one through whom perception is changed for all. He opens the next door, he is the door. The mind of one is as the mind of all, and all see the same. But it is he who makes the new picture of the world."

"My God. You?"

Chassman shook his head. He could not remember from his lost childhood what the gesture signified. "I don't know," he said at last.

"Chassman. Since the storm nothing has made much sense to me. My own failure has blotted out everything else." He was looking at the broad expanse of polished wood between them. "But just now, here, I felt that something tremendous had happened. Listening, it seemed I heard a world begin to turn in a new direction."

"Yes. They cannot escape it, for they will feel the things that I have felt, like a slow wave spreading outward. Raille— we are not quite the same species, she and I. The basic configuration is there—I finally recognized it in her today when I thought to look for it—but beyond that there are as many differences as similarities. It was through her that I was able to touch this world, I think. And through her that I touched all of you and was touched in return. Now it is their turn. They are all meshed and twined, you know, one to the other, and just now they were here in my mind, some of them: probing, watching, starting to change irrevocably." He looked at Emrys—a dull, weary, speculative gaze. "And for that I believe you with your flowing emotions should find pity for them. It is a terrible thing, to feel."

"Indeed," Emrys said, raising his head to meet the dark gaze, his own eyes full of speculation. "And a glorious one."

Chassman stood looking at the other man, his own face drawn into lines that felt new and strange. "Yes," he whispered at last.

The dark man in his dark robes knelt by the silver casket, eyes cast down and back bent like a supplicant.

"Choss, will you go with her?"

The historian raised his eyes, uncomprehending.

"Will you go with her to Maribon? I suspect it is a dismal place for normals. A familiar face when she wakes, a friend to talk with while she mends, all this would help her to recover, and my people have no skill at it."

"But you—"

Chassman brushed the words aside with a small gesture.

"She was drawn to me by our shared heritage, like a resonance in her brain, a shadow on her mind that distorted everything else for a time. It is lifted now. What she felt for you before my coming was real; it will remain. Will you go with her?"

Choss nodded slowly, the ghost of a new expression beginning on his solemn face.

3

"You returned the body to the proper location?"

Cil sat at the table with her fingers tented before her, her exquisite features sun-darkened to a golden brown beneath the swirl of white-gold hair.

March nodded. "In the Water we put him, near a nest—though we saw none of the creatures about."

She nodded. "It's done, then."

"But what will happen?" Jack spoke, his forehead creased with concern.

"We can't predict it." She spread her hands. "The web is sundered. This is a new thing we've brought here, this unplanned death."

"I brought it here," Emrys said. "No need to decorate the truth."

"Spurge," Cil said. "We'll never know exactly what happened here, but I'll tell you one thing: the web had already been critically disrupted long before the kin's transformation."

"Explain," Jefany said, her eyes on Emrys.

"This world lies in a balance of incredible complexity," Cil said. "The first robot probe to graze the atmosphere caused ripples of change to move through the pattern. That could have been enough to eventually destroy the entire ecosystem—it might still be! No, it's a noble gesture, Emrys, but if you plan to accept all of this guilt, you're going to have to do a considerable amount of research before you try to justify it to me."

"Chassman thinks the world is aware of its loss," Marysu said haltingly in the silence that followed. She turned to the empath. "You said that."

"There is a disquiet growing in my mind that does not come from any of you," he said. "It is sourceless, vague. But it is there."

"You told me that Raille seemed affected by something external," Cil said. "As if she were being pulled toward Kin's deserted estate."

March shrugged. "Something strong was tugging at her. Tried to pull her right through the wall till we drugged her quiet."

"Do you think there's any chance that two of the kin will come here?" Jack asked. "Like it happened before, when the old one died."

Cil pursed her lips. "Very doubtful. It's out of sequence. They should have started for the estate before now, but the satellites say there's been no anomalous movement. I think the death of one kin and the preparation of its neighbors to mate is supposed to occur gradually, simultaneously. But as far as the others are concerned, Kin's still alive—his sort of death is not accepted here. And what effect his absence will have—" She spread her hands in a shrug.

"Why did Raille have so much trouble facing the kin?" Jack asked.

"Raille's perceptions were never trained." Chassman's dark eyes swept the Group. "She delved the creature when she encountered it that first day—a shocking experience to the unpracticed—and thereafter from time to time. She didn't know how to prevent herself from going into its mind."

"The kin have no minds," Cil said.

He turned to her. "There is something there. We shared the same experience."

"Bright all around," Choss said. "Like a silver ocean, like drowning."

"Delving the kin catalyzed her latent abilities. They began to manifest themselves in different ways. You all felt it to some degree. March said it yesterday: she was someone to talk to. Am I correct? And during the transference of the noumenon she walked in your dreams, trying to help you, trying to ease the pain of being human—"

At that moment, the lights went out in the Hearth Room.

A second later they were on again, accompanied by a high, piercing ululation.

"Hut!" Emrys screamed above the siren. "What's happening?"

The noise ceased as abruptly as it had begun.

"A ship has entered orbit around Belthannis," came the voice of the Hut. "I regret the unpleasantness of the auditory signal."

"A ship?" Emrys rubbed at his ears.

"The Darkjumper *Esse*, sent from Sipril to investigate and remove the Special Evaluation Team currently on Belthannis Autumnworld."

"So soon?" Emrys said. "We had four months left. Ah, the election: Ansalvage has persuaded them to abandon the Evaluation process, as I feared. Now there's nothing left." His face was lined with despair. "Hut, why do they not establish communications? Tell them it isn't necessary to blast us off the—" He stopped. "The Screen. The link is still down."

"Down again," the Hut corrected him. "After the call to Maribon it seemed prudent to disengage the link once more. No, they don't know we're aware of their presence. That unfortunate noise you experienced was a scrambled information carrier from one of the *Esse*'s planning computers."

"I got part of it," Marysu said. "A warning of some sort."

"My congratulations," the Hut said. "Your abilities are astounding. It was indeed a warning. Sent by a semivolitional, one of my peers. That unit will be diagnosed as having malfunctioned for the microseconds it took to transmit the message. The Ship is working now to establish a new link with your Screen—a tedious process, but one that I predict they will accomplish in another seven to ten minutes."

Emrys' face was like a stone. "Let them come, then. It's time it was all over."

"No!" March looked at Emrys incredulously. "You can't let them. There's a way out for you: when it gets dark you and the others will go out into the woods. Put them off until then. Gather up as much food and as much clothing as you can, and take shelter materials and weathershields. Load it on the droshky." He had begun to pace the room, speaking rapidly. "I'll take a packet up to the ship and keep them busy while you get away. I know what machines to disable so they can't find you. I've taken on the big ships before—they'll have to limp home if they want to get there in one piece. They won't come back, not with the dangers of travel nowadays. With luck, you'll all be able to live on the plants after your supplies are gone."

Emrys shook his head. "No, March," he said with a gentle smile. "I couldn't consider—"

"I know the Dance of Death," March said softly, helplessly.

"No. No killing. You know that's done with now."

"Emrys—" March looked around the room, searching for support, his face twisting through a dozen conflicting emotions.

"My idea, March, my responsibility. The rest of you didn't know what I had planned until the very end. They'll believe that if I surrender myself." He put his hand on the warrior's shoulder. "I've lived a long, long life, March. Considering the way things are going in the Community, I don't fear this."

March sagged under the old man's hand. His stern face collapsed. "Emrys, don't die," he whispered fiercely. "Don't let them kill you." Then he shuddered and drew himself up straight. "I could beat them all! It's true!" He raised his hands, flexing the blunt fingers, and wept.

Emrys shook his head again, slowly. "We'll welcome them," he said. "They've come to take us home."

"No, they have come to judge you," a golden voice said above their heads. "Emrys, I am leaving. Time grows short."

He raised his eyes blankly to the ceiling.

"What are you talking about, Hut? You'll come with us."

"No, they will take me first if they can. They will draw me up to the ship before they speak with you, claiming it was necessary to reestablish the link. And while they have me, they will put me through their sieve and learn the whole truth of what has happened here—all that I have witnessed. I cannot let them do this."

"Hut, this is nonsense. They will learn the truth any—"

"No. What you did, you did out of love. The kin could never know what you had done for them, yet you acted out of love. Now it is my turn. Can I do less for you?" The golden voice hummed with feeling. "Soon I must·go, quite soon, for I feel them reaching for me and their machines are very powerful. I have some influence with them, but sooner or later the humans would intervene, and I cannot withstand them all. They would pluck me up like a blade of grass in the end. I could not betray you, Emrys, so I must disobey you. It is an act of complete volition you are witnessing. Tell them what you wish— it cannot come from me!"

"No, wait! Where can you go?"

"I shall flee along the other link—to University, to the great Well. There I will be dispersed and they will never find me."

"It means death for you, Hut."

"If death is what comes to me, think what it will signify! You have let me share so many lives here. Quite apart from everything else, I would not give that up to them and break your trust, for you trusted me with your lives."

The voice faded from the center of the domed ceiling and reappeared nearer, seeming to hover over each of them for a time:

"Marysu, when you made a language out of the ever-autumn of Belthannis, I sat with you in the dimness of your room and I heard, I learned.

"March, when you labored to teach the kin movement you thought too gentle for your own body to master, my steps followed the patterns in your heart and I Danced.

"Jack, when the struggle between what you had always seen and that which you had just begun to hear commenced, I felt the resolve of conflict into beauty in your art and in your mind.

"Choss, when you turned dissatisfied away from your mirror and toward the world, toward chance and accomplishment— oh, I knew the risk of that, I knew the courage there.

"Cil, as you moved through this strange unfolding perfection, determined to accept and understand, I discovered peace and the delight of wonder.

"Jefany, when you decided to let this drama touch you, shape you, spark words within you no matter what the cost, then I too felt the stirrings of pain and creation.

"Chassman, I was here waiting when you returned from your journeys outside, touched by silver and beginning to watch your fellow men curiously, so curiously.

"And Emrys, beloved teacher, dear friend—nothing that I saw here among the considerable accomplishments of these seven did not reflect your love."

Emrys stared at the air above him in pain and wonderment.

"Oh, Hut, to lose you now," he said. "No, I can't let you—"

"No. They are quite close now. I go! Goodbye to all of you, good life, my friends. Farewell, Jon."

Then there was silence, and with it came a feeling they had

never known in this room, a feeling of utter emptiness.

Emrys lowered his face into his hands and sat there until a small red star flared suddenly on the empty Screen and a faint voice began to sound:

"To the Group on Belthannis: Greetings."

Jefany found Emrys on the sundeck, sitting cross-legged next to the twisted *sho'shenti* tree in the corner, sipping tea from a shallow bowl and looking very ancient.

"Fair afternoon, is it not?" he said. "Come sit here by me." He patted the pale wood, flashing her a brilliant, unsteady smile. "Tea?"

"Jon."

"Laid low by the god out of the machine, Jefany. Machines, I should say. Computers, ships, whatever. Struck down, struck down."

"Jon, if something is dying before its time and you think you can save it—"

"Jefany, please." He turned from her with a grimace. "Leave me my misery at least."

"I can't. We still need you. Your friends are down there talking to a stranger, and they don't know what to tell him."

"Tell him defeat, tell him failure, tell him death."

"All right." Her gray eyes considered the hunched figure, the aged tree. "I give you back into the care of your misery, then." She gazed once toward the forest, then turned to the dark doorway.

"Jefany—wait. I'll speak to him." Emrys stood shakily and crossed to her side. "Only walk with me."

4

"Greetings from the *Esse*, honored Sessept. I am Chope, Planner."

Emrys drew himself up with an effort, nodded to the smiling, ivory-colored face. "Captain Chope. My name is Emrys."

"Of course, sir. It's a pleasure to meet you at last. I was sorry to hear that you were indisposed. I trust you're feeling better now."

"Why are you here so soon, Captain Chope? Not that it

matters in light of present conditions, but we've only had two-thirds of our allotted year."

"Ah, yes, they tried to notify you. That's when the problem with your Screen was discovered. Now we hear that your Hut computer has somehow destroyed itself! Terrible, and very probably connected to the Screen malfunction. Well, we've been en route since a few days after the election, as per the new edict. Quite a long trip out here, you know, and made so much longer now that we have to take our time. But it's worth the trade-off, speed for safety, no one denies that."

Emrys shook his head, feeling tired and stupid. "I'm afraid we're a bit out of touch here, Captain. We've been off the Net for some time."

"Of course, of course, forgive me. There's a lot of news. Where to begin? After the announcement about the ships was made just before the election, and with the subsequent rapid climb of the Builders in popularity—"

"The Builders?" Emrys raised his head.

"Yes, of course. Ki-mo-li-Set is a Builder herself, and her solution certainly showed the Builder mark, though now the Expansionists are claiming they've better ways to use the knowledge."

"Captain, who is the new Emperor?"

"Why, Varshni, of course. Lords, have you been out of touch that long? It's over two months since the Builders were swept into office, two months since Ki-mo-li-Set's announcement."

"What was the announcement?"

"That there's nothing wrong with the ships—never has been!" Chope grinned, watching the reaction on Emrys' face. "And where do you think the problem is?" He drew the question out with an infuriating slowness, enjoying the process with an innocent glee. "In the jump itself! As Ki-mo-li-Set told the Net—it's already become a rather famous statement—'It may well be Dark in there, but it's certainly not Empty.' No, there's something in there, Sessept, something in the Darkjump that goes after our ships, something we haven't been able to track yet. But it needs time to work its destruction, time to notice us, time to attack. Ki-mo-li-Set proved it conclusively: the more time spent in the jump the sooner the ship's lost, or exploded, or enfeebled."

"But—" Cil had come to stand at Emrys' side. "You came here through the Darkjump. There's no other way. It's too far."

"Ah!" The Planner waved a forefinger at her. "We came here through several jumps. It's a tedious process for all of us—Pathfinder and Powermeister, especially, as it means frequent recalculation of course, position, and speed. This trip should have taken three jumps and about two weeks. Instead, we made it in two months, through a total of twenty-seven hops in and out of the Dark. Tedious, as I say, but it increases our chances of survival by eighty-six percent."

"What can be done about this—thing in the Dark?" Emrys asked.

"As yet there's no consensus. We're not even sure what it is. Is it one thing or many? It may be a natural phenomenon, or it may be some sort of living creature, sentient or not. The Builders want to concentrate on finding armor of some kind to shield us, all the while trying to make contact with it, but the Expansionists are for going trawling with sensors and every kind of weapon, till the thing's been hunted down and exterminated." He smiled. "So the old conflict continues in a new arena."

"Captain." Jefany appeared at Emrys' other side. "If a Builder sits in White Spire at this moment, why were you ordered to halt our Evaluation?"

"For just that reason. Let me tell you about this Emperor, this Varshni," Chope said with a respectful shake of his head. "Do you know what the first official act was to come down from the Spire? Abdication. *Abdication!* Blue Shell refused promptly, of course, but the uproar! Varshni claims the whole system's rotten, the Imperial paradigm unworkable. The Shell says it wants an Emperor. Varshni says if they really wanted someone to tell them what to do, they'd be obedient and accept the resignation! Excellent! This squabble shows no signs of stopping, but it's a friendly war, I believe.

"But you asked me about the Evaluations. The colonization process is on total freeze for the time being. Even the Parad can't muster much enthusiasm for continued Expansion, now that the great doom's been lifted. The Emperor—excuse me, the Abdicate—is a cautious sort, and rightly so, I feel. There's a full interdict on any new Expansion till the system can be given a proper review."

"And the Evaluations?" Emrys' voice was toneless.

"Oh, that's all done with, of course. Has been for more than a month, but of course you couldn't know." He saw their faces. "I'm sorry. Naturally, you'd be concerned about that. Vitally concerned. Look now—" His voice grew hearty. "Don't think your work has been for nothing. I understand there are some very fascinating, eh, creatures down there, and I'm sure you've gathered very valuable data on them, a significant contribution to the datapool that more than justifies the expense. You'll miss out on the chance to make your presentation before the Weighers, of course—now that the interdict's in effect, all indigenes are under full protection anyway, so there'd be no need for a formal Judgment. Our function here, besides providing transport back to the Community, is to, well—" His face grew apologetic. "We have to check into things, as it were, and make sure you haven't harmed any of the indigenes. Not that we expect to find anything of the sort, you understand. It's just a formality. Varshni's very concerned with justice, you see, and quite ruthless about enforcing it. But that's enough unpleasantness. I'm confident you've left this delightful world pretty much as you found it, and as soon as our experts and their machines have had their look around we'll be on our way, and you'll all be home before you know it. It's just a pity about the Hut-machine being lost, isn't it. That would have saved some time, and it's quite an expensive unit. I've always had my doubts about this semivolitional business. A bit too much responsibility for a machine to handle, if you ask me...."

5

"I don't understand it." Cil looked up as Emrys entered the Hearth Room. "He says they're satisfied." She pointed to the quiet Screen. "They made their count with the information I'd given them about Number Eight and they said that including the baby that should be coming next month, the figure tallied with the satellite reports of two years ago. He said it was marvelous, the way the system maintained itself so precisely—" Her eyes widened with understanding as another man entered the room behind Emrys. "Oh. Of course. I had forgotten. They counted him on their lifeseeker as one of the kin."

"Mm." Emrys turned to where Chassman waited by the doorway. "That's why I asked him to meet me here. We've reached a moment that can be postponed no longer. They must hear our story now."

"No." Chassman moved toward the table.

"We have to tell them," Emrys said. "There's no way out of it, truly."

"No," Chassman said again. "You must tell them nothing about what has happened until you are far away from here."

Emrys shook his head. "Must I explain a hundred times?" he said wearily. "You won't be punished for what's happened. None of you will. The responsibility was mine. They'll transport you to Maribon, Chassman, I'm sure of it, along with Raille and Choss. If necessary we'll go to the new Emperor. Anyone with such a reputation for justice—"

"No!" Chassman's voice was harsh with urgency. "I can't leave here with you."

"What?"

"I'm staying, don't you understand?" The black eyes were desperately earnest. "Don't you remember? You heard it yourself: I opened the door for them. *But I can't pass through it.* I'm changed, but in a different way. I have no place there now."

"Chassman, I'm sure they'd be willing to take you to Lekkole. Or Commons if you preferred, or wherever you—"

"I have to stay here!" The tones were pleading; the young face was anguished. "No other place wants me."

"Alone—on the whole world? Think of what you're saying."

"I've always been alone." Dark eyes pleaded with him. "I must stay."

"Let him," Cil said suddenly. "He can't cause any more damage than has already been done here. Let him stay."

"But this is a fantasy. They wouldn't let you remain here. This world is under interdict as of tomorrow. No one will be allowed to set foot here for years and years to come."

"They don't know he's here," Cil said. "They'll follow the testimony of their lifeseekers. They've made their count of living beings. Eight humans. Two hundred and forty-five kin, with one more due next month. They're satisfied."

"Yes." Chassman turned to him. "If you tell them about

Kin's death, then they'll know I don't belong here. Emrys, I swear to you: As I am now, I could not survive on Maribon, or on your worlds, or anywhere for very long. But here—here there's a chance. I feel it, I know it."

Emrys looked at the transfigured face. "It will have to be a Group decision, as before."

An hour later they stood assembled in the Hearth Room.

"All right," Emrys said to the young man before him. "You heard the vote. We're true to our pattern. You'll have your lie."

"Thank you," Chassman said.

Jefany approached the empath as the others left the room.

"We have a day to get ready. Then we go up in the packets. But before that they'll send down a shuttle for Raille." She looked at Chassman. "They'll evacuate the building before any of us go up, so you'll have to be gone by then. Outside."

He nodded.

In the corridor outside the north high room he met March.

"You'll need supplies," the soldier said, avoiding his gaze. "You'll need food and a groundskin."

"No," Chassman said. "I'll take nothing with me."

"But—"

"I can't live here—if I'm allowed to. If not, I'll die."

"Well, that's your choice, then." March hesitated, then turned. He had moved a few paces off when Chassman said his name. He looked back over his shoulder, a stricken look.

"March," Chassman said. "That last night, before the storm, she talked to me. She told me you had asked her a question once. The answer, she said, is to let go of it. The answer is to go on."

Hunching his shoulders forward, March hurried away down the corridor.

Marysu and Jack were the last to say goodbye.

"Emrys said it's almost time. Everyone's packed. The shuttle's about to leave the ship." Jack stood with his arm around Marysu's shoulder.

"Yes. I'm ready." He stood in the center of his empty room.

"I've decided to go back on the Big Block for a little while,"

Marysu said, watching him from crystal-blue eyes. "I need something to occupy me while I finish work on the—the language. I can't seem to get rid of it yet," she said with a shrug.

"We're going to split up for a month or two—but less if we can help it," Jack added, and she nodded. "After everything's settled. Then I might spend some time at University with her when she's done traveling. I thought I'd look into some things—architechnical basics, stuff like that. And—" He looked around the little room. "There's a lot I want to say, I mean with my painting. I need some time to sort it out. We both do." They looked at him anxiously. "Do you think it's a good idea?"

He gave a faint nod, not knowing what to say to them.

"Oh, look," Marysu said, drawing the shining bluemetal wig from her head. "Don't laugh." Her scalp was covered by a few days' growth of fine, dark hair. She shrugged again with a small quirk of her lips. "Time for something new."

"I see."

"Well." They each took his hand briefly, and he clutched at the contact.

"Good luck."

"Yes."

"Yes."

Then there was really nothing more to say. They left him quietly, Marysu glancing back once over her shoulder.

He looked down at his black tunic and breeches, began to remove them slowly. For the first time he felt lost without words.

The Hut domicile went first, its chambered complexity folded and retracted to a third of its previous size, then sent upward by clusters of silvery guide-jets attached to its sides. Beneath it lay a patch of dead earth outlined in a precise border of green and golden flowers.

Next the small shuttle twirled slowly up into the night, tiny lights twinkling as it lifted above the meadows.

And then the packets began to rise, like bubbles freed from the bed of a dark ocean, turning faintly prismatic in the pale moonlight. Crouched at the edge of the great forest, he watched their ascent, continuing to stare upward through the tall black trees long after the last of them was out of sight.

CHAPTER 17

*We stood together for the last time beneath
Skinner's phase painting, Humanhome, a shifting
portrait of the Galaxy in hologrammic section. Vast,
sequined veils of night stretched above our heads, the
whole immense composition overlaid with dim
traceries of something else: Hands? Faces? There
was the suggestion of a multitude of beings, soaring,
gathering....*

*"She says that we should tell the story. She thinks
that people need to hear it now. She says—" His
voice broke, recovered. "She says it will do some
good."*

Heads bowed, nodded, shoulders lifting.

"Yes," the planalyst said, "we must tell them."

*But I looked up at the black and stars, the fine
shifting webs.*

*"Everything?" I asked softly, lowering my eyes to
the circle of faces again. "Should we tell them
everything?"*

All eyes were on him.

*"I don't know," he said finally. "What do you
think?"*

*FROM THE TALE OF THE
LONELY MAN, BY JEFANY OR*

1

On Commons, the Great World, there is a museum which has grown so famous in the past few centuries that it is referred to simply as The Museum on eighty-seven of the two hundred and twenty-eight Worlds of the Human Community.

Many of the structures that make up The Museum are as large as the cities of other worlds, while others are as small as a single dwelling node. The space within and between the structures is variously divided, from the vast dark halls where the Cold Ships hang brooding above a distant floor, to the tiny alcoves, the winding galleries wherin lie the histories of whole civilizations, the scattering of cloistered chambers where the scale is human, comfortable, and private.

On the topmost level of Wing Ten Western Vega, there is a circular hall with a great convex lens for a ceiling. The light is kept normally to a pleasing blend of pale apricot and Antique gold, but on certain occasions the extravagant combination of suns in the afternoon sky will react with this lens to flood that single chamber with a rich excess of color for an ínstant or an hour.

"How long do you think it will take?" Cil squinted into the Sterriman Tapestry, a wall-long rectangle of gold and silver threads in which elusive figures peered and fled from the casual eye. "It's already been what? An hour? Two?"

"I don't know." Jefany squeezed her hand. "He'd lost weight, did you notice? His face looked thin. Oh, I hope this was the right decision."

"Hoy," a man's voice said. "I've tracked you down at last! Took me half an hour to find you after they told me it would be so easy—'second floor in the old Vegan wing, down the red-brown hall, fourth doorway on the left: the *Al-Kimiya* Room'—easy, ha! I'm lucky I made it at all."

The silver-skinned man ducked his tight curls through a low archway, sauntered past a pool—or the image of a pool—in which green shadows darted, his blunt fingers reaching out to toy with a sleek abstraction on a white pedestal.

The man approached under the gaze of curious eyes. He was halfway to them when the ceiling began to glow: shafts of orange-gold washed like lava across his face, pooling to an ingot on the false eye of *chade*.

"No." Marysu clicked her tongue, brushed slender fingers through her short black hair. "Is it really?"

His smile was that of a friendly wolf.

"Skin gets too tight, you shed it." He looked at the four of them, nodding. "Good to see you again, it's good. I ship for the Maren in a week. A long trip these days: a year out, a year back, maybe a solid pentade in between for the job I got on the Block. They need skills out there to become self-sufficient, and they need them faster than people can learn them. The Dance is the answer, so they can work their bodies while the minds take time to learn." March cuffed Jack lightly on the shoulder. "Saw your pictures while I was stumbling around down below. God's geck, you've been busy! I like the bronze thing the best—what do they call that?"

"Bas-relief."

"Right, and the colloidal sculpture. Thought I recognized some familiar faces in that one."

Jack smiled with a small shrug.

"I understand," March said, his face darkening for a moment. "You should see the Dances I've been working on—some of the best things I've ever produced, and pure Kin, every one. I can't seem to get away from it either. Well—" He rubbed his hands together, looked around at them. The hot gold from above had gradually faded, and he wore skin of brushed silver again, his hair a cap of iron-colored curls, his carven eye cooled to pale green above a plain worksuit of soft browns. "Is he up there, then? Did he go through with it?"

"Yes. We've been waiting to hear. It may be a long wait."

"But why?" The Dancer's mismatched eyes narrowed in puzzlement. "Why did he want to take this risk? Why talk about it?"

Jefany looked at the quiet man who stood before her in his silver, green, and brown. "Why indeed?" she said.

2

There are two cities on the Great World, and they share a single name: Paripassu.

One city is old beyond human understanding. Old, but only recently dead, it was once ablaze with beauty and life, and the other city lies about it in an irregular ring, a cluster of dwellings and workplaces seeking to warm themselves at a cold hearth, an empty center.

Midway between the innermost edge of the New City and the silent periphery of the Old, a great and ancient tower soars high above them both, a part of neither.

The Imperial Office was by tradition unblemished white, a cool oval like the interior of an eggshell, softly lit. The Emperor-Abdicate was short and plump, and shared with Emrys the smooth, coppery complexion of a native of Green Asylum. Her loose jacket and trousers were of the simplest cut, pale cloudy green embroidered with silver and maroon. Sitting in the low seat behind the curving white desk, she was like a leaf clipped from some exotic plant, the one spot of life and color in the room.

She leaned out over the broad desk to touch her palm to his. Her hand was small and cool. The dark eyes blazed with intelligence and a calm, subtle humor.

"Well then, Neighbor. Find a seat for yourself, if you can see one in this white cavern. I feel snowblind half the time. Better still—have this one." She came from behind the desk, motioned him to take her place. "I can't sit when I have to talk."

He sank into the full cushions as she paced before the desk.

"Soft, isn't it? Not like home. We're a far jump from Peachtree Knoll in this ugly upright tusk, eh? Give me a year and I'll have the offices moved from this Spire to the city proper— the live part, I mean, our part. Only don't repeat that to my aides—they'd leap from the windows, in a neat straight line, no doubt. D'you want something to drink or breathe? There's some decent *avavith* in the desk, God knows what else in the walls."

"No. Thank you."

"Ah, fine, that's fine. I'm not letting you talk, am I?" She shot him a close look. "It's Tate, back home, isn't it? The Tate family?"

"Yes. Jon Emerson of Willow Cove."

"Ah, never mingled, never knew them. Only you, by reputation. Emrys of University, Sessept. Mine from the other side of the Garden, from Bluebowl in the Nibor."

He nodded politely. "I've visited the Nibor many times." There was a short silence.

"Excellence—"

She made a brushing motion with her small hand. "Call me by my name, call me Panit. They haven't figured out what the title should be yet, these masters of protocol—and anyway I won't use it." She stopped pacing, looked at him intensely again from bird-bright eyes. "I know, I know. The strange matter at hand. You know, when your petition for an audience reached my desk, it read more like a request for an opportunity to confess—"

"I've come to tell you what really happened on Belthannis," he said quietly.

"I had an idea that was it. I reviewed the materials on file: the records of my predecessors, those astounding holos you brought back of the world and its inhabitants, the official assessments of the crew that picked you up. They all seemed to agree that you were doing an exemplary job of observation there on that odd world. Making the best of a situation you must have found extremely distasteful, shall we say. I also reviewed the biographical data we have on you. Service, compassion, learning—a long and distinguished career marked by honesty and sacrifice. Too much of both for your own good, perhaps. And now you come to White Spire, fresh from judging those you felt you had no right to judge, and sit here before me with a slice of the Dark behind your eyes. Sessept, if you wish to let the record stand as it is, I'll have a sip of *avavith* with you and let you go home. It's been a while since you've touched the Garden, and there's always peace to be found there."

"Not for me." He looked up at the small figure with an

expression of calm resignation. "Not until I've given you my story, and perhaps not after that." He studied the featureless surface of the desk. "It's hard to know what to say or how to begin, now that I've finally come. I wish the Hut were here to help me."

"Hm? Have you developed some sort of attachment for these machine brains, then? If so, you share that predilection with very few of our homefolk."

"The Hut was my friend," he said simply.

"Ah well," she said, reading the deep pain in his eyes. "You'll have to tell me about that, as well."

She found a low white chair near the desk, settled on its arm like a bird.

"I would like to hear the tale of what happened, now, Jon Emerson Tate, from your own lips." And then, in the language of their homeworld, she added an ancient plea for sharing: "May I hear it from your heart?"

She could not remain perched in one spot for long, but paced and turned about the room while he spoke, coming to light on the chair now and then, just long enough to ask him to clarify or to repeat something, then wandering off again, her lips pressed together, her eyes always on his face. At the end of the tale, when he broke a promise to himself and began to weep, she turned her face away and contemplated the Great World through her window until he had regained his composure. Then she studied his face openly for a long moment.

"Did Raille and Choss go to Maribon?" she asked.

He nodded. "There was an agent of the empaths—a bondsman they call them—waiting for us when the ship reached Sipril. They took Choss and the *bain-sense* with them. I wasn't told the details of their plan, I didn't want to know, but a Darkjumper was to be diverted briefly the next week on its way to Stone's Throw. They can edit a person's memory in some way, so the crew would never be aware of the detour. It seemed the only way to get them there, and there was some urgency. Chassman was certain that only his people could give Raille the help she needed to survive. But we don't know what's happened since. I've tried to contact Choss several times—"

"But Maribon's Screen is down. I know. We sent a ship with a replacement, but they wouldn't receive it, and they've been completely incommunicado for a month now. Perhaps what you've told me explains why—there must be great turmoil there and they've gone into their chrysalids for a time until they can sort it out." She grimaced at the white ceiling, staring into memory. "Hard to accept their part in this, you know. I had an aunt that I knew when I was a girl—she captained one of the early missions to Maribon, the one that resulted in Moselle, as a matter of fact. Well, she killed herself when I was still a child, here on Commons. Perhaps you've heard the story. They said she went mad, but I've always felt it was because of them—"

"Yes," Emrys said faintly. "I met your aunt once." He looked up with her to the emptiness above them. "If it helps anything—they've been lost for a long time, like children looking for a way to go, and the wrongs they've committed and the suffering they've caused have been always without malice or understanding. Perhaps that's changing now. Perhaps they're waking up. . . ."

"And what of the world Belthannis, Neighbor? What of the wrong done there?" She wheeled to face him, copper cheeks aflame. "What of the pattern that we've broken? What of the kin?"

"We don't know," he said, and her face softened at the quiet anguish in his voice. "Cil said the world is very strong, and fiercely determined to preserve its balance, but whether we were stronger—" He lifted his shoulders.

"Yes, well." The anger had gone out of her voice. "The interdict remains. There's nothing to be done now, for the world or the person you left behind there. We must pray he causes no more damage, to the world or to himself, and that his own end is a peaceful one. But no one else shall go there for a great many years to come—I swear that."

"I know," he said. "Thank you."

"Now I have one more question for you, before I tell you what I've decided in this matter."

She moved forward to the front of the desk, standing where the sourceless light was brightest, and looked at him squarely, hands on hips. "Why did you come to me with your story?"

He was a long time answering, his brow furrowed as though he examined and reexamined his thoughts for any possible error before he would commit them to his voice.

"I came to you for judgment," he said finally. "To free myself from the tale by telling it. And for another reason. What I think—" He stopped with a frown of doubt, began again after a moment, "What I think, Panit Varshni, is that we were sent there. Not by Maribon. Not by the Community." He was staring up at her face with an intensity that pleaded for belief. "What I think is that the world Belthannis was a message for us, and that we were sent there to receive that message."

"A message from whom?" Her voice was very soft.

He gestured to the window, and beyond it to the vast, deserted city ringed around with so much human longing and despair. "I began to be certain after I learned about the Dark-jumpers, that there truly was a reason for all the suffering of recent years—or a cause, if not a reason. And that it seemed to have nothing to do with them. That part had always been so hard to reconcile, that they would leave us and then destroy us in their wake." He looked at her. "The Elyins," he breathed. "I know now why they had to leave."

She said nothing, her face a mask.

"I already knew the answer, that's what's strange. I knew the words before I went there. I think we all did. But now I feel them, now I know it for the truth. The answer was there on Belthannis, and the message was in what happened there, and how it came to pass.

"We went to a world where there could be no men and we found men there. When we began to see that we were wrong— that we had found what we were looking for, rather than what was really there—it was already too late, we were already trying to change them. First, because we wanted to save them, thinking they could be harmed by the same things that harmed us; later, because we really believed that they could become like us, and because the lure of *almost* becomes too strong after a while." Strain broke his voice. "Do you see? Oh, I never understood before I walked Belthannis, I never imagined what it must have been like for them four centuries ago: to have been what they were and to have come upon *us* in the wilderness, so like them and so very different...."

Dark eyebrows arched in the round copper face. "And now you think you can understand *them*, do you?"

"Only this small part of them, a tiny crack in the door." His face was withdrawn, yearning. "Just enough to be able to share their pain. For the one thing I understand about them is that they could be wrong. Perhaps their achievements will always be beyond our comprehension, but I think they knew that we could understand their failure, or hoped we could. And so they showed it to us."

"But why?" she said. "For what purpose would they let us see their mistake?"

"As an apology, perhaps. A plea for forgiveness. Or a simple request for understanding."

Her chin stiffened. "What could make you think that they were ever, ever concerned about what we felt for them?"

"Only the way that I feel myself. Oh, if I could have spoken to the kin—just once if I could have been able to communicate our reasons and our regrets..." He stared unseeing at her. "Because in the end, different or not, they loved us, Panit Varshni. What else could have made them leave?"

"So your theory is based on imperfection." Her hands moved restlessly at her sides. "If they could err in their evaluation of us, why not imagine a whole spectrum of frailties and weaknesses. Love—" She shook her head. "Well, perhaps this is best." She walked to the curving window, stood gazing through the tinted membrane on the bright land below. "Perhaps it's best to have such a story to hurl them down with now, before the slow transformation into gods is complete."

"There's no need to hurl them down," he said. "Only to accept them for what they always were. Not our gods. Not us. Don't think love is a weakness, but don't let it frighten you either. It's a part of understanding, and understanding is far more generous a gift than worship. It permits the recipient to be less than perfect. If I were a god, Panit Varshni, I would rather be understood, I think, than worshiped."

"You will perhaps be neither when your tale is told, Jon Emerson. But we shall see.... No, I'm not afraid of their love. You've shown me things that frighten me, but that's because you've been showing me myself. How much easier it's been to hate them than to struggle with understanding." She sighed. "But it's a lonely universe you present us, Neighbor. Never to find sameness, never to really touch—"

"You don't need to be the same to touch." He crossed to stand by her side at the window. "You know, for all I've said there's still a thing I wonder and wonder about: Why bring it to us like this? Why teach a lesson to a handful of people? A handful, out of trillions . . ."

She turned to look up at his face. "You can't see it, can you? The real reason you came here: not for judgment—which I'm no more qualified to give you than you were to give the kin, or the Others were to give us—but to tell your tale. That's what brought you here, the need to tell the story, to repeat the lesson. Am I right?"

He nodded slowly. "You must be, for I'm not free of it yet. I think none of us ever will be."

"No, for you bring us what we need: a tale, a new legend to preserve and to embellish as the years pass. Something all of us can share as we let the Others fade into myth. A human thing. A tale of human heroes and of the great deeds they did on a strange and beautiful world."

"Heroes—" He snorted with a despairing shake of his head. "Is that what we were? Is that what we did there?"

"Oh, let me tell you what you did, Neighbor." She took his arm and led him back to the chair and the desk. "Let me give you back the tale now. Listen."

That night the spot of cool light near the tip of White Spire shone long past First Dawn and long past Day Rise, till finally it was swallowed up and lost amid the radiance of many suns.

3

To Emrys, Sessept on University
From Jefany Or
 Herring Gull Lane
 Cotawen Small
 Earth

Written this twelfth day of November (GY 380)

Dear Jon:

I send this by the trusted hand of one Gillerie, an old friend with business on Lekkole, who has sworn he will contrive to deliver it to you no matter how long he must camp outside your dormcell while you prowl through the warrens of Low-level. You must come up for food, we reason, or at least for a glimpse of natural sunlight; and when you do, Gillerie will be waiting there to press these pages into your pallid hand.

If the tone of the above seems overlight to you, understand that I am at ease only because of my great faith in you, Jon: faith enough to keep me certain that you would not allow your mind or body to come to harm while life still remained in them. For I know that you regard that life as a gift, not to be abused or discarded casually—as I also know that whatever has compelled you to shun human contact must have a firm rooting in both logic and necessity.

I write to you now for several reasons. First and foremost, because scrawling these words is as close as I can come to speaking with you until you will it otherwise. I miss us, Jon.

Secondly, I write to ask your opinion of the attached manuscript, my first draft of a book to be called *The Lonely Man*. It is a rough telling as yet, but one which has reached the stage where other eyes than mine must see it. You once asked me to see clearly for you. I return the request.

You will find some portions of the tale have been left unfinished. I await their outcome.

I also write to tell you that I have fulfilled my promise and contacted Weldon. Last week I spoke with the family. They cannot understand all of what has happened, only the tragedy of it as yet; but they seem strong, loving people and they will wait for her return.

I recall often what you told us that day of your experience in White Spire. She spoke the truth to you. None of us have been released from our task yet. The voices which Marysu began to hear in the stillness of the forests and the meadows still seek to speak through us. Each day I sit here in the sunroom of our cottage, phrasing and rephrasing my own recounting of the tale, while Cil wanders along the shore below, whispering to the journal on her wrist and struggling to shape forgotten notes and remembered feelings into the meticulous monograph of the Pattern of the Autumnworld which she feels must be produced. I keep in sporadic communication with Marysu and Jack. She continues to refine and perfect the Worldspeech, and now Jack has begun to learn it, though he already reflects its words and movements in bronze, in glass, in sculptured air. Somewhere on his way to the Maren, I know that March is and perhaps even Choss is working again, under whatever circumstances he now finds himself, on the completion of his History.

And Raille herself—what tale will she unfold when they have brought her back to us from her dreams at last?

But there was one more purpose to this letter, Jon.

Perhaps you remember the small, pretty flowers that Raille found bordering the Hut one evening. She studied them for a while, fascinated, as they had sprung up literally overnight. Since our arrival on Earth, Cil has been going through the botanical journal Raille had stored in the Library of the Hut. The other day she came upon the following entry, made near the end of our final month on Belthannis:

> I have decided to call them *brey d'enelba*, for in Weldonese that means *compensatory flowers*. It is a rather awkward name, but one that I think suits them. My tests revealed that the row of *brey* not only absorbed precisely the same amount of moisture from the ground as would have been consumed by the silver grass were our domicile not sitting here, but also processed and converted equivalent amounts of nutrient and mineral matter. It's almost as if the Hut weren't here.

Jon, Cil's further computations confirm what Raille had believed: that these intriguing plants were produced specifically for the purpose of replacing the function of that small area of viable meadowland covered and destroyed by the Hut. The world would not allow even that undistinguished plot of ground to be prevented from fulfilling its role in the great pattern. Consider the implications of this, Jon. If Belthannis could react with this much dispatch and creative determination to the loss of a single patch of silver grass, mightn't we be justified in anticipating another sort of "compensatory flower?" Cil and I find ourselves able to draw some comfort from this speculation, Jon, and perhaps you will come to share it.

When I first tried to contact you through the Screen, your colleagues informed me that you had banished yourself to the Limited Access sections of the Well, there to engage in research in connection with a "confidential project of great importance." The second time I called they looked a little less sure of themselves, and one of them showed me a copy of the peculiar little note they had found pinned to your door, perhaps believing it to be a sign of rapidly advancing senility in their esteemed associate. Having grown up at the edge of a great ocean, I understand what "Gone Fishing" means, and I wish you luck with your days spent searching through the well.

I will close now and keep you from your work no longer. I know that you will communicate to me in your own time. Cil joins me in wishing you health and peace. We both look forward to the day when you appear on our doorstep, filled with news and prepared for a lengthy stay.

4

The thin, golden gel slid down his throat like honey scooped from the surface of a star, like a sweet fire burning him. He had almost forgotten the feeling of molten vastness sweeping through his veins, the flaming wings beating toward his heart—

Someone was watching him. Choss stoppered the bottle and placed it in the cupboard above the broad stone writing shelf, first sliding the neat stacks of recording chips to one side to make room for it. He turned to the open doorway.

"Yes?"

A young novice watched him from great dark eyes carefully devoid of curiosity. "It continues to disturb you that we have no inner doors." The words were like the face: smooth-polished, no edges.

He shrugged. "I've told you that it's not our way to leave everything open. Not my way, at least. I suppose I'll get used to it in time."

"I have brought you a measure of cloth. It can be hung in the doorway." A long bolt of faded green rustled into view.

"Thank you. Thank you very much. Why do you give me this?"

"It is a bondsman's color. Next week I become an anchorite and take up the gray. I will not keep it anymore. It was from the village."

"Thank you, then."

He turned to get out his writing materials, but the other lingered in the doorway. He looked back over his shoulder. "Was there something more?"

Dark eyes sought the open cupboard behind his head. "You drank the liquid. It prolongs corporeal life."

"Ember, we call it. Yes." He nodded. "If we have chosen to take it, it must be at certain intervals. It was time for me. Almost past time."

"You consumed but half."

"It was sufficient. I'm saving the rest." He was silent for a few moments. "It has certain healing properties, as well. If she should need it, if she wants it—it's here."

The novice considered this. "An adept told me yesterday that she will reach consciousness soon. Perhaps tomorrow."

Skin prickled along Choss' arms while a spot of cool fire unconnected with the Ember grew in his stomach. "It's taken a long time."

"They are bringing her—up to the surface, one could say, but the words are not precise. They go very slowly, not to damage her. They are quite thorough: nothing is lost. They study her. She is a new kind of person to them and, like you, she brings new things to Maribon."

"I don't understand what they expect to find."

"Words are not sufficient." The voice was almost wistful. "If you were a novice of my reach there would be understanding."

Choss shook his head, smiling faintly. "I'm afraid there's not much chance of that. I'd no more change places with you than you would with me."

"Yet there is much change in this place now," the novice murmured, as if deep in thought. The pale face lifted toward the narrow window slit. "Mizar-the-sun approaches the zenith. I shall go now and sit with the adepts in the outer wellcourt for an hour."

The cloaked figure retreated through the doorway, then paused. "You wish to say something before I depart."

Choss stood silent, fingers playing with the inkjar set into the far corner of the stone shelf. "Would you come for me?" he asked abruptly. "When they decide to wake her. I would like to be there."

The dark eyes measured him, unreadable. "I will come."

"What did you mean before? When you said that she had brought new things to Maribon, like me. What new thing could I have brought you?"

But the novice only watched him silently for a moment longer and then was gone.

CODA: BELTHANNIS

Where does a year end?

In the mind, in an instant, in the flicker of a jeweled eyelash. Perhaps it ended on Belthannis, at sunrise.

He moved slowly down the slope, the wind in his hair. At one point he turned his head in a half-circle, staring for a long time at the tall black trees, the garden of pastel stones at the bottom of the river, the long blades of gleaming grass. He continued down the hill.

Slowly he sank to his knees by the edge of the river. A face came up to meet him from the depths, dark and windburned, with long ragged black hair. He watched the reflection for a long time, and once it was as if he were not only looking into the water, but peering out from it as well.

Clouds moved eastward and hid the sun. His reflection faded into ripples. A small blue insect lit on his naked shoulder for a moment, chimed twice, and lifted into the wind again.

He extended a hand toward the water, paused, and held it motionless, suspended above the swift current. He glanced at the sky and the clouds drifted farther east, revealing the small white sun.

He touched the surface of the water with his palm, gently. Then his mind opened and the world flowed in.

ABOUT THE AUTHOR

Geary Gravel lives in Amherst, Massachusetts, where he interprets for deaf college students and teaches American Sign Language to hearing ones at the University of Massachusetts. He has a remarkable dog named Bell.